COFFEE TEA THE CARIBBEAN & ME

CAROLINE JAMES

RAMJAM PUBLISHING COMPANY

COPYRIGHT

Cover Design

Alli Smith

First Edition Published by Ramjam Publishing 2016
ISBN 978-0-9573782-8-5

A CIP catalogue record for this title is available from the British Library.

DEDICATION

For my lovely mum, who always taught me that...
"The time to be happy is now!"

With love

AT THE BEGINNING ...

"The time to be happy is now, let the universe show you how..."

Jo never forgot John's words...

LOOKING BACK...

Jo stood at the kitchen door and looked out at the fells beyond. In the distance, a tractor chugged through a field, while birds hovered overhead and a dog ran in circles chasing their shadows. The last few months had been tumultuous and Jo wondered how she'd got through them. From complete despair, she'd fought to keep her sanity and diminishing family close and as the sun warmed her upturned face, she closed her eyes and remembered.

1

Hattie Contaldo held her breath and sucked in her stomach. She gathered copious folds of bedroom curtain around her body and closed her eyes as the window-cleaner daubed his limp chamois half-heartedly across the glass.

Of all times to clean the sodding windows! Hattie prayed that he hadn't seen her.

A heap of clothes lay piled on the bed, the packaging strewn to one side. Hattie had been trying new outfits that she'd ordered online and was stripped down to support pants when the window-cleaner's sudden and unexpected arrival disturbed her. Unable to streak out of sight through the door on the other side of the room, she buried herself in the curtain.

"Morning, Hattie," he called out, "off on 'yer holidays?"

Hattie gritted her teeth and glared at the ruddy-faced man. A limp roll-up hung from his lip and smoke curled in a wispy haze, past half-closed eyes and bushy brows. She adjusted the fabric around her ample body and wished that she'd had time to move the Magi-Sculpt swimsuit, with scaffolding-like panels, that lay on the counterpane.

"Hurry up Reg!" Hattie yelled, "Or I'll have you up as a peeping Tom."

"Hardly likely, I've known thee forty-odd years," Reg retorted in a broad Westmarland accent and nodded towards the swimsuit, "but I could use that contraption instead of me ladder." He raised his eyebrows and grinned, then gave the window a final flick, "Leave me money in the usual place."

Hattie watched Reg descend and fought back the urge to open the window and send him flying. She untangled herself and stomped towards the bed, then grabbed the offending garment and thrust it back in its packaging. That was the last time she'd order anything from Fabulous Fifty Plus, she vowed. There was nothing fabulous about being fifty plus, it was all downhill from here. Hattie stared at her naked breasts in the full length mirror and sighed, she'd have to stand on her hands to make them pert and upright again. As she reached for her housecoat, she wondered if she'd still got time to knock a few pounds off before booking a holiday, maybe give one of those drink-only diets a whirl. She yawned and decided to pack up the garments later. Right now she was thirsty and fancied a coffee.

Hattie filled the kettle from a tap at the kitchen sink and stared out of the window, where tightly packed houses sprawled before her on the Westmarland estate. Early morning sunshine glinted off grey slate roofs and her gaze followed the distant fells as they sprawled towards the village of Kirkton Sowerby, where Jo, her friend of many years, lived in an old manor house. Hattie wondered what Jo was up to and knew that she was probably out walking with her daft mongrel. She'd never understood Jo's love of animals, especially dogs.

Hattie flicked the kettle on and reached for a mug then took a spoonful of instant coffee and was about to stir it into hot milk from the microwave, when the words MAURICE'S MUG, painted in large letters across the crockery, seemed to shout at her and she flung the offending object into the sink. It shattered into several pieces and Hattie stared at the jagged edges, remembering that Jo had told her on numerous occasions that Maurice was playing away from home, but it had taken Hattie months before she took any action.

"Bloody men!" Hattie cursed and searched for a cup and saucer.

She looked out of the window again and wondered if Jo might fancy a bite to eat later on. Hattie decided to give her a ring, but not until she'd had her coffee.

Jo DOCHERTY STOOD at the window in her lounge and looked out at the road beyond the wrought iron gates of Kirkton House. A heavy chain linked the bars, joining the gates with an imposing steel padlock.

There was little traffic since the new by-pass had been built and the road was rarely used. Jo wondered at the passing of time, where had all the years gone? Until recently, Kirkton House was a thriving hotel that she'd run for more than two decades. But today the old manor stood quiet and foreboding at the edge of the village of Kirkton Sowerby and it seemed a lifetime since she'd burst through the gates - an innocent young woman with a will to survive and a passion to bring life to the decaying old building.

An old American craft clock on a nearby mantelpiece ticked loudly.

Time's heartbeat!

Jo shuddered as she stared out at the deserted village and silent road. The clock had been a wedding gift many years ago when she'd married Greg, her first husband and father of their son, Thomas James or Jimmy as he was now known. The clock was the only thing to survive their union - a relationship that had been short and sharp and made way for her blissful marriage to John, the handsome Romany, who'd been her rock and given her Zach, a second beloved son.

A door banged on an upper floor and an icy chill floated down the stairs. Jo shivered, rubbing her hands over goosebumps under the fine wool sweater that covered her thin arms.

She half expected John to come running down the stairs and smiled as she remembered him, all those years ago, making his way through the hotel gates on a snowy New Year's Eve, to find her alone on the frozen pathway. The sound of a distant dance band and merry revellers echoed in the night when Jo momentarily escaped from the party. She couldn't believe her eyes, oh the joy of seeing John! To be engulfed in his strong embrace and covered in kisses, just when she thought she'd lost him forever.

Torn between his love for Jo and marrying out of his Romany culture, John turned his back on his family to wed Jo and their years together had been blissful. He bought love and laughter into her life and in time his family forgave him, as they too, learnt to love the gorger, a non-gypsy, who'd stolen the heart of their precious son. John was successful in business; the days of following his father's cart as they tinkered around the country, long gone. He invested in property and bought and sold well and was proud of his new wife and her bustling hotel.

Jo remembered how the hotel came alive when John walked through the gracious Georgian rooms, smiling and chatting to visitors, whilst keeping a gleam in his eye for Jo as she went about her work.

But now the house seemed barren and Jo wondered how she would ever get through the long days and years that lay ahead.

All her men had gone.

Indents on the gravel marked the spot where Zach had parked his car and she wanted to reach out and touch the tiny stones to assure herself that Zach would return before sunset, that he'd merely slipped out and soon she'd hear tyres crunching and footsteps racing as the door flew open and his larger than life character, so like his father, burst into the room.

Her heart ached and she let out a deep sigh as tears pricked at the corner of her eyes and began to cascade down her cheeks. Kirkton House had been a place of love and laughter for so many years but now every ancient beam seemed to groan, laden with sadness, as if feeling Jo's emptiness. She reached for a tissue from the pocket of her jeans and dabbed at her puffy eyes.

Meg, a black Labrador, placed two paws on the window seat

beside Jo and let out a howl. As if sensing distress in her mistress, Meg too searched the road for Zach.

The plaintive cry was unsettling and Jo reached out, "We have to let go, Meg." More tears slid down Jo's pale cheeks and dripped on the dog's head, "Zach's only gone to London, not the other side of the world."

The dog licked anxiously and nuzzled the hand that offered comfort.

As she rubbed the soft warm fur, Jo thought about her sons. Jimmy at twenty-six, lived in the Caribbean, where he'd opened a bar on the popular island of Barbados. It was an eight hour flight and at that moment, felt like another planet. Zach, three years younger than his brother, was on his way to London. He'd left that morning and was hoping to use his talent as a chef to forge a career in the city. Jo glanced at a photograph next to the clock. Taken two summers ago, the boys stood either side of their parents and surrounded by her family, with Meg at her heels, Jo smiled happily at the camera.

It was the last image of them all together.

Meg turned suddenly and leapt on her box under the stairs. She began to scramble at the crumpled blankets until she emerged with a scruffy worn lead and tossed it in the air. With her tail wagging excitedly, the old dog bent low in a pounce position and stared at Jo.

Jo wondered at the creature's ability to lift even the darkest mood and reached for the lead, "Very well, you old rascal," she said, "Let's walk this off."

She followed the excited dog into a utility area and selected a quilted jacket from a selection of outdoor wear that hung above a pile of muddy Wellingtons. As she thrust her arms into the man's jacket, Jo's felt her heart lurch. A faint trace of John's aftershave caught her unaware and she bit on her lip. She thought of the times she'd buried her face in the worn fabric and snuggled into John's embrace. The pain of losing him wracked through her body and her hands shook as she pulled at the zipper.

With a sigh, she stepped outside.

Spring sunshine greeted them and Meg hurtled through a pretty walled garden. They meandered past dense herbaceous borders and along a gravel path to a gated meadow, then over a rickety wooden stile to the fields beyond.

Ahead, the Westmarland fells that formed the end of the Pennines, lay soft and undulating and invited the walker to spend a leisurely afternoon hiking along the many nooks and pathways of the popular tourist county.

As she followed the dog, Jo picked up her pace and gave herself a telling off. It was no use moping around feeling miserable! After all she had a roof over her head, money in the bank and good health. But as the vastness of the countryside surrounded her, Jo wanted to scream. John, the pulse of her existence was gone and her life would never be the same again. How would she survive the darkness that stretched ahead?

She stopped and looked back at Kirkton House. Bathed in a pinkish and mauve light, the house stood proudly under a slow-moving sky, which framed the scene and reminded Jo of the photo-graph in the agent's draft sales details, where the accompanying words stated:

Formerly the principle residence of the village, Kirkton House dates back to the 17th and early 18th centuries with an elegant front wing added in the 19th century. The resident owner has carefully renovated the property and created an award-winning, stylish country house hotel. The property has en-suite rooms and a fine dining restaurant and, until a recent family bereavement, traded most successfully.

In what felt like another life, a young Jo had stood on this same spot with Robert Mann from, Mann & Co, Estate Agent for Country Living, who'd been astounded at her impulsive decision to purchase the crumbling old property. But Jo had explained her vision and he'd gradually understood. In the months that followed she invested every penny of her settlement from Greg and Kirkton House opened its doors to the public. When Hattie turned up on her doorstep, Jo sensed her desperation and immediately offered Hattie a job, for

Hattie too had been abandoned for a younger model and Jo was determined to give her a chance.

It was an act that created an enduring friendship and Jo thanked whatever wind that had blown Hattie to her, even though she was avoiding her friend these days.

Robert had long since retired but his son Rob, much to Hattie's disgust, was now keen to get Jo's instructions to go ahead with the sale of Kirkton House. The whole village had been talking about it and everyone, including a disgruntled Hattie, wondered if Jo would stay in the old place on her own.

So much had changed.

Jo resumed her walk and tried to imagine what John would tell her to do.

Suddenly, a ghostly wind blew across the deserted fells and his voice seemed to whisper, "The time to be happy is now..."

Jo stopped. As if struck by an epiphany she realized that John's haunting words were right! What on earth was she thinking? Life does go on! Somehow she had to lift the gloom and embrace the future and if it meant selling Kirkton House, she would clear the way to enable a fresh start. After all, everyone said your fifties were the new forties these days and Jo determined to stop moping around.

She must find fresh challenges to focus her life on.

Feeling encouraged, Jo hastened her pace and Meg, sensing a lifted spirit, ran joyously beside her.

2

Hattie balanced her coffee in one hand and a tin of assorted biscuits in the other and headed for the La-Z-Boy chair in the lounge. The recliner, which had been Maurice's idea - a true lazy boy if ever there was one, was large, comfortable and inviting. Hattie straddled the cushion and wriggled her behind into place then pressed a switch and as she watched her legs rise, her moth-eaten old slippers fell to the floor.

"I'm drowning in Draylon..." Hattie mumbled as the chair engulfed her. She placed her cup in the holder and closed her eyes.

She thought about Maurice.

He'd had a decent business as a flooring contractor and had never been mean with money, but why had she stayed with him for so long? Years ago, Jo had warned Hattie about Maurice's philandering ways, but for some reason Hattie had hung on in the vain hope that things would improve. They hadn't and Hattie's patience finally ran out when she caught Maurice laying more than a new vinyl floor, at the home of a divorcee from Marland. At least they'd not had kids and he'd been good with her two boys – offspring of her disastrous marriage to an Italian, when she was a mere slip of a girl. She was grateful that she'd never married Maurice and there was no messy divorce to go through. The house was her own, bought many years ago with the money she'd inherited from Bertie, the only man she'd ever truly loved.

Ah Bertie...

Hattie flicked the lid off the biscuits and grabbed a handful. She closed her eyes again and munched happily as she thought about the heady days of the hotel, when Kirkton House was packed with anyone who was anybody in the county and visitors came from far and wide.

Hattie had adored her job. As assistant manager to Jo, Hattie careered from one disaster to another, helping her boss ride the storm of recession in the early 90s to a more prosperous millennium and in the years that followed, the business flourished as they went about their day to day in the lovely old manor house that Jo had restored. Hattie chuckled as she dunked a custard cream.

By gum, they'd had some fun!

Two young women, whose friendship had grown from the first day that Hattie had knocked on the door of Kirkton House Hotel, fresh from the job centre with a crumpled application form clutched anxiously in her hand. Hattie was gob-smacked when Jo offered her a job and determined that she would do all that she could to make the business flourish. It had been the happiest time of her life and when Jo was ricocheting from pillar to post, as her illicit relationship with John developed, Hattie met Bertie - a charismatic Dubliner, who was staying at the hotel for the annual horse fair. He'd fallen head over heels for Hattie from the moment he laid eyes on her ample chest, "You're my storm in a D-cup!" Bertie would mutter lovingly as he endeavoured to pin Hattie down.

Hattie thought about Bertie's farm and his beloved horses. The kids had adored the place. But a sudden and fatal heart attack whilst Bertie was cantering along a beach, had sadly curtailed their wedding plans and in the dark days that followed, only her job and Jo's friendship had pulled Hattie through.

Hattie reached for her cup and dunked another biscuit.

Bertie's family had been generous and Hattie paid off her mortgage but it wasn't long before Maurice caught her on the re-bound, while she was still grieving for Bertie. The relationship was good in its day and she was fortunate that she'd had the sense to keep everything in her own name. Hattie knew that she'd never be rich but a small savings account would ensure that she'd manage.

Hattie sighed and wondered how many lovers Maurice had laminated since she'd kicked him out. She sat up and adjusted her housecoat then took a sip of coffee and reaching for the remote, turned the television on. She flicked through the stations, past house-building projects and heir-searching experts and stopped when she found her favourite.

Rickinson's Relics had just begun.

As she watched the screen, Hattie idly wondered how many hours the host spent applying fake tan, he seemed to blend into a set of mahogany furniture and Hattie wondered if he buffed his complexion with bees wax.

The adverts appeared and Hattie sat up. She ran her fingers through her mop of curly ginger hair and wondered what to do with the day. It was such a shame that Jo had shut the hotel. Hattie had loved working there over the years and, until it closed, still put in a few hours every week. The job had given her a purpose, especially since her boys had grown up and moved away.

Hattie remembered that Zach, Jo's youngest, was heading south and no doubt Jo would be feeling lost without him. She envisaged Jo wandering miserably around the gloomy old house, with that daft dog trailing behind, and decided that she'd give her friend a call when the programme finished.

She glanced around the living room and realised that she'd soon settled into single life. There wasn't a trace of Maurice anywhere, unlike Jo's rooms at Kirkton House, where John's presence seemed to haunt the place and Hattie wondered if Jo would ever get over her loss, for his death had been catastrophic. Given only a few short weeks from diagnosis, the once proud Romany, who'd overcome so much, couldn't fight the cancer that attacked his body and he died within days, shocking and shattering his family.

Hattie, who had watched Jo's sons grow up and alongside her own, felt that they had all been like one family and she remembered their agonising despair. John had been a wonderful stepfather to Jimmy and raised him as his own, encouraging Jimmy when he announced that he'd bought a bar in Barbados and Hattie wondered if Jimmy was working flat-out to mask his grief. Hattie knew that Zach couldn't stand to be at Kirkton House, where memories of his father oozed from every corner and hadn't argued when Jo made the sudden decision to close the hotel. Jo had bravely assured her sons that she would be fine, but Hattie knew that despite the months that had passed since John's death, Jo was far from fine and Hattie didn't know how to help her friend. She'd been thinking about a holiday to Spain as she'd far too much time on her hands and suddenly, Hattie had a flash of inspiration.

That's it!

Hattie sat up and knocked the biscuit tin onto her lap. Never mind moping about in that empty old building, what Jo needed was a holiday! A change of scene would do her the world of good. Hattie rammed her finger onto the La-Z-Boy's switch and was abruptly catapulted off the sofa. The biscuit tin went flying, narrowly missing the heavily tanned image that filled the television screen.

"You won't be the only one with a face like a coconut," Hattie shouted happily at the presenter as she gathered the housecoat around her ample chest and struggled to her feet. "It's time to pay Jo a visit and book a holiday!"

Hattie turned the TV off and made her way up the stairs. She'd a summer wardrobe to plan and maybe she'd try that swimsuit on again!

∼

JO WALKED BRISKLY along the tree-lined banks of the River Bevan, which curved around the perimeter of the little town of Butterly and hoped that the sharp spring air would lift her mood. Her thoughts during her morning walk with Meg had been positive but as the day progressed, her feelings had declined and she was pleased when Hattie called, to ask if she fancied a Sunday afternoon stroll and a cup of tea.

"Bleedin' hell, can you please slow down a bit?" Hattie yelled as she puffed and panted and tried to keep up. Jo and Meg were twenty yards ahead.

"Sorry, Hattie," Jo said and stopped in her tracks. She remembered that Hattie's idea of exercise was to lift a large gin and tonic repeatedly with one hand, whilst stretching out with the other to snack on a selection of crisps.

"I'm gasping," Hattie replied, "let's go and get a cuppa, sod this walking lark."

"It's important to keep fit," Jo said as she waited for Hattie, "do you want to head into your next decade on a stick?"

"Only if I use it to hook the back of your collar, you go far too fast." Hattie caught up with Jo and took her arm. "Let's have a nice chunk of sticky toffee pudding with our tea, it will give me an energy boost." She eyed Jo up and down as they stepped off the pavement, "Mind, if you lose any more weight, you'll slither through a grid." There was hardly anything to Jo these days. She'd lost a great deal of weight since John had died.

"I never seem to be hungry," Jo tugged on Meg's lead, discouraging her from sniffing every inch of an adjacent lamp-post. "Even Zach's cooking..." She trailed off and stared blankly at shop windows as they headed to the Lemon Drop Cafe.

The cafe was busy but they soon found a table for two by the window. Jo sat opposite Hattie and shoved Meg into the recess between their legs. She dropped the dog's lead onto the slate floor.

"Shouldn't allow animals in the place," Hattie moaned and jerked her foot as Meg licked the bare skin protruding above Hattie's trainers.

"This is Westmarland, not the West End," Jo said. "You're probably the only household that's animal-free." She looked around and smiled as one or two furry heads showing an interest in Meg's arrival, peeped out from chair legs and tails thumped.

Hattie ignored Jo and gave their order to the waitress then sat back and stared at her friend. She'd planned a speech to entice Jo on holiday and with the well-rehearsed words at the ready, took a deep breath.

"I know it's only early days," Hattie began, "and it probably doesn't seem five minutes since you lost John, what with Jimmy and Zach being off your hands too," she watched Jo carefully as she spoke the dreaded words, "but are you sure about selling up?"

Jo spread her fingers on the pretty cloth covering their table and traced tiny stitches that formed daisy chains across the fabric, enthralled by the effort that had gone into the stitching. The waitress produced a tray of tea with fine bone china and Jo caressed the crockery; she loved the current fashion for all things vintage.

"Are you listening to me?" Hattie broke into Jo's thoughts.

"I'm sorry, Hattie, what did you say?"

"For goodness' sake, get a grip, you're like a zombie," Hattie spooned three heaps of sugar into her cup. "I know you don't want to hear it and there's no one but me can say it, but are you absolutely sure about selling up?" She stirred the tea rigorously and took a sip. "I seem to remember you thinking the same thing twenty odd years ago, but you held on and it all came out right in the end."

Jo fiddled with a spoon and looked thoughtful as the waitress placed bowls of warm sticky toffee pudding before them.

"What have I got to keep me here?" Jo said, "Jimmy and Zach are gone and will never return." Her eyes began to fill. "I feel such emptiness as I rattle around Kirkton House. I can see, feel, smell and hear John in every room, around every corner, in every building and over every blade of grass. He loved the old place as much as I did and although he let me get on with the running of the hotel while he dealt with his own business, the walls seem to talk – they whisper his name and it haunts me." Jo caught her breath and a tear trickled down her cheek. "It's time to move on, start again."

"Start again at our age?" Hattie asked incredulously. "Where would you go? You've loved living in Westmarland and your friends are all here, including me." She reached out and took Jo's hand.

"I need a fresh start," Jo replied, "and I'm not short of money."

"Oh, to hell with money," Hattie snatched her hand back and reached for her pudding. "You're sitting on a tidy sum at Kirkton House, even though you've foolishly closed the business and the buildings will go to rack and ruin." She spooned the toffee sponge into her mouth. "You'll be like a fish out of water in a strange place and will lose your marbles in no time without me to nag and prod you along."

"I've made a decision, Kirkton House has to go," Jo was adamant. She pushed her untouched pudding to one side and thought about the silent rooms filled with antiques and fine furniture, covered with dust sheets which added to the eerie hostile atmosphere.

"It's not as if you'd be short of company in time," Hattie thought about Pete Parks, a local business man who had lost his wife the previous year. "Pete would be round here in a flash if you let him."

"Pete is just a friend and always has been," Jo said, "he might have taken a shine to me once but that was years ago."

"Like a bee to the honey pot now you're both foot loose and fancy free."

"How can you even think that, with John's death only months ago," Jo began to well up again.

"Alright, but will you do one thing for me before you make any decisions?" Hattie braced herself and forged on; she didn't want Jo blubbering all over her pudding.

"It depends what it is."

"Let's have a holiday, a few weeks in the sunshine with nothing more taxing than deciding where the next gin and tonic is coming from." Hattie challenged Jo and waited for her response.

Several minutes ticked by.

"Women our age don't go on holiday on their own," Jo said.

"What?" Hattie pulled a face.

"I'd feel awkward without a man..."

"Oh, for crying out loud," Hattie was furious.

"People might get the wrong impression?" Jo's argument was weakening.

"Get a grip, girl! This isn't the Victorian era - I'm not asking you to wheel the bathing huts down a beach and romp out in your modesty vest and knickers."

"Well, I don't need a holiday," Jo said finally. "I haven't worked for months and want to do something meaningful and move on."

"Well I do!" Hattie was cross and raised her voice. "You forget that I haven't exactly had an easy time of things lately and I for one would like a break and if you want to do something meaningful for the benefit of mankind, you can make sure that I have a marvellous time!"

The cafe was silent and several diners leaned sideways to catch Jo's response.

"Oh God, I'm sorry," Jo looked distraught, "I've been so wrapped up in myself, I never thought about anyone else."

Bull's-eye! Hattie thought and heard a collective sigh of relief as cups and saucers clattered and the cafe resumed business. She grinned and leaning over the table, reached for Jo's pudding, "Is that going spare?"

Jo watched Hattie tuck in. Hattie loved her food and had always been first in the kitchen to sample the hotel menu. She was such a dear friend and they'd been together through thick and thin over the years. Jo felt guilty that she'd neglected Hattie.

"Where would you like to go?"

"Spain, Nerja has our name all over it."

Jo winced and thought back to her only memory of Nerja and a long weekend with Hattie and Maurice a couple of years ago.

It had been a disaster.

"What about somewhere different?" Jo tentatively suggested. She knew that Hattie rarely went out of her comfort zone.

"Where are you suggesting?" Hattie licked sauce off her lips and eyed Jo suspiciously.

Jo didn't know where she wanted to go but perhaps they should consider somewhere further afield?

"What about Barbados?" Hattie said suddenly and held her spoon mid-air.

"Barbados?"

"Yes why not? You had a great time there with John last year, before he was ill. Jimmy would be thrilled to see you and I'll soon fit in." A piece of sponge fell off the spoon and dropped onto Hattie's lap.

"Jesus!" Hattie yelled as two Jack Russell's flung themselves on the sponge. Meg growled and leapt up causing the table to lurch, which sent tea flying everywhere. The commotion created uproar in the cafe as the dog's owners descended over broken crockery to retrieve their soaking animals from the depths of Hattie's crotch.

Jo began to giggle.

"Bloody animals!" Hattie stood up and stared at her wet gusset. Meg, who'd seen the terriers off, began to lick milk from the floor.

"You owe me, Jo Docherty," Hattie glared. "I hadn't even finished me pudding!"

Jo beamed, it had been a long time since she'd laughed and she'd forgotten how funny Hattie was. Perhaps a holiday wasn't such a bad idea?

"I take it that's a yes, then?" Hattie began to smile too.

"Better get your bikini packed," Jo replied.

"If it means getting you on holiday, I'll wear soddin' support pants on me head!" Hattie punched the air then flung herself back on her chair and proceeded to finish Jo's pudding.

3

Pete Parks sat in his office at the back of the car showroom and surveyed the activity on the forecourt of his garage.

It was busy for a Sunday evening.

His business lay just off a motorway junction at the Gateway to the Lakes, a popular tourist destination on the edge of the town of Marland, seven miles from the village of Kirkton Sowerby. As Pete studied his customers, he thought that the surge in trade was probably due to weekend holidaymakers. No doubt the hoards who queued for fuel had made the most of the fine spring weather and now filled up their vehicles before beginning their homeward journeys.

Pete closed his eyes and leaned back in an old battered chair. He thought about Jo, alone at Kirkton House and memories flooded back.

My, how the years have passed!

Jo was as attractive to him today as she was when he'd first caught sight of her many years ago, a bonny young woman who'd been abandoned by her two-timing husband.

Pete's heart raced as he remembered.

He'd always had a reputation as a womaniser but in truth, Pete thought it was a misguided notion. Married at eighteen, he'd stayed with his wife long after the kids had flown the nest. A Cumbrian man has values and to leave the lass that had given her life to him wasn't an act Pete had ever considered, despite the fact that he'd fallen out of love years before. His lass had died of cancer last year - a sad and painful end and it had been a difficult time as he nursed her through her final grip on life. Pete understood how Jo must be feeling.

But at least it had been quick with John.

In the early days, Pete had been suspicious of John whose mysterious gypsy background and fine looks had swept Jo off her feet. But as the years crept by, Pete put his concern to one side and got to know John. Their respect for each other grew and Pete thought John was the salt of the earth, an honest man who cared deeply for his family and they'd become friends. John's death had been a huge shock - at a time when Pete was already reeling from his own traumatic experience.

A car horn blasted, disturbing the peace of the office. It tooted repeatedly and woke Pete from his day-dreams. He hurried to see what was causing the commotion.

Hattie stood by a fuel pump and waved a credit card in the air.

"What's all this, Pay at the Pump, nonsense?" Hattie shouted. "It says me card isn't valid."

Pete shook his head and smiled as he walked across the forecourt, modern technology was lost on Hattie Contaldo.

He took the card and read the date, "Expired last month."

"Well it were alright in the Lemon Drop Cafe this afternoon," Hattie said primly and snatched the card back.

"Still got the slide machine, have they?" Pete replied and changed the screen on the pump to, Pay in Kiosk. He reached for the nozzle and began to fill Hattie's car.

Hattie turned the contents of her handbag onto the hood and rummaged around for alternative payment. "I'll have to get some cash," she said.

Pete replaced the nozzle and secured the fuel cap, then nodded to the assistant on the desk in the forecourt shop. The dials on the pump cleared.

"On the house, that should get you down the road for a mile or two," Pete watched Hattie bundle a cracked powder compact, an old pair of tights and a sachet of Slimfast, back into her bag.

"Very kind, I'm sure," Hattie snapped. "It'll make up for all the times you've had your hand up me skirt in the restaurant at Kirkton House."

"In your dreams, Hattie," Pete smiled.

"Talking of dreams, you might want to get over to see Jo," Hattie fiddled with the buttons on her blouse and stuck her cleavage out. "She's talking of selling up and moving on."

"Aye, I heard."

"Be a pity that, with you both being single again."

Hattie lit the blue touch paper and stood back.

Pete shook his head and sighed, Hattie never changed. She'd always been a mischief maker.

"We're both still in mourning for those we've lost."

"What nonsense," Hattie snapped and held her car key poised. "Life's too bloody short, Pete Parks, you should realise that. Still, I'm getting her away on holiday and if I have my way, she'll be taking up with a wealthy widower who can keep her in the style she's accustomed to." Hattie reached for the door and continued, "She'll be running down the road to happiness, not waiting for you to get a motor on your walking frame. Time you retired, you daft sod, and had some fun." Hattie flung herself into the car and started the engine and Pete leapt back as she thrust the car into gear and sped away.

He stared at the retreating vehicle as it shot in front of a line of traffic, causing several vehicles to brake. Hattie was probably right, he mused, he'd more than enough money and the garage would sell in a flash - wasn't it time to tell Jo how he felt about her and see if there was a chance of them making a life together? Perhaps he'd have a run over to Kirkton House tomorrow, it promised a fine day and he'd nothing else pressing. For the first time in months he felt a spring in his step as he wandered back to the showroom.

JIMMY DOCHERTY OPENED the door of the American refrigerator and rummaged through the neatly stacked provisions until he found a bag of bread and a bowl of barbequed fish. Closing the door with his bare foot, he took a roll, split it open and placed a fillet of spiced fish into the doughy layer. He grabbed a bottle of water and holding the sandwich and drink in one hand, stepped out of the kitchen into the dazzling Caribbean sunshine.

Jimmy wore faded denim shorts and his bronzed muscular body was toned and strong. At six foot three with closely cropped hair and fashionable stubble on his chin, he cut a handsome figure.

The cement on the patio was hot underfoot as Jimmy strolled barefoot then turned left out of a gate and onto the beach. He stopped and looked out at the turquoise sea. The sparkling water glittered in the morning sun, reflecting tiny diamonds of light on waves that broke into gentle rolling surf before embracing the pure white sand.

Jimmy sighed with pleasure, Barbados is for Lovers! He thought and was reminded of travel posters at the airport that greeted new arrivals. He began to stroll along what he called his 'back garden'.

It was a relief to get out. The humidity was high for the time of year, especially within the walls of his pretty beach house. Despite open shutters, no air circulated onto the ceiling fans and the only cool place was in the tiled wet room, where jets of soft tepid water caressed and reduced body temperature. Jimmy didn't mind the heat and was acclimatized to it now, but he knew that Hattie and his mum, who were due to arrive in a few days' time, would find the beach house far too hot and he'd reserved an air-conditioned apartment further along the coast.

Jimmy took a bite of his lunch and munched hungrily as he walked. He'd been surprised to get Hattie's call earlier. She'd talked Jo into a holiday and wanting to act before Jo changed her mind, booked their flights online and asked Jimmy to sort out accommodation. He was looking forward to their visit, it seemed ages since he'd seen them, the last time at his father's funeral, where Hattie had comforted Jimmy and Zach, telling tales of John in his prime and how she'd not wanted Jo to marry the mysterious gypsy, but in the end, all had turned out for the best. Jimmy thought about his parents, their marriage had been happy and Kirkton House a perfect family home.

John had been a wonderful stepfather and his death had pole-axed Jimmy.

He struggled to imagine how his mother was coping and hoped that this holiday would be beneficial, away from all the memories in Westmarland. Maybe a little bit of island life would give her time to relax and get some clarity. Jimmy wished that he could be more supportive but knew that only Jo could examine her life and decide on the way forward.

He sat down on a flat-topped rock and stared up at an Air Canada jumbo jet which had commenced its descent and glided smoothly along the coastal flight path of the south coast of the island. Taking a swig of water, Jimmy wondered if the Toronto Tigers ladies volleyball team would be in his bar that night. The leggy beauties had blown his bar staff away last month. Nineteen female twenty-somethings, all over six feet tall, had marched up the steps and over the deck to the bar of the Lime Inn then demanded that the shots keep coming.

Jimmy shook his head as he recollected the crazy night that followed.

Visitors leave their inhibitions at home when they land in Barbados and his bar, situated in a busy area known as the Gap, played host to it all. At least he wouldn't have to worry about his mum and Hattie, they'd be tucked up in bed as these nights were beginning and it was probably just as well. The bar made its money as day turned to night and a carnival of characters stepped out in their finery to embrace all the pleasures that were on offer.

He took another swig of water and glanced at his watch; he had a meeting with a promoter in an hour. Jimmy had other business interests which included an arena, at the back of the bar - a venue that specialised in large musical events. The legendary rock singer, Long Tom Hendry, was coming back to the Caribbean and Jimmy wanted to be sure that he secured the singer's gigs.

A tall handsome fellow, with waist-length dreadlocks and a beautifully defined body that shone like ebony, approached and raised his hand.

"Yo, Rasta!" Jimmy smiled and they touched knuckles in greeting.

"Yo, Jimmy, you mek sport?" the man asked.

"No, man, I have to work," Jimmy replied. "Are you coming to the bar later?"

A popular reggae band was playing live music on the deck that evening.

"Sure t'ing, sweet fuh days..." The man waved and strolled casually along the beach. He pointed towards another plane that was descending along the flight path, "I see you later!"

JO SAT on a rocker by the fire in her lounge and stared at the dying embers in the grate. The room felt cold and she contemplated teasing a fresh log into life but the effort was too much and gathering the folds of a blanket from the back of her chair, she wrapped the soft wool around her shoulders.

Meg, sensing movement, looked up.

The old dog stretched and yawned and when no activity was forthcoming, buried her head into her blanket and went back to sleep.

Jo was lost in thought.

Hattie had bullied her into a holiday and now that she'd agreed, Jo was beginning to have doubts. Was it too soon to be thinking about pleasure? Could she really allow herself the opportunity to go away and forget about Kirkton House and all its memories? She half expected John to walk through the door at any moment and his death was still raw, was she making a big mistake?

Jo sighed and shrugged her cold body. It was hard to know what to do these days, her mind jumped all over the place and what seemed right one moment, felt completely wrong the next.

At least Zach was happy.

Jo had spoken to her youngest son earlier and listened with interest as he told her that he'd arrived in the capital and settled into his temporary digs in a pub recommended by Jimmy. Jimmy had worked in London for several years before a beginning his business in Barbados and had been pleased to help his brother.

Jo glanced at the family photograph on the mantelpiece above the fire.

Zach was the image of his father. Tall, dark and handsome with a mop of curly black hair, almond skin and deep blue eyes. He was a brilliant chef and Jo marvelled at his talent. As a young boy, Zach had spent all his time in the kitchen, hungrily following all the recipes that Sandra, the cook, prepared for the restaurant and after leaving catering college the young apprentice spent his holidays working in Michelin starred restaurants, before returning home to gain stars of his own at Kirkton House. A week before Zach's departure, Jo had taken a call from an agent in London who wanted to meet with her son. She'd encouraged Zach to set up an appointment and this evening, had reminded him to confirm the meeting, now that he was in town.

Jo wondered what London had in store for Zach. It could only be better than spending his days cooped up here. They'd argued about the closure and Zach had said that his mother was mad to give up the business, especially as things were going so well. But Jo knew that Zach would never progress beyond the gates of Kirkton House if things had stayed the same and she no longer had the heart for hotel life after John's death. Her decision to close, despite her families protestations, had been easy.

But Hattie had talked Jo into a holiday and in a few days' time they would be leaving for Barbados.

Jo stretched her legs and wriggled her toes into Meg's warm tummy. Whatever was she going to do with her dog? Perhaps someone in the village would take her in? Jo only had a few days to sort things out and realised that she had much to do. The hotel was shuttered up but the garden needed attention; she'd airport pickups to arrange and must dig out some holiday clothes. Hattie wanted to fit a shopping trip in too and was planning a whole new wardrobe.

Jo yawned. Was it worth all the effort? Couldn't she just sell up and move away?

It was getting late and Jo gathered the blanket from around her shoulders and folded it neatly onto the chair. Meg, fearing that she was about to be booted out into the cold for a bedtime constitutional, opened one eye and watched Jo suspiciously.

"Come on Meg," Jo said and pulled on the dog's collar but Meg was determined to stay put.

"Even you don't want to move do you?" Jo sighed and shook her head and deciding that it was pointless to drag the reluctant old dog outside, tucked a rug around the sleeping body and turned off the lights.

Tomorrow is another day... She whispered to John's ghost and wearily made her way upstairs.

4

———

Pete sat in his office and scrolled though the list of contacts on his phone. He searched until he found the number for Rob Mann at Mann & Co Estate Agent but his finger hovered and he hesitated.

Now that the call was imminent, his confidence suddenly evaporated.

He'd been thinking about Hattie's comments, when she stopped at the garage a couple of days ago. Since then he had been determined to put the business up for sale.

He knew Hattie was right.

If he could live out his years in the company of a woman he'd always hankered after, what was he waiting for? His marriage had been happy and he'd done all that he could for his wife at the end, but if truth be told, had Jo not married John and she'd given Pete even half a chance, he would have grabbed it with both hands.

He'd always loved Jo and no doubt always would.

Hattie said that they were going away and Pete knew that he couldn't afford to miss any opportunity to speak to Jo and tell her about his feelings.

It was a risk, but at his age what had he got to lose? The alternative looked grim. Rambling around alone, in his big old house at the foot of the fells, with occasional visits from his kids, putting in an appearance at work when the fancy took him and generally living out his days in solitude as he declined into old age, wondering what might have been.

Pete leaned back in his chair and thought about the previous evening. He'd decided to act on impulse and taking Hattie's advice, called in at Kirkton House on his way home from work. He'd stopped at the village shop to pick up a bottle of champagne then parked at the back of the hotel. He knew that Jo was unlikely to answer the front door and leaving his car on the cobbled pathway in front of the old coach house, had wandered past a number of outbuildings to the ornamental gates that led to a walled garden. He found Jo barefoot, kneeling on the patio as she pulled at plants buried deep in a stone urn.

Meg lay alongside, watching Jo's every move.

Pete stopped and stared at the vision before him. Jo was simply dressed in a cream cashmere sweater and pale blue jeans and the evening sun caught strands of gold in her chestnut hair. Her delicate skin was flushed as she tugged at a stubborn bulb.

Pete was shocked. Jo was a shadow of her former self.

The voluptuous woman who'd confidently run her business and lived life to the full had diminished in the last few months.

Pete remembered John's funeral, where Jo stood between her sons and followed the entourage into the crematorium to say their final farewell. Zach was sobbing and Jimmy deeply distressed as John's coffin disappeared behind a velvet curtain, but Jo was calm and dignified as she reached out to comfort her sons. She'd taken Jimmy's hand and placed an arm around Zach as final prayers were said and Pete, watching from the sidelines, had been in awe of her dignity and strength. But as he stared at Jo now, he could see that her strength had given way to grief and she wore her loss openly, her heart clearly broken. He yearned to scoop her into his arms but her frailty alarmed him and he held back.

Jo sat on her heels and stared at the urn in frustration.

Pete watched her forehead crease in a faint furrow, as she bit on her lip and placed a trowel beside a shallow wooden trug. He longed to smooth the frown away. She was a striking woman; time had been kind and now, in her middle years, she could still turn a head. But as Pete stared across the patio, he felt her despair and yearned to take Jo in his arms and reassure her that everything would be alright.

He took a step forward and reached for the latch on the gate, then tentatively pushed it open.

Jo spun round and stumbled, knocking the trug on its side. Meg leapt to her feet and began to run in circles.

"Gosh, Pete," Jo exclaimed, "I didn't see you there."

"Look out!" Pete replied, "You've got soil all over your feet," he rushed forward and placing his bottle on the stone slabs, leaned in to manoeuvre Jo into a sitting position then began to brush the soil from her toes with his fingers.

"That tickles…"

Pete looked up and saw that Jo was giggling. The years suddenly lifted and he was back in this same garden, in the months before she married John.

"Do you remember when I stood in the mud?" Jo asked, her memory drifted back to that time too.

"Aye, you messed up your fancy shoes, I don't expect you ever wore them again."

They stared at each other with affection and remembered a time when life had infinite possibilities and their worlds were waiting to be conquered. Pete had declared his love then but had settled for friendship. He wondered what the world was offering the two of them now.

"Are you celebrating something?" Jo pulled her foot away. She nodded towards the bottle and began to stand.

Pete leapt up and held out his hand to assist her. Suddenly, he was embarrassed. It no longer seemed the right time to talk to Jo about his feelings.

"Hattie says you're off on your travels," Pete said. "I thought I'd wish you bon voyage."

"Oh that's kind," Jo took Pete's hand, "let's find some glasses."

Jo ran her fingers through her hair and the curls lay softly on her shoulders. Pete longed to touch the glossy locks but instead reached down and patted Meg's head. The dog had settled at his feet, her tail thumped, sending wayward soil flying.

Jo walked ahead.

Pete looked at Meg and shrugged his shoulders. The dog rose and together, they followed Jo into the hotel.

It was dark and gloomy as they entered the cocktail bar and Pete shook his head as he looked around. It saddened him to see the signs of finality, as he noted boxes stacked on tables and chairs. Dust sheets covered comfortable old sofas surrounding an open fireplace, where the grate was cold and dark. A ghostly shiver ran down Pete's spine and he longed to walk to the stone mullioned windows and pull back the curtains to bring light and life back into the room. He'd had so many happy evenings in this bar, on nights out with friends and family.

"Is it cold or shall I get some ice?" Jo asked as she hunted for glasses.

"Aye, ice might be a good idea," the bottle was warm and clammy in Pete's hand.

Jo returned a few moments later with a silver bucket. She reached out and took the bottle then pushed it into the ice. "Let's go and sit in the house where it's far more comfortable."

Pete followed Jo through the bar and into an even darker room which had in its day, been a restaurant. A lovely room with wooden panels and low, beamed ceilings; filled with tasteful antiques and carved mahogany furniture. Like the bar, the room was now dismantled; all signs of the busy, successful restaurant wiped clean and packed into crates.

"You're packing up then?" Pete asked as he stood in Jo's lounge.

"Have a seat," Jo ignored his comment and indicated that Pete should sit in a low backed rocking chair. Meg sat beside him and placed her head on his knee, while Jo expertly popped the cork and began to pour. Handing a glass to Pete, she raised a toast.

"To my holiday," Jo said, "if that's what this is all about."

Pete wasn't keen on champagne but knew that it was Jo's favourite tipple. He took a drink and stroked Meg's head as he looked around the cosy room which felt far more welcoming than the hotel rooms, but still lacked Jo's usual warmth.

"So you're selling up?" Pete tried again.

"Looks that way, have you come to talk me out of it?" She was brusque and Pete knew that he needed to tread carefully.

"No, lass, if that's what you want, I wish you all the best."

"Well, I didn't expect you to say that," Jo was frosty as she continued. "Everyone thinks a for-sale sign will go up any day now, I'm told it's the talk of the village."

"Can you blame them?" Pete asked. "This place has been the biggest part of their lives for years; they'll not want some property developer to knock it all down and throw up a couple of housing estates or turn it into a rabbit-warren of fancy apartments." Pete knew this would happen should Jo sell. Marland was expanding and the council keen to build new homes.

"I can't be responsible for other people."

"No, you have looked after folk all your life, now you need to look after yourself." Or let someone else! Pete thought.

"I've told Hattie I'll make up my mind after the holiday, but it's already made up."

Pete watched Jo pace around the room. Now was not the moment to tell her of his feelings, she was so wound up he might just forfeit the friendship that still held firm.

They'd finished the champagne.

"Can I take you out for a bite to eat?" Pete asked hopefully.

"No, I'm fine thanks."

Pete moved Meg to one side and stood. He had to say something! If Hattie had anything to do with things, Jo would soon be sailing the coast of Barbados on the yacht of a wealthy widower and Pete's chances would be overboard.

"Look Jo," Pete began, "I understand how you're feeling. Grief is a strange thing and makes you do things you might not normally do."

Jo stopped pacing and watched Pete.

"Don't do anything hasty with the hotel, eh?" Pete raised his eyebrows and took a step forward. "I've been through this too and maybe a break is all you need."

"I'll think about it," Jo conceded, "but if Rob Mann has any viewers they can look around while I'm away."

Pete sighed, he wasn't going to change her mind, but there was a glimmer of hope if he could buy some time. He placed his hands on her arms.

"I'll be here when you get back, perhaps we can go out for a meal?" he asked tentatively, hoping that Jo would thaw.

"That would be nice." She closed her eyes and reached out and Pete wrapped her in an embrace.

Softly, softly lad...

"Is there anything I can do for you while you're away?" Pete longed to bury his face in Jo's hair and run his hands over her body, but managed to restrain himself. "I can look in on the place and keep an eye on things."

Meg leaned against their legs.

"Well, yes... actually," Jo pulled away, "there is something you could do but I hardly like to ask."

"Just ask."

"Could you look after Meg?"

"Meg?"

Hearing her name, Meg jumped up and began to circle.

"I really don't want to put her in kennels."

Meg stopped and in a deft movement placed her front paws on Pete's chest and began to wag her tail.

"Well, aye, alright. I can hardly say no, can I?" Pete sighed and smiled at the dog. "Down you go, old girl. There'll be none of that at Park's Palace, it'll be tough love where you're going," he ruffled the fur on Meg's head and shook his head.

"Oh, I can't thank you enough," Jo exclaimed, "that's such a relief, to know that she will be well looked after."

MEG WASN'T the one he wanted to look after, Pete thought as he reflected on the previous evening, but if the route to Jo's heart was through her dog, it was a path he'd willingly tread.

He stared at his phone, where his finger still hovered over the contact list and with a renewed confidence, pressed the number for Rob Mann. After all, Pete told himself, he'd got plenty to do while Jo was away and it was time that he made a start!

"BRING BACK DOROTHY OSBOURNE!" Hattie yelled from the changing room in the ladies department of a store in Carlisle. Jo stood outside and held the curtain as Hattie's bottom protruded through the gap.

"There were none of these postage stamp cubicles in Dorothy's day; you can't swing a cat round in here," Hattie complained as she handed Jo a mass of discarded sundresses.

Jo began to work through the tangled items, hanging them neatly in order. She nodded her head in agreement and remembered the delightful dress shop that had sourced many stunning outfits for them both in days gone by. Service was everything at Dorothy Osbourne Designs and Dorothy had instinctively known what was right for her clients. An afternoon's shopping had been a pleasurable experience, combined with sherry, dainty sandwiches and a selection of cakes. Jo smiled as she thought about Dorothy who'd long since retired to the Greek island of Lesbos with her partner.

"This will knock 'em dead," Hattie announced and pushed past Jo to look in a full-length mirror.

"Or out..." Jo mumbled as she looked Hattie up and down. The lime green jump-suit that stretched dangerously over Hattie's curves was tight where it had no right to be tight.

"You're just jealous of my hour-glass figure," Hattie said as she paraded up and down.

"What about a pashmina to go with it?" Jo suggested as Hattie's ample chest oozed over the top of the bodice.

"Far too hot in the Caribbean," Hattie swept past. "I'll take this in all three shades."

Jo closed her eyes. She thought of the red, yellow and green jump-suits and wondered if Hattie had chosen the reggae colours deliberately.

All she needs is cornrow braids!

"Never mind standing there with a stupid grin on your face, we've still got to find your stuff."

"The clothes I took last year will do."

"And look like Orphan Annie?" Hattie eyed Jo's considerably reduced figure, "I don't think so." She flung herself into the cubicle, "I'll pay for this lot then we'll make a start."

Jo caught the jump-suit as it flew past the curtain.

"Let's have a bite to eat?" Hattie called over her shoulder as she eased into her clothes and gathered her bags. "I shall faint if I don't have something soon."

Jo thought of the mid-morning refreshments they'd shared an hour ago. Hattie had made light work of a basket of Danish pastries and two milky coffees.

"Got to keep your strength up for the holiday," Jo said.

"Never a truer word and we need get some flesh on your skinny hips."

As they made their way through the store, Jo thought it ironic that she'd spent most of her life worrying about her weight, always trying to lose a few pounds and now she needed to gain them. Perhaps she'd get her appetite back in Barbados.

They found a table in the champagne bar on the fourth floor and ordered a bottle to celebrate.

"Next time we'll be drinking champagne, it will be at thirty-five thousand feet," Hattie said and raised her glass.

Jo stared at the golden bubbles and remembered the previous evening, when she'd shared a bottle with Pete Parks.

"At least you've still got a taste for champagne," Hattie smirked. She'd seen the empty bottle and two glasses by the sink in Jo's house that morning. "Pete was always a white wine man, he's obviously changed."

Jo's head shot up.

"Don't go reading anything into it," Jo said. "Pete's a good friend."

"A friend minus a wedding ring," Hattie smirked, "who gets a lump in his trousers whenever he sees you."

"You have to spoil things," Jo snapped. "We've both been though a lot."

She took another sip of her drink and thought about Pete. Many years ago he'd promised that he'd always be there for her and to this day, he'd kept his pledge. He'd had a terrible time when his wife died and refused to admit her to a hospice, caring for her at home alongside the palliative nurses. Jo wished she'd been able to do the same for John, but he'd been rushed into hospital and neither of them had known that his end would come so quickly. It had been hard to be strong when all she'd wanted to do was scream at the injustice. Pete understood this; he'd been through it too and his reassuring words the previous evening had been comforting as he told her that he'd be waiting when she got back from her holiday and if she needed anything, she had only to ask.

"Maybe you should give Pete a chance?" Hattie reached for the bottle and topped up their glasses.

Jo looked up. Was she hearing Hattie correctly? Pete had been in her life for more than two decades, but as a friend not a lover. Surely Hattie must know that Jo would never get over John and had no intention of trying? She'd be happy to have a meal or two with Pete but there would never be anything more to their relationship; why didn't Hattie understand that?

"You've still got a lot of life to live," Hattie continued and popped a plump olive into her mouth. "Pete's a nice man. He's got plenty of money, a decent property and his flirting days are most likely over."

"But he's not for me," Jo said firmly, closing the subject. She pushed the bowl of olives towards Hattie and reached for the menu, "Are you still hungry?"

"I could manage a bite," Hattie perused the main menu, trailing her finger over the embossed page. She stopped on, Surf 'n' Turf Burger.

"My treat," Jo said, she'd already chosen a Caesar salad and hoped that she had the appetite to eat it. "The seafood in Barbados is amazing, you'll love it."

"Yep, I see food and absolutely know that I'll love every mouthful." Hattie topped their glasses up again, "Here's to our holiday."

"Here's to our future," Jo smiled at her friend and as they chinked glasses, she wondered what the future had in store. Perhaps now was the time for them both to find out.

5

Bob Puddicombe sat on a banquette at his favourite table and looked out at the crowded restaurant. He loved The Wolseley and could never understand why his business partner, Hilary Hargreaves, preferred to entertain at the more casual Ranchers Restaurant, in Covent Garden, which in Bob's opinion was filled with far too many media luvvies and celebrity gazers.

Bob glanced at his watch and noted that his guest, Zach Docherty, was running late.

He thought about his call to the north, a couple of weeks earlier. Hilary had been adamant that Bob track down a hot new chef, who had two Michelin stars and had recently closed his restaurant in a village called Kirkton Sowerby. Bob thought it sounded like the back of beyond but had spoken to the chef's mother, a charming woman by the name of Jo, who had been pleased to arrange a meeting with her son.

News of the young chef's two Michelin stars was quite the talk in hospitality circles and Hilary was keen to sign him to their media agency, but since her recent marriage to rock star, Long Tom Hendry, she had been away from the office for weeks and delegated the task to Bob.

Bob had been ecstatic when Hilary made him a partner at the agency a few months ago and was more than happy to take over the running of the business. After all, he'd worked for Hilary for years and there was very little that Bob didn't know, but Hilary had a trained eye for talent and if she spotted a chef with potential, she'd make damn sure that Hargreaves & Puddicombe Promotions were first in line to sign them up. Food journos around the country were raving about Zach's abilities as a break-through young chef and to be awarded two Michelin stars in such a short space of time was unheard of. Like everyone else, Hilary was astonished when the restaurant suddenly closed and she dug out an article in Caterer Online and emailed it to Bob with the subject line: "FIND THIS CHEF AND SIGN HIM UP!"

Bob reached for a string of prayer beads wound tightly around his wrist and stroked the smooth droplets, as he quietly repeated a few soothing chants, letting his mind focus on his inner core as he thanked his god for bringing him safely to this meeting.

"Mr Puddicombe, your guest is here." A smartly dressed waiter with a long black apron tied at the waist, bowed slightly and stood back.

Bob opened his eyes and stared at the young man who stood before him.

"My God," Bob told himself, "he is absolutely stunning!"

Bob stifled a gasp and sprang to his feet.

"Hello Mr Puddicome, my name's Zach Docherty."

"Oh, please call me Bob, don't stand on ceremony," Bob pumped Zach's hand.

"I'm so sorry that I'm late," the chef began but Bob waved his hand, dismissing the apology.

"Not at all dear boy, I hadn't even noticed," Bob said. He was struggling not to stare at the hunk who sat opposite, the young man oozed sexuality, in a rough and tousled way.

"Now what would you like to drink?" Bob composed himself.

"I'll stick with mineral water, if that's OK."

"Same for me," Bob said and instructed the waiter. He wondered if the chef was tee-total as he gazed at the magnetic blue eyes and thick mop of dark wavy hair and imagined legions of gagging fans.

Bob needed to get Zach signed to the agency as fast as possible, before their competitors swooped in! His mind raced ahead and he visualized the chef hosting a TV show, at book signings and travelling the country to demonstrate at festivals and events. Zach's culinary skills were clearly without question and anyone with two Michelin stars knew their way around a kitchen. But had he got personality? Or would this be something Bob would have to work on in their bid to make Zach a household name, thus ultimately reaping the benefits of a generous percentage of Zach's earnings.

"And what are your plans now that you are living in London?" Bob made small talk.

"I want to keep my options open, but I'd like to be back in a kitchen as soon as possible."

"Have you ever thought about compiling a cookery book to celebrate your success in the restaurant at Kirkton House?" Bob studied Zach.

"Oh yes, my recipes are in order, including my signature dishes, there's at least three hundred written out in my journals," Zach said. "Our hotel cook, Sandra, made me keep detailed files of everything I ever created," he looked whimsical, "cooking is a religion to her and she taught me a great deal of what I know."

Bob reached for his prayer beads and said a silent, Thank you. Zach was a publisher's dream!

"And would television appeal?" Bob broke a warm roll in two and spread creamy white butter over the soft dough.

"I've never really thought about it, the local TV station was interested in me but I never had time."

Bob bit into the bread and smiled. A comforting glow tingled through his body as he visualised their new protégé making his first appearance on, Saturday Morning Cooks, in a few weeks' time.

The meeting boded well and Hilary was going to be delighted!

~

"By heck, this is the life!" Hattie tucked her bag into a storage area as a stewardess placed a glass of champagne and a packet of savoury snacks on a table between their seats.

"Ah, business class, the only way to travel." Hattie raised her glass and eased into the comfortable leather surround. "How long is the flight?" she asked and rummaged around for an inflight magazine, "I think I could settle on here for days." She tossed a cashew nut into the air and deftly caught it with a wide-open mouth.

"Don't smudge your lipstick," Jo said as she watched Hattie repeat the process.

"Virgin Atlantic," Hattie read the headline, "that's us – two virgins crossing the Atlantic."

Jo fastened her safety belt and breathed a sigh of relief. They'd made it to their seats with only a few minutes to spare before take-off. Hattie had lingered in the duty-free shop, oblivious to the final call for passengers Docherty and Contaldo and it had been a frantic rush to get to the boarding gate.

"What time are they serving dinner?" Hattie asked as the stewardess reached above their heads and closed the overhead locker.

"I think they might want to take off first," Jo smiled at the pretty girl in her tailored red uniform.

It had been a frantic dash to get to the airport. Jo had hoped for a leisurely journey but Hattie had thrown a last minute panic and insisted on repacking her cases, adding five more outfits that Jo had never seen before. Combined with Hattie's need to have a cooked breakfast, "For the journey, you don't know when we'll get fed again..." They'd left an hour later than planned. Pete had offered to give them a lift and as he was collecting Meg that morning, it made sense to accept.

He'd arrived in his Mercedes saloon and stared at the mountains of luggage on the driveway at Kirkton House.

"How long did you say you're going for?" Pete asked.

"It's all Hattie's," Jo replied as she placed her solitary case in line and wondered how on earth it would all fit in.

"I'm not sitting with that scruffy mongrel!" Hattie threw herself onto the front seat and slammed the door. She lowered the window and glared at Meg who was sitting morosely by the suitcases, her head nudging Jo's legs as Pete began to load bags into the car.

"You look like one of the Beverly Hillbillies," Hattie said sarcastically as she watched Jo clamber into the back and squeeze next to Meg, amidst mounds of luggage. "Barley sugar?" Hattie reached for a bag of sweets, deep in the depths of her bulging handbag.

Relieved that the cases were safely stowed, Pete slid into the driver's seat. "I wish I was coming with you lasses," he said as the engine roared into life and he pulled onto the main road.

"Well I'm very glad you're not," Hattie replied rudely. "We don't need a chaperone where we're going." She turned and gave Pete a salacious wink. "Ever thought of opening a kennels when you retire?" Hattie nodded towards Meg, who'd snuggled on Jo's knee.

Jo put her arm protectively round the dog.

"Let's just hope that the good folk of Barbados understand your warm Westmarland wit and humour," Pete commented wryly as he took a barley sugar and began the journey to Manchester airport.

THE PLANE TOOK off and Jo and Hattie were finally on their way to Barbados. With eight hours to kill, Hattie fiddled about with the inflight entertainment and Jo closed her eyes and thought about the conversation she'd had with Zach the previous evening. He'd told her all about his meeting with Bob Puddicombe and explained that Bob, who seemed likeable, was very spiritual and wore several rows of prayer beads on his wrists. He seemed to consider good karma an integral part of running a successful business and Zach had thoroughly enjoyed the meeting. Jo didn't think that karma was a criteria Zach needed worry about, but she listened carefully as Zach explained Bob's ideas and plans then asked Jo for her advice.

"What do you really want to do?"

"I'd like to work with Bob but don't want to be out of a kitchen for too long, there are loads of opportunities in London."

"Well, try and combine the two," Jo suggested. "If Bob can raise your profile and get you media coverage it would significantly help when you do open a restaurant. But don't sign anything without legal advice."

"OK, I'd like to give it a shot. He wants me to start with some training, how to cook and talk in front of a camera, deal with the press – that sort of thing," Zach had replied and they'd ended the call with the decision agreed.

Jo turned her head and ignoring Hattie's fumbling and cursing, stared out of the window. The plane had risen steeply and now levelled off to cruise above the clouds, where a deep blue horizon stretched as far as the eye could see. She sipped her drink and wondered if she was dreaming? Was she really going on a Caribbean holiday as a single woman? After a lifetime of being escorted by a man, this was something that she had never imagined and the thought filled her with anxiety, even with Hattie's company. How Jo wished that her beloved John was here, holding her hand, and for the zillionth time she wondered if the pain of loss would ever ease.

"These bleedin' earphones don't work!" Hattie punched wildly at her control panel.

"Have you tried plugging them in?" Jo asked and taking the wires from Hattie's fingers, connected the sound.

"Ouch!" Hattie shouted as the opening music to a feature film blasted her ear drums, "Get us another drink Jo - I need to steady my nerves before I start watching, Twelve Years A Slag."

Jo closed her eyes and smiled. Whatever would she do without her friend? Hattie was like sunshine on a rainy day and Jo had a feeling that this holiday was going to be eventful. Was Hattie ready for Barbados, but more importantly, was Barbados ready for Hattie?

~

PETE STRODE BRISKLY over the fells behind his house with Meg ambling alongside. It was a lovely night, light for the time of year and a pleasure to be out walking after being closeted up in his office at the garage all day. A plane soared high in the sky, trailing a golden vapour against the setting sun and Pete wondered where it was heading. He checked his watch. Jo and Hattie would have landed by now and no doubt be settling into their apartment.

Pete had never been to the Caribbean. He'd had several family holidays in the sun, mostly in Florida, and imagined that he'd probably enjoy Barbados if he ever got the chance. He occasionally travelled with his mates, who shared his love anything to do with engines and Motor GP. An ex-biker himself, Pete's interest in bikes had never waned since winning the famous TT race on the Isle of Man many years ago and he still sponsored up and coming riders, hoping to give them the opportunities that he himself had received as a penniless young man.

But with any luck, the opportunity for island holidays may come soon.

Rob Mann had been ecstatic when he received Pete's instructions to sell. The garage was to be marketed immediately and the estate agent had assured Pete that a buyer would be found in no time. Despite lean economic times, there was a big demand to build new housing and the land that the garage occupied was perfect for that purpose. Pete would have the choice of selling it either as a going concern or building land and could more or less name his price.

Meg bounded over to a mossy overgrown stream and Pete shouted for her to come back but the dog ignored him.

Typical female!

Pete thought about Jo on an island that was sure to be full of temptation. Had he left things too late? Only time would tell. At least he had her dog to look after and she'd no doubt be on the phone to find out how Meg was faring. He'd look in on the hotel too and as Jo had left her keys with him, he'd make sure that the old place was safe while she was away.

A muddy lump moved towards him and Pete stopped in his tracks and sighed.

"It's no use wagging your tail!" he bellowed at Meg as he jumped out of the way. If it was his dog, she'd be out in the barn tonight but he thought about the soft wool blankets and luxurious towels that Jo had left alongside Meg's big padded bed, and the huge bags of toys, treats and dog food that stood in Pete's utility room. He'd better get the animal showered down when they got back, there was sure to be a bottle of doggy shampoo amongst her belongings.

Pete sighed. Whatever it took!

He kept walking.

6

"Where's my factor fifty?" Hattie yelled as she swept into the arrivals hall at Barbados International Airport and fanned her face with her passport.

"We've only walked across the tarmac, try and calm down!" Jo said as Hattie made exaggerated gestures and feigned heatstroke, whilst looking around at her unfamiliar surroundings.

The airport was busy and as they waited to have their passports checked, Jo filled in their immigration papers. Hattie smiled at a customs officer and tried to decipher his many questions. Then, having established their length of stay and address whilst on the island, he stamped her paperwork and wished them both a pleasant vacation.

"Blimey, does he want to know my shoe size too?" Hattie snapped and shoved her paperwork into her bag.

"Welcome to Barbados, momma." A porter wearing a red baseball cap drew his trolley alongside Hattie and beamed. "Yu want help?"

"Right now I need a very large drink," Hattie replied, "who turned the heating up?"

"We're in an air-conditioned building and you must wait while I get our bags." Jo moved towards a conveyor belt, where luggage from the Manchester flight was beginning to appear.

Hattie mopped her forehead with a tissue and looked around. There was a huge throng of people on the move from returning locals to excited holiday makers, weary from their journey and anxious to retrieve their belongings and begin island life. Hattie removed her jacket and stuffed it into her bag, then adjusted the bodice of her dress and ran a coat of pink gloss over her lips. She thrust her chest out and followed Jo, who with the aid of the porter, had managed to gather all their suitcases.

"I hope I'm not strip-searched," Hattie said as she entered the nothing-to-declare lane.

"Well you won't have much to take off," Jo glanced at Hattie's chest, encased in a thin cotton fabric that strained to contain her ample bosom.

"You're only jealous," Hattie smirked and sailed past Jo and the porter, through sliding glass doors and out into the airport complex. "Where's our ride?"

"AUNTY HATTIE! OVER HERE!"

Jimmy stood behind a barrier and shouted. He wore knee-length shorts and a black vest and his tanned and handsome face stood out amongst the crowds waiting to greet the incoming flight.

"JIMMY!" Hattie bellowed and dropping her bag, ran at full force. She almost knocked Jimmy over as she leapt over the barrier to engulf and smother him with kisses.

Jo bent down to gather the contents of Hattie's abandoned bag, where the passport and paperwork were scattered amongst half-eaten packets of sweets, a packet of condoms and several lipsticks.

Hattie was crying hysterically.

"I always get emotional at airports," she blurted and dabbed at her eyes as she held onto Jimmy's arm. She sniffed and wiped her cheeks then stood back and poked his muscles, "By heck, you're a right stunner."

Jimmy grinned then turned to his mother and held out his arms. Jo threw herself into her son's embrace.

"Hello, my darling," she choked back tears, "it's so good to see you."

"It's wonderful to see you too, Mum." Jimmy said as he hugged his mother. "Have you had a good journey?"

"Bleedin' hell, can we cut the chatter?" Hattie had composed herself and produced a battery operated fan from her bag. She turned it on and moved her head from side to side, "I'm gasping..."

"I bet you're both ready for a rum punch," Jimmy guided the women to his waiting vehicle and settled them into the air-conditioned interior. He gave the porter a tip then jumped in beside them.

Thrusting his foot onto the accelerator, Jimmy headed for the highway and joined the evening traffic. "Welcome to Barbados!" he yelled above the noise of Hattie's whirring fan. "Do you want to go straight to your accommodation or would you like to stop for a drink?" Barbados was four hours behind UK time and he wondered if Jo and Hattie might be tired.

"Do pigs fly?" Hattie called out as she lowered her window and let the warm balmy air caress her skin, "Hell, it's hot, but I love it already!"

Jimmy turned off the highway and wound his way through a series of small roads that ran parallel to the coast then pulled into a car park, behind a bamboo building. A wooden platform with a rope rail led to a bar. Jimmy stood back to let Jo and Hattie enter and smiled as he watched Hattie's face light up.

"Oh my..." Hattie gasped. She gazed beyond the bar where several steps dropped down to the beach. A fire pit was roaring and sent sparks shooting into the night. The smell of burning drift-wood was sweet and combined with a strong aroma of ozone as waves crashed along the shore.

"I thought the sea was calm in Barbados," Hattie said as a barman appeared with their drinks.

"The west coast is calm," Jimmy replied, "but this is the south where the Caribbean meets the Atlantic and it's perfect for surfing." He held his drink up and toasted their holiday.

"I'm not sure that we'll be surfing," Jo said as she gazed out at the view.

"Speak for yourself," Hattie replied. "Blimey, this stuff is nectar." She raised her glass and took another slug then tipped the glass back and drained it. "Can I have another?"

"Aunty Hattie," Jimmy said and put his arms around Jo and Hattie, "you are on holiday and can have anything you want." He planted a kiss on both their foreheads.

"I won't tell you to go easy," Jo linked her arm through Hattie's, "but the rum is strong and can be deadly."

"It doesn't seem five minutes since we used to start and end the day with a stiff drink," Hattie said and stared out to sea. "We had fun days when the hotel was just starting." She turned at looked at Jo. "But we didn't have a clue, did we?" The two women shook their heads and laughed. "And I loved every moment in the years that followed, I wish you hadn't closed the hotel."

"Yes, we had some laughs."

"And we could have plenty more."

"There are too many memories," Jo said, "we can't go back."

Jimmy returned with several friends who'd just arrived. He wanted to introduce everyone to his family and as the bar began to fill, the barman turned up the reggae music.

"I'm being bitten to death!" Hattie shouted above the noise and slapped at a mosquito, "But I couldn't care less!" She grabbed another rum punch from a passing tray. "Fancy a dance, Jo?" Hattie grinned and hitched up her dress. "I haven't had a cigarette in years but could murder one."

Jo eased herself up onto high stool, where she could watch the evening's activities as the place came to life. It was so good to be back on the island! The tropical air and cooling sea breeze was like balm on her skin and the rum was making her mellow. Jo felt herself relax and she stretched her fingers out and smiled.

"Happy?" Jimmy asked.

"Yes, I am. It's so good to be here."

They watched Jimmy's friends as they danced and drank and encouraged Hattie onto the dance floor.

"Please may she not learn to twerk on her first night," Jo muttered.

"Twerking may be the least of your worries," Jimmy said, remembering that he'd seen Hattie puffing on a joint when she'd asked a local for a drag of his cigarette.

"Oh well, you know what they say..." Jo looked at Jimmy and joined him as he replied, "What happens on the island stays on the island!"

THE BEDROOM in Jo's apartment felt cold and she shivered as she swung her legs over the side of the bed and glanced at her travel clock.

It was early, the day was just beginning.

She stood and turned off the air-conditioning then flexed her arms above her head and stretched for several moments, before stepping into the bathroom.

A fluffy towel hung on a rail and Jo wrapped it around her naked body. She squeezed paste on her toothbrush and as she began to scrub, stared at her reflection in a mirror that lined the wall above a deep marble sink.

Jo looked exhausted and it was no wonder. The local rum had finally got the better of Hattie and most of what was left of the previous night had been spent administering aid as Hattie retched and swore that she'd never drink again. She'd finally settled and with only a few hours left before daybreak, Jo had managed to grab a couple of hours sleep.

As she rubbed anti-ageing cream into her face, taking care to smooth it gently into the dark circles around her eyes, she thought about the holiday ahead.

The first thing Jo wanted to do was swim.

The beach lay just beyond the apartment and Jo looked forward to reacquainting herself with the glorious stretch of silvery white sand and turquoise blue sea. She ran a brush through her tousled hair then searched for a swimsuit and pulled it on. Grabbing a sarong, she opened the bedroom door and the humidity hit her as she walked through the ground floor rooms. Jo tugged a cord which hung from the central light fitting and stood for a moment to bask in the cool air as a fan began to turn.

Tip-toeing over to Hattie's room, she gently opened the door and peeped in.

The cover on the double bed rose methodically and loud snores reverberated from the thin cotton. Hattie's head was visible, her skin pale and eyes tightly closed and Jo breathed a sigh of relief. Hattie was sleeping soundly and it was safe to leave her. She gently closed the door and went to the desk in the hallway where she found the apartment key. In the lounge, she pulled aside a long muslin curtain and unlocked the patio doors, then stepped out onto tiles which were hot beneath her bare feet.

Jo walked along a winding path that led through the gardens of the apartment complex. Her route was surrounded by pretty plants, the grass neatly cut and sprinklers positioned at intervals to shower the flowering vegetation. It was a beautiful morning and Jo breathed deeply, she wanted to fill her lungs with the clean rejuvenating air.

"Mornin', madam," a middle-aged lady with scarf tied around her head, strolled along the path. She smiled when she saw Jo, "Yu' came back!" she cried, her dark skin glistening and smile radiant.

"Hello, Gloria," Jo said. "It's lovely to see you again."

Gloria held a bucket in one hand and a broom in the other and as she passed, she frowned, a look of sympathy on her face, "Yu' too, honey, we sure sorry to hear 'bout your husband."

Jimmy must have told the staff about John.

"That's very kind, Gloria, thank you."

"Yu' enjoy yo' swim, yu' hear?" Gloria nodded. "Anything you need, jus' ask."

Jo hoped that she wouldn't need more of the help that she'd acquired in the night from another staff member. Cecil, the night watchman, had helped support Hattie, who'd fallen prostrate and giggling at his feet, when he'd opened the door of Jimmy's truck.

"She's had a long journey," Jo hastened to explain as she reached out to preserve Hattie's modesty by tugging at her dress, while Cecil and Jimmy scooped Hattie's paralysed body into a fireman's lift and hauled her into the apartment.

"De jet-lag play hell with de balance," Cecil commented as they'd placed Hattie on her bed.

Jo shook her head as she remembered the performance; Hattie would certainly suffer for her exploits today!

She had reached the beach and stood in the shade of a row of Casuarina trees that lined the edge of the complex.

Nothing had changed.

White sands stretched in a curve around the bay and palms swayed over a row of sunbeds and umbrellas that lay waiting for the day's tourists to descend. Beach folk were setting up their water sports equipment and several life-guards, wearing red shorts and yellow tops, began morning exercises beside their headquarters, a wooden structure on thick poles, with shutters open to a panoramic view.

Jo gazed at the green and blue sea and wriggled her toes in the sand. The scent of coconut oil wafted by on the breeze and she closed her eyes and remembered the tanning oil that she'd rubbed onto John's muscular shoulders the previous summer.

Tears began to threaten.

The last time she'd stood on this beach, she'd been holding John's hand. Their holiday had been like a second honeymoon, blissful and relaxing in this tropical paradise. Had it been a mistake to stay here again? So many memories flooded back and the pain suddenly seemed to engulf her as she choked back tears and tried not to sob. Stop it! Jo told herself, she was so fortunate to be in this beautiful place once more, she must not feel sorry for herself!

Jo stepped onto the beach and began to walk quickly. As she reached the row of beds, she tugged at her sarong and dropped it on the woven fabric, then turned and ran into the sea. The warm water was welcoming and as Jo began to swim out, she turned her face to the sun.

It was heaven.

She rolled onto her back and with a burst of energy, began a furious backstroke. After a few minutes, she turned and swam back. The swim was wonderful, it was so good to release pent-up energy and as Jo repeated her routine, she knew that Barbados would be healing over the coming weeks, how could it not? The gentle way of life, beautiful scenery and quiet days ahead were just what she needed and Jo intended to enjoy it all. She gazed at the horizon as she swam and filled her head with soothing thoughts.

"WATCH OUT FOR SHARKS!" A voice bellowed out from the beach.

Jolted out of her daydreams, Jo saw a figure standing in the shallow surf; it seemed to be gesticulating and waved frantically.

Sharks? Jo thought anxiously.

Not wishing to take any risks, she scrambled through the surf to head back to the beach as fast as she could. Gasping for breath, she soon reached the shore then stood and looked around. The figure had moved up the beach and seemed to be causing a commotion. Jo stared as the voluptuous body collapsed on a sunbed and indicated to the beach attendant to alter the angle of the umbrella.

The penny dropped and Jo walked out of the sea.

Hattie lay on a bed. She wore a vast, sleeveless cotton ensemble, straw hat and sunglasses and her face, smothered in factor fifty, was as white as snow.

"I thought you might be drowning," Hattie said as she made herself comfortable. "Get some of this on your face; it looks as though you've dipped it in a chip pan." Hattie threw the tube of cream in the air and Jo caught it.

"You were comatose when I left the apartment," Jo stared at Hattie in disbelief. "How on earth have you managed to get here?"

"It's me strong Westmarland constitution," Hattie replied as she applied red lipstick. "I was just telling my friend Malibu here, how much we'd enjoyed the rum punches last night," she beamed at the beach attendant who peered from under his knitted hat and fussed about as he placed a table conveniently beside Hattie. Malibu returned the smile and thanked her as she placed a five dollar bill in his hand. Hattie dropped her lipstick onto the table and flopped back on the bed.

"You look like The Joker from Batman," Jo said and began to giggle.

"Can't be too careful with this sun," Hattie touched the waxy cream on her face then flexed her legs and scratched a mosquito bite. "Anywhere where we can get some breakfast? I'm starving."

Jo picked up Hattie's abandoned towel and began to rub her wet hair.

So much for a quiet morning on the beach.

7

J immy sat in a courtyard, under the shade of a large canvas umbrella and tucked into his breakfast. He was hungry and the cheese and bacon omelette, which had been cooked to order in the little cafe, was delicious.

The promoter, who sat opposite, sipped a black coffee and waited patiently as Jimmy ate. He lit a cigarette and blew smoke into rings, then watched them dance high above the chattel house shops that surrounded the popular dining area.

"I'm happy with the deal," Jimmy announced and pushed his plate to one side. He caught the eye of a pretty waitress and with a smile, asked for a drink. As if by magic, a tall frosted glass of freshly squeezed juice appeared.

"Usual set up," the promoter said. He stubbed out his cigarette and went to light another, "Smoke?" he asked.

"No thanks," Jimmy wiped his mouth with a napkin and took a long drink of the juice. "He's a good crowd-puller," Jimmy said, referring to Long Tom Hendry, the famous rock singer who was booked to gig on stage in Jimmy's arena, courtesy of the promoter. "Bajans love his reggae vibe." Jimmy thought about Long Tom's best-selling album, No More War, which had been re-mastered by his record label. Radio stations in the Caribbean played it day and night. "I like him," Jimmy said and sat back to admire the shapely curves of the waitress as she leaned over to clear an adjacent table.

"Nice booty," the promoter grinned.

Jimmy's phone vibrated constantly and as he drank his juice he scrolled through emails and messages.

"Tickets are sold out," the promoter said. "Long Tom arrives soon and his crew will want all the usual sound checks."

"He's welcome to set up and rehearse any time," Jimmy read his mail and as he worked, thought about the aging rock-star whose come-back tour had started at the Lime Inn the previous year. Jimmy had spent time with Long Tom in between rehearsals. "Is he still sober?"

"As a judge," the promoter replied. "He got married too."

"Cradle snatching?" Jimmy envisaged a young wannabe model, no doubt a clone of Long Tom's previous wives.

"On the contrary, some business woman from London, she won't see forty again."

"Hell, I didn't see that coming," Jimmy put his phone down and looked up.

"Neither did his fans."

"Are we done?" Jimmy asked.

"Good to go, my friend." The promoter stood and shook Jimmy's hand. "The contract will be emailed today, increase your security - the old man is a legend these days."

"Already sorted," Jimmy smiled and tapped his phone. He sat back and watched the promoter wander through the tables, high-fiving a couple of people as he made his way to the road.

Jimmy looked forward to welcoming Long Tom back to the arena and knew that the two events had sold out within hours of tickets going on sale. Gigs like this were rare on the island and both would enhance trade. Jimmy rubbed his hands together, he loved being busy!

He picked up his juice and wondered how Hattie was that morning, she was probably still out cold. Last night, she'd drunk enough rum to sink a pirate ship and Jimmy thought it highly unlikely that she'd surface today but he'd ring and make sure things were OK, they might want some food sending down a little later. At least Jo could chill out and get some rest, he was concerned by her weight loss and she looked so tired, perhaps the holiday would help get her over the pain that she so obviously felt. He missed his stepfather too and it still felt strange not having John on the end of a phone, always interested and keen to offer help and advice.

He drained his glass.

"Can I get you anything else?" The waitress hovered. She had one hand on her hip and pursed her lips provocatively.

"No thanks, just the bill." Jimmy reached for his wallet and placed some dollars on the table, aware of the attention. Women seemed to fall at his feet and as he picked up his receipt and left a generous tip, Jimmy sighed. He longed for the thrill of the chase, for someone to actually make him do all the running. Island life had a pattern and if you had half decent looks, money in your pocket and a willing smile, you could have the time of your life in Barbados. But Jimmy was bored with romance that only lasted the length of a holiday and no longer wondered what the next plane would bring. Occasional flings fulfilled his needs but until the right girl came along he would focus on his business; at least that gave him a buzz.

Jimmy walked through the courtyard and decided that he would drop by the apartment to see what meds Hattie needed then visit the pharmacy and stockpile. He had a lot to do that day and checking his watch to make sure that he was on schedule, jumped in his truck and headed off.

"By gum, I enjoyed that." Hattie said and pushed her plate to one side.

They sat in the shaded restaurant of the Tropical Palms Hotel, which overlooked the beach. In the middle of the room, a buffet was set out on long tables where a selection of hot and cold food was covered by silver domes. Casually dressed guests meandered around and helped themselves to the breakfast items.

"You made light work of your eggs," Hattie commented as she buttered a slice of toast. "Haven't seen you eat so much for ages," she stared at Jo's empty plate.

"I think it must be all the swimming," Jo replied and bit into a warm croissant, "and the fear of being hacked to death by a shark."

"Don't want you getting complacent; you looked like you might be enjoying yourself."

The two women glanced at each other and laughed.

"Oh, Hattie, it's so good to be here," Jo said. She turned to gaze out at the beach, which had begun to fill with holidaymakers settling down for the day.

"It certainly is," Hattie wiped crumbs from her lips.

"What do you fancy doing?"

"Should we spend a day on the beach and go somewhere nice for a meal tonight?"

"That would suit me," Jo thought of the sunbed with longing, "but I have to go back to the apartment and get my book and sun cream."

"Get a hat too; your face is as red as a raspberry." Hattie looked around for a waiter, "Shall we pay the bill?"

They made their way out of the restaurant and past the hotel swimming pool where the cool blue water looked inviting.

"I think I might have a dip," Hattie said and pulled her dress over her head to reveal a scarlet swimsuit.

"That's a stunner!" Jo stood back and admired Hattie.

"Thought I'd give Pamela Anderson a run for her money," Hattie dipped her toe in the water. "Bloody hell, I'm not getting in that, it's freezing." She retrieved her bag and dress, "Come on, the sea calls." Hattie led Jo out of the hotel and onto the beach, where they went past the lifeguards, who lounged around by their wooden HQ.

"Keep walking," Hattie thrust out her chest. "They think we're from Baywatch..."

Jo marvelled at Hattie's confidence.

Back at the beach beds, Hattie made herself comfortable.

"I'm just popping back to the apartment," Jo said. "Can I get you anything?"

"Only as long as it comes in a chiller box with lots of ice and is easy on the mixer," Hattie lay back and closed her eyes. "I'm ready for a little livener."

Jo began her walk and smiled at two local ladies who were brushing the sand with long-handled brooms. They swept little green pods that had fallen from a nearby almond tree, into neat piles.

"Hiya Mum!" a voice called out and Jo looked up. Jimmy was heading towards her, "Don't tell me Hattie is conscious?" he asked incredulously as he reached his mother and placed an arm around her shoulders.

"She's conscious, full of breakfast and requesting a drink."

"And I was about to check her medical insurance," Jimmy laughed.

They fell into step and Jo told Jimmy of her plans for the day.

"If you need anything, just give me a call." Jimmy held the apartment door, "Mattie can drive you tonight." Jimmy referred to Mattie, the driver for the Lime Inn. "Why not try the lobster restaurant at the end of the Gap?"

"That sounds lovely," Jo said and collected her things.

"You could come by after dinner and have a drink at the bar? There's a jazz band playing that you'd like."

"Sounds like a plan," Jo kissed Jimmy's cheek then stepped into the sunshine as he locked the door.

"Catch you later, enjoy your day," Jimmy dropped the key into Jo's bag. "Love you!" he called out.

Jo watched her son as he walked away. He was so charismatic, just like his brother. Her heart swelled with pride, how lucky she was! She reached for her sunglasses and placing them on her head, turned to find the pathway leading to the beach.

As she walked, Jo silently thanked Hattie for insisting that they come on this holiday. By the time they returned home, there was a good chance that she would be ready to sell the hotel and move on. She thought of Pete's anxious face, her decision was the last thing he wanted, it was only a matter of time before he expected to be taking her out and it would be very easy to let him, but did she want a relationship again?

The time to be happy is now, let the universe show you how...

Jo heard John's words and stared up and the sky, "Don't worry, my darling," she whispered, "that's exactly what I intend to do."

PETE SAT at the table in his kitchen and stared at the unopened letter. He dabbed a chunk of bread into bacon fat that had begun to congeal on his plate and took a bite.

The stable door crashed open and Meg, smelling bacon, bounded across the room to fling herself across the stone floor until she skidded to a halt beside Pete's legs. She was wet and muddy and her coat had the faint aroma of cowpat.

"Oh, bloody hell, Meg!" Pete pushed his chair back and looked at the dog with exasperation. Was it a Labrador thing or did all dogs gravitate to the smelliest area they could find when you let them out for their morning constitutional? She'd obviously been rolling in something foul and now thumped her tail with expectation, eyeing the remaining bread in Pete's hand.

Pete was on the point of giving up. It was hopeless trying to keep the dog clean and he wondered how the hell Jo managed. Meg was always silky and shiny when she was with Jo, and he realised that it must take a great deal of time to groom the mischievous old animal.

"Aye, you can have it," Pete sighed and held out the bread then watched Meg gobble it down in one gulp. He searched for an old towel and was on his knees wiping the fur on her tummy, when the phone rang.

"Hello?" Pete said as he held the phone to his ear and arched his aching back. The dog would be the death of him, he thought as he looked down. Meg lay with her back to the open doors of the wood burning stove, basking in heat.

"Morning Pete," Rob Mann said cheerily. "Have you opened your post?"

"Just about to, but I got waylaid." Pete glared at Meg who was very close to the stove.

"They've offered the full asking price," Rob announced. "It's all in the letter I've sent and I hope you will accept, Pete Parks Autos could soon be the Marland Fields Estate."

"By heck, that was quick." Pete looked around anxiously, could he smell scorched fur?

"Completion subject to planning permission, no need to worry about selling as a going concern, the builder wants the land and has the planning in his pocket." Rob added, "With a shortage of new property in Marland, the council will push it through in no time."

"It's burning!" Pete yelled and rushed to the hearth where Meg lay.

"What's that?"

"You prat!"

"Well, I've done the best I could, I thought you'd be pleased," Rob sounded peeved.

"No, sorry Rob, not you – this damn dog has gone and burnt her backside and doesn't seem to have noticed." Pete gripped the rug that Meg lay on and pulled it away from the open flames, then slammed the doors of the stove shut. He rubbed her back and tail where the fur had singed and hoped that it would grow back quickly.

"Where there's no sense, there's no feeling?" Rob asked.

"Aye, but don't go telling that to Jo, she'll have a fit."

"You're dog sitting then," Rob stated the obvious.

"I'll be dog throttling if it keeps this up," Pete sighed and sat down. He picked up the letter and resting the phone in the crook of his neck, ripped it open. "Well that's a great result, Rob."

"Shall I accept on your behalf?"

"No point in holding off, we'll not get a better price."

"I'll start the paper-work, congratulations."

"Aye, I suppose so, thanks."

Pete replaced the phone and stared at the letter. It would be the end of an era. He'd started the business when he was nineteen and had never known anything else. Pete thought about his kids, he'd better tell them. Not that they'd bother, his daughter worked in the city and his son was in the army. Both had families of their own to worry about, but at least it would clear the way to spend some time with Jo. After all, he'd have plenty of time on his hands, perhaps he should take up a new hobby? Pete sighed. He liked to tinker about with old tractors but the only hobby he really wanted was to wine and dine Jo and take her to places he'd only dreamt of. He wondered what she was doing at that moment, it was agony to think of her in the company of wealthy widowers and as Hattie quite rightly suggested, Jo probably won't be on her own for long.

Meg looked up then trotted across the kitchen to rest her head on Pete's knee. She gazed at him with soulful eyes and howled. Was the dog so perceptive? Did she know that Pete was thinking of Jo? Pete stood and opened the door and waited as Meg hurled herself on her box to retrieve her lead, then bounded past Pete into the yard.

I shall be a fit as a bloody fiddle if I keep this up. Pete thought as he followed. At least something good is coming out of all this.

8

B ob looked at the thick contract and slowly began to unscrew the cap off his Mont Blanc fountain pen. On the opposite side of Bob's desk, Zach leaned forward in his chair and stared at the same paperwork.

The boy looked doubtful and for a moment, Bob was anxious. Hilary would kill him if he didn't get a signature soon.

Things had escalated in the past few days and it was imperative to have the paper work nice and tidy before Zach started work. Bob knew that Zach had been reluctant to sign without checking over the finer details with his mother, who was on holiday in the Caribbean and sadly unavailable and Bob had suggested that Zach take legal advice, but the Docherty family solicitor had retired and Zach didn't know of anyone else.

"There's no pressure," Bob had said, "but after your successful screen test, there are opportunities coming up that I'd hate you to miss and we need to have an agreement in place before you start working with us."

He'd watched Zach closely, pen poised, and reminded him that he'd pulled in favours to secure a debut appearance on Saturday

Morning Cooks, this coming week, and it was a wonderful opportunity.

"Where do I sign?"

"On the last page," Bob said breathing a sigh of relief. "Both copies, please."

Bob watched Zach and felt elated. Hilary would be thrilled! Now they could really go to town and get things moving, this was a recipe for success!

"Poppy dear," Bob spoke to his assistant, who hovered by the desk, "could you witness Zach's signature and ask Lottie to come in and witness mine, then I'd like you to call Ranchers Restaurant and reserve Hilary's table for lunch, she said she would be joining us."

"Your press release will be going out today," Bob said to Zach. "Several recipes are scheduled in mainstream magazines and they all want an interview with you within the editorial." He studied his computer screen and continued, "Fenums TV saw your screen test and are interested in filming a pilot and a meeting has been arranged with a publisher on Friday to discuss your book. I also want you to work with Poppy to set up social media accounts."

Bob watched Zach make notes in his new leather-bound notebook, he seemed to be distant and Bob saw that Zach had drawn a row of vegetables across the top of the page.

"No time for day-dreaming, dear boy," Bob stood up. "There's much to be done." He grabbed his jacket from the back of an ancient captain's chair, "Taxi for Ranchers Restaurant!" he yelled to Lottie, their office administrator, and held the door open for Zach. "After you."

Bob winked at Poppy, who had appeared in reception with a freshly made-up face and was joining them for lunch.

"Tally ho!" Bob cried and gathering his party, swept down the stairs of Hargreaves & Puddicombe Promotions and out onto Wardour Street, where Lottie had commandeered a taxi to whisk them to Covent Garden.

"Have fun," Lottie grinned as she watched them pile in.

"You must tell your mother the good news," Bob said as they sped through the lunchtime traffic. "She'll be delighted that you are now officially part of our agency."

Or she'll crown him for not taking legal advice... Bob thought and reminded himself of the first lesson in business that Hilary had drummed into him, never sign anything you don't understand!

LONG TOM HENDRY lay on a wooden swing on the verandah of an old plantation house and swayed gently as he stared out at the landscape before him. High above sea-level, the building enjoyed an excellent view of the east coast of Barbados, where the Atlantic crashed along the rugged coastline. Huge mahogany trees lined the perimeter of the plantation and as the heavy branches swayed their cooling breeze was welcome. Doors and shutters lay open allowing balmy air to circulate through the hot and humid rooms.

Long Tom was enjoying himself.

Reclining on the swing, with several cushions supporting his head, a Stetson hat was tilted on his forehead and his long fingers laced loosely across his naked chest. He'd arrived on the island the previous day and checked into his favourite hotel on the west coast and with a good night's sleep under his belt and an early swim, in the calm Caribbean waters that lapped his luxurious beach-fronted room, he'd made an early start to be driven to the plantation and meet with his band.

He loved this old house and the studio, which had been added by his friend Eddie, a Bajan musician who'd bought the property several years ago. Musicians from all over the world craved to record here, but it was by Eddie's invitation only and much sought after.

Long Tom had known Eddie for years. They were successful artistes and in the 80s, their hey-day, had been hell-raisers, leaving years of drug and alcohol addiction in their wake. Now, in later life, both had found sobriety which had enhanced their friendship and saved their lives. They knew the demons that had previously destroyed them and discovering that life could go on without the aid of substances, were determined to enjoy their sunset years with clear heads and open minds. Eddie spent most of his year on the plantation with his family, travelling only when work took his fancy or a faraway city called.

As Long Tom swayed gently, he thought about his own family, which consisted solely of Hilary, his wife. They'd not been married long and to date, things seemed to be working out. It was the first marriage that Long Tom had entered sober and he could barely remember how the previous two had ended. He wished that Hilary was with him but she'd little interest in lazing around in Barbados while Long Tom prepared for his forthcoming gigs. Hilary's business in London kept her busy, as did the renovations on the manor house, Flatterly Manor, in Ireland, Long Tom's country home. Hilary had fallen in love with the crumbling old pile and with the help of a top London designer, set about returning it to its former glory.

Long Tom couldn't see what all the fuss was about.

The manor house had been his retreat when he came out of rehab and he'd spent several comfortable years there, living as a recluse, until his record company brought out a reggae version of his best-selling album, which suddenly became a huge hit in the Caribbean and he was forced out of retirement to promote it.

Long Tom sat up and removed his hat. He shook out his shoulder length hair then reached for an ice-cold soda and as he savoured the refreshing drink, he contemplated his return to fame. Meeting Hilary had helped him to compose songs; with love in his life he was able to write again and was working on a new album. What better place than Barbados to record it?

"Comin' for a stretch across the yard?"

Long Tom looked up. Eddie stood beside him and motioned towards the huge expanse of land that surrounded the house. He wore a tracksuit and his hair was neatly braided, the thick dreadlocks flowed halfway down his back.

"Don't mind if I do," Long Tom replied.

Some yard! He thought and heaved himself upright.

Long Tom grabbed a shirt from the end of the swing, then slipped his bare feet into a pair of old sneakers and fumbled about in the pockets of his shorts to retrieve his sunglasses. He crossed the verandah and went down wooden steps to walk through an area which had been restored to replicate a traditional 17th century herb garden. He soon fell into step alongside Eddie as they wandered through the culinary and medicinal herbs.

"This place has history everywhere you go," Long Tom commented. "You can feel it in the air." A pair of Moluccan cockatoos screeched and reminded Long Tom of his own beloved peacocks in the garden at Flatterly Manor.

They passed an enormous sandbox tree which gave shade to the courtyard and Eddie explained that the tree was over three hundred years old.

"Imagine the history it's witnessed," Long Tom commented as he watched a frog hop into a crevice and merge with the gnarled bark. He tried to envisage the tree as a sapling, when the plantation was fully operational with scores of slaves working in the surrounding cane fields.

They continued their walk and wandered through a gully, where lush green terrain was home to many varieties of indigenous flora and fauna and ancient silk cotton trees lined the pathways.

The remains of a windmill stood on a raised patch of land.

Eddie stopped and looked up at the imposing structure. "The plantation kids used to hang off the sails when the windmill was operational," he said. "It was sport for them and broke the monotony of work."

Long Tom felt a shiver run down his spine as he stared at the ghostly pile. He tried to envisage little bodies hanging onto huge wooden sails that powered the mill, as grinding stones inside crushed and harvested the cane.

"Many of them fell and received terrible injuries," Eddie whispered. "Probably my forefathers."

The cries of children from another century seemed to echo and Long Tom squinted as he cast his eyes over acres of surrounding land

and tried to envisage the plantation when it was fully operational and slaves toiled monotonously under a scorching sun.

"If only they could have seen into the future," Long Tom said. "Now look who is boss."

They continued their walk through the plantation grounds, then turned and headed back to the house, where lunch was about to be served.

Eddie and Long Tom entered the dining room, a large colonial room with polished wood floors, covered in antique rugs and a wealth of period furniture. Modern artwork hung on the walls, interspersed with more traditional pieces. Eddie was an avid collector but he also liked to paint abstracts and some of his work was displayed.

"Something smells good," Long Tom said.

Eddie's wife had prepared a meal and fussed around a long refectory table, placing piping hot tureens on hessian matting and bowls of salads and side-dishes alongside. Eddie pulled out chairs for his guests and their children chattered excitedly as members of Long Tom's band, who had taken a break from the studio, joined them. The table was piled high with traditional fare and everyone tucked in.

"Lookin' forward to your gigs?" Eddie asked as he dunked a fish cake into a bowl of pepper sauce.

"Yeah, it's a cool place to play," Long Tom replied and cut himself a slice of macaroni pie. He thought about the Lime Inn, it was a good venue and held a large crowd. As he ate, Long Tom studied his fellow diners and thought how fortunate he was to be with this loving family, back on the island. The last time he was here he'd been so nervous, it had been the start of the comeback tour and after years of isolation he'd been unsure of his ability to perform stone cold sober in front of a big audience. But his worries were unfounded and with Eddie's encouragement and support the tour had been a huge success and received warmly.

Eddie's children bantered and giggled with the band as they fought over the last of the spicy shrimps, while Long Tom looked on, munching coconut coleslaw and fried breadfruit. He remembered the windmill and said a silent prayer of thanks. Thank god these children knew better times.

"We will all be there to support you," Eddie said as the children scrambled onto his knee and hung off his muscular torso.

"No pressure then," Long Tom smiled.

He finished his lunch and excused himself, then went out onto the verandah and as he leaned on the railing and gazed out at the view, he thought of Hilary. He missed her and wished that she'd come on this trip, there was so much to experience on this island. But she'd dismissed it as a beach holiday and not being one to sit all day in the sun, told him that her time was better spent at work in London and taking care of matters at Flatterly Manor. Hilary didn't need to work, they had no financial pressures other than the vast amount of money she was spending to restore Flatterly Manor, but she loved her business and was reluctant to delegate everything to her co-director, Bob. Long Tom hadn't put up an argument, after all, this trip was work for him too and he longed to be back on stage, the buzz from a receptive audience was as good as any chemical or alcohol high. But something was missing in his life and he wished that Hilary were here to share it with him.

Barbados gets in your bones...

Long Tom heard the family laughing whilst they cleared the meal away and he thought about the affection that Eddie and his wife showed to each other.

A man needs his woman beside him!

The sun was setting in Barbados and it would be lunchtime in London, Hilary would be busy. Long Tom made a mental note to call her later, maybe she'd have a change of heart.

The sky above the Atlantic had changed from glorious shades of red and gold to inky blue and black, but as he stood on the verandah and listened to wave's crash on a distant beach, he knew it was unlikely that his wife would be joining him.

With a sigh, Long Tom wandered back to the studio to continue with his work.

9

Jo and Hattie soaked up island life. The holiday had progressed well so far and they were enjoying lazy days on the beach, interspersed with trips to tourist attractions and points of interest that Jimmy recommended.

They'd struck up a friendship with Mattie, who had his own taxi company and worked as a driver for Jimmy. He was a knowledgeable guide, born and raised in Barbados, and knew all the hidden treasures that could only be found by veering off the beaten track. So far, they'd discovered deserted beaches that seemed to come straight from the pages of Robinson Crusoe and eaten with locals at pop-up events in rickety rum shops and tiny chattel houses, all tucked away in remote communities dotted throughout the eleven parishes that made up the geography of the island. Mattie would manoeuvre his vehicle down a particularly tricky incline, or hairpin bend in a road, while Jo and Hattie clung on tightly only to whoop with relief as they emerged at yet another deserted hamlet nestling precariously on the side of a hill. The locals they encountered were warm and friendly and always happy to stop for a chat, especially with Hattie who loved their lilting patter and hung off their every word.

"Did you know that suck-a-bubbi, is a drink you buy from a vendor, usually an old woman sitting with a cart beside the road?" Hattie asked Jo. She sat on a comfortable patio recliner with her feet resting on a footstool. "And pick-pick is the penis." She looked over the top of her reading glasses and held out, Bajan Words Explained, a pamphlet she'd picked up in a nearby gift shop.

Jo ignored Hattie's offering and turned the pages of Barbados Today, the local paper that Cecil left by their door each morning. She perused the events section.

"That's handy to know," Jo vaguely replied, "interesting phrases that we can try next time we're out with Mattie." She reached out and poured a coffee. They'd eaten breakfast earlier and the remnants remained on the table.

Jo turned another page and yawned. It was nearly lunchtime and they'd yet to decide what to do with the day. "Jimmy says that Long Tom Hendry is performing in the arena and he's reserved us VIP tickets."

"I'd expect nothing less than VIP treatment from your Jimmy and I have always liked old Long Tom. Can you remember him in the 80s?"

"Not really," Jo was distant. "Do you fancy going on a catamaran cruise on Sunday? If we got up early and head to Bridgetown we could get one from the pier." She examined an advert in the paper, "This one says you can swim with turtles and enjoy a traditional Bajan lunch on board."

"Safe man, safe," Hattie replied.

Jo looked up and raised her eyebrows.

"It means: cool, OK, good," Hattie grinned. "Let's do it."

"You have to book," Jo scanned the paper for a telephone number. "I wonder if Jimmy wants to join us?"

"The lad will jump at the chance of escorting a couple of bronzed beauties," Hattie commented and waved at Gloria, who passed by with a trolley stacked with freshly laundered sheets and towels. "Yo, Glo!" Hattie called out.

"I'll call him and check," Jo muttered and went in search of a phone.

Hattie lay back and contemplated their adjustment to island life since their arrival in Barbados. Most mornings were spent on the beach and after a brisk walk before breakfast they would lounge around in the sun until lunchtime, with Jo taking frequent swims while Hattie paddled on the shore. In the afternoon they often went for a drive with Mattie, followed by dinner in a local restaurant and a few late drinks at the Lime Inn, where there was always live music and a welcoming atmosphere, before retiring tired and happy.

She looked out at the well-maintained gardens and saw George, the head gardener and handy-man, who was watering a tightly packed border. It was covered in brilliant bougainvillea and a large leafy plant, which Mattie had told her, was named Lady of the Night and gave off a powerful and intoxicating scent when the sun went down.

Hattie ran her fingers through her hair.

Earlier, she'd applied treatment oil which, if the label be believed, would bring lustre and shine to dry and damaged locks. It was a gift from Mattie, who'd assured her that the oil had magical properties and would restore the sun-damage in no time. Hattie wasn't so sure and knew that with the heat and oil combo, she could fry a couple of kilos of chips in her hair and she was anxious to rinse the oil off.

"All booked," Jo said as she returned. "Jimmy wants to come on the catamaran too and suggests that Mattie drives."

Hattie pulled a face and fiddled with her hair.

"You'll be able to wear it up soon," Jo said, noting that Hattie's hair had grown rapidly since they'd arrived.

"Must be this slimy stuff Mattie gave me, he says it's full of vitamins." Hattie examined her greasy fingers and frowned. "Let's go and have a swim, I can sandblast it off."

They gathered their things and locked the apartment, then made their way to the beach. It was another glorious day and as they arrived at their sunbeds, Malibu hurried over with a table which he placed on the sand, then arranged an umbrella to give Hattie shade from the scorching sun.

"Rain comin'," Malibu announced and pushed the beds closer together under the umbrella.

"Fuh' true?" Hattie looked doubtfully at the sun-drenched sky.

Jo listened to Hattie chat with Malibu as she spread her towel out and undid her sarong.

"Malibu says it will be pouring by this afternoon, there's a storm on the way," Hattie flopped down, her brightly embroidered kaftan billowing over the lounger.

"Better make the most of it then," Jo replied. "Coming for a swim?"

"Nope, I've asked Malibu to get us a couple of pina coladas, they are full of fruit and we haven't had our five-a-day yet." Hattie grinned. "Off you go, watch out for sharks."

Jo spent the next twenty minutes swimming in the gentle surf. She enjoyed her routine and knew that the daily exercise was doing her good.

"You're beginning to look half-decent again," Hattie commented as she watched Jo stroll up the beach and pat herself down with a towel. It was true; Jo had gained a few pounds and at last, seemed to have an appetite. Her tan was deepening, as was her confidence and she'd even cast her swim-suit to one side and now wore a pretty bikini.

"Sup up, you're getting behind," Hattie sucked her drink through a straw and ran her finger around the top of the glass. "Bloody love-ly..." she sighed and bit into the cherry garnish. "Two more of these, when you get a mo," she called to Malibu, who was happy to oblige. Hattie's generous tips were going towards his scooter fund and he hoped he'd soon be mobile.

"Crikey, these drinks get stronger every day," Jo said and reached for her book. "It's absolutely delicious though," she took another slurp.

"Good, eh?"

"Wonderful."

They touched glasses.

"Cheers!" Jo said and raised her glass, "To us."

"Too sweet," Hattie sighed and with a grin spreading across her sun-kissed face, closed her eyes.

~

"And, action!"

Bob stood on the set of the pilot, Foraging with Friends by the Gypsy Chef, and watched Zach look into the camera.

As the lens focused on his face, the young chef grinned.

His blue eyes twinkled and thick curly hair, nestling on the collar of his crisp white t-shirt, gleamed under the hot arc lights as he grabbed a knife and with a deft flick, began to chop a bunch of nettles. He tossed them into a pan to sauté, alongside finely diced wild garlic as several female members of the crew gazed on, mesmerised by the chef's muscular forearms that diligently stirred and gesticulated as he cooked.

Bob thrust his hands into the pockets of his Barbour jacket and felt smug. Fenums TV, on discovering Zach's Romany background, had pushed ahead with filming and invented a foraging angle, confident that the public would lap it up.

"The boy is an absolute natural," the director told Bob when they took a break for coffee. "Housewives will be salivating over their screens and running to the garden to bag a handful of weeds to whip up in a wok for hubby's tea."

They stood in the director's garden in west London, which had doubled-up as a set for the day and Bob stared at the untamed mangle of vegetation that was being used to improvise as a deserted heath in the countryside. Zach had spent the morning pretending to forage for food as he grubbed about behind the Victorian house. The programme, a pilot to entice the TV channel commissioners, was being filmed on a low budget, at the expense of the production company, Fenums TV, who had seen no need to fund their crew to move out of London to capture the essence of The Gypsy Chef. Bob had skirted over the fact that it was actually Zach's father who was the gypsy, Zach merely his offspring who'd inherited classic Romany looks. But given the success of all things with the word, 'gypsy' in the title, Bob considered the hook useful.

A young researcher was on his hands and knees and with great effort, dragged a child's tricycle from under a bush, while everyone waited patiently.

"I wondered where that had gone," the director said as he examined the flaking paint and broken seat then indicated to the researcher, who was covered in dirt and brambles, to put the battered object out of sight.

"Let's nail this take, people!" the director called out and Zach sprang into action to dunk a wild crayfish into a pan of boiling water, on a makeshift stove. The crayfish, which had been purchased by the crew's home economist from a west London delicatessen that morning, was supposed to have been found in a countryside stream. Zach tapped the shell and explained to the camera that the clever little fish even had his own coat of armour.

"Good job you never cleaned that pond out," Bob commented as he watched the playback with the director. "I feel as though I'm knee-deep in the Shires."

"It's a wrap!"

Everyone applauded the end of the shoot and began to pack up.

Bob made his way over to Zach and stepped over yards of untidy cabling that wound through the garden. He wished he'd worn Wellingtons and not the immaculately polished brogues that were now covered in mud.

"Brilliant, dear boy," Bob said and slapped Zach on the back. "It's certain to be commissioned and I'm confident that you will get a series." Bob grinned. "It's a format that we could roll out to any country."

They watched the crew pack away the cookery equipment and portable camping table.

"I'm going to head off," Bob said. "Let's catch up in the morning, bright and early, there's a publishers meeting at lunchtime, so make sure you're suited and booted."

Bob watched Poppy hold Zach's jacket and as he thrust his arms into the sleeves, the chef asked her if she'd join him for a drink to celebrate. Keen to accept, Poppy went to find her jacket.

"Better not make it a late one," Bob said as he watched them climb into a taxi. "You have a busy day tomorrow and need to prepare for your appearance on Saturday Morning Cooks."

The taxi moved off and Bob watched the pair settle back into their seats, their heads close as they chatted about the filming. Bob wondered if Zach had paid any attention to the clause in his contract about fraternizing with agency staff. It was something that Hilary was adamant on. In-house relationships were a no-go and both staff and clients when signing their contracts, were bound by this rule.

Bob sighed, he was sure it was just innocent and with no more thought to the events of the day, he signalled a taxi for The Wolsely, where he was meeting his partner for dinner. Anthony would have a glass of Bob's favourite wine waiting.

Time to relax!

Bob grinned happily as the taxi sped away.

10

"F uckety, fuck fuck fuck!" Hattie yelled as she skidded across the wet patio and fell in a heap by the apartment door.

The contents of her beach bag spewed across the tiles.

"Oh my god..." Jo mumbled and staggered as she teetered towards Hattie. She tried to regain her footing but she'd stepped on a bottle of Hattie's hair oil, which squirted violently onto her feet. As the sticky substance adhered to Jo' bare skin, she lost her balance.

Within seconds, she joined Hattie on the floor.

Thunder crashed and lightning streaked across the darkened sky as torrential rain flooded the holiday complex.

"We'll drown if we can't get upright!" Hattie shouted above the storm.

Jo's head was in line with Hattie's knees and she frantically reached out to find something firm to hang onto.

"I knew that last drink was a mistake," Jo muttered. Her head was spinning and she felt unsteady as she grabbed Hattie's leg.

"It's like a tsunami," Hattie giggled. She lay immobile, staring up at the ceiling. The level of water on the patio had risen as the storm continued to rage.

"I don't know whether to laugh or cry," Jo gripped Hattie's knee.

"Don't bleedin' cry, I don't want to drown in your tears." Hattie felt anxiously at the ground around her prostrate body. "Did I put the key in my bag?" She turned her head and tried to focus on anything that resembled the shape of a key amongst the sodden leaves, sand and debris that was sloshing about on the patio.

"Can you get up?" Jo asked.

"Doubt it."

The last drink had gone straight to Hattie's head and despite all her best efforts; the large amount of rum had paralysed her. She prayed that Jo could stand.

"Don't mind me!" Hattie yelled as Jo skidded to her feet and landed her left foot in Hattie's face. She winced in pain as another crash of thunder threatened to bring the ceiling down.

Jo grabbed a beach towel and stuffed it into an untidy bundle which she shakily placed under Hattie's head.

"Mustn't let you dwown," Jo slurred.

"Bollocks to that, just find the sodding key!" Hattie shouted.

"Lordy, lordy, ladies! What de hell goin' on here?"

Like saviours sent from heaven, Cecil and George appeared, silhouetted against darkened skies, complete with black garbage bags protecting their uniforms. Their arms struck out through make-shift holes as they scrambled across the patio to assist.

"We lost the key and Hattie fell over," Jo grinned foolishly.

"De rains play havoc with de balance," Cecil said solemnly as he placed a master key in the lock and helped Jo into the apartment. George reached down and began to haul Hattie to her feet.

Within moments, they found themselves side-by-side on the sofa as George placed the missing key on the hall table and with a courteous nod joined Cecil, who was brushing flood water and debris away from the apartment.

Hattie's kaftan was drenched and bright red dye seeped over her arms and legs, spreading up her neck to her face, "I look like a crime scene," she said.

"Fuckety fuck," Jo muttered. "We're alive!" She swung her legs onto the sofa and lay her head on Hattie's damp shoulder then closed her eyes.

Hattie looked at her friend and could see that Jo had fallen into a deep asleep. "Another day in paradise," Hattie muttered softly then closed her eyes and within moments was snoring gently.

PETE WAS deep in thought as he drove along the main road towards Marland and hardly glanced at the countryside as it flashed by. Meg sat alongside with her head hanging out of the passenger window and barked loudly whenever she saw a sheep.

The garage sale was going through and Pete had several matters to tidy up in the coming days. He'd a stock of vehicles that he needed to sell off, staff redundancies to sort out and ties with the petrol supplier to end. Everyone was hoping for an early completion and Pete didn't want to hold anything up.

"There's new life on the wind, lass," he called over to Meg. The dog's tongue lolled and her ears flapped, she seemed to be laughing as they sped along.

They approached the village of Kirkton Sowerby and Pete slowed down then made a turn. A cluster of neat, honey-coloured houses lay in a curve above the green and he noted that there were very few folk about.

It was so different from days gone by.

When Kirkton House was open there was always a buzz about the place. Many residents in the village worked at the hotel and if they weren't coming and going, they were often to be found at each other's gates, gossiping about the activities within the busy Georgian property. It played host to guests of notoriety and most of the events in the Westmarland social calendar. Any overspill from the hotel, which was frequent, had been eagerly caught by the bed and breakfast hostelries dotted around. Situated just off a major trunk route from north to south, Kirkton House Hotel had been an ideal stop for travellers in need of refreshments, a destination for foodies who wanted a Michelin starred meal or an oasis of comfort for those in need of cosseting, whilst spending a few days in the beautiful countryside.

Pete thought about all the hard work Jo had invested to build her business, which had been recognised far and wide and sighed as he approached the gates of the hotel.

It filled his heart with sadness to see the windows dark and unwelcoming, curtains drawn and lights extinguished, with a 'closed' notice pasted over the sign hanging from a large oak tree.

The place looked forlorn and depressing.

He drove onto the gravelled driveway and climbed out of the car. Meg, recognizing her home, leapt across the seats to shoot past Pete, barking as she raced from door to door. Gravel flew in her wake.

"There's no one there, old lass," Pete said as he grabbed her collar and clipped on a lead. The dog would go through a window if she kept that racket up!

He walked around the outside of the building and inspected the property, checking that all the doors and windows were locked and intact. Satisfied, Pete strolled under the archway to the side of the house and made his way to the back. He repeated the process on all the outbuildings and glanced through windows, where familiar signs of closure remained the same, with boxes stacked and dust covers in place. There was little to be done today, no doubt the gardener would be along to tidy the lawns and borders, which already bore an air of neglect.

Pete shook his head as he led Meg back to the car. It was a tragedy to see the old place this way and he thought of happier days when the garden was full of life for a party or wedding. His daughter had trod on the welcoming red carpet at the front door, after nuptials at a nearby church, followed by a reception in the hotel and it had been a wonderful occasion.

Carried away by his memories, Pete didn't notice a sleek car glide to a halt on the drive. He was startled when a voice called out.

"Is this the place that's up for sale?"

A yuppie looking type in a striped suit with a split-parting hair-style got out of the car. He stood tall and confident as he stared up at the house.

"Not to my knowledge," Pete replied, taking an instant dislike to the man who was clearly not from these parts. The stranger walked forward to try the front door.

"It's closed at the moment," Pete said.

"I can see that, do you know where the owner is?"

"Who's asking?"

The man produced a business card and held it out. But Pete ignored the gesture and leaned down to let Meg off her lead.

"I own a property company and am looking to invest in the area, what can you tell me about this place?"

"What you see is what you get," Pete watched Meg sniff around the man's legs with suspicion and decided that he was very much at one with the dog.

"I see a soon-to-be derelict building that I could breathe new life into," the man replied. "This is ideal for apartments, investors are crying out for second homes in the area."

Leaving local folk with no chance of a crack at the property market! Pete thought with dislike.

"I understand a widow owns it?" The man looked slyly at Pete and winked. "I know it's not on the open market yet but if you can help me in any way, I'll make sure it's worth your while." He thrust the card into Pete's jacket pocket. "Call me anytime."

Meg began to bark and the man shooed her to one side with his hand. Pete half hoped that the dog would bite it, as he watched the stranger climb back into his car and roar away. He reached for the card and read the gold embossed lettering: Julian Struthers, Property Investments. A London address was detailed. Pete was tempted to rip the card up, but instead he returned it to his pocket.

"Come on, old lass," he called out to Meg, who'd slumped miserably by the front door. "Your mum is a long way away and it's not forever, but judging by the look of folk sniffing round here, the longer she stays away the better."

He pulled the dog to her feet and led her to the car, where with a howl and a heavy sigh, Meg collapsed on the seat.

She'll be back! Pete whispered to the house and with a confident nod, got back in his car and headed to his business in Marland.

11

The heat was blistering and down by the dock in Bridgetown there was hardly a breath of wind as Mattie pulled in to the dropping-off lane.

"Jump-up, Momma's," Mattie said as he helped his passengers climb out.

"Bleedin' hell, it's a relief to get out of that weed wagon," Hattie complained as she slammed the car door and fanned her face furiously. "Twenty minutes in there and I'm jammin' in the name of the Lord."

"You could have opened the window," Jo said, but had to agree that the aroma of weed was strong in Mattie's taxi today. She helped Hattie straighten the top of her lime green cat-suit and wondered if Hattie had made the right choice of outfit for their day on the catamaran.

No doubt they'd soon find out.

Jimmy appeared from the ticket booth and held out four boarding passes. "Are you ready for the off?" He waved to Mattie, who had parked the car and now joined them. Jimmy took Jo and Hattie's arm and together, they strolled past the waiting boats.

The Jolly Roger, an old wooden pirate ship that ran cruises for tourists, was moored alongside several sailing vessels and the crew looked up and called out:

"Lady, come and walk the plank with me!"

"In your dreams, sailor," Hattie grinned and thrust her chest out. "And you can pack your parrot away!" She winked and nodded at the deckhand's tight-fitting shorts.

They continued along the wooden decking beside the marina until they arrived at the catamaran. Holidaymakers, dressed in colourful swimwear, were being helped aboard by a smartly attired crew who wore white logoed T-shirts, khaki shorts and leather belts embossed with anchors.

"Mornin', darlin'," a man said as he held out a hand to help Hattie. "Watch the slippery surface now, beautiful." His sun-streaked hair contrasted sharply with a deep tan, several gold piercings, tattooed arms and a smile as wide as the bay. "Call me Raymondo," he grinned as Hattie climbed aboard, her chest mere inches from his sparkling eyes.

"Don't mind if I do, Raymondo, where's the bar?"

Jimmy led them into a large open cabin and found seats by a corner table.

"Are you getting changed?" Jo asked as she sat beside Hattie and slipped off her sarong and doubled it to make a skirt over her bikini.

"Not likely," Hattie said as she took off her sandals and stowed them under the seat.

"It will be hot on the water and you won't want tan lines," Jimmy said as he removed his shirt. "You can't swim in a cat-suit and we'll be swimming with turtles in a bit."

"Who said anything about swimming?" Hattie eyed the bar.

The cabin gradually filled and as guests prepared for the day, applying generous layers of sun cream; juice, coffee and rum punch circulated.

Several friends of Jimmy's arrived and introduced themselves and everyone laughed and joked as they anticipated the day ahead.

"There are a few housekeeping rules," the captain announced as the crew prepared to set sail. "The toilets are port side and you need to pump hard," he indicated the front left of the catamaran. "Only leave when the crew allow and always wear a life-jacket." He gripped the tiller and began to manoeuvre away from the dock as the crew loosened ropes and jumped on-board.

"The bar is now open and we ask that you drink sensibly," the captain called out as he turned the yacht to face the open sea. "And remember - no friggin' in the riggin'. It disables the crew and we need them to get you home safely." Giggles rippled through the cabin. "Have a great day folks, anything yo'all need, just ask."

Calypso music began to beat out and the catamaran gained speed. Soon, Bridgetown was far behind and the west coast of the island lay ahead.

"This is the life!" Jo cried as she climbed on the netting at the front. The sea bounced beneath them and she could see deep blue water and frothy crests as she looked down. Jimmy reached out and helped Hattie get comfortable beside Jo. She'd placed a wide brimmed straw hat on her head and wore large plastic sunglasses that spelt out, Groovy Baby in white and pink lettering around the lens.

"They're very fetching," Jo said as Hattie reclined beside her.

"I'm a natural style icon." Hattie sipped her rum punch and looked at the assortment of bodies on the deck.

Mattie began to gyrate and with half-closed eyes, swayed his hips to a Bob Marley tune. His shorts were half-mast and as was the fashion, designer boxers were visible on his trim waist. Gold chains and wooden beads hung across his muscular torso and he'd tied his long dreadlocks into a neat roll on top of his head. With outstretched arms he joined Jimmy's friends and soon the front of the deck was filled with dancing bodies as the catamaran skimmed the waves under the heat of the blazing sun.

Jo leaned back and breathed in the salty air. Her body tingled in the heat and she slipped her foot through the net and let the sea spray pound against her skin as she dangled her lower leg.

She felt wonderful.

The holiday was the best thing she could have wished for and she was having a glorious time. Kirkton House was a million miles away and all thoughts of the dark and gloomy building were buried as she watched her son dancing with his friends, while Hattie lay sunbathing beside her.

A flush of guilt swept over Jo. Should she really feel so good?

What could be better than a day spent like this? It was a perfect Sunday and as they sped along she tried not to think about the call she'd received from Rob Mann that morning, He'd told her that a property developer had heard that the hotel might be coming on the market and wanted to view. Jo had agreed. There was no harm in the viewing, she told herself, after all, it didn't commit her to anything and if she did she decide to sell, she'd have a buyer lined up.

But she refused to think about that today.

Jo held up her head and as the wind whipped at her hair, she stared at the white sandy shores where paradise beckoned. Properties built for millionaires, nestled in secluded beach-fronted gardens and palm trees swayed, as the turquoise waters lapped and Jo caught sight of people strolling along the beautiful beach. She was a long way from Westmarland and the mountains and rain and suddenly felt a sense of freedom that she hadn't experienced in years.

It was exhilarating!

"Dreaming of George Clooney?" Hattie sat up and nudged Jo, "You look like the cat that's got the cream."

"I feel so relaxed, Hattie, I can't explain it."

"Well that's good news," Hattie said as she eyed Raymondo approaching with a tray of banana bread. "I put it down to my good company, a couple of weeks of sunshine and a barrel of rum." She reached out and took a slice of the proffered cake. "Pass a slice over here for Orphan Annie," Hattie indicated towards Jo. "Jimmy, get your arse over to that bar and fire up a couple drinks," Hattie held out her glass.

"Too sweet," Raymondo observed Hattie as she munched her cake. "I like a woman with an appetite."

"I have a voracious appetite, my friend." Hattie removed her sunglasses and winked as Raymondo wriggled his bottom in time to the music, postulating perilously close to Hattie's eager face. He raised his eyebrows and winked back, then continued to circulate with the cake.

Hattie eyed his pert behind as he moved away.

"Earth to Hattie," Jo said as she watched the sexual performance.

"Fuh real..." Hattie mumbled and took her drink from Jimmy. "That boy can go-so."

The boat began to slow and the captain gently cruised into a secluded bay. He announced that anyone wishing to snorkel and swim with turtles should assemble at the front and put on a life jacket.

"Oh, I can't wait," Jo said as she scrambled to her feet and reached for a snorkel and flippers.

"I'll watch from here," Hattie said and sat back.

"You don't know what you're missing, are you sure you want to stay here?"

"Perfectly happy, thank you, I'll look after the drinks." Hattie peered over the top of her sunglasses and watched Mattie's hips as he continued to sway to the music. "Seen one turtle and you've seen them all," she observed and tugged the brim of her hat over her forehead.

Jo let Jimmy help her climb down the steps and once in the water, began to swim towards their group, who were hovering around a crew member sitting astride a float. He paddled with his feet and removed strips of raw bacon from a pack around his waist.

Jo was entranced.

As she moved along the surface of the water she looked through her mask where a magical world lay below. A shoal of yellow and blue angel fish darted in and out amongst the coral, their long dorsal fins trailing like shimmering gowns, a dark patch resembling a crown speckled their foreheads as they fed on sponges, oblivious to human bodies circulating round. She stared in awe at snapper, chub, parrot and trunk fish, schooling amongst the reef; the tropical colours of sea-life almost blinding as the sun raked through the water.

Jo kicked her legs lazily. She was lost in a subterranean world, and was startled by a tug on her flipper.

Jimmy beckoned her to follow him.

They rejoined their group and as Jo looked around, she saw several turtles swimming alongside. The gentle giants fed hungrily on bacon and seemed comfortable amongst the snorkelers. Jo was fascinated and as a baby turtle brushed past she reached out and stroked the green and grey shell. It felt tactile and smooth and mesmerised by the creature, Jo was unaware that her snorkel was filling with water. She gasped and quickly surfaced to shake it out.

A crew member swam over to see if she was alright and Jo paused to ask a question.

"I noticed the turtles wear tags?"

"Yes, indeed," he replied. "They're a rare species and we are protective of our turtles. You're swimming with Hawksbill and Green Turtles, which are critically endangered and only one in a thousand of the young hatching's live to reach adulthood."

"Oh gosh," Jo was dismayed. "Do they breed a lot?"

"Breed?" The guide was aghast. "Lady these turtles do nothing else! They love to fuck. If they can fuck all day and fuck all night, they will, it's a way of life for them and they never stop..."

The guide was interrupted by the sound of shouting and splashing behind them.

"I WANT TO BE A TURTLE!" A voice cried out.

Jo turned and her eyes fell on a pair of sunglasses bobbing on the surface of the water.

Groovy Baby was making quite a commotion!

Hattie, still in her green cat-suit, gripped a long polystyrene float in one hand and a rum punch in the other.

Horrified, Jo hurried to Hattie's aid.

"Why aren't you wearing a life-jacket?"

"Must'a fallen in," Hattie grinned foolishly and allowed Jo and Jimmy to take either side of the float and drag her back to the catamaran. The captain and Raymondo reached out from the steps as Jimmy and Jo pushed Hattie from below and with some considerable effort they managed to haul her safely back on deck.

"Well that's buggered me outfit up," Hattie said crossly as she climbed out of the cat-suit and revealed her red halter neck costume. "Good job I've got a couple more."

"Look after her please, Raymondo," Jo said as she shook out her hair and reached for a towel.

"Be my pleasure." Raymondo grabbed Hattie's hand and led her into the cabin where lunch was ready.

"Hungry Mum?" Jimmy asked as he applied oil to his golden brown skin. He was surrounded by bikini-clad girls of different nationalities, who proffered limbs to be drenched in lotion.

"Starving," Jo replied and headed below deck.

A Bajan feast was laid out on a buffet table by the bar. Platters of spiced couscous and macaroni pie sat beside a shrimp and seafood medley with tasty salads, roast chicken and breadcrumbed flying fish. Jo spooned black-eyed peas onto her plate, as Jimmy forked a sweet baked potato and added a spoonful of golden apple chutney.

They found a seat and began to eat and Hattie, who'd already consumed a plateful, danced with Mattie around a central pole in the cabin. Mattie wore Hattie's sunglasses and encouraged Hattie to bump and grind to the music.

"She's certainly having a good time," Jimmy said as he tore the juicy flesh from a chicken thigh. Jo nodded, she was enjoying the meal and the swim with the turtles had given her an appetite.

Jimmy's friends joined them as Hattie finished her dance.

"Hattie, do you remember Wilma?" Jimmy paused to introduce a tall lean woman. "You met her at Chicken Rita's last week."

Hattie nodded curtly, she did indeed remember Wilma. The woman had made a cutting remark about the size of Hattie's impressive cleavage.

It had hurt Hattie.

Only Jo's prompt intervention at the time had prevented Hattie from retaliating to the jibe.

"Yes, of course," Hattie smiled sweetly at Wilma and gave a little wave. Hattie whipped a lipstick out of the top of her swimsuit and thrust her chest into Wilma's face then smiled as she applied the deep red gloss to her lips. "How could I forget her?"

Jo tensed. She pushed her plate to one side and braced herself as she watched Wilma. The attractive brunette had struck a pose in her miniscule bikini and leaned forward to whisper in Hattie's ear.

"Honey," Wilma began, "I need to tell you that you have a little camel-toe going on down there and there's lipstick on your teeth," she straightened up. "Woman to woman, you understand," Wilma whispered, loud enough for anyone within an arm's length to hear.

Jo looked at Hattie. Her friend had gone as red as her costume and seemed about to explode. Fearing that Hattie was about to grab Wilma by the throat and manhandle her over the side, Jo grabbed Hattie's hand and dragged her away.

"Come and help me tie my sarong," Jo muttered as she shoved Hattie down the stairs to the ladies room.

"BITCH!" Hattie hissed as soon as they entered the tiny toilet and locked the door. "I would have punched her, but I wanted to make sure that there isn't a little camel toe going on down there." She reached down and adjusted her costume.

"Of course you haven't," Jo said crossly. "The bloody woman can't bear anyone else taking centre stage and you, my dear, are gorgeous." Jo thought about Wilma and her latest escort, an attractive boy half her age who followed Wilma around like a lapdog.

"Don't let her spoil your day," Jo stroked Hattie's arm.

"You're right," Hattie said and checked herself in the mirror. "The old bag is jealous of my wonderful English complexion and youthful appearance. She's obviously threatened by my animal appeal to men."

"Yes, Hattie," Jo agreed. "That's exactly what it is."

They returned to the deck where several people had dived into the water and swam ashore to walk along the beach.

The next couple of hours were spent basking in the sunshine.

Hattie lay with her head on Mattie's chest and snored gently as the boat bobbed about on the water, while Jo and Jimmy took turns to dive off the steps.

When it was time to leave, the captain called everyone on board and set his return course for Bridgetown. The music was cranked up and more drinks flowed as they soared across the waves.

Hattie, with Raymondo's help, straddled the bow and balanced precariously and as Raymondo reached for her outstretched arms, they imitated a scene from the film, Titanic, before leaping back to lead the rest of the passengers in a dance that involved a great deal of limbo and twerking.

"I don't know where she gets her energy from!" Jo called out as she tried to maintain her balance. The wind whipped at her hair and salty spray bounced off her sunburnt limbs as she joined in with the singing and dancing. Raymondo and the crew jammed around the deck and encouraged everyone in a series of energetic moves to the music.

As Bridgetown approached, the noise from the catamaran reverberated around the dock and tourists and workers waved at the boisterous party.

"A quiet and gentle arrival into Bridgetown..." Jo said to Jimmy and giggled as she watched people fall off the catamaran, and still singing, make their way unsteadily along the wooden decking to waiting taxis.

Hattie was wrapped around Raymondo and as she thanked him profusely for his hospitality, Jo was relieved to note that her friend hadn't noticed Wilma go by.

"Swell gal," Wilma said to Jo and nodded in Hattie's direction. She smiled sweetly as she clung on to her toy boy and Jo, returning the smile through gritted teeth, resisted the urge to trip Wilma into the water.

Mattie appeared and leaned over to help peel Hattie from Raymondo.

"Thank you, Raymondo, that was a sh'well day out," Hattie slurred as she reached to fasten the neck of her cat-suit. Raymond had dried the garment by hoisting it onto a flag pole, where it flapped about in the hot Caribbean wind, but the suit had shrunk and Hattie winced as she tugged and pulled at the fabric.

"Walk in front of me!" Hattie hissed at Jo then tugged at the camel-toe forming around her crotch. "Mattie, get the car around here as fast as you can!"

They stumbled, single file, along the dock.

Jimmy, who'd held back to thank the captain, caught up with the party, "Enjoyed your day?" he asked and glanced at his watch.

"Couldn't be better," Jo smiled.

"Are you looking forward to Long Tom's gig tomorrow?"

"I can't wait, it will be fun."

"It should be, its a sell-out, make sure you get there in plenty of time."

"Don't worry, we will."

They reached Mattie's car where Hattie jumped into the passenger seat. Jo stifled a yawn and hoped that they'd go back to the apartment soon; she was tired and needed a shower.

A gleaming open-topped sports car skidded to a halt on the opposite side of the road and the driver, an attractive blonde, called out to Jimmy, "Are you ready?"

Jimmy waved to the girl.

Jo remembered the girl from the catamaran and gave Jimmy a little shove, "Go and enjoy yourself," she said, "thanks for a perfect day."

Jimmy leapt into the vehicle and the couple roared off.

Jo watched the car disappear then wearily climbed into the back of the weed wagon. In front, Hattie and Mattie discussed life in the Caribbean and were oblivious to Jo as she stretched out her legs and settled down.

Jo thought about Zach in London and hoped that everything was going well. She'd spoken to him in the week and he'd chatted happily about his new life and an agent, called Poppy, who worked for Hargreaves & Puddicombe Promotions. They'd been out for a drink and had a great time then Zach reminded Jo to watch his appearance on Saturday Morning Cooks, if she could find it on cable TV.

As the old colonial buildings of Bridgetown sped by and locals stepped out for the evening, Jo remembered Pete. She had asked him to record the cookery show, so she would be sure of catching it, and after assuring her that he would, Pete went on to say that Meg was in fine fettle, eating him out of house and home and had a favourite spot in front of the fire.

She suddenly had a vision of being cosily ensconced with Pete, beside the wood burning stove, with Meg curled up on the rug and as Mattie's vehicle headed for the highway and the sun began to set, Jo shuddered.

She wasn't ready to settle for a quiet life, even though Pete would make a wonderful partner. Somewhere, a fresh challenge beckoned and despite John's death, or perhaps because of it, Jo knew that she had a second chance to achieve something. Maybe something to help others, but right now, she had no idea what it might be.

Mattie turned off to drive along the side roads and Jo looked out at little chattel houses and rum shops that seemed to pop up round every corner, with music booming out of open doors and windows. Street life slowly emerged as darkness came down and a scrounging mongrel, inspecting the ditches along the sidewalk, reminded Jo of Meg and she hoped that the old Labrador was comfortable with Pete. What would Pete do now he was single? He was an attractive man with many good years ahead of him and an army of willing females beating a path to his door for a moment of his company and, Jo thought wistfully, a glance from those irresistible blue eyes.

They had arrived back at the apartment and Jo began to gather her things. Hattie, still squirming in her tight cat-suit, ran ahead with Mattie who was loaded down with bags. The rich aroma of Lady of the Night wafted across the complex and Jo paused to take in the intoxicating smell.

She stared up at the clear starry night.

Home seemed a million miles away but as she heard the gentle sawing of cicadas and watched the sky changing from red gold to inky black, she remembered John's favourite words and smiled.

The time to be happy was most certainly now.

12

J o lay in bed and listened to the loud tick of the clock on her bedside table. She peered hopefully into the gloom and searched for shadows to pass by the window, her senses alert for the sound of footsteps on the patio and a key turning in the lock.

Where the hell was Hattie?

After their day on the catamaran and a quick shower and change of clothes, Mattie had arrived to take them to the Lime Inn, where a popular jazz band played. The music was loud and pulsated across the club as drinks flowed and people, including the band, leapt onto tables and danced around the deck.

But a full day and too much sun had caught up with Jo and she was tired.

A headache that had been threatening began to pound and Jo longed to be back in the cool apartment with a glass of iced water and a couple of pain killers.

"I think I might head back," Jo shouted to Hattie over the beat of the music. "Are you coming with me?"

Hattie didn't seem to hear.

"What did you say?" Hattie yelled.

"I'm going back to the apartment!" Jo shouted back.

"OK, I'll catch you later, I don't want to miss this..." Hattie waved her arm in the direction of the throbbing crowd. A man grabbed her hand and twirled Hattie into a dance.

Jo was reluctant to leave but as she watched her friend twist and turn in time to the music, she could see that Hattie was having the time of her life. Jo caught the eye of the manager and asked him to summon a cab.

Hattie was old enough to look after herself.

As Jo climbed gratefully into the back of an air-conditioned vehicle, she felt relieved. Soon, she would be safely tucked up in bed and she could nurse her headache and sleep easily.

But in reality, sleep had been a million miles away.

Jo tossed and turned and imagined Hattie in all sorts of precarious situations, even bundled into a car and taken into the seedy part of Bridgetown, where god knows what might happen. Jo knew that security should never be taken lightly and a single woman needed to be careful, especially after dark.

She shouldn't have left her friend!

The night wore on and Hattie didn't return. Unable to sleep, Jo got out of bed and headed for the kitchen to make a cup of tea. Her mind raced and she hoped that Hattie had stopped drinking, the local rum was lethal and weakened the hardest defence.

Jo became more and more anxious and at seven o'clock began to make calls.

Jimmy's phone was off. Mattie didn't answer and a messaging service picked up at the Lime Inn. Jo had no idea who to call next. She considered going to see Cecil, who would soon be off duty, but after their many drunken exploits she knew that Cecil would be unable to take her seriously. Hattie had only been gone for a few short hours and it was too soon to place her on a missing persons list.

Jo paced the apartment and wandered in and out of Hattie's bedroom. The bed was pristine and freshly laundered towels lay on the neat cotton counterpane. Jo was taut with anxiety as she stared at the unusually tidy room; she longed to see Hattie's slumbering bulk and hear her drunken snores.

In frustration and with no better plan in her mind, Jo decided that she'd head for the beach. A brisk swim might help work off her worry. She found a bikini and changed quickly then grabbed a towel and hurried through the gardens. The complex was deserted and the sand ahead smooth from a gently rolling surf, undisturbed by footprints. Jo deposited her towel on a lounger and scanned the water's edge, hoping that the tide hadn't washed up a lifeless body.

Where the hell was Hattie?

She plunged into the water and began to crawl furiously through waves that seemed stronger than normal that morning.

Jo swam for the best part of an hour. She pounded up and down but kept her eye trained on the entrance of their complex, knowing that if Hattie returned she would appear, having read the note Jo left on the patio table, telling her that she was swimming.

But as the morning wore on, there was no sign of Hattie.

Jo was exhausted.

Having missed a night's sleep through all the worry, she suddenly felt weak and waded out of the sea to wander back up the beach to retrieve her towel. She sat down and buried her face in the soft fabric and choked back tears as she tried not to imagine Hattie in a perilous situation. Her mind searched for solutions to the problems that would unfold as the day progressed and Hattie remained absent.

An unusual noise alerted Jo and she dropped her towel in her lap. She looked around at the empty beach and felt sure that she could hear people singing. A happy song could be heard close by.

"Brown skinned girl stay home and mind baby..."

Jo strained to hear the voices.

"I'm going away on a sailing ship and if I don't come back..."

Jo was mystified. The beach was still deserted and only the local lifeguards were to be seen as they slowly wandered to their station and began their daily rituals.

Now, the voices were louder!

"Brown skinned girl stay home and mind baby..."

Jo spun round.

Striding along the back of the beach in the shade of the palm trees, Hattie approached. She was hand-in-hand with Mattie and they sang as they walked.

Oh Christ... Jo sighed as the penny dropped. Not Hattie and Mattie!

Hattie wore the same outfit as the evening before, a red cat-suit. Her hair had been braided and lay in tight corn rows across her head; plaited with colourful beads. Mattie held her shoes and bag in his free hand.

"Mornin' darlin'," they said in unison and flopped down on the sand beside Jo.

"Don't bloody mornin' darlin' me!" Jo yelled. "Where the hell have you been?"

"Take a chill-pill momma," Mattie said and stroked Jo's arm. "Me and the lady had some talkin' to do," he smiled at Hattie and her face lit up. She was glowing!

Guilt hit Jo.

What on earth was she doing? She was ready to read the riot act to Hattie, who was old enough to be a grandmother and more than capable of looking out for herself. But Jo was angry, she'd missed a night's sleep and her brain was in turmoil. After all, Hattie was aware of the gossip about tourists hooking up with locals and getting thoroughly fleeced and she could at least have called to say where she was. Jo knew that Mattie was a decent man, but even so.

"I'm going back to the apartment," Jo said angrily and stood up. "See you later!"

"I think she might be annoyed," Hattie chuckled.

Jo grabbed a towel and swiping it in Hattie's direction, stomped across the beach.

"Fuh' real," Mattie smiled and placed his arms around Hattie's shoulders, drawing her into his strong arms.

"Fuh' real..." Hattie whispered and snuggled into Mattie's embrace.

13

Pete sat in the Lemon Drop Cafe in Butterly and tucked into his lunch. The all-day breakfast that he had chosen from the limited menu, filled a large oval plate and as he dipped a chunk of Westmarland sausage into the golden yolk of a lightly poached egg, he sighed with pleasure. The spice of the well-cooked meat was delicious.

Meg sat under the table and patiently waited for a tit-bit. Every now and then she nudged at Pete's leg and when nothing was forthcoming, thumped her tail and placed a paw on his knee.

"You'll get me thrown out," Pete mumbled unconvincingly as he held out a piece of freshly buttered toast and watched the old dog scoff it down.

It had been a successful morning and Pete felt pleased with himself. A colleague of many years, who had a garage in Butterly, had agreed to take all of Pete's surplus car stock. The vehicles would go for a knock-down price but Pete was glad to get them off his hands. Redundancy payments had been agreed with the staff and as the settlement was generous, everyone was happy. A multi-store complex was due to open in Marland soon and most of his workers would find themselves in new employment in no time. Rob was working hard to get a completion date for the sale of the garage.

All in all, things were moving along nicely.

Pete pushed his empty plate away and reached for his coffee. He grimaced as he took a sip, the tasteless liquid was cold.

"Can I hot things up for you?" A waitress stood by the table. She wore a frilly white apron and a suggestive smile.

"Ay, Marlene, you could bring this back to life," Pete pushed the coffee to one side.

"Anything else you want bringing back to life?" Marlene whispered as she leaned over and gave Pete an eyeful of wrinkled cleavage.

"I'm alright, lass, the coffee will do fine."

Pete watched the middle-aged woman saunter away and wondered what her husband would think. What was it about running a garage? The throb of an engine and pulsating pound of red-hot pistons fired up in the dark depths of an oily workshop seemed, for some females, irresistible. Women had always offered more than Pete asked and many a service account had been settled with payment that included a private phone number scrawled on a scrap of paper and thrust into Pete's hand. Not that he'd been a saint all his life, but those days were well and truly over. Pete knew that his middle years had treated him kindly and had been told that he'd aged well and was still attractive. But now, with an abundance of time threatening, like a gaping hole in his future, he knew that he'd have to find a pastime to fill it, or he'd rapidly be heading down the road to senility as he rattled around in his house in the country.

Pete thought about Jo and glanced at his mobile phone. It would be early in Barbados but there was a chance she'd be up, perhaps he would call her? Seizing the moment, Pete located Jo's number, she should be at the apartment and he might catch her in.

The phone rang for several moments and Pete was about to hang up when a click on the line indicated that he'd got through.

"Yes," a grumpy voice said.

"Er, hello?"

"What? Stop pissing about!"

"Er, I only wanted to see how you were," Pete mumbled and held the phone close as Marlene placed the fresh coffee on the table.

"Who is this?" Jo said.

"It's me, Pete, and I've got someone here who wants to say hello," Pete grabbed Meg's collar and held the phone to her silky ear. Meg look curiously at the object then began to lick it all over.

"Bloody hell, Meg!" Pete cursed as he retrieved the damp object and tried to ignore the stares of other diners.

Why was he behaving so stupidly?

"Oh, I'm so sorry, Pete!" Jo exclaimed. "I thought it was Hattie."

"No, it's me and Meg, sitting in the cafe and wondering how you were getting along."

"Is Meg OK?" Jo sounded anxious.

"Aye, as right as rain, she's just had some toast," Pete said. He was peeved that Jo's interest clearly lay with the dog.

"Oh good, I really miss her."

"How's your holiday?"

"It's progressing," Jo replied curtly. "I can't say without mishaps and moments of anxiety but we're still in one piece."

"That's good then." Pete found himself lost for words.

"Sorry Pete, I'm tired. Was there anything else?"

"No, lass, you make sure you enjoy yourself, all's fine this end."

"Good, I'll speak to you again soon."

Jo hung up.

Pete stared at the phone and began to wish he'd never made the call, Jo sounded so distant and not just by miles. Had she found someone already?

"Can I get you anything else?" Marlene raised her painted eyebrows and placed one hand on her hip.

"I'll settle up, thanks," Pete said and tucked the phone in his pocket.

The bill arrived and Pete reached for his wallet. As he read the figure he noticed a phone number had been scrawled along the bottom of the receipt. He left a generous tip and taking Meg by the lead, stood up and made for the door.

"See you soon," Marlene leaned over the till and winked.

Pete raised his free hand and waved.

In your dreams, Marlene! He thought and headed out onto the street.

Jo CLATTERED ABOUT in the kitchen and made herself a cup of tea. Even though Hattie had finally turned up, there wasn't a chance that Jo would get back to sleep and her tired nerves were fractious.

She thought about Pete's phone call. What a time for him to phone! Didn't he know that it was only breakfast time in the Caribbean? Most people were still asleep and certainly not clamouring for an early morning, 'how-are-you-today', call.

Jo stomped across the patio and threw herself onto a chair. The tea she was carrying spilt onto her sarong and she cursed as she rubbed at the stain.

"Mornin'!" Gloria called out in greeting. Jo spun round and saw Gloria's face light up and as she smiled, the woman looked as beautiful as the day beyond. Jo waved and forced herself to smile back. Everyone was so damned happy on this island, why couldn't she take a leaf out of Gloria's book?

She smoothed the damp cotton over her knees and a wave of guilt hit her.

What the hell she was doing?

Poor Pete had received an earful and Jo didn't even ask how he was. Just because she felt exhausted, Jo knew that she shouldn't take it out on everyone else. The tiredness was of her own making, after all, Hattie could do whatever she chose and Jo had no right to be judge and jury. If Hattie wanted to stay out all night, it was entirely up to her. Who on earth was Jo to be so righteous?

As Jo admonished herself she took a sip of her tea and sighed. She needed to get a grip. Here she was on a paradise island where everyone was going about their daily life and having a good time, while she was working herself into a right old stew.

Enough! She'd make some breakfast and force herself to cheer up. Jo picked up her empty mug and headed for the kitchen.

She broke two eggs into a bowl and added seasoning and a dash of milk then beat hard with a whisk. She tossed a square of butter into a hot pan and poured the mixture onto the bubbling fat. Reaching for a slice of bread, she placed it under the grill then flicked the radio on and began to hum as music filled the kitchen with happy sounds of a local reggae band. The song came to an end and the presenter announced that the radio station would be at the Lime Inn to support Long Tom Hendry and his band. The biggest event on the island in months. Jo thought about the upcoming gig and was deep in thought when a timid voice rang out and startled her.

"Please Sir, can I have some more?"

Jo spun round. Hattie stood at the edge of the kitchen and held out an empty plate.

"Bloody hell, Hattie, you made me jump!"

"Look out, your toast is burning!" Hattie leapt across the open space and grabbed the grill pan.

They collided in the middle of the kitchen.

"You haven't got dressed."

"You've had your hair braided,"

"Am I in trouble?"

"I sincerely hope not," Jo raised her eyebrows. "No glove, no love..."

"No you silly cow - have I upset you?"

Jo stared at her friend. Hattie cheeks glowed and her eyes were bright. She looked better than she had in years and Jo was suddenly furious for being upset with Hattie. Hattie was the best friend anyone could possibly have and had every right to chance her hand at happiness.

"Of course not," Jo smiled. "You should be mad at me for being such a grump."

"Oh, I'm used to that," Hattie said and reaching for the toast, slathered it with butter. "You don't improve with age." She took a bite and smiled.

"Want some scrambled egg with your toast?"

"You bet!"

Jo spooned the egg onto a plate and pushed it towards Hattie then, as she heard Bob Marley sing out, raised the volume on the radio.

"We're jamming'," they both sang. "We're jamming' in de name of de Lord..."

"Better not bring the Lord into things," Jo said and smiled as she cracked another two eggs into a bowl.

"Oh, I expect He jams too," Hattie replied and with a shake of her hips and a flick of braided hair, jammed her way happily out onto the patio to eat her breakfast.

~

THE ARENA at the Lime Inn buzzed with activity as Long Tom's road crew prepared for a rehearsal. Today was the final run-through before the weekend gigs.

Equipment was in place on stage and with wires taped down and guitars tuned, the last sound and lighting checks were about to begin. On the floor, event staff went about their tasks and called out to each other as they stocked bars and checked security arrangements.

In the VIP box, overlooking the main stage, Jimmy and the promoter leaned on a railing and looked on.

Long Tom suddenly appeared from his dressing room and calmly strode through the arena. He wore jeans with a black T-shirt, cowboy boots and a trade-mark Stetson low on his forehead; his flowing hair tied back. He acknowledged everyone as he made his way to the stage, where the backing band warmed up and technicians made final adjustments. Satisfied that everyone was ready, Long Tom moved to the centre of the stage and reached for the microphone, then stared out at an imaginary audience.

The arena hushed.

Long Tom took a deep breath, "Hello," he said, "my name's Long Tom Hendry."

The band struck the chords of No More War, his most popular hit and as the music filled the arena, Long Tom began to sing. His deep throaty voice rumbled slowly and as he headed towards the chorus, it ricocheted off the walls and embraced the huge empty space.

"He's going to bring the house down," the promoter announced. He smiled and lit a cigarette and studied the smoke rings that drifted up into the clear blue sky.

"The old man's a star," Jimmy replied. He was in awe as he watched Long Tom move around the stage in his characteristic manner.

Jimmy sipped a strong black coffee and stifled a yawn. He hadn't had a great deal of sleep, having slipped out of the Hilton Hotel an hour earlier, where the Canadian flight attendant he'd met the previous day was staying. As he watched Long Tom rehearse his set Jimmy took another drink, he'd need buckets of caffeine to keep going today.

Long Tom wrapped up the rehearsal and Jimmy raced over to meet him.

"What can I get you?" Jimmy asked.

"Just my usual thanks." Long Tom said. "Hell, it's hot." He wiped his face with a towel and sighed as he wrapped it around his neck. The arena was empty but Long Tom knew that the gigs would be a hundred degrees hotter than it was right now, when two thousand pulsating bodies would send the temperature soaring.

"Shall I bring it to your dressing room?"

"No, let's go on the deck, it's cool out there."

The artiste dressing rooms were air-conditioned but Long Tom made his way to the front of the Lime Inn, where he could watch the world go by from the elevated area. Jimmy appeared with a fruit punch in a tall chilled glass and Long Tom took a grateful swig.

"Anything else I can get for you, something to eat?" Jimmy asked.

"No, my friend, this is perfect." Long Tom held his drink and looked down at the road below. Bright bougainvillea trailed across the terracotta walls that surrounded a beach-fronted restaurant and palm trees lining the road swayed in the hot morning breeze. Tourists wandered along in search of brunch and a uniformed postman climbed off his bike and raced up the stairs to deposit the day's mail. Two burly security guards stepped out of the shadows and watched the postman return to his bike.

"Got the boys in?" Long Tom asked.

"All bases covered," Jimmy said. "You're a big act and we need to look after you."

Long Tom grinned and finished his drink. "Hot as hell out here today, I'm going to head to the beach." He placed his glass on a table.

"I'll get your transport sorted." Jimmy disappeared in search of Long Tom's driver.

Long Tom sat under the shade of a canopy and thought about the day ahead. He'd go back to the hotel and have a swim, then rest up. The next few days would be busy, spent up at Eddie's studio, working on a new album. He made a mental note to check when his manager was arriving and to call Hilary too. They'd spoken each day but he'd not been able to persuade her to fly out.

Long Tom sighed. He missed his wife.

He longed for the comfort of her body and sharp wit of her mind. The run up to a gig could be difficult and in days gone by, Long Tom knew that he'd have a good supply of Colombian marching powder in one hand and a bottle of whisky in the other. But he'd been clean for the last few years and had no intention of fighting his demons again. He'd get through the days and walk onto the stage as sober as the day he was born, which in many ways, he thought, made things so much harder.

"The driver's here," Jimmy appeared. "He's at the back entrance."

Long Tom stood and thrust out his fist, "Thanks my friend, catch you later." The men touched knuckles.

Jimmy watched Long Tom climb into the waiting vehicle. The singer wore sunglasses and the brim of his hat was low as the car pulled away; tinted windows shrouded him from the glare of the sun and inquisitive eyes. Jimmy's stomach did a summersault and adrenalin pumped through his veins. He needed to get on! This gig was big and he had much to do before the weekend.

With all thoughts of tiredness light years away, Jimmy reached for his iPad and began to check every last detail. He grinned as he paced through the arena, how he loved his job!

14

In the austere and clinically efficient meeting room of Quanter Publishing, Bob sat back and watched the activity as the Editor in Chief and Cookery Editor argued about the content of Zach's new book, while other creative experts chipped in and tried to keep abreast of the argument. An illustrator doodled on her notepad, whilst the photographer and food stylist sat back, wondering why they had been called into the project at such an early stage.

Nancy Nevis, the company's Managing Director, an old sparring partner of Bob's, had called her team together for the Monday morning breakfast meeting and was positioned at the head of the boardroom table. She drummed scarlet tipped nails on the polished surface and her steely gaze bore into Zach as he frantically scribbled notes on a pad and tried to keep up.

Bob stared at his client and noted the dark circles under the boy's eyes and tousled hair that looked as though it hadn't been near a shower in days. Zach had dark stubble on his chin and in Bob's opinion, looked even more attractive than normal. Clearly, the boy had been burning the candle at both ends and Bob wondered how much of that had involved Poppy.

Bob had removed Poppy from the account that morning.

Office gossip had filtered back and it seemed that that pair had been inseparable since the day of the shoot. Bob had read Poppy the riot act and in no uncertain terms spelt out that her job was in jeopardy if she continued to fraternize with Zach, a new and much valued client. If Poppy valued her position, and she was well on the way to being one of the company's most successful agents, she would stay well clear.

"And what does Chef think?" Nancy cut through the argument. She tapped her talons on the table and stared at Zach.

Zach at that moment was clearly thinking about Poppy and Bob gave him a sharp prod with an elbow as Nancy raised an eyebrow and waited for a reply.

Nancy Nevis ran her company with a rod of iron and staff trembled when she summoned them. Known as Cruella of the Page, she had the reputation of being the best in the business and publishing wannabes, hoping to gain recognition on their resumes, flocked to her doors for the opportunity to work in the hallowed offices. Most of the top names in the cookery world were published by Quanter Publishing, who had an enviable catalogue of best-seller titles under their belt. Bob had agreed Zach's contract, which was generous for an unknown talent, and Nancy wanted to be sure that she was getting her money's worth. She was heartened by Bob's assurance that this was a winning project; the television show was more or less in the bag and they both knew that with TV running alongside, Zach's debut book was guaranteed to be a huge success.

But Bob could see that Zach was out of his depth and knew that if he didn't step in soon, Foraging with Friends by the Gypsy Chef would take on a whole new concept and Zach would be foraging with the enemy.

"I think our chef feels that a lot of great ideas have been put on the table today," Bob smiled warmly at the assembled audience. "He will need to digest all your comments and discuss more in a follow-up meeting." Bob noticed Zach look gratefully in his direction. "I think that's enough for today," Bob continued and gathered his paper work. "Let's reconvene next week and in the meantime, everyone exchange summary thoughts."

"Very well," Nancy said.

She remained seated and watched Zach pick up his belongings and file out of the room with the rest of the team.

"The boy is an idiot," Nancy announced coldly.

Bob took a deep breath. He'd had enough of Nancy and her debilitating remarks. He zipped his document case and stood. Without saying a word, Bob strolled over to the door, closed it firmly and turned to face Nancy.

"The boy is overwhelmed," Bob said through gritted teeth, determined not to take any nonsense from this hawk-faced crone, for he knew too much about her. Nancy's relationship with one of Hargreaves & Puddicombe Promotions most successful female clients was top secret and neither woman, who both had respectable spouses, would wish to have exposure to the press. Bob had smoothed the path of many an indiscretion between food writer Prunella Gray and Nancy Nevis.

They both owed him, big time.

Bob would not have his young protégé annihilated simply because Nancy had got out of bed the wrong side that morning and Bob chose not to think whose bed that might have been.

"Zach has a great deal on his mind," Bob said. "He's hardly hit the city's cobbles after a life-time in the sticks and is doing a sterling job of keeping up with everything that's being thrust upon him."

Nancy, who hadn't moved a muscle as she watched Bob pace around the room, reached into her bag and produced an electronic cigarette. "He's got the looks," she conceded, inhaling deeply.

"He's got more than looks, my dear, he's got more talent than you've ever had wander through your offices," Bob gripped the back of a chair and glared. "If you treat him like that again, I shall take both copies of his publishing contract, which incidentally are still sitting on my desk, and rip them into shreds!"

Bob was furious and a protective instinct for his young chef made his pulse pound. He involuntarily reached for the prayer bracelet wrapped around his wrist and took a deep breath, then waited for his composure to return. "Do we understand each other?" Bob asked.

"Perfectly," Nancy smiled sweetly and stood. "I'll send a courier over for our copy of the contract." She stared at Bob, "Don't break your beads."

Bob resisted the urge to smack Nancy across her smug face and silently called on his karma. "We'll be in touch," he said and reaching across the desk for his case, turned and flounced out of the room.

He found Zach in reception and guided him hastily down the stairs and into the nearest wine bar, where he spent the next hour restoring Zach's confidence. As he wrapped up their meeting he leaned forward and lowered his voice.

"I've moved Poppy on, as you know," Bob said. "It's for the best. I really couldn't give a rat's behind who you sleep with, but agency staff are strictly out of bounds. Hilary would have a stroke if she found out."

Zach sighed and looked miserable.

"Heidi, who is very experienced, will be working with you going forward and you need to find a permanent place to live. I've asked her to source a few options, and she's confident that she's found some-where. With your book advance you can easily manage and it has a large kitchen, which will help your work."

"I appreciate all your help," Zach stood up.

"All in a day's work, dear boy," Bob replied and shook Zach's hand. He watched the young man walk out of the wine bar to merge into the crowds on the busy city street.

Bob settled the bill and gathered his belongings. He tried to remember what young love felt like but it was far too long ago.

All in a day's work, he reminded himself as he headed back to the office.

∼

Jo and Hattie were spending a day on the beach. They lay on loungers, shaded from the hot sun by a faded canvas umbrella. Hattie idly flicked the pages of magazine and Jo observed the ebb and flow of beach life around them.

It was another lazy day in paradise.

A short distance away, under the branches of a casuarina tree, a gaggle of locals sat around a make-shift table. Their game of dominos was vocal as they slapped tiny tiles heavily on wood. A group of life-guards stood on the edge of the water and studied the bay while two bikini-clad girls passed by and flirted with the guardians of the water.

Jo looked up as a plane came into view; the soaring bird flew low as it descended.

"That will be the Gatwick," Hattie called out and checked her watch, "right on time!"

It was a daily pastime of Hattie's to check the incoming flights and she was now an expert on insignia and aircraft. Jo watched the London flight and as it cruised along the coast and disappeared round the south of the island, she thought of Zach and wondered how he was getting on. Jo missed her youngest son and longed to hear all about his new life. Jimmy had searched the internet and managed to find Zach's appearance on Saturday Morning Cooks and they had all gathered around Jimmy's laptop to watch. They shrieked when Zach was introduced by the host and began to cook a recipe that they'd all enjoyed at Kirkton House.

Jo felt a wave of pride for her youngest.

"Fancy a game?" Hattie asked and placed her magazine on a small plastic table.

Malibu and a friend stood a few feet away, they wore bright shorts and beanie hats and both held a bat in one hand. The pair played with skill as the ball travelled at great speed across the beach. It was a fine performance as both players swooped and dived to keep the ball out of the water.

"If you like," Jo replied and began to sit up, "I'm sure Malibu would let us use their bats."

"Are you mad? It's making me dizzy," Hattie pulled her hat over her eyes. "I meant the, how-fast-can-you-drink-a-pina-colada game." She flexed her legs and yawned. "It's time we had a livener."

Jo swung her legs over the side of the lounger and gathered her sarong.

"I'll go and get them," she said and rising nimbly to her feet, picked up her purse and set off for the cafe.

A delicious smell of coconut oil accompanied Jo as she passed a line of tourists, settled comfortably for the day, with nothing more arduous to consider than topping their tans up and frolicking in the warm sea. The beach was busy and all of Malibu's beds were occupied. Jo waved at the man who owned the jet-skis and shook her head when he made encouraging motions. She was grateful that Hattie had yet to take him up on his daily offer and imagined Hattie astride a powerful machine.

The engine would be burnt out before Hattie got into the bay.

"Yo, lady!" A man carrying a suitcase of jewellery called out and encouraged Jo to look at the selection of shell necklaces and pretty paste earrings that he'd shaped into turtles. She politely declined.

"Yu, have a good day now," he said and waved cheerfully.

Jo flopped down on a bar stool in the cafe and nodded when the waiter asked, "Your usual?" She watched him prepare the drink, crushing ice in a blender with a large slug of rum and pina colada mix. He poured the thick alcoholic cream in two large beakers and topped both with cherries and a slither of pineapple. Jo thanked the man and placed some dollars on the bar and with a drink in each hand, headed back to Hattie.

"Thought you'd got lost!" Hattie called out from the shade of her umbrella as Jo approached. She wore several shell necklaces on her wrists and ankles and pointed her fingers and toes for maximum effect.

Tiny turtles twinkled from her ear lobes.

"Very nice," Jo said and held out a drink. "How much did that lot cost you?"

"What makes you think I bought them?" Hattie replied mischievously and took a sip. The thick cream made a frothy moustache.

"They can spot you a mile off," Jo said as she sat down, "you're a soft touch."

"Such a cynical madam," Hattie licked her lips. "A bit of male company might sort that out." She smiled at Jo and winked.

"I'm more than happy to sit back and let you cast your charm over the legions of male admirers," Jo said. "I get exhausted watching you."

"Well, I could certainly give you a few pointers, you've been out of the dating game for a hell of a long time."

"I'm not sure that I was ever in it?" Jo reflected and counted the number of men she'd slept with, including two husbands, on the fingers of one hand.

"Time you used both hands," Hattie shook her head, "and a few toes. Blimey Jo, you couldn't be in a better place for a bit of a romp."

"Bit of a romp?" Jo raised her eyebrows. "I doubt I'll ever have a bit of a romp again."

"Well more fool you. You don't know what you're missing."

As Hattie rambled on, Jo sipped her drink and thought about their holiday, they were halfway through another week and despite the lazy pace of island life, their days seemed to pass quickly.

A woman in bright yellow shorts strode along the edge of the water and a dog ran alongside, tail wagging as it followed its mistress. Jo thought longingly of Meg. A dog's love was unconditional and constant, how she missed the old girl!

Hattie had noticed the dog too. "I expect Pete will have the grooming gear out at Park's Mansions," she said. "He won't want Meg in a mess... more than his life's worth."

"I'm sure he's taking good care of her," Jo slid the pineapple from the side of her beaker and took a bite.

"He'd take good care of you too, if you'd let him."

"Don't start all that up again, Pete won't be short of female company, with all thoughts of me far from his mind."

"Aye, there's another pig flying over the waves," Hattie stared out to sea.

Jo turned and looked at Hattie and both began to giggle as another plane cruised overhead.

"That'll be the Air Canada from Toronto," Hattie said, checking her watch. "Your Jimmy will have his hands full tonight."

Jo looked at her friend fondly.

Barbados is for buddies, she thought and silently said a prayer of thanks that she'd come on this holiday.

15

On the other side of the island, Long Tom dived gracefully into the crystal clear water of Eddie's infinity pool. He took long languid strokes and swam for several lengths then stopped at the mosaic tiled steps, perfectly positioned to admire the view.

The sun caressed Long Tom's back and a warm breeze soon dried his skin as he stared at the east of the island. It lay shrouded in a haze of heat, beyond which, lush green countryside rolled down to the coast and distant waves roared forcefully to the rugged shore.

Long Tom smiled happily and thought of the outing he'd enjoyed that afternoon with Eddie and his family.

HE'D ARRIVED at the plantation early and worked with the band in the studio. By mid-afternoon they called it a day and Eddie suggested an excursion. Long Tom helped load the kids into Eddie's pick-up and they headed for Martin's Bay, where the village tavern served a host of goodness fished straight from the sea.

They'd sat by the beach, at a plastic picnic bench, under the shade of a torn umbrella and munched happily on snapper, conch and pickled shrimp – eaten piping hot with their fingers as they ripped into the juicy flesh. The kids giggled when Eddie insisted that Long Tom try deep-fried chicken gizzard, which was considered a great delicacy, and in disgust Long Tom had pulled a face. Locals joined the queue for drinks from an open counter and swayed to loud music piped from speakers perched precariously in corners of the bar, with wires sticking out in all directions.

Long Tom felt completely at ease with Eddie and his family. He tilted his Stetson to protect his head from the scorching sun and reached for another portion of fish as the kids were excused and ran across the grass to play, under Eddie's watchful eye.

"You ready for the weekend?" Eddie had asked.

"Ready as I'll ever be," Long Tom replied and took a drink from his ice-cold bottle of water.

"Your new album is good," Eddie said. "The songs sure are sweet."

The two men discussed the time they'd spent in the studio that week. The new material was working, giving Long Tom confidence in the songs he'd written.

"Words flowing again, man," Eddie looked out to sea, "takes a clear head."

Eddie too had struggled with his creativity during his years of addiction and like Long Tom, was grateful to have come out of the darkness to a world where he could be productive and clean. He had collaborated on the album and was proud to be a part of it.

"A day at a time, brother," Long Tom said.

"Amen to that."

Eddie stood and beamed at his children. A football landed at his feet and he joined in with their boisterous game.

Long Tom walked over to a shaded spot and leaned on the hull of old fishing boat. A fisherman sat on a rock nearby and nodded as he set about repairs to his nets. Long Tom watched the surf roll along the rocky beach and thought about the week. It had been perfect and they'd achieved a great deal in preparation for the new album which would be released later in the year. To have Eddie on the credits was an honour and Long Tom felt a rush of warmth for his friendship with the recording artist who, like Long Tom, had recovered from the demons of addiction.

He looked at the family playing on the grass with a pang of envy.

How he longed for a family of his own! He'd not been blessed with kids and put that down to drug abuse causing infertility. But he had a new wife, a loving partner to support him at this stage of his life and as he stared at the Atlantic, he wished, yet again, that Hilary was by his side. Had he been blinded by love when they'd met the previous year? Was he on the rebound from rehab? He'd been smitten at the first sign of something good but certainly hadn't antici-pated spending so much of his married life on his own. Hilary loved her business in London and spending time at Flatterly Manor. Long Tom was grateful that his reincarnation as a rock singer bought earn-ings beyond his wildest expectations and he could fund her extrava-gant refurbishment of his Irish mansion. Not that money mattered to him; he was happy with the simple things in life and couldn't imagine Hilary wandering barefoot along this primitive beach. The west coast and its suave moneyed way of life were far more in keeping with her style.

"Are you ready to hit the road?" Eddie called out. He had a weary child draped over each shoulder.

"You got it." Long Tom scooped another child from the grass and swung the wriggling body into the back of the truck to join its siblings, then climbed in alongside. He banged on the side of the cab where Eddie sat behind the wheel.

"Wagons roll!" Long Tom called out and settled back as they made their way up the perilously steep and winding road that led to Eddie's plantation.

THE SUN DIPPED low over the horizon as Long Tom reflected on his day. He stood and climbed out of the pool and reached for towel from a pile nearby.

Barbados is for families...

Long Tom remembered the kids snuggled happily against him in the back of the truck and felt blessed to be on this beautiful island.

PETE PACED the full length of the car showroom, his footsteps echoing around the cold empty space. He was perturbed as he looked out at the dark deserted forecourt, for he'd witnessed something earlier that had made him quite anxious and he was unsure how to handle the situation.

On his way to the garage in Marland that wet afternoon, Pete had decided to take a detour through Kirkton Sowerby and visit the hotel. He knew that he didn't need to go so frequently, but Jo hadn't phoned back and he had an instinctive urge to check on her property. As he pulled into the gates, he saw two vehicles parked on the drive.

A sleek and sporty vehicle sat beside a Volvo estate.

Pete recognised the car - Julian Struthers! The Volvo belonged to Rob and it wasn't rocket science to work out that Julian had inveigled his way into finding the agent who handled Jo's affairs and was now viewing the property.

Pete pulled in and came to a stop by the large bay window and Meg, who was lying on the passenger seat, sensed that she was home. With an ecstatic woof, she leapt over Pete and flung herself out of the car.

Gravel crunched noisily underfoot as Pete made for the hotel entrance and Meg ran round in circles. He ignored the bell and reached for a large brass handle. The door was unlocked and the handle turned easily, allowing Pete to step into the cold hallway.

Clearly, the viewing was already underway, despite the silence in the deserted rooms. Meg was nowhere to be seen, she'd raced ahead in search of Jo and nothing would have stopped the dog in pursuit of her mistress.

Pete stood still and listened for voices.

He thought he heard a door creak upstairs and grabbing the oak banister began to climb the wide curved staircase that led to a first floor gallery and bedrooms beyond. Meg, who had completed her search of the rooms downstairs, pounded past and disappeared down a corridor while Pete strolled across the gallery and popped his head round the doors of the front bedrooms. Both were dark and silent, the furniture and four-poster beds covered in dust sheets and window shutters closed to the outside world.

"Agh!"

A distant yell alerted Pete and he turned, wondering where the sound was coming from.

"Call the damn thing off!"

Meg was barking furiously and Pete ran, following the sounds of commotion until he found Julian Struthers pinned to a wall at the back of the hotel. Meg had her paws on his chest and was about to rip into the lapels of his Saville Row suit. Pete stifled a grin and took his time as he reached for the dog's collar and clipped her lead into place. With a tug, he ordered the dog to sit.

"I'll bloody sue you!" Julian screamed. His mop of hair had fallen forward and he fumbled to rake it back into place with shaking hands.

"What for?" Pete asked and stared at the saliva on Julian's suit. "A dry-cleaning bill?"

"Is everything OK?" Rob asked anxiously. He had appeared from the back staircase and was surprised by the scene that met him. "Hello Pete," Rob said. "Are you on caretaker duty?"

"Aye," Pete replied, glaring at Julian, "just passing."

"Mr Struthers is viewing the property," Rob stated the obvious. "I checked with Jo and she's quite happy for him to do so."

"And I want to continue," Julian snapped. "Now if you'd be so kind as to call off PC Plod and his vicious brute, I'd like to finish the viewing." A hand-tooled leather loafer kicked out in Meg's direction and she lurched forward to bite it.

"Easy girl," Pete soothed and pulled the dog away, "you've eaten better dinners."

"Right, let's check the garden and outbuildings," Rob guided

Julian down the stairs and through the conservatory and Pete watched them stroll out and over the croquet lawn.

He shook his head.

That bastard is going to get his hands on it! Pete thought angrily and imagined the old house being demolished and rebuilt with swish modern interiors that suited the townie time-sharers, who would flock for a slice of country living. Local folk could kiss goodbye to any thoughts of future employment while they watched property prices rocket and youngsters move away. Had Jo no notion of what she was doing? Did she not feel any responsibility for the environment that had taken her to its heart and given her a living and a good life for so many years?

Pete ran down the stairs and when he reached the bottom, turned his back on the garden. He could hardly bear to watch Rob point out the merits of Kirkton House and the acres that could be utilised in so many ways, including the development of apartments, car parking and leisure amenities. He stormed through the ground floor rooms, dragging a reluctant Meg, who was still hell-bent on finding Jo.

"She's not here and she may as well never come back!" Pete shouted to the silent rooms before flinging open the front door. He thrust his car into reverse and sped away so quickly that gravel ricocheted and to Pete's delight, pebble-dashed the immaculate paintwork of Julian's car.

But now, as Pete stood in the empty showroom, which would soon belong to a builder, he stared out at the night traffic on the road beyond and knew that he had over-reacted. It broke his heart to think that Jo would be leaving and time was running out to gain her affection. Grief would eventually lift, if it hadn't already in her Caribbean idyll, and she'd move on. How he longed for the opportunity to take her out, look after her and show her that life in Westmarland could blossom again.

Was it already too late?

But Pete was a fighter, he'd come from nothing and made a good life and he determined that where there was a will there was a way. As he turned off the lights and locked up his premises, he vowed that he'd never give up.

Meg, who was curled up in the office, slid off Pete's chair and stretching her body, thumped her tail as she watched him approach.

"Come on, old lass," Pete smiled, "it's time to go home."

He buttoned his jacket and headed off across the forecourt with Meg trotting happily alongside. He wondered if he should call Jo and ask if Rob had been in touch after the viewing, for Julian was sure to have made an offer, but Pete decided that he'd ring in the morning and plead his case and in the meantime there was a nice bottle of red at home and a welcoming fire.

Meg sat on the passenger seat as Pete drove through the countryside. She seemed to share his optimism and reached out a comforting paw. As they sped past Kirkton Sowerby, Pete rubbed the dog's head and thought of Jo in Barbados.

Barbados is for Lovers...

Pete remembered the words of a travel advert and hoped that in Jo's case, the words would prove untrue.

16

Rain pelted down on the streets of east London and the sharp deluge bounced like cold needles on the melee of folk fighting their way through the crowds to get out of the downpour.

Zach stood at the window in his kitchen and stared down. He was oblivious to the weather and rubbed his hands together as he turned his back on the street and looked around the spacious loft apartment.

He loved his new home.

Heidi had found a gem. She'd taken the task very seriously and had determined not to have Zach wasting his time trailing all over the suburbs looking at accommodation as varied as inhospitable new-builds by the river, to split-level housing that seemed to be no more than rabbit warrens strung together for an extortionate rent. Zach had fallen in love with it as soon as he walked through the door and moved in straight away.

The newly renovated apartment, which comprised of the top floor of the property, was laid out in an open-plan and the jewel in the crown of the living area was the kitchen. On a raised platform, nestling between stylish brick walls, an array of space-saving units made of re-conditioned pine, surrounded a central cooking station.

Double doors opened onto a small balcony with a panoramic view of the surrounding gardens.

"You'll be able to have herbs growing in pots outside," Heidi said as she fastened the doors against the beating rain and walked over to an office area adjacent to the kitchen. "This place is so well planned, it's perfect for you." Heidi admired the bank of shelving, imagining Zach's cookery books stacked neatly above his laptop and printer.

"I need to go shopping," Zach said. He walked over to the break-fast bar and sat on a tall stool then began to make a list of equipment and supplies.

"Well, no excuses for not getting on with your book." Heidi ran her fingers over the ceramic hob and grinned. "Nancy will have you doing all the food photography in here, the light's so good, think of the saving on her budget."

"Nancy can get stuffed," Zach replied. "This is my creative zone and only the chosen few can enter."

"Don't forget duvets, sheets and towels," Heidi reminded Zach as she checked the bathroom and bedroom. The flat was furnished and everything brand new, but Zach had none of the basic items required for day-to-day living. "It's going to cost you a bomb to kit this place out."

Zach was totting up his list and nodded his head in agreement. The kitchen kit alone would eat up most of his book advance but Zach knew that whatever he spent it would be worth it and at last he had somewhere he could call home.

"Fancy a bite to eat at the pub?" Zach asked. "It's too late to do any shopping."

"Very kind of you, but I have to get back. My other half will have dinner waiting and our little one ready for bed." Ever efficient, Heidi kept to her schedules. "I'll call tomorrow and go through your diary for the next few weeks. Have a good night."

With a wave, she was gone.

Zach listened to Heidi's footsteps fade as she trotted down the stairs, then eased himself off the stool and wandered around.

Suddenly alone, his thoughts soon turned to Poppy.

How she would love the apartment and how perfect it would be to have her here with him. Zach wondered what Poppy was doing and sighed with frustration and guilt.

How easily he'd given her up!

He'd never felt this was about anyone before, even though they'd only had a few stolen hours together. Was his career really worth it? And why had he signed that damn contract? He could have continued with their relationship and made a living by opening a restaurant, in charge of his own destiny and not under the thumb of those who thought they knew best and looked set to gain from him.

But Zach knew that he'd never have met Poppy if he'd not joined the agency and knowing Poppy for the brief time they'd had was better than never knowing her at all.

Zach longed for someone to talk to and decided to call Jo.

There was no reply to the phone in Jo's apartment and as Zach ended the call, he searched for his brother's number and was dismayed when Jimmy failed to pick up.

Zach needed a drink! He needed to shake the cloud of gloom that had descended since Poppy's departure and get his act together. He'd made his bed and he must lie in it. He looked around for his jacket and found it slung across a wide leather sofa in the lounge. As he pushed his arms into the sleeves, he made his mind up to put all thoughts of Poppy to one side.

Bob was right.

Zach had the world at his fingertips and was in a position to conquer it, if he got his head down and worked hard. There was no time for long-term relationships right now.

He picked up his keys and locked the door and as he stepped onto the street, Zach's stomach reminded him that he was hungry. He increased his pace and headed towards the local pub.

The bar was heaving as Zach entered and every table taken.

A group of girls, paying for a round of drinks, had secured a table in the corner of the bar. They nudged each other and asked Zach if he'd like to join them.

"Don't mind if I do." Zach replied and grabbing a pint, followed a shapely figure that guided him to the table. Suddenly, things seemed brighter, there was no harm in a bit of female company and he had an evening to kill.

"Cheers!" Zach said.

"Are you the gypsy chef that was on the TV the other day?" A blonde fluttered her eyelashes, while her friends leaned in and bombarded him with questions.

"Er, I've only been a guest on one show." Flattered, Zach made light of the comment. "I didn't think anyone had seen it."

"Everyone's talking about it and now we've actually met you," the girls chorused.

Zach smiled when the girls insisted on a series of selfies and another round of drinks and as the evening wore on, the blonde got closer and Zach's arm rested comfortably on her shoulders, all thoughts of Poppy and work far from his mind. He thought of his family and wished that he'd been able to speak to Jo or Jimmy but they were an eight hour flight away and no doubt partying. Feeling quite mellow, Zach decided that he'd join them in spirit.

The girls were drinking shots and Zach held out his glass.

"To absent friends," Zach said.

"And new ones..." The blonde whispered.

FOUR THOUSAND MILES AWAY, on a bright and sunny day, the late morning traffic was heavy as Mattie carefully drove the weed wagon along the coastal road. Hattie sat alongside, with Jo perched in the back.

They were heading for Bridgetown to buy fresh produce for a barbeque later that day, and Jo raised her eyebrows as she listened to Hattie grumble that it would have been far easier to nip over to the mini-market over the road from their apartment, never mind haggling with locals in a steaming hot market hall.

Mattie steered the car into the bustling area of commerce and found a space to park. "Come an' meet my Aunty Jasmine," Mattie said to Hattie, "then you will understand de magic of de market."

He led the women past a multitude of outdoor vendors, nestled closely together on the side-walk, where tables and boxes overflowed with fresh produce, bought in from farms and plantations all over the island. Tomatoes, peppers, sweet potatoes, okra and plump bananas looked tempting but Mattie kept walking, guiding them into the market hall past little huts and alleyways, where they caught the drift of incense and occasional ganja. Jo was enthralled by the glorious colours of the mounds of vegetables and herbs and she stopped at a table full of spices, with trays of shark oil, essences and bay rum. She picked up a handful of nutmegs and the little nuts gleamed through layers of skin-like webbing.

"Don' take too much," a vendor beamed, "yu sho' get high!" As she laughed her whole body wobbled and a bright cotton apron, spread tightly across her mid-drift, strained at the ties. Mattie explained that nutmeg, taken in large quantities could cause euphoria and hallucinations.

"No more rum punch for you," Jo said to Hattie as she thought about the thick layer of delicious spice that locals grated generously on the surface of the drink.

Aunty Jasmine sat in a row of pea vendors in a far corner and called out as Mattie approached.

"Yu lookin' for me hunni?"

"I sho' am, Aunty," he leaned down and pecked her plump, shiny cheek. "Yu' still here?"

"I ain't gin nowhere 'til de day de Lord call me," Aunty replied, balancing a wooden tray on her voluptuous lap. Her thick fingers moved deftly over a pile of dried green vegetables and as she worked, she shook her head from side to side. Picking up an old pewter pot, she filled it to the brim then waved her hand for Hattie to hold out her basket. As she poured the pea-like objects, Aunty gave instructions on how to make a soup or add the peas to rice.

Jo was enthralled and asked if she might take a photo.

"Sho, yu tek picture," Aunty said and grabbing Hattie and Mattie in her huge arms, sat them comfortably on each knee and beamed at the camera. Her face lit up as she smiled.

"I'll send that to Zach," Jo said as the trio left the pea-picking corner.

They wandered through the gaggle of stalls and added to Hattie's basket. Soon it was bursting with fresh ginger and herbs, salad ingredients, breadfruit, mangoes and guava.

"Enough to feed the whole bleedin' beach," Hattie moaned and handed the basket to Mattie. She'd smelt a food court and set about finding it.

They sat on tall stools at a long wooden counter and nibbled on salt fish. Mattie chewed a slow-braised lamb neck and licked the tasty juices that ran over his fingers.

"It will be lovely to have a barbeque," Jo said, "we'll pick up fish from Oisten's market on the way home."

"You can pick up anything you like," Hattie replied, "I'm going to have a lie down, I'm exhausted."

Jo was more than happy to potter about and finish the shopping in preparation for the meal. Jimmy was coming over later with a group of his friends and she was looking forward to seeing them all and playing host. It seemed light years since she'd entertained - something that had come so naturally to her when she ran the hotel and, for a moment, Jo felt a pang of nostalgia and knew that she missed it. How tempting it was, on this sunshine carefree island, to fantasise about starting again - doing something new with her lovely old manor house. But her last memory was of dark and foreboding rooms, with John's ghost seeping from every corner and crevice and as the sharp pain of loss threatened, Jo banished all thoughts of staying at Kirkton House.

It was time to move on and she knew that her decision was right.

Rob had emailed with details of an offer from a London property developer and it was too good an offer to refuse.

"Well I think that's a great idea," Jo turned to Hattie as they left the market. "You rest up and get your beauty sleep and I'll make us all a lovely meal."

"I am quite tired," Hattie yawned and settled her tired limbs into the comfort of the car and as Mattie pulled away from the heat-drenched streets, her head slipped to one side and she slept.

Sleep sweetly, Jo thought and smiled as Hattie's snores reverberated round the weed wagon and winking at Mattie, who grinned in the rear-view mirror, Jo settled back to enjoy the drive home.

17

A bell in Zach's apartment pierced the afternoon gloom. The sound was loud and persistent and woke Zach from a comatose state. He reached out a hand and fumbled on the carpet to try and find his phone.

But his search was in vain and the bell kept ringing.

"Christ..." Zach muttered as he dragged himself into a sitting position and tried to focus through the gloom, his head pounded and his throat was as jagged as a rock.

Something woolly was wrapped around his legs. He seemed to be covered by a coat.

Zach swung a wobbly leg over the side of the bed and listened. The bell had stopped and in the distance, a door slammed.

"What time is it?" A lump moved under the coat and a blonde head peeked out.

Startled, Zach looked away and tried to recall the events of the night before. Nothing was registering, but the body in the bed needed no explanation.

Suddenly, the door flew open and light burst into the bedroom.

The blonde sat up and squinted as she tried to focus, while Zach jumped to his feet and yelled out, "Who the bloody hell is that?"

"Do you have any idea what time it is?" A voice replied, "It's me, Heidi."

Realising that he was completely naked, Zach grabbed the coat but the blonde was having none of it and tugged hard.

"Your phone is off and Bob is trying to get hold of you," Heidi blurted. "It's three o'clock in the afternoon and you should have called him at nine, he's going mental." She stepped into the room and threw the blinds open.

A chaotic scene greeted her.

Clothes were strewn across the floor and glasses and an empty bottle of vodka were upturned on a chair. Zach, who'd lost the coat battle, had jumped back into bed to cover his nakedness and sat wide-eyed and speechless in the cold light of day.

"I suggest you have a shower then find a taxi to take you to the office," Heidi told him.

"But it's late afternoon!" Zach protested.

"Who cares? Your TV series has been commissioned and Bob wants to tell you personally and sign the contract."

Zach stared back, his face a mixture of emotion clouded by a stonking hangover.

Heidi, knowing that this was probably the best that she could accomplish, hoped that he'd sort himself out and have a plausible excuse by the time he hit the office in Soho. As she retreated, the spare set of keys jingled in her pocket. Thank goodness she'd kept them!

Heidi turned to depart and, glancing back at the bed, called out, "I'll pick up a duvet set on my way home..."

PETE SAT in a corner of the Red Lion with Rob alongside and sipped a pint of best bitter. They were enjoying an early evening drink. A couple of feet away, Meg lay basking in the warmth of a roaring log fire and rolled over as the occupants of the next table, a couple with a small child, reached out and scratched the dog's tummy. The child giggled as Meg twitched her leg in rhythm to the scratching.

Pete smiled. The old dog knew which buttons to press. She'd be rolling her eyes next and making sorrowful glances towards the child's plate, which was stacked high with chicken nuggets and chips.

"He's made an offer then," Pete said. He nursed his drink and as he thought about Julian Struthers, he watched Rob's face light up.

"Yes, it's a very decent price too," Rob replied enthusiastically, "Jo would be mad to turn it down."

"Have you spoken to her?"

"I emailed the news and thought I'd give her a call on my way home." Rob drained his glass and glanced at his watch, "Mind, she might be out for the day, perhaps I'll try later." He stood up and skirted around Meg, who sat upright and held out a paw as the giggling child fed her pieces of chicken.

"You'll be closing the kennels soon," Rob smiled and nodded towards Meg.

"Aye, it's time she went back to her mistress." Pete watched Meg roll onto her back. Her tail thumped as she theatrically caught a large chip. "Not that she'll have the gardens to roam in for much longer; no doubt she'll be cooped up in a flat somewhere," he added bitterly.

"Not if we know Jo," Rob said, "she'll have a new venture in the pipeline before the contract on Kirkton House is signed." He buttoned his jacket and winked at Pete, "I'm surprised you haven't closed a deal in that department."

"Be off with you," Pete replied half-heartedly. "You spend too much time buggering people's lives up with your fancy sales, bringing in outsiders where they're not wanted."

"It's called progress, Pete."

"Aye, I know," Pete sighed as he watched Rob retreat through the bar. He finished his pint and felt the warmth of Meg's head resting on his knee.

The family had gone.

"And you're as bad," Pete said, stroking the dog's head, "playing up to anyone with a better offer."

Meg's fur was soft and warm under his touch. He would miss the old girl more than he cared to admit and remembered Rob's insinuation that the village was gossiping as they watched Pete and the dog moon around the hotel. He wondered what Jo's reaction had been when she'd read Rob's email.

No doubt she was ecstatic.

Jo hadn't phoned lately and Pete was miserable. Clearly, life in Kirkton Sowerby was the last thing on her mind as she enjoyed herself in the Caribbean.

She hadn't even called to check on her dog.

Pete motioned to the lass behind the bar and in moments a fresh pint appeared before him. Marlene, the waitress from the Lemon Drop Cafe, who worked part-time at the Red Lion, fussed around the table.

"On yer own?" Marlene asked.

"Nope," Pete replied and took a sip of the beer. He wished that Rob was still with him.

"You're spending too much time with that daft mongrel," Marlene said and nodded towards Meg, who had resumed her position in front of the fire and now snored gently.

"Aye, looks that way," Pete muttered.

"I could keep you company," Marlene whispered as she leaned over to place a mat under Pete's pint. The neckline on her blouse was cut dangerously low and she hovered in what she thought was a tantalising pose.

"You'll get repetitive strain if you stay like that for long," Pete said. "How's your Jack since his prostate operation?"

Marlene flounced off and Pete breathed a sigh of relief as he drank his pint and let his thoughts drift back to Jo. He envisaged her on a beach or sitting at a bar, sipping a cocktail, hopefully without a man in tow. Pete imagined Jo with a cracking suntan and thought of her soft skin, he longed to touch it and wondered if the sun had lightened her copper hair. Jo would tell Hattie of her news and they'd soon be celebrating together or with anyone else she'd no doubt met!

Pete shook his head. It was no good. Time was running out and he had to do something to stop the tide of change that was racing in. He couldn't get Jo out of his mind and felt that he'd never even had a chance. If it wasn't for Meg he'd be on the next plane out there. Hattie's words about happiness rung in his ears and he feared that he'd left it too late.

Pete made a vow to call Jo, but in the meantime decided to drown his sorrows. He finished his drink and preparing to dodge Marlene's attention, headed to the bar for a refill.

THE FOLLOWING MORNING Pete realized that his decision to drown his sorrows had been a big mistake.

He sat at his kitchen table and held his head in his hands as the radio presenter announced the time. He wished he had the strength to turn the damn thing off but he had the hangover from hell and moving was not an option.

Meg paced around the room and went through a repertoire of tricks to try and encourage Pete to butter the toast that lay uneaten on a plate, beside a mug of cold coffee. After thrusting about with every moth-eaten and chewed toy she could find, she placed a paw on his knee and howled.

"Aye, alright old lass," Pete raised his head and squinted at the dog. He picked up the toast and held it out. Astonished that a whole piece was being offered, Meg gently took it and retreated to her place by the fire.

"You can keep that noise down," Pete grumbled as the dog thumped her tail on the mat. He reached for the coffee and grimaced as he took a gulp.

For some reason, Pete had gone on a bender the previous evening. After several pints at the Red Lion, he'd walked to a mate's house on the way home and they'd drunk the best part of a bottle of malt whisky. His friend, also a widower, had been delighted to have a drinking partner and they'd sat up half the night, airing their views on problems both at home and world-wide. There had been talk of Jo too and his friend didn't need a crystal ball to see which way the wind was blowing Pete's affections. He'd encouraged Pete to either get on a plane and go and talk to her or failing that, pick up the phone, which is exactly what Pete had gone and done.

He opened his eyes and stared at Meg and thought about his call to Jo.

How he regretted making it!

Never make an important call when you've had too much to drink... Pete vowed as he patted the dog's head and tried to remember what he'd said.

He'd given Jo all his news and kept the conversation light and cheerful, even when she showed surprise that he'd sold the garage. Trying desperately not to slur his words, Pete found himself asking about Julian Struthers and when she admitted that he'd made a very generous offer, Pete pleaded with her not to sell up and move away. He remembered, through his boozed up prattle, that he'd told Jo that he loved her and begged her to stay, assuring her that he'd look after her. But she'd suggested that he'd had a tad too much to drink and she'd speak to him in the coming days.

Pete groaned. He took a swig of the cold coffee and shook his head.

Meg sensed activity and ran to the door. She raised herself up and nudged at the latch.

"Aye, all right." Pete dragged himself to his feet. "Let's see if a bit of fresh air will clear my head."

With a sigh, he shrugged on his jacket and followed the dog.

18

B ob leaned back in his ancient office chair and stared out of the window to Wardour Street. The morning traffic was heavy and shoppers and pedestrians, anxious to shelter from the rain, ran along damp grey pavements, drenched with muddy spray from vehicles pounding along the road. He reached for a string of prayer beads wound tightly round his wrist and began to chant, fondling the smooth droplets as he mentally balanced his inner core.

Bob thought about Hilary, many miles away in Ireland. She seemed happy to leave the day-to-day running of their business to him now, as she decorated Long Tom's Irish pile, which had taken precedence in her life. Bob still received daily calls and anything to do with their latest signing had to be immediately relayed to Hilary, she had high hopes of Zach Docherty.

As indeed did Bob.

The Gypsy Chef! A smile crept across Bob's face as he idly watched the traffic below. The boy had appeared in the office, the previous day, looking as though he'd crawled out from one of the forests he so happily foraged in. Zach had fallen into Hargreaves & Puddicombe Promotions, fearing for his future and after giving him a mild telling-off, Bob detailed the offer of the television series that had miraculously been commissioned with some haste by a mainstream TV channel. Zach's shaking hand had signed on the dotted line and Bob had taken him out to celebrate. As they settled amongst the media luvvies at their table in Ranchers, it amused Bob to witness the attention Zach received. Females found any excuse to stop by and chat and Zach, naïve to his rising success, was happy to accommodate them.

Word was out that he had a lucrative TV series and book deal.

"Hair of the dog, old boy?" Bob had asked, as a waiter arrived to take their order. Zach looked hesitant but after Bob ordered champagne to celebrate Zach's success, the two men soon found themselves halfway down the bottle.

As Bob reflected on that evening, he wondered where Zach had spent the night. He'd left him just before midnight, in the company of several females who were keen to go clubbing, and Bob was in no doubt that his client, who had miraculously come back to life, obliged. Bob wouldn't stand in his way. Zach was more bankable when available and would soon have legions of adoring fans hanging off his every recipe, a celebrity with a wedding ring had less appeal.

Thank goodness he had stemmed the romance with Poppy.

Bob turned back to his desk and called to Lottie that he was ready for his coffee. He glanced at the appointments page on his diary and made a note to speak to suitable sponsors for the Gypsy Chef. Zach's profile would soon be as good as printing out bank notes and Bob needed to make sure that he found the most attractive deals possible.

"Have you seen Twitter today?" Lottie inched round the door, balancing a cappuccino in one hand and a chicken panini in the other. She wore a short bubble skirt and thick red tights and as Bob looked up, he refrained from telling Lottie that she looked like a lollipop.

"Do I need to?" he asked.

"Check out hashtag gypsy," Lottie bit her lip and focused on placing her offerings on Bob's desk and not in his lap.

Bob ignored the clatter of china and whipped out his phone. As

Lottie retreated, he punched #gypsy into his twitter account and gasped when he saw the stream of tweets - Zach had gone viral! The Daily Mail had photographed the chef falling out of a nightclub in the early hours and it had made their online news.

Bob was horrified.

And to make matters worse, the photos showed Zach in the company of one of the younger royals and several scantily dressed females.

They were all three sheets to the wind.

The heading read:

Right Royal Forage for the Tipsy Gypsy Chef!

"Hilary on line three," Lottie called out from her desk in reception.

Bob picked up the phone and held his breath.

"How in god's name did you engineer that?" Hilary bellowed into the phone.

Bob reached for the coffee, his hand shaking.

"He's absolutely off his trolley and wrapped around royalty."

Bob closed his eyes as Hilary's voice pounded in his ear.

"The timing's perfect." Hilary laughed. "I couldn't have done better, imagine the viewing figures for the TV series. Make sure you get Princess Pie in his book or something with a royal slant, what an endorsement."

Bob sprang up, spilling the coffee. He reached for his prayer beads and breathed a sigh of relief then beamed as Hilary ranted on about possible sponsors and Zach's earning potential. Bob couldn't remember a time when he'd encouraged a client to get into trouble; normally he spent most of his time digging them out. But Zach was hot-to-trot and with his handsome face and just-tumbled-out-of-bed look, Bob knew that there would be a media frenzy. The public loved a good scandal with celebs behaving badly and Zach was clearly up for the role.

"Shall I get Zach on the phone?" Lottie peeped round the door as

Bob said goodbye to Hilary.

"No," Bob replied, "let the boy sleep, I'm sure he needs it." He beamed at Lottie. "Fabulous outfit, darling, do you come in several flavours?"

AS THE SUN went down in Barbados and Jo and Hattie prepared for Long Tom's gig, Jo lay in her bath and thought about the email she'd received from Rob Mann.

The offer from Julian Struthers was way over what they'd considered a good asking price and Jo was stunned.

Rob had left a phone message too and she knew she'd have to call him back but wanted to have the weekend before accepting. She considered telling Hattie, but decided against it - nothing must spoil her friend's holiday.

Hattie stood in front of the bathroom mirror and carefully undid her hair.

"I thought you could leave them in for ages?" Jo said as Hattie pulled on the tiny plaits and untangled her locks.

"They've been in for days and are bleedin' killing me, they're so tight," Hattie mumbled as she stared at her reflection and fiddled with the snake-like braids, "I look like Medusa!"

"A look you might take back to Marland?" Jo teased.

"You can piss off and not be so righteous," Hattie snapped as her sun-kissed titian hair, released from its bindings, billowed around her head and beads rolled across the tiles.

"I thought it suited you," Jo nudged the tap with her toe and added more water to the bath.

Hattie scooped her hair into a band and pulled it back, then filled the sink and began to wash her face, squeezing her eyes shut as she lathered.

"Pete called," Jo said casually and rubbed a sponge over her tanned arms, "I was quite sharp with him, I must call him back and apologise."

"Nothing he's not used to." Hattie groped for a towel.

"To be honest, he sounded a bit the worse for wear."

Jo had already made her mind up not to tell Hattie that Pete, through slurred words, had pledged undying love. He also knew about the offer on Kirkton House and begged Jo not to move away. She hoped that in the sober light of day he might have forgotten the content of the call.

"He's probably drowning his sorrows."

"He say's Meg is fine."

"There's a surprise."

"Kirkton House is still in one piece and he's paid the gardener."

"That's alright then."

"Oh, and he's sold the garage, it looks like an offer is going through and it's going to be a housing estate."

"What?" Hattie dropped the towel and stared at Jo. "Got your priorities right?" She shook her head, "He's about to make a massive life change and your first worry is your dog."

Jo ignored Hattie. She didn't mention that he'd already told her he'd had an offer and as she sat up, she reached for the plug and pulled.

"So has he told you what he's going to do? Did you ask?"

"Well he kept asking if I'd made any decision on the hotel and urged me not sell it. Why do you think that Pete's future has anything to do with me?" Jo snatched at the towel Hattie held out. "I may be moving on myself one day and what he chooses to do with his life is his own affair."

"Suppressed emotional feelings..." Hattie mumbled and turned back to the mirror. She picked up a bottle of body lotion and generously applied the thick cream to her legs. "You can't see a good thing when it's standing right in front of you. There'll be many a lass in Marland falling over as they beat a path to his door. I can't understand why you would want to move away."

"Hattie, I'm not in love with Pete," Jo snapped, "he's a good friend and that's all."

"Time you put him out of his misery and told him then," Hattie sloshed perfume over her neck and breasts. "Now, what shall we wear tonight?" she said and strolled out of the bathroom.

Jo gathered the towel and rubbed her body briskly. She was thankful that she hadn't enlightened Hattie to Pete's confession of love, but Hattie was right, Jo really must speak to Pete and make it clear that their friendship would never be anything more. The last thing on Jo's mind was romance and she doubted that she'd ever have a relationship again, even though Pete was attractive and a very kind man. As she walked into the bedroom, the phone began to ring and Hattie threw herself on the bed to answer it.

"There's a taxi for Docherty and Contaldo in thirty minutes," Hattie told Jo, "that was your Jimmy on the phone. He said to thank you for the barbeque last night. Everyone enjoyed it, even that gobby cow, Wilma."

"Oh that's good," Jo said as she rubbed her hair with the towel and remembered that she had spent most of the night keeping Wilma and Hattie apart. A fierce exchange over the pulled pork had left Jo wondering if Wilma was aware of the barbeque sauce that Hattie had flicked over Wilma's retreating back, as Jo stepped in to calm the situation.

"We'd better get a move on," Jo said.

"Not until we've had a livener, then I can focus on my outfit." Hattie tucked a sarong around her body and disappeared to make a drink.

Jo thought about the evening ahead, it was going to be fun and she couldn't wait to see Long Tom Hendry, the headline act. Everyone had been talking about it last night at the barbeque. She knew she should call Pete back and apologise for being curt, as the last thing she wanted was to hurt his feelings. He was a huge help in looking after Meg and keeping an eye on Kirkton House and now that she had an offer on the hotel, her mind was awash with confusion. But as she opened the wardrobe door, Jo pushed all thoughts of Meg, Kirkton House and Pete firmly out of her mind. After all, she thought as she chose a long red evening dress, she was still on holiday.

"By gum, that's a stunner!" Hattie returned with two highball glasses, filled with rum cocktail, and stared at the flimsy dress Jo had hung on the closet door. "Remember what happened last time you wore a long red dress?" Hattie grinned as she sipped her drink and thought back to the night of Jo's engagement to John.

"In another life, Hattie," Jo said whimsically and stared at the dress, remembering that enchanting night. The dress she'd worn had been a ball gown and far more fancier.

"Time you got laid."

Jo shook her head. She doubted that she'd ever get laid again.

"Come on, we'll be late," Jo grabbed her drink from Hattie's outstretched hand and winced as the alcohol hit her. "Hell, that's strong!"

"Made with Mattie's special coconut water, he says it makes you randy," Hattie drained her glass.

"No more for you, then," Jo giggled.

"Well you could do with another," Hattie took Jo's glass and as she headed for the kitchen, began to sing, "This is my island, in the sun..."

Jo finished getting ready.

After carefully applying her make-up, she opened a drawer and chose a red lacy thong then stepped into the dress and smoothed the luxurious garment over her body.

When Hattie returned, she let out a long wolf whistle, "Oh my, I feel trouble ahead, red for danger?" She stared at her friend and shook her head. The change in Jo was remarkable. Since they'd arrived on the island she'd lost the drawn and haunted look that she'd carried for months and in its place, the ravishing Jo of old had suddenly returned. Combined with a glorious suntan and the addition of a few extra pounds, Jo looked as sexy as Hattie had ever seen her.

"You look amazing, Barbados suits you," Hattie said, "thank heavens that miserable old widow in mourning has finally been laid to rest."

Jo ignored the mixed compliment and turning to a full-length mirror, studied her reflection. The dress looked marvellous and the tight halter top enhanced her curves as the silky fabric caressed her hips and fell to the floor. Jo reached for a jewellery box in the drawer of the bedside table and chose a single diamond on a fine gold chain. It was the first gift John had given her and as she fastened the clasp and let her hair fall around her shoulders, she knew that it was a perfect match - simple but stunning. She smiled and touched the precious stone.

"Stop looking so smug and find some slippers, Cinderella," Hattie said as she threw her sarong to one side, "our carriage will be here any time."

Jo found a pair of flat gold sandals and slid her feet into the soft leather. She looked up and asked Hattie if she needed any help.

"Brace yourself!" Hattie cried and flinging the closet door open pulled out a multi-coloured cat-suit. The psychedelic pattern made Jo's head spin.

"You sneaked that one in..."

"I hope the bloody thing fits," Hattie cursed as she wriggled into a pair of support pants that finished under her bust. "Mattie will get whip-lash if he has a fumble in these."

With Jo's help she manipulated her body into the torturous looking garment.

"You'll be on stage with the backing singers with that suit and your hair," Jo smiled as Hattie climbed into the cat-suit and paraded around the room. She'd fluffed out her hair and it shone like a magnificent halo.

"Ladies, your driver awaits!"

A voice called out from beyond the patio doors. Mattie, handsome in a designer shirt and smart trousers, stepped into the lounge and as Jo and Hattie emerged from the bedroom, he wolf-whistled and held out his arms.

"Cheese on bread," Mattie said, "the heavens sent two angels."

"Never mind all that Bajan bullshit," Hattie snapped as she bustled past, "just get us to the gig on time."

Jo and Mattie looked at each other then, breaking into laughter, followed the colourful cyclone out to the car.

"Have you locked up?" Hattie called from the front seat.

"As safe as houses," Jo replied as Mattie held the door.

"Let's see what sort of show your Jimmy can put on."

Jo settled herself into Mattie's car and hoped that the weed wagon would get them there quickly. She was excited, this was a big event for Jimmy and her pride swelled as she thought of her eldest son.

But there was something more.

As the car crawled along the busy road and passed sidewalks packed with people heading to the venue, Jo accepted that there could be a life without John. So far she hadn't dared to contemplate it, for to be happy had felt wrong as her grief combined with guilt. After all, she'd survived hadn't she? Months of wondering why he'd been chosen and not her evaporated, as the hot humid air and sweet smelling perfumes of the Caribbean night heightened Jo's senses and she allowed herself to embrace the air of excitement and expectancy.

It felt almost sexual and Jo's skin tingled with anticipation.

Perhaps Mattie's coconut water was taking effect? For the first time in ages, a surge of happiness was bubbling, life did go on and Jo had been granted another chance. She touched the diamond at her throat and smiled.

They arrived at the back of the arena where Mattie pulled into the reserved parking area. Jimmy, immaculate in a sharp three-piece suit, met them.

"Wow, you both look amazing," he said and grinned from ear-to-ear, "come this way." He guided Jo and Hattie up the steps, ushering them past several security guards who lined the entrance. They walked along a dark corridor towards a set of double doors marked, 'VIP Area'.

"Go through and I'll catch you later," Jimmy pecked Jo's cheek and she sensed that he was nervous as she watched him hurry away.

"Well," Hattie asked, "are you ready?"

They could hear muffled sounds of an excited crowd as music thundered out from the acts already on stage.

"I can't wait," Jo said and tossing her head back, grabbed Hattie's arm and threw open the doors.

"Let's go!" they both cried excitedly and burst into the party.

19

Back-stage at the Lime Inn, Long Tom Hendry was in trouble. He sat in front of a mirror, where harsh light from surrounding bulbs lit up his deathly complexion. Despite the chilly air blasting out of the air-con unit in the dressing room he was sweating profusely, his head ached and nausea threatened.

Long Tom had spent the afternoon on the beach at his hotel on the west coast where, from the comfort of a padded steamer chair, he stretched full-length and watched the world go by. He contemplated the evening ahead, conscious that he was due on stage at the Lime Inn in a few hours' time and despite nerves, which were normal pre-concert, he was looking forward to the event.

Well-heeled guests in designer beachwear sat alongside, or wandered along the edge of the soft white sand, their perfectly manicured toes touching the turquoise waters that lapped the glorious beach. A sun deck was moored in the bay and as Long Tom lay back he heard the sound of swimmers as they swam out, then dived off the rig and splashed around. He ordered a club sandwich and having enjoyed his lunch, settled down to read a book. Lulled by a balmy breeze and the gentle sounds of beach life, Long Tom soon fell into a deep and sophomoric sleep.

"Wake up! You're going to be late..."

A hand reached out and shook Long Tom's shoulder.

Long Tom heard Boss, his manager call out and as he gradually woke and focused on the anxious face before him, silhouetted in the setting sun, Long Tom realised that he had been asleep for several hours. He raised himself into a sitting position and reached for his shirt then hastily followed Boss across the cooling sand to his suite to get ready.

But now, as he sat in his dressing room, with the concert less than an hour away, Long Tom's head pounded and he felt dizzy and sick.

"I think you may have sunstroke," Boss said as he stood beside Long Tom and stared at the troubled face in the mirror. The singer had been quiet in the car on the way to the gig and now appeared to be rapidly deteriorating. Boss cursed under his breath and knew that he should have flown in earlier, not left it until the day of the first concert. Where the hell was Hilary? This wouldn't have happened if she'd been here.

"I feel ill, Boss," Long Tom mumbled.

Jimmy who'd been summoned to the dressing room stood along-side. From the moment Long Tom had stepped out of the chauffeur driven car and stumbled on the steps at the artiste's entrance, Jimmy had known that they had a serious problem.

He reached into his pocket and held out a small bottle.

"What is it?" Boss asked.

"A Bajan remedy, I got it from a certified doctor." Jimmy crossed his fingers behind his back.

"No alcohol?" Boss looked suspicious and imagined voodoo remedies but Jimmy looked at him with disgust.

"You don't honestly think I'm that stupid," Jimmy said angrily.

"Guys, this is no time to argue," Long Tom had begun to shiver. "Whatever you have in that magic bottle had better work fast." He wondered how he could have fallen asleep in the sun. If Hilary had been with him he would have been under an umbrella, coated in layers of factor fifty; she was paranoid about exposure to the sun.

Damn the woman, she should be here!

Long Tom held his head in his hands and groaned. There was no way that he would make the stage that night.

"Now or never..." Jimmy said.

"You're absolutely sure?" Boss asked suspiciously.

Jimmy glared at Boss then turned to Long Tom. He was concerned about his act, but far more concerned about the promoter's reaction if Long Tom pulled out of the show. The arena was already full and they could hear the warm-up bands playing to a pulsating audience that would go crazy if Long Tom failed to show.

"Down in one, my friend," Jimmy unscrewed the top off the bottle and held it out.

"Been nice knowing you..." Long Tom looked up through puffy eyes and took the mixture. He gave it a sniff, shook his head, then tilted his head back and drank.

Boss and Jimmy held their breath.

Both were paralysed with anxiety as they watched Long Tom's body shudder. His head slumped forward and he buried his head in his arms on the dressing room bench.

"Jesus Christ, you've killed him," Boss hissed.

"Give him a minute," Jimmy held his breath.

The backstage manager knocked on the door, "Thirty minutes to show time!"

"We're fucked," Boss said.

Long Tom's body was still and he seemed to be sleeping.

Jimmy silently cursed the old woman who'd given him the potion. He'd raced round to her chattel house as soon as he'd realised that Long Tom was ill and it had cost him a hundred dollars to raise her from the back porch and into her kitchen. Jimmy had watched as she reached a wrinkled, leather-like claw hand into a dusty cupboard and produced the cure-all medicine. It had raised Jimmy from the dead on more than one occasion but he needed a miracle this time.

"Yu, tell him no more sun!" The old woman called out as she

cackled through broken teeth and shooed Jimmy away, "Dem white boys sho are stupid."

Stupid or not, Long Tom was in trouble and Jimmy found himself praying.

"He's moving!" Boss whispered.

They held their breath.

"Twenty minutes to show time!" They heard another menacing thump on the door.

Long Tom shook his head and sat up. Colour had returned to his face and he stared in the mirror at Boss and Jimmy, "You two look like you've seen a ghost," he said and reached for his Stetson, "let's get this show on the road."

"How do you feel?" Boss asked in wonder.

"Never felt better," Long Tom replied as he pushed his hat down on his head and stretched out his arms.

Jimmy closed his eyes and said a prayer to every voodoo effigy he could conjure up and threw in a few Christian ones for good measure.

"We'll have a case of whatever that was," Boss cried and pumped Jimmy's hand. Jimmy thought Boss might change his mind if he'd smelt the fish guts, herbs and other odious ingredients that had boiled for days on the old woman's stove, but not wanting to dampen the mood, returned the hand-shake and breathed a sigh of relief.

"Fifteen minutes, guys," Jimmy said with a nod in the rock star's direction.

Long Tom winked back.

Jimmy hurried from the dressing room to assure everyone they were on schedule and was met by the promoter.

"Everything OK?" the promoter asked.

"He's in great form."

"That's what we want to hear, you'll make a killing out there tonight."

They looked around at the packed bars, the place was pulsating and people danced and swayed as they watched the acts. It was hard to be heard above the noise.

Jimmy reached into his pocket, where he'd stored a back-up bottle of magic potion. He fondled it lovingly and decided to hang on to it as he looked out at the well-oiled machine that was his business and smiled.

Only in Barbados!

~

IN THE VIP box there was a ripple of excitement. The long-awaited night had come and in moments, Long Tom Hendry would step out onto the stage.

Jo and Hattie stood side by side and stared down at the throng below, both too tense to sit down. The atmosphere was electric, compounded by the hot and humid night and dozens of people around them moved forward to get a better view. Jo gasped as she saw a famous Bajan musician and his family lean over the adjacent rail.

"That's Eddie Plant..." Hattie whispered excitedly, nudging Jo's arm, "and I'm sure that's Rhiana's family talking to your Jimmy." She pointed to a group who could be seen chatting in the wings.

Hattie and Jo looked around the private bar area and noticed many well-known celebrities who owned exclusive homes on the island. A drum roll roared and the promotor bounced onto the stage. He grabbed a microphone and held his hand up.

"OK folks, this is the moment you've all been waiting for..." Whistles and whoops came from the crowd. "It is my greatest pleasure to welcome this act back to the Caribbean, he knows you love him and we know that he loves you!" Deafening cheers went up amid yells and stamping feet. "So let's give a massive Lime Inn welcome to the one and only... Long Tom Hendry!"

The lights went out and the stage was black as the band began to play Long Tom's most famous hit. The crowd became silent as the music of No More War began.

Suddenly, a spotlight pierced the gloom and illuminated a solitary figure in the middle of the stage.

"Hello," the figure said softly, "my name's Long Tom Hendry."

He stared out at the audience as the familiar music could be heard, then closed his eyes and began to sing. The rich gravelly drawl started slowly and as he headed towards the chorus, it roared out and sent spine-chilling waves that reverberated around the arena.

The crowd went wild.

"Oh, my..." Hattie cried and grabbed Jo's arm. They swayed in time to the music. "He's amazing." Her words were drowned out by the noise as everyone joined in with the chorus and Long Tom took command of the stage.

Jo looked down and saw Malibu with the lifeguards from the beach. They were on the front row and reached out as they sang along with Long Tom. In a far corner, Cecil, George and Gloria, surrounded by their families, smiled and clapped their hands and Raymondo and the crew from the catamaran wriggled around wildly. Wilma and her toy boy were buried in the frenzy and Hattie leaned over the rail to wave.

"Just so she can see us in VIP!" Hattie yelled.

A waiter appeared and placed a bottle of champagne beside Hattie and Jo. He topped up their glasses then eased himself back through the crowd of the packed bar.

"This is the life!" Hattie threw back her drink and grinned.

Jo tasted the cold bubbles that popped in her mouth - it was as delicious as the atmosphere and sounds from the stage. As the night pulsed with expectation and they watched Long Tom sail through his numbers, Jo wanted to pinch herself. Could she really be this happy, so soon after losing John? For tonight she felt special, as if her life had somehow begun again and as the champagne took effect, she determined that any thoughts of loss and regret were to be banished, for nothing was going to spoil the evening ahead.

Long Tom was on sparkling form.

He'd removed his Stetson and taken off his jacket and strode around the stage. For some of his numbers he played a guitar and jammed with the band and for others, he sat at a piano and let his fingers caress the keys as he sang songs of love and happiness.

You don't need a million dollars
To wake up on a sun filled morning
To feel my arms around you
You're here,
Right here, right now, with me...

"I wouldn't mind waking up with him on any morning," Hattie announced as she listened to Long Tom sing his most recent hit.

"He's quite a dish isn't he?" Jo agreed and stared down at the man whose charisma and talent had the audience in the palm of his hand.

The concert was drawing to a close. Long Tom had been on stage for two hours and as he came to his final number, he graciously gave thanks to everyone who had supported him, then turned to the side of the stage and to the amazement and joy of all, beckoned Eddie Plant to join him. The audience went wild as Eddie, their local hero, stepped out and sang with Long Tom. The cheers reverberated up into the night sky as the concert ended and Jo and Hattie found themselves linking arms with everyone, as they all joined in.

When Long Tom left the stage and the final cheers died down, a strange silence fell over the arena. An unspoken understanding of being in the right place at the right time seemed to ripple through the crowd.

A local band had set up on stage and now played familiar reggae music and soon, everyone was once again swaying happily to the music.

"That was fantastic," Hattie said as she turned from the stage and glanced around. Members of Long Tom's band, the promoter and Jimmy had entered the bar and were shaking hands with the VIP guests.

Mattie appeared and put his arm around Hattie, "Fuh' real?" he asked, "some show eh?"

Hattie was still pumped up from the music and champagne and having earlier spied a dance floor to one side of the bar, grabbed Mattie's hand and led him away.

"Mum, come and meet Eddie," Jimmy grabbed Jo's hand and she

let herself be drawn into the group of people surrounding the Bajan artiste. Eddie greeted her warmly and said he could see where Jimmy got his looks from. Jo was pinned tight into the crowd as everyone wanted to talk to Eddie and the band. The conversation was deafening as Jo savoured the moment of being so close to a music legend.

"And here's someone else I want you to meet..." Jimmy reached for Jo's shoulder and turned her round.

Jo came face to face with Long Tom Hendry.

"Long Tom, I'd like to introduce Jo."

Jimmy's words were distant and the crowded bar blurred as Jo looked into the dark eyes of the man before her.

Time seemed to stand still.

Long Tom reached out and took her hand. His warm fingers caressed her skin and Jo gasped as his raw gaze burned into her.

"The pleasure's mine," he said, his deep voice gravelly.

Jo's heart raced and she wondered if her knees were going to buckle. Her body offered no resistance when Long Tom pulled her to him.

"Don't let me lose you," he whispered in her ear, "come back to the party..." His free hand wandered over the silk at her hips, like flames scorching into her skin and his warm breath sent electrifying shivers down Jo's spine.

But in moments he was gone.

"Blimey, was that Long Tom?" Hattie threw herself in front of Jo and stood on her toes to catch a glimpse of Long Tom, who'd been moved on to meet and greet sponsors. "He's very good looking, when you get close," Hattie turned, "and you couldn't have got any bleedin' closer, what did he say?"

Jo felt as though she'd been hit by a missile and still gripping her glass, took a hefty swig. A long forgotten sensation was flooding through her body and as feelings of sexual anticipation coursed through her veins, her face burned.

"He said something about a party."

"Party?" Hattie cried. "Hell, you've only gone and got us an invite back to his bash on the west coast!"

"Well, perhaps Jimmy has arranged it," Jo muttered and held her glass out for a refill.

"I've no doubt he has, but to get an invite from The Man himself," Hattie held up her hand and high-fived Mattie, who'd slid alongside. "No wonder you're as red as a rooster," Hattie laughed.

Jo was wondering what had just happened to her. Two minutes ago she had been normal, now she was on a rocket to the moon. She shook her head and tried to focus on what Hattie was saying but her eyes anxiously searched the room for Long Tom. The noise was deafening and the crowd closing in seemed denser and Jo suddenly knew that she had to get some fresh air. She indicated to Hattie that she was going to find the ladies room and handing her glass to a waiter, headed for the doors that they'd arrived through and slipped into the darkness.

It was cooler in the corridor but the night was still humid and sticky. Jo closed her eyes and leaned against the wall; she took deep breaths and tried to calm her rapidly beating heart.

Long Tom stood in the shadows and stared at the woman before him. He'd managed to keep track of her as he mindlessly made conversation in the bar and accepted praise, but when a flash of scarlet shot through the crowd, he made his excuses and followed. Now he wanted to reach out and touch her again. There was something intoxicating about her and like the drugs that he'd resisted for so long, the addict in him craved to satisfy his need.

He stepped forward.

Jo heard a footstep and opened her eyes. Before she had time to think what was happening, Long Tom had reached out and was kissing her passionately. His arms wrapped around her body and she found herself melting into his embrace.

It felt so good!

"Wow," Long Tom said, "you're some lady."

Jo was speechless as Long Tom held her in his arms and stared searchingly into her eyes.

Suddenly, a door opened at the far end of the corridor and a voice called out.

"Long Tom, are you there?" It was Jimmy.

Jo winced, she was mortified that he might find them and wriggled out of Long Tom's arms. "He mustn't see me," she whispered, anxious that her eldest son didn't catch her in a compromising situation.

"Come to the party," Long Tom whispered back. "Please!" He couldn't remember the last time he'd pleaded with anyone.

"Your car's here!" Jimmy was getting closer.

Jo pulled away. She ran to the door and disappeared into the bar.

Long Tom stared at the door as it closed. The last thunderbolt that had struck him came after three bottles of Jack Daniels and many lines of coke. He'd woken up in Las Vegas with a wedding ring on his finger and a famous model by his side.

This one had come when he was stone cold sober.

He'd been sober for years and would never go back but even his relationship with Hilary had never felt like this. He sighed, then turned and called out to Jimmy that he was on his way.

Would she come to the party?

He'd soon find out.

20

J immy watched his security team surround Long Tom as the singer stepped into the back of the arena and signed autographs for a queue of adoring fans. When he'd finished, Boss helped him climb into the back of a waiting vehicle that would whisk him away to the west coast. Long Tom was hosting an after-show party at his luxurious hotel and the invitation list had prompted a closely guarded security operation.

Jimmy had ensured that Jo and Hattie were on the list.

But as he watched the car pull away, he caught the eye of Long Tom and knew that Jo had no need for Jimmy's priority invitation.

Jimmy was as sharp as a razor and was aware of everything that happened on his turf. He'd seen the chemistry between Jo and Long Tom from the moment their eyes met and when Jo disappeared and Long Tom followed, Jimmy made sure that the security team, who were glued to Long Tom's every move, gave the couple some space.

Now, as Jimmy double-checked procedures to ensure that all his VIP guests were safely escorted off his premises, he thought about his mother.

She wouldn't want him to know.

Long Tom was married and would be totally off limits in Jo's mind. But Jimmy knew that strange things happened on the island and the explosion of emotions that he'd witnessed wouldn't die down until they'd been satisfied. Whatever happened he would protect his mother and with luck, she'd never know that he knew.

Jimmy shook his head and wandered through the arena and into the Lime Inn, where the bar was still packed and the dance floor heaving. He stood and watched the happy drinkers and gyrating bodies and reminded himself that Barbados was a holiday destination.

What happens on the island stays on the island...

AT A BAR on a beach in an exclusive west coast resort, Hattie sat on a tall stool and sipped a cocktail. The party at Long Tom's luxurious hotel was in full swing.

Guests from the concert had arrived and made their way through the marbled foyer, down gently sloping steps, to a canopied gazebo laid out on the private beach. Bright orange flames from giant torches leapt out into the starry sky as pale cotton muslin, bunched around pillars, escaped and billowed in the humid night breeze. A popular steel band played calypso songs and uniformed staff circulated with dainty canapés and cocktails.

"By heck, this is the life," Hattie said as she watched the movers and shakers from the music industry and world of celebrity. Nearby, a group of super-models air-kissed each other and Hattie pulled a face. "That lot could do with a decent meal," she frowned.

"Fuh' real, Momma," Mattie replied idly, his dark eyes drinking everything in.

A barbeque had been set up beside a long table, laden with island delicacies and a pig roasted on a spit as guests wandered by to feast on the midnight buffet.

"Ah, here comes Cinderella," Hattie said as Jo walked across the sand to join them.

Jo was barefoot and the silk of her dress seemed to float as she moved. Her hair shone in the glow from the torches and several heads turned to follow her progress.

"Big-up, Momma," Mattie said in greeting, "too sweet..." He smiled lazily at Jo.

"Never mind the compliments," Hattie nudged her laid-back lover, "get Cinders and me something tall, dark and strong to be supping on." She held out her empty glass.

"How beautiful this is," Jo said as she perched on a stool next to Hattie, "I've never seen anything so decadent and luxurious."

"It beats Marland on a wet Monday night, half the guests are off the tele..." She gawped as judges from a popular talent show make an entrance. "Blimey, he's surrounded by all his ex-girlfriends," Hattie shook her head as she watched the performance before them.

The band stopped playing and a faint drum roll could be heard.

Long Tom appeared at the top of the steps. Barefoot, he'd changed into a pair of faded jeans and white cotton shirt, the sleeves rolled back to reveal deeply tanned arms. As he made his way onto the beach, the guests applauded.

Jo was transfixed.

Long Tom smiled and shook hands with his guests. He seemed perfectly at ease and with magnetic appeal, was soon completely surrounded. As Jo watched Long Tom laugh and smile, she wondered if she'd been dreaming. Had he really followed her into the corridor and kissed her so passionately? Engulfed by beautiful women half Jo's age, Long Tom could pick and choose and he had a wife back home in London, Jo reminded herself reluctantly.

"Jump-up, Momma?" Mattie had returned and placing fresh drinks down, indicated that Hattie might like to dance, the band had struck up a well-known tune.

"Too-nuff!" Hattie leapt off her stool and taking Mattie's hand, sashayed off to dance.

Jo turned away from the party and looked out towards the sea where a rake-thin girl in a wisp of a dress, stood at the edge of the beach. She leaned down and scooped warm salty water into her hands then splashed it playfully over the adoring Adonis who stood beside her.

Jo suddenly felt her age. Years ago, she too would have flirted and teased, but these days she didn't know where to begin.

The couple held hands then made their way back to the party and Jo slipped away from the bar and walked to where they'd been standing in the water. It was a beautiful night and stars, high above in the inky black sky, twinkled across the sea. A new moon shot a beam across the bay where, far away on the horizon, lights from a cruise ship shone as the floating giant made its way to the Grenadine Islands.

A wave lapped and Jo wriggled her toes as her feet sank in the pure white sand. She imagined Long Tom's strong arms snaking around her waist and his kisses on her neck. The Caribbean was tantalising! A place where illicit encounters seemed acceptable, where emotions flowed with the tides of the seas and dreams became real for a few stolen moments.

Dare she still dream? Could life still conjure up surprises, still offer hope?

Jo thought about home.

She remembered the cold closed-up rooms and shuttered windows at Kirkton House. The old house oozed sadness and now, as the weeks passed, would soon show signs of neglect. What had she to go back for? In her mind she could see her beloved Meg and hoped that Pete was looking after the old dog, who was demanding in her twilight years. Why was Jo avoiding Pete? Was he too embroiled in her past? He was a good man and now, after his admission of love, Jo knew that he'd do anything to be closer, so why was she pulling away? She turned from the sea and looked back at the party where the piercing sound of a tree frog mixed with the beat of steel drums. Silhouettes danced in the torch-lit shadows and happy guests mingled by the bar, beneath a row of lanterns hanging from almond trees lining the beach.

Jo looked up at the sky and thought about John. What would he tell her to do? She sighed, for John was gone and, at this moment in time, she no longer knew what to do and part of her was angry at his passing.

Jo turned and searched for Long Tom and could see that he was, as always, surrounded. Jimmy stood on the steps; he cut a handsome figure and was soon joined by two pretty girls. Eddie Plant had picked up a guitar and joined in with the band and Jo noticed Hattie and Mattie dancing nearby. Hattie's body swayed happily as Mattie gyrated around her and Jo felt envy for her friend's ability to live in the moment and embrace life's pleasures without fear or guilt. Jo moved away from the party and gathering her dress to stop it trailing in the water, began to wander along the beach.

Amongst so many, with so much luxury surrounding her, she felt very alone.

The excitement of earlier had gone and as she paddled in the warm water and stepped out into the night she became lost in a confusing mix of emotions. Being single in your middle years wasn't what it was cracked up to be and the confidence of youth was, at that moment, light years away.

"Want some company?" A voice whispered.

Jo froze.

The deep silky tone of Long Tom's lazy drawl hung in the humid air.

"Is my party not good enough for you?"

Jo began to speak but Long Tom had reached her side and placed a finger gently on her lips. He'd rolled his jeans and the water rippled against their bare legs. Jo looked up, mesmerised by his dark sparkling eyes as they held her gaze.

She offered no resistance when his arm reached round her waist and drew her to him.

The rush of sexual adrenaline from earlier coursed through Jo's body and she closed her eyes as they began to kiss. The moment seemed to last forever. Languishing in Long Tom's strong arms, Jo completely succumbed.

Time stood still as Long Tom nuzzled into her neck. His hands stroked her back and sent shivers down her spine as he whispered in her ear, "There's more privacy in my room."

He took her hand and led her along the beach, where neatly trimmed hedges of Lady of the Night surrounded a private terrace, the powerful sweet aroma of the native plant as intoxicating as Long Tom's touch. Unlatching a gate, he pushed it to one side and they stepped onto a tiled verandah. Security guards slipped into the shadows and Long Tom gave a dismissing nod in their direction as he opened the door to his suite.

"Won't you be missed?" Jo asked.

"They've had their money's worth." He smiled lazily and pulled her into a candle-lit bedroom.

As if in a trance, Jo followed.

"Would you like a drink?" Long Tom stood by a table laid out with soft drinks.

"No..." Jo whispered, "Just you..."

She slipped out of her dress and lay down on the bed.

21

A clock on the mantelpiece chimed the hour and woke Pete. He was slumped in an armchair by the stove in the kitchen and as he slowly gathered his thoughts, he realised that he'd been there all night. Heaving himself into an upright position, he remembered his call to Jo.

What a fool! He'd made a right mess of things.

Pete stared at the clock and mentally calculated the time in Barbados. It would be very early in the morning, perhaps Jo was up? He knew he needed to apologise and with a sigh he shook his body to bring some life to his limbs then stood.

Meg, sensing movement, looked up from the comfort of her box.

"Here we go again, old lass," Pete said as he reached for the phone.

The phone connected and taking a deep breath, Pete listened to the dial tone. It was answered on the second ring.

"The Shagging Shack, may I help you?" A voice spoke.

Pete was confused. Mystified, he held the phone tightly to his ear, "Er, I think I've got the wrong number."

"Bleedin' hell, is that you Pete Parks?" Hattie shouted.

Pete winced as he heard Hattie's voice.

"Don't tell me they've finally got a satellite signal hooked up to your love nest," Hattie continued, "you'll be surfing t'internet next!"

"Aye, very funny," Pete replied. "I take it the holiday's going well?"

"Sure t'ing, sweet cheeks, has something happened to the dog?"

"No, nowt like that, Meg is fine - I wanted to have a word with Jo." Pete drummed his fingers on a side table and Meg, hearing her mistress' name, got up and came to sit next to him. There was a hesitation on the other end and Pete wondered if he'd been cut off. After a long pause, Hattie replied.

"I think she's gone for a swim, she was up early this morning." Hattie had stopped joking. "Should I tell her you called?"

"Will she be long?"

Another pause before Hattie replied.

"Erm, hard to say, she likes her swimming."

"Well, tell her I'll call back later." Pete was about to hang up but he too paused and asked, "Is she OK?"

"Oh aye, never been better, I'll pass your message on." Hattie hung up.

Pete stroked Meg's head and contemplated the call. Hattie sounded strange but Pete thought he was probably reading something into nothing and decided that he'd ring Jo when she was back from the beach. Hattie had indicated that Jo was cheerful and feeling slightly heartened, he reached for Meg's lead.

"Come on, let's walk this off," he said to the wriggling animal, "we want to be on top form when we speak to your mam." He picked up his jacket and unlocked the kitchen door, then walked out across the sunny yard. "Barbados isn't the only place with glorious sunshine," Pete mumbled as the pair made their way to the fells.

HATTIE TOO CONTEMPLATED THE CALL, as she placed the phone back on the desk. Pete wasn't the only one who was wondering where Jo was.

She wandered into the kitchen and poured a glass of orange juice, then went out to the patio where the sun scorched across the gardens. Hopping across blistering tiles, Hattie slipped her feet into a pair of Jo's abandoned flip-flops and placed her juice on the table. She looked up as Cecil appeared with the morning paper.

"Yu' enjoy de show?" Cecil smiled as he handed the neatly folded pages over the patio wall.

"Sure t'ing," Hattie replied.

"Made de front page," Cecil muttered and wandered away.

Hattie threw the paper onto the table and nestled her bottom comfortably onto a chair. She smiled as she looked at the headline,

Long Tom Triumphs at the Lime Inn!

There was a photo of the singer on stage surrounded by adoring fans. Hattie was pleased for Jimmy, the publicity was wonderful. She picked up her reading glasses and peered closely at the photo. Long Tom was a handsome bugger and no doubt as charismatic as his stage act.

Hattie sat back and thought about the call she'd had from Jimmy, right after breakfast. Jimmy had told Hattie not to worry about Jo; she was fine and would be in touch later.

I bet she bloody will! Hattie thought and smiled. Talk about the pot calling the kettle black! Hattie giggled. Who would have thought it! Miss, 'I'll-never-get-laid-again,' had surpassed herself and was tucked up in the arms of one of rock's most famous sons, no doubt in the lap of luxury at his west coast retreat. What would the media make of that! Long Tom's addictions return with yet another middle-aged woman in tow. Wasn't his wife clocking up the years?

Long Tom clearly enjoyed the charms of a more experienced hand, Hattie thought as she finished her juice.

A little bullfinch was hopping about on the wall, waiting for Hattie to make crumbs with the remnants of toast on the table. The tiny tame birds were regular visitors and Hattie, much to Jo's annoyance, would normally shoo them away. But now, she observed the industrious creature as it edged closer and with confidence, balanced on the plate and began pecking.

The sharp beak made light work of the hardened bread.

The act of watching another eat made Hattie's tummy rumble and she decided that she'd stroll along the beach and have a gander at the breakfast buffet over at the Tropical Palms Hotel. It seemed ages since she'd had a couple of rounds of toast with her first cuppa and she'd no company to worry about, with Jo making hay on the west coast and Mattie busy with an island tour.

Hattie knew that Mattie would be occupied all day.

Tourists loved Mattie's off-road experiences and paid handsomely for the thrills and spills of a day out in the weed wagon, finding places completely unknown to the glossy brochures, stacked high on reception desks of every hostelry offering accommodation. A day out with Mattie made memories that sent recommendations soaring on Trip Advisor, for those who'd survived the round of rum shops and still had the memory to recall.

Hattie wrote out a note saying where she had gone and left it on the table for Jo to see when she returned. She remembered to add at the end that Pete had phoned and would be calling back later. It wouldn't surprise Hattie to hear that Pete was boarding a plane - he'd sounded so dejected and forlorn and Jo's absence clearly made his heart grow fonder. But there was the daft mongrel to consider and Hattie knew that there was little chance of Pete leaving her. Jo would have a stroke if Meg was put in kennels.

Hattie yawned and glanced at her watch.

She'd better get a wriggle on - the brunch buffet would finish soon. Grabbing her purse and lipstick she locked the apartment and headed for the beach and as she set off on her walk, she hoped that Jo would put in an appearance soon. Hattie wasn't cut out to play solo and lest anyone think she was Billy-no-mates, she gritted her teeth and smiled at bemused sunbathers and swimmers, before flopping down on a cushioned chair on the terrace at the Tropical Palms.

Hattie ordered a restorative drink and looked out at the bay ahead where a sleek speed boat skimmed the waters beyond the reef.

"Happy days Jo," Hattie smiled and raised her glass, "wherever you are..."

A SHORT DISTANCE AWAY, Jo leaned back on soft leather cushions and spread her arms along the deeply padded upholstery of the luxurious boat that soared across the calm Caribbean waters. Standing tall at the helm, Long Tom steered with skill and dexterity, his hair billowed out in the warm sea breeze and as he turned to race the boat across the bay again, he smiled at Jo.

"Happy?" he called out.

"Delirious!" she beamed back.

Jo tucked her red dress high and flexed her legs in the sun. The silk dress was ruined from the water and salt spray but it was a small price to pay.

Long Tom slowed the boat and with the shore in sight, dropped anchor and cut the engine. He reached under a seat and pulled out a large wicker hamper. The hotel had provided a wonderful brunch, as well as use of their speedboat and as Jo watched Long Tom assemble their make-shift meal, she marvelled at the power of money.

"Where did you learn your boat skills?" Jo asked and sat forward to take a porcelain beaker of piping hot coffee. She ran her fingers over a gold embossed logo.

Long Tom sat close and placed his arm around her shoulder. Dressed in faded denim shorts, his skin was warm and inviting.

"There's nothing to it, steering this babe around the bay is easy," he said. "But I've sailed many a sea in the past, it's the most freeing thing you can do, alone with only the elements for company." He looked thoughtful as he recalled days gone by. Exactly where he had sailed was blurry, as his travelling companions had generally been a crate of Jack Daniels and a barrel full of weed.

How he'd ever survived was a mystery.

He turned and began to nuzzle Jo's neck. Oh the joy of a warm and loving woman! It surpassed any chemical high and as his hand caressed her soft skin, all thoughts of Hilary lay a zillion miles away. Jo was real with curves in all the right places and skin that wore her past well. No chemicals smoothed her freckled face or plumped her soft lips and faint lines appeared when she laughed. This woman was sensuous and as natural as the water that lapped around the boat.

Jo put her beaker down and closed her eyes. She sighed contentedly as Long Tom's mouth and fingers awoke sensations she'd long suppressed. Under the heat of the glorious sun, gently rocked by the placid sea, Jo's senses sprang awake and succumbed to the pleasure of the moment.

They'd spent a heaven-sent night together, experiencing highs that only two perfectly matched people could enjoy. It had been wild and thrilling but tender and romantic too. In the soft light of day he'd gently stroked her hair as she woke and she'd jumped at the chance of his suggestion of a picnic on a boat. They'd waded into the water, where Jo allowed herself to be helped aboard, as hotel staff discreetly wished them a pleasant morning and Long Tom fired up the engine.

Now, as they made love yet again, Jo allowed the drug that was Long Tom take hold. Long Tom had spoken to Jimmy earlier and Hattie would know where Jo was. For the first time in as long as she could remember, Jo didn't think about the future or the past.

The time to be happy was now.

22

*Z*ach pulled the collar of his jacket tight around his neck and kept his head tilted from the force of the driving rain as he hurried to find shelter in the warmth of the local pub. He'd spent the last hour on the phone with Nancy Nevis, who seemed to take it for granted that he'd be working at the weekend. To Zach's surprise, she'd been helpful and even agreed with some of his ideas for the format of his book. Zach intended to spend the next few days at his laptop, his head was buzzing and he needed to commit the thought process to paper.

But first he wanted a pint and some hearty pub grub.

"Watcha Mate," the barman called out as a sodden Zach removed his jacket and settled on a stool at the bar. Zach looked round at the cosy pub which had become his regular haunt. It was full of punters, happy to be out of the rain.

" 'Tis the tipsy gypsy!" The cheeky barman, who recognised Zach, grinned and whipped a newspaper out from under the counter and pushed it forward, headline facing.

"Very funny," Zach said glaring at the offending object.

"Mixing with some heavy duty babes, dude?"

"I honestly can't remember most of what happened that night,"

Zach said and glanced at the newspaper, regretting that he'd had so much to drink.

"Think of the money and the women," the barman said and drifted off to serve another customer.

Zach cringed as he read the article.

Since his brief relationship with Poppy, he'd gone right off the rails. Women seemed to be throwing themselves at his feet and it was difficult to resist the temptations.

Zach took a drink of his pint and looked up when the barman, who had returned, nodded towards the door.

A girl had entered the pub and walked purposefully to the bar.

Zach froze.

"Is that yet another hair of the dog?" Poppy asked. Her voice was cold.

Zach shoved the newspaper to one side and felt the tensions and frustrations of the last few days fall away and as he looked into Poppy's lovely eyes, he automatically held out his arms, reaching for her embrace.

But Poppy pushed him away brusquely.

The barman, who was familiar with the staff from Hargreaves & Puddicombe Promotions, stepped forward.

"Can I book a table for tonight?" Poppy asked. "It's Heidi's birthday and we want to celebrate."

"Sure you can. How many are dining?" He smiled. The agency often used the pub for celebrations.

"About ten, I think, Bob said you can charge it to the office." She watched as the barman made a note of the booking.

"Is everyone invited?" Zach asked.

Poppy ignored him then turned and walked out of the pub without looking back, her hair flowing across her shoulders, catching the light as she opened the door.

"Jesus..." Zach mumbled. His heart seemed to leap from his chest and drag painfully in her wake across the bar floor.

Zach thought of Poppy's long legs and glorious green eyes and sighed. If he had any sense he would leave the pub now and head back to his flat. He had a ton of things he should be doing and lingering here wouldn't help matters.

"One for the road?"

"Just the one," Zach said and pushed his glass across the bar, "then I really must get going."

"Yes, mate," the barman poured the refill.

Zach looked at his watch. Poppy's party would be here in a couple of hours and knew that he should do the sensible thing and move on.

"Cheers!"

Zach shook his mane of tousled hair and attacked the drink. It tasted like nectar and slipped down his throat in record time.

It looked like another interesting evening ahead.

JIMMY STOOD at the door of his beach house and stared out towards the sea. With little enthusiasm, he contemplated a run and his eyes searched up and down the beach, checking the day's traffic.

There wasn't a soul about.

A phone rang in the kitchen and feeling relieved that the decision to run had been temporarily taken from him, Jimmy turned to pick it up. He listened to the caller and with a courteous thank you, replaced the phone.

Jo was still on the west coast.

Jimmy looked at his watch and wondered if she'd be making a weekend of it. Knowing what he did about females, he was fairly sure she'd be heading back to the apartment soon for a change of clothes. He picked up his sunglasses and walked out to the beach then and with a sigh, began to run.

Fishing boats bobbed about in the bay ahead, their stark white hulls a sharp contrast to the aquamarine sea as the vessels made their way to a quay further down the coast, where a crowd waited to inspect the morning's catch.

Jimmy settled into a comfortable pace and as he ran, he thought about his mother.

It felt strange to be her protector. Uncomfortable in a way and he wondered if she knew what she was getting into? A relationship with someone like Long Tom was high maintenance and with any luck it would be no more than a fling. Jimmy knew that he didn't have the right to judge; he was no saint himself and lurched from one romance to the next, as holidaying females came and went. But he'd an image of his mother at home in Westmarland, with a dog at her heels as she went about a gentle life in the country, playing the widow's role. He'd never expected Long Tom to single her out, god knows what it would do to her and Jimmy regretted having made the introduction. Surely there was some steady fellow in Westmarland that would be glad of Jo for company?

He'd reached the end of the beach and slowed to mingle with locals and visitors, all crowded around the fish market where stalls and benches were set under tattered awnings and tin roofs.

"Man, wuh' yu want today?" An old man with a waxed apron tied over his shorts, swung a huge cutlass, slamming it across the head of an enormous snapper. "Don' giv me no trouble now..." The head of the fish dropped into a bucket, its glazed lifeless eyes stared up as Jimmy approached.

"Whatever you got, boss," Jimmy said as he watched surrounding vendors weigh, scale, clean and cut the fish to order. "Send the lot."

Mistress Nysha, the chef at the Lime Inn, was an expert with fish and the specials board that night would be oozing with chowders, pate, catch of the day and a host of delicious dishes made from the fish Jimmy bought.

"Sure t'ing," the old man said and reached for a half-finished beer, "mind yu'self, do." With a broad grin he raised the bottle and gave a salute. Jimmy thanked the man and returned the gesture.

In a corner of the fishery a woman called out, "Yo, big man! Yu want flyin' fish?"

Jimmy wandered over to a board that read, The Fish Girls, where Liz and her sister Carnetta spent their days cleaning and gutting the popular local fish, before packing them into polythene bags and layering on packs of ice in large coolers. They wore rubber aprons, sticky with guts and mismatched wellingtons and beamed as Jimmy approached.

"Eff yu please!" Liz chortled and indicated a packed cooler. The order for Jimmy's business was about to be dispatched and she wanted him to appraise their hard work.

"Looks good to me," Jimmy said as Carnetta wiped her bloody fingers on a rag.

"Dem flyin' fish scarce," Carnetta muttered, her ample body swaying as she spoke, "dem like de other islands more dan we."

Jimmy examined his order and after thanking both women, said his goodbyes and hurried back to the shore. He glanced at his watch and taking a deep breath, began to run again.

Long Tom had another gig that evening and Jimmy had much to do.

With work his main focus, he set off for the beach house and made plans for the night ahead. He thought of his mother and decided that she would, no doubt, return at some point.

As long as Jo was happy, Jimmy would be happy too.

Jo STEPPED out of the shower onto a pale cream marbled floor and reached for a towel from a stack nearby. She hugged the thick fluffy cotton and ran her fingers through her damp hair.

It was a mass of unruly curls.

A basket of expensive toiletries lay on the double sink and Jo reached tentatively for a jar labelled, Marine Cream, knowing that the singular pot probably cost more than a lifetime supply of her regular lotion. Oh, how the other half live! Jo smoothed the cream onto her fingers and applied it to her face and as she gently rubbed, she thought about Pete.

His phone call had unsettled her.

Jo knew that he was three sheets to the wind when he professed undying love, but she had a nagging feeling that he meant it. He'd begged her not to move away when she told him that she'd received a generous offer for the hotel and Jo wondered if she was in danger of losing a friendship that had sustained for many years.

Jo sighed. She couldn't think about Pete now.

She turned and reached for a hanger on the back of the door, where a simple but exquisite dress hung under a layer of tissue. An embossed label stuck out and informed Jo that the item had come from a designer shop in the hotel lobby. As she slipped into the sleeveless ensemble, she could hear Long Tom talking in the adjacent room.

"Hello gorgeous," Long Tom said as she appeared from the bathroom. He put his phone on the table and came towards her, "Nice dress."

"And somehow a perfect fit," Jo smoothed the fabric over her hips and smiled as he took her into his arms.

"Clever concierge," Long Tom tucked a strand of damp hair behind Jo's ear and kissed her cheek, "your red dress is being cleaned."

"I really should be getting back," Jo said, "you need to prepare for tonight."

"I have time." His hands ran over her buttocks.

"My friend Hattie will wonder where I am."

"I think she has a pretty good idea."

Long Tom edged Jo towards a sofa, where several newspapers were scattered on a side table. With little willpower to resist, Jo tumbled into the soft cushions and gave in to Long Tom's caresses as he began to slip the dress over her thighs and nibbled on her neck. She turned her head to one side and dreamily cast her eyes over the table, where an overhead fan gently turned, causing the pages of the day's news to flicker.

A newspaper headline screamed out.

Right Royal Forage for the Tipsy Gypsy Chef!

Jo gasped as she read the words and opened her eyes wide to read on. "Bloody hell," she said, "that's my son!" Jo jumped up and grabbed the paper.

Startled, Long Tom leaned over her shoulder to study the headline. "Good looking boy," he said and stood. He reached for a carafe of iced water and poured some into a glass.

"He's fallen out of a nightclub!" Jo was mortified.

"And your point is?" Long Tom took a swig of his drink.

"It could ruin his career."

"Or make it."

Jo looked up. Long Tom was grinning and gave her a wink.

"Cut him some slack, babe. A man has to learn his own way."

Jo folded the paper and sighed. Long Tom was right. It was none of her business to get involved in the personal life of her sons, but if they were all over a major tabloid? Whatever had Zach been getting up to? She decided she'd deal with it later, she didn't want to spoil the moment with Long Tom but perhaps she should be on her way.

"I better get going, I must look a sight."

"You look beautiful."

"You have things to do."

"Will you come to the concert tonight?"

"Well," Jo hesitated, "I hadn't thought about it." She must get back to Hattie and she wanted to know what the hell was happening with Zach but as she looked at the man before her and his warm endearing eyes, her heart gave a sudden lurch and she longed to fall back into his arms.

A knock on the door made them both turn.

"Long Tom?" A voice called out. "It's Boss, I need to see you."

"My manager..." Long Tom held up his hands in a frustrated gesture. "Come to the concert, we can catch dinner later?"

"Alright, that would be great." Jo picked up her bag and retrieved her sandals and holding them in one hand, stood on her toes to kiss Long Tom on the mouth. "I had a wonderful evening, thank you for everything."

"Me too, babe," he whispered.

The door to the suite opened and Boss walked in. He nodded as Jo hurried past.

"Sex and drugs and rock and roll..." Boss said as he watched Jo disappear down the corridor.

"Leave out the drugs," Long Tom replied and with a grin as wide as the bay that lay beyond the terrace of his suite, began to prepare for the evening ahead.

23

The pub in east London was heaving and in the main room of the pub, Heidi was enjoying her birthday party. Surrounded by friends and colleagues, all gathered round a large table, she gasped with delight as a waiter brought a huge birthday cake and laughed as everyone began to sing.

"I didn't have enough matches to light all your candles!" Lottie called out and gestured towards the solitary candle on Heidi's cake.

"Just strike yourself..." Bob mumbled and looked meaningfully at Lottie's outfit. She wore a tight cream body stocking that emphasized every bone and a bright red bob-hat. The ensemble reminded Bob of a giant match and he hoped no one held a flame near her head.

"Make a wish!" Someone called out as Heidi cut into the cake.

Bob wished that Heidi had chosen to have her party anywhere but the pub, which Bob knew, was now Zach's local. She'd the whole of London to choose from but for some reason had decided that the pub would be a perfect place to celebrate and the bar staff, used to the agencies gatherings, would take care of them.

Bob didn't agree.

Had he known that the event was to be held at the pub, he would have stepped in to stop it. But Poppy had been dispatched to book the table and it wasn't until Bob sat in the back of a taxi with Lottie that he learnt of their destination.

"It's handy for Zach," Lottie said as she whipped out a compact and slathered ruby gloss over her lips. "Doesn't Poppy live near the pub too?"

Bob sighed as he stared out at the slow-moving traffic. Lottie would latch on in time, but at the moment was oblivious to the chef's relationship with Poppy and the office manoeuvrings to put an end to it.

Now, as Bob sat at one end of the table and watched the sexual tension being played out before him, he sincerely hoped that his protégé made good his promise and kept his hands off Poppy. The young lovers were blatantly ignoring each other, but as one looked away, the other stole a furtive glance and it wasn't rocket science to see which way the wind would blow if Bob didn't step in soon.

"I hate to break up the party," Bob announced and stood up.

"Then don't!" a voice said and everyone laughed.

"Some of us have work to do in the morning, even though it's a weekend," he glanced pointedly at Zach, "books won't write them-selves." Bob gathered his coat and as he went to kiss Heidi goodbye, he stopped beside Poppy.

"You're at Britain's Best Baking Show tomorrow, with three of our clients and I expect an early report from backstage," Bob held Poppy's gaze, "don't let me down." With a wave to the animated party, Bob told the barman to send the bill to the office and made his way out of the pub.

Zach watched Bob leave.

He breathed a sigh of relief and reached out to top up his wine. As he tilted the bottle he caught Poppy's eye. She looked away quickly and for a moment Zach thought he saw a flash of longing in her eyes.

He must be imagining it.

After all, after his recent antics, which had made the papers, she'd be out of her mind to want him back. The conversation over dinner had been full of jovial remarks about the newspaper headline and bets were being placed to see what he would do next to make the pages of every scandal rag, both on and offline. Heidi had been inundated with requests for interviews for the Tipsy Gypsy Chef. His recent escapades were public knowledge and must have been hard for Poppy to read. Zach knew that he couldn't make any moves on Poppy and was conscious of Bob's disapproving stares, but his heart was playing emotional ping-pong every time he looked at her and the pain was unbearable.

"Let's move on to a club!" someone suggested and as the birthday party finished their drinks, taxis were arranged and they all tumbled out of the door.

"I think I'll call it a night," Zach said to Heidi as they stood on the pavement outside the pub.

"Good idea, Bob will kill you if you don't get some chapters ready soon."

"You have a great night, got your dancing shoes on?" Zach asked.

"Oh, I'm heading back too," Heidi replied, "I've got a husband and little one snuggled up at home and I can't wait to sneak in and join them." She smiled as she thought of her family.

Two taxis came to a stop and everyone began to pile in.

"Remember what Bob said," Heidi whispered in Zach's ear. They both turned and stared at Poppy who sat amongst the noisy party goers in the back of a taxi.

"Yes," Zach sighed, "I will." He pecked Heidi on the cheek and waved as she was driven away. Poppy's taxi roared into life too and Zach stood with his hands in his pockets and watched as it made a wide arc in the road.

A face appeared in the rear window and Zach saw that Poppy had looked back.

He groaned as the taxi disappeared into the night.

～

Jo RAN barefoot across the garden at the apartment. She clutched her sandals in one hand and didn't notice George, who stood on a path holding a hose pipe. He turned the nozzle and water shot across the grass, dancing in a rainbow as sunshine caught the fine spray.

It also caught Jo as she rounded the corner and within seconds, she was soaked.

"Lordy, Lordy!" George called out and threw the hose to the ground.

"Oh!" Jo squealed as the water hit her new dress. "Don't worry," she grimaced, gritting her teeth, "it's no problem."

"I go fo' towel," George stared at Jo but made no movement to go anywhere.

"I'm absolutely fine," she assured him and hurried by, longing to get into the apartment.

Hattie, who had been lazing on the sofa, came out to the patio to see what all the noise was about. She folded her arms across her chest as she watched Jo's walk of shame.

"Bleedin' hell, it's Miss Wet T-Shirt. Nice threads." Hattie admired Jo's dress.

"It's ruined!' Jo snapped and threw her sandals across the tiles. She grabbed a beach towel from the back of a chair and flopped down.

She felt exhausted.

Her journey had taken ages. As Long Tom's driver negotiated the drive south, the west coast traffic was heavy; no doubt the hoards were heading to the concert.

"Fancy a livener?" Hattie asked.

"Yes please, make it a large one."

Jo put her bag on the table where a copy of the tabloid was opened to the article about Zach. Hattie had obviously seen the headlines.

Hattie appeared with a tray and sat down beside Jo. She deposited two highball glasses on the table, beside a dish of olives.

"Cheers!" Hattie said and took a sip of her drink.

"Oh, I needed that," Jo sighed and closed her eyes.

"One night of abstinence with an ex-alcoholic or are you are bracing yourself for the media madness surrounding your son?" Hattie nodded towards the paper and took a handful of olives.

"Christ knows. I wish I could wind the clock back."

"Whatever for?" Hattie asked, her cheeks bulging as she munched. "You've played a blinder."

"Oh don't go on," Jo didn't need a lecture on sleeping with a married man. It had been a wonderful night and she was determined not to feel guilty.

"Your lover's wife is your son's boss." Hattie sat back and let the words sink in.

Jo was stunned. Her mouth fell open and she stared at Hattie, grasping for comprehension. "What did you say?"

"You heard," Hattie chuckled. "I've been bored this afternoon and have been surfing the web, and it's amazing what turns up on t'internet."

"Long Tom's wife is Zach's agent?"

"You betcha, lovely article in the trade papers about Zach's signing to Hargreaves & Puddicome Promotions and an even better piece on their website."

"But his agent is called Bob..."

"Bob Puddicombe - business partner of Hilary Hargreaves, Long Tom's dearly beloved."

Hattie flicked an olive stone across the table and it bounced over the garden wall.

"Oh hell!"

"Aye, not even your Jimmy will magic you out of this one."

"Hilary mustn't find out," Jo said, "it could ruin Zach before he's even got going."

"I take it we're not going to the concert tonight, then?"

"I think we should leave the island."

"Bugger off, just because you cock it up, in more ways than one." Hattie reached for her glass, "I've still got a holiday to finish and am not going anywhere." She tossed the drink back. "Long Tom's a player and he won't come looking for you. Men like that don't do the chasing." Hattie stood up. "Might as well have another drink, I suppose we'll be stopping in tonight."

As Hattie disappeared into the kitchen, Jo thought about her friend's words. She was probably right. Men like Long Tom don't do any chasing. But as Jo remembered the last few hours and her time with the charismatic rock singer, a nagging doubt threatened to surface.

Men like Long Tom also got what they wanted and last night he'd wanted Jo.

Jo closed her eyes and tried to think. She couldn't do it to Zach, if Hilary found out there would be hell to pay. After all, they'd only been married for five minutes! Jo's head throbbed, one minute she'd been so happy and now she was a nervous wreck!

"Shall I heat up the barbeque left-overs?" Hattie called out.

Might as well, Jo thought as she dragged herself out of the chair and headed into the apartment. Please may it not be all over for Zach!

PETE HAD DECIDED NOT to make any more calls to the Caribbean. He'd waited patiently all day for either Jo or Hattie to call him back, but neither had bothered and pride forbade him to further make a fool of himself. Jo had no doubt accepted Julian Struthers' offer and was out celebrating, with all thoughts of Kirkton House and Westmarland firmly pushed to the back of her mind.

There was nothing Pete could do.

He walked across the yard and headed to a large barn at the side of his house, where a collection of vintage tractors was stored beside a workshop. Pete spent many an hour tinkering away with machines that he'd rescued from derelict farms and auction sales, and knew that soon, he'd have plenty of time on his hands to restore many more.

Meg followed and watched Pete flick the barn light then remove a plastic sheet off a newly painted Massey Ferguson. As he ran his hand over the immaculate body-work, Pete smiled. He got a great deal of pleasure from bringing aged machinery back to life and this little number was a dream.

"Come on, old lass," Pete patted Meg's head and pushed the barn door to one side. He hopped up onto the tractor and reached out to grab Meg's collar, hauling her onto the running board, where she plonked herself down and waited to see what he proposed to do next.

Pete turned the engine and it roared into life. With a grin, he accelerated forward and with Meg braced between his legs, they headed out and across the yard.

It was a warm evening with only a gentle breeze blowing in from the fells and as Pete negotiated the lane beyond his property and the tractor chugged along, he smiled and looked around. Never mind the Caribbean, he thought, you can't beat the glory of Westmarland! Jo was misguided if she imagined she could start over somewhere new and Pete hoped that whatever she decided to do, she'd soon yearn for the beauty of this countryside and come back to home turf.

And when she did, he'd be waiting.

He parked the tractor outside the Red Lion and with Meg trotting alongside, headed into the busy pub.

"You've heard the news then," Marlene stood behind the bar. She thrust her chest out and smiled as Pete ordered a drink.

"I'm not interested in gossip," Pete diverted his eyes from her bulging blouse and picked up a well-read newspaper.

"You'll be interested in that," Marlene nodded towards the head-line and skilfully pulled a pint of draft ale. "That young chef from the fancy hotel that's closed down is making a quite name for himself in the smoke."

Pete reached for his glasses and scanned the story.

Right Royal Forage for the Tipsy Gypsy Chef!

By gum! Pete smiled. What would Jo make of it this?

"Good looking lad," Marlene pushed the glass towards Pete, "Westmarland breeds 'andsome men," she whispered and ran a rough finger over Pete's hand.

"It's none of our business and folk won't thank you for gossiping," Pete snatched his hand away and reached for his pint.

"I'd like to give 'em something to gossip about!" Marlene was miffed. "It's not normal you having that daft dog for company, when you could have a lot more..." She gave Pete what she considered her best come-hither smile.

"You want to watch that the wind doesn't change," Pete said, leaving some money on the counter. "Keep the change." He turned and went into the snug where Rob sat beside a roaring fire.

He too, had a copy of the newspaper.

"I don't remember any tipsy gypsies falling out of Kirkton House." Rob looked thoughtful. "That's the city for you," he said as Pete sat down.

The two men stared into the fire and sipped their pints. Rob picked up a packet of pork scratchings and held one out for Meg.

"Have you heard from Jo?" Pete asked.

"No, nothing, have you?"

"Nowt to report, good job she's not seen this," Pete nodded at the headline.

"You never know, when she agrees the sale, she might move south and set Zach up in a restaurant, where she can keep an eye on him."

Pete shook his head. That was all he needed to hear! But at least Rob had no confirmation that things were going ahead with Kirkton House, perhaps Jo hadn't made her mind up yet?

"Is that your Massey Ferguson outside?"

"Aye, I thought I'd give her a run out."

"Nice machine. I've walked down, can I grab a ride home on the running board?"

Meg rested a paw on Rob's knee and rolled her eyes.

"That's if there's room," Rob said, glancing at the dog.

"Aye, no bother," Pete replied and watched Meg devour her treat.

"Fancy a game of darts?"

"Why not," Pete said and sighed as he settled in for yet another scintillating evening in the Red Lion.

Come home soon Jo, Pete thought as he selected a set of arrows. Before it's too late!

24

Long Tom headed backstage and out of the back of the arena, where a vehicle was waiting to whisk him away. His second concert had been another roaring success. After the celebrity party of the night before, he'd done his duty for the promotor with a post-gig meet and greet in the VIP bar for an excited mix of revellers, who'd paid handsomely for the privilege of meeting their idol.

Now he wanted to get away and looked around for Jo, but she was nowhere to be seen. Long Tom knew that Jimmy was close on his heels and wondered if it was appropriate to ask him.

Jo was, after all, Jimmy's mother.

"She's at her apartment," Jimmy said, he'd called the apartment earlier and Hattie told him that they were having a quiet night in. He held the car door and watched the mystified expression on Long Tom's face.

"Got the number?"

Jimmy watched as Long Tom tapped into his phone.

"Thanks man," Long Tom said, "I'll look after her."

"You'd better," Jimmy said, unperturbed at the tone of his reply as he watched the rock star hold the phone to his ear and climb into the back of the car, then speed away.

Long Tom sat back and waited for the phone to pick up.

"Tipsy Gypsy Fan Club, who's calling please?"

"Just an old reformed rocker," Long Tom told Hattie.

"Bleedin' hell, is that really you Long Tom?"

"It was last time I looked, is Jo there?"

"She's in the bath having a soak," Hattie mumbled. "You'll have to call back."

The phone went dead.

Long Tom was puzzled. Jo had said she'd come to the concert, she'd agreed to have dinner too. They'd had a perfect night together and he longed for her company and didn't want to be alone. Coming down from a gig wasn't easy. One minute, as you stood in the limelight, your adrenaline pumped so hard you felt like you'd explode, then it all stopped and people who wanted a little of the glory and attention you'd received, flocked like flies. Long Tom loathed it and in days gone by would be so smashed that he didn't care, with booze and drugs replacing the highs he experienced on stage and any woman would do.

Now he was sober, it was different.

Hilary had called to wish him luck and sent a hamper of his favourite foods. He made the right noises during their conversation but was quietly angry with her, he didn't need a hamper. He needed a warm and loving woman, someone with a brain and experience of life, someone who asked no questions but understood how he operated and Jo had been just that.

Long Tom wasn't used to being turned down and leaning forward, he instructed his driver to find Jo's address and head on over there.

He reached for his Stetson and sat back, he'd soon get to the bottom of this.

~

JO BRUSHED her newly washed hair and clipped it into a pony-tail. She felt so much better for her bath. Doused in a favourite perfume and with her tanned skin smooth from lashings of rich moisturiser, she dressed casually in faded denim cut-offs and a thin lace vest.

Thank goodness she'd stayed away from the concert.

It was unthinkable to see Long Tom again, imagine the consequences! The slightest whiff of their indiscretion reaching Hilary Hargreaves could cause Zach untold problems and Jo was embarrassed at the thought of having to explain herself. Far better that they pretend last night had never happened. After all, Jo tried to convince herself, Long Tom was probably already hooked up with someone else; there was always a multitude of available females keen for the green light from anyone with celebrity status, just look at what was happening to Zach!

Jo ran a light coat of gloss over her lips and wandered barefoot into the lounge, where Hattie stood by the open patio door with the phone in her hand and stared out across the dark garden.

"I must give Pete a ring," Jo commented as she sat in a bucket-shaped wicker chair.

"Aye, keep him up to speed with your shenanigans," Hattie said and turned to place the phone on the table.

Jo ignored the comment. She decided it best not to go over Pete's inebriated phone call, although Jo had no doubt that Hattie wouldn't be surprised that he'd declared undying love.

"Who was on the phone?" Jo asked.

"Long Tom."

"What?"

"I can't believe that I've spoken to a real rock star..."

"Hattie! What did he say?" Jo leapt to her feet.

"Not a lot, I put the phone down on him."

"You did what?"

"I thought you didn't want to see him?"

"Oh Christ, I never thought he'd ring," Jo paced anxiously around the apartment.

"I don't know what your problem is," Hattie flopped onto the sofa, "who the hell is going to know if you have a couple of nights' hanky-panky? His missus is probably used to it."

"Oh thanks! That makes me feel a lot better."

"Get real Jo, he's spent his life pulling women, why should he change? Personally I think you should have a bit of fun," Hattie smiled. "What happens on the island stays on the island and all that."

"There's absolutely no way that I am going to see him again." Jo was adamant.

"Well, if I had the look you had when you crawled in this morning, I'd be in a taxi heading up the west coast highway right now."

"That was before I knew about Hilary being Zach's boss." Jo sighed and faced her friend. "Oh Hattie, I had the best night ever and after all the pain of last year, it was magical to let myself go. I never thought something like that would ever happen to me, at my age..."

"Age is just a number."

A soft voice sounded from the darkness beyond the patio and both women spun around.

Long Tom stepped out of the shadows.

"Jesus..." Hattie whispered.

"No, only me," Long Tom smiled and removed his Stetson. He stared at Jo and thought how lovely she looked.

"I'll get myself a drink," Hattie mumbled. "If there's any chance of an autograph before you go?" She looked at Long Tom hopefully but he didn't seem to hear. "Well, no, perhaps not," Hattie disappeared into the kitchen.

"You didn't come tonight," Long Tom spoke.

Jo bit her lip. It was no good pretending - she had to speak the truth.

"Your wife is my son's boss," Jo said.

"I worked that out."

"Then you can see my dilemma, on top of the fact that you're married. I'm sorry if I'm a bit old fashioned."

"She won't know. I have people around me - it's what they're paid to do."

Jo remembered Long Tom's security guards and thought about

Jimmy and how he always seemed to know what was happening before it had even happened.

"It doesn't seem right."

"Things are never right, babe, like your husband dying suddenly of cancer."

Jo gasped. How did Long Tom know?

"Take a chance, live in the moment," Long Tom implored.

In the kitchen, Hattie held the door ajar, squeezing herself into a corner as she strained to hear the conversation. She too implored Jo to get some sense and live a little.

"Dinner?" Long Tom asked.

For goodness sake, say yes! Hattie rolled her eyes and crossed her fingers.

"I know a great place by a beach," Long Tom urged.

Perfect! Your old cut-offs will do for a trip across the sand... Hattie resisted the urge to storm into the room and shove Jo through the door.

"Well, if it's just dinner..."

Halle-bloody-lujah! Hattie let out a sigh and reached for a bottle of rum. Her nerves had been ripped to shreds and she badly needed a drink. All this tension was making her hungry too.

Hattie poured herself a drink and rummaged around in the fridge. In the distance a car engine purred into life and she heard the patio door close. Hallelujah! she said to herself then glanced at her watch and smiled, Mattie would be finishing work soon. Taking her drink and a plate piled high with food, Hattie headed to the patio to sit and wait for him.

JIMMY SAT in his car and stared at his mobile phone. He dialled Zach's number and waited for the phone to pick up.

"Hello?" Zach answered. He sounded tired.

"What's happening little bro'?"

"Oh Jimmy, it's so good to hear from you."

"We saw the headlines, are you OK?"

"Oh that, yes, I'm fine. Did Mum see it?"

"Yes."

"Shit, is she worried?"

"She's a little preoccupied at the moment," Jimmy scratched his chin. "But she's fine, they're having a great holiday."

"When do they head home?"

"Not long now."

"I can't wait to see her, perhaps she'll come up to London and spend some time with me, I've got a new place and I'd love her to meet the people I work with."

"London? Yes, I'm sure she will." Jimmy shook his head.

"I really miss you guys. So much is happening here and it all feels a bit lonely at times."

Jimmy wished that he could magic himself to London and give his brother a huge hug. So much had changed for Zach and he was, after all, still young and quite naïve despite oodles of talent and gorgeous good looks. He'd lost his father so suddenly and now his family was dispersed far away.

"I promise to make a trip really soon, or you get yourself out here? Perhaps when Mum gets home," Jimmy added as an afterthought. God forbid that Zach should turn up whilst Jo was in cahoots with Long Tom. There was bound to be a clause in Zach's contract about shagging the agency staff, even if it was a relative that was guilty.

"That would be great and it would give me time to write this damn book." Zach sighed. "But I've tons of work to do and will start filming soon. I've got interviews and appearances lined up for months."

"Sounds like the celebrity life style, no wonder you're falling out of night clubs," Jimmy chuckled, "spoilt for choice eh?" He was about to ask Zach about the royal connection but could hear a bell ringing in Zach's apartment.

"Damn, there's someone at the door, can I call you back?"

"It's OK, it's really late for you, let's catch up later in the week?"

"Yeah, I'd like that. Maybe I can pick your brains for some of the things Dad taught us, about stuff we foraged? I want the book to be personal."

Jimmy assured his brother that he'd be pleased to help then said goodbye and hung up.

He was thoughtful as he stared out at the nightlife milling around the bars and clubs. The Lime Inn would be busy after the concert tonight, what a great week they'd had. Long Tom could certainly attract attention, in more ways than one.

Jimmy knew that Jo was out with him again tonight and had known from the moment Long Tom's vehicle headed south. Best that Zach doesn't find out, Jimmy thought as he started the engine and his truck came to life. Jimmy saw every type of relationship come and go on the island and that's exactly what would happen to this one, it would come and go. As long as Jo was happy, what was the harm? And Zach had enough to deal with without further complications. Look at Hattie too! Heaven knows what Marland would make of Mattie should she ever choose to have him visit, but they were all adults and had their own choices to make.

Thinking of choices, Jimmy wondered which direction to take.

The Canadian flight attendant had extended her leave and invited him to her hotel. Alternatively he could check back at the club then take the managers for a post-gig drink and debrief. He flicked his phone to Club Cameras and watched the CCTV lens scan around his club. It was still busy. There was time to go calling.

Jimmy pulled out into the slow-moving traffic and headed for the hotel.

25

J o and Hattie linked arms and stepped out onto the beach. It was their last day in Barbados and they wanted to make the most of the final hours. Jimmy was taking them to lunch then it would be time for goodbyes, before boarding their early evening flight.

A plane overhead flew low and Hattie looked up.

"That's the Manchester flight arriving," Hattie said glumly. "We don't have to go home." She tugged on the brim of her sunhat, securing it against a playful breeze coming in off the sea.

"Oh I think we do," Jo smiled. "It's been a wonderful few weeks but all good things come to an end."

"I'm not sure that I've anything good to be going back to," Hattie said and sighed as she waved at the lifeguards who looked out from their wooden platform and with broad smiles, waved in return.

"Of course you have, you've got your lovely house and lots of friends and you can go and visit your boys."

"Hardly going to change the course of world events is it?" Hattie was miserable. "No one actually needs me, Mattie will be moving on to the next plane load of tourists and you'll soon be buggering off to god-knows where."

To Rob's joy, Jo had decided to accept Julian Struthers offer and had told Hattie her news. Solicitors had been instructed to push ahead for an early completion date. She hadn't a clue what she was going to do but the urge to forge ahead with something new was as strong as ever.

"Perhaps you'll saddle up and ride off with Pete Parks?" Hattie asked.

"He'd never leave Westmarland."

Jo thought about her call to Pete. She'd phoned him back as promised and tentatively mentioned that she was going ahead with the sale. He'd expressed little emotion, simply asking what date she'd be back and assuring her that he'd be waiting at the airport. He never referred to the call he'd made when he'd been half-cut.

"Another heart you've broken," Hattie moaned.

"I didn't mean to," Jo replied and looked wistfully out to sea, "it's just that I need to do something new and Pete wants everything to stay the same."

Hattie stopped at one of Malibu's sunbeds and removed her hat, "Come on let's have one last swim." She shrugged her kaftan off then turned and ran down the beach.

Jo was astonished.

In all the time they'd spent in Barbados, Hattie had never put a toe in the sea. Now she bounced along in her brilliant red swimsuit and plunged into the water. The lifeguards stood up to look out at the figure bobbing along.

"Marvellous!" Hattie called out. "Get your arse in here!"

Jo soon joined her friend and together they jumped and body surfed on the crest of white plumed waves, which carried them to and from the shore.

"I should have done this weeks' ago," Hattie said as they sat in the shallows and relaxed. She held her freckled face up to the sun and Jo thought how well and happy Hattie looked, Mattie had given her a new glow. The holiday had been good for both of them.

Jo thought about Long Tom and smiled.

IT HAD LASTED for four days, four glorious days where she didn't think about the outside world, nor worry about anyone else.

In their time together, Jo talked to Long Tom about her past, and began to realise that she'd worried about everyone else for the biggest part of her life, from bringing her children up to taking endless care of both her parents until they died. She'd pampered and nurtured guests at the hotel and been heavily involved in the welfare of her staff and their families, supportive through all their trials and tribulations. When John died, his death had knocked her sideways, teetering into depths of despair and she'd doubted that she'd ever be happy again. But this holiday had brought her back to life and she was grateful to Long Tom, he'd listened patiently and assured her that it was alright to be indulgent, to recuperate and mend.

She hadn't allowed herself to think of his personal life. Perhaps that was selfish? But he'd insisted on it and whatever happened with Hilary would be his own choice. There was no reason for Hilary to ever find out about Jo and that being the case, no repercussions for Zach.

Jo had loved her hours with Long Tom and their blissful, uncomplicated days together.

He'd taken her to Eddie's plantation, where the family had left for a holiday in America and the band had returned to the UK.

They'd spent evenings on the verandah and he'd strum on a guitar as they listened to the nocturnal chirruping of cicadas and chatter of monkeys, hidden in branches hanging over sweet-smelling orchids, ginger lilies and gardenias in the garden below. In the day, they swam in the pool then wandered down to the east coast, to sit and watch rain fall like drift smoke over huge volcanic rocks that had withstood centuries of crashing breakers, while the majestic Atlantic rolled the slate-blue sea to the shore. They ate at rickety rum shops, dotted along the many bays; gorging on freshly caught fish with yellow rice and garlic-smothered plantain and drinking coconut water with fresh lime. They marvelled at humpback whales that leapt out of the water, before landing with a theatrical crash, as if to satisfy the lens of tourist cameras that clicked from the boardwalk, along the north point of the island.

And at night, Long Tom would play the grand piano, positioned in a corner of their guest suite. He'd written a new song and sang softly to Jo, as stars sparkled in the dark sky beyond the plantation windows.

THE SUN IS GOING down on this great unknown
    I'm out of sight and all alone
    Don't forget me!
    Don't forget me...

They made endless love in the mahogany four-poster bed, savouring the pleasure of two bodies perfectly tuned in the act of passion, before watching the sun rise beyond open doors that over-looked the dramatic coast line below.

Jo had been happier than she'd been in a very long time but knew that the interlude couldn't last and their stolen time must end.

Long Tom had to return to London, where dates had been announced for a European tour to coincide with the launch of his new album. He had much to do and they'd parted with no plans to stay in touch, both knowing that they had to step back into their own lives. But Jo was grateful for the affair and as short as it had been, it had restored her confidence as a woman and given her a renewed energy and determination to find something meaningful to occupy her time.

"IT'S NOT SO bad being a boomer woman, is it?" Hattie interrupted Jo's daydream.

"What's a boomer woman?" Jo looked up.

"I read it somewhere," Hattie trailed her fingers in the wet sand. "I think it means women at our time of life who are pretty comfortable with what they have. They're good at business and often on their own through divorce or whatever, but they haven't given up on life and men."

"You mean emotionally?" Jo asked.

"Yes and financially. They've put the work in and often raised families and invested in themselves so they can sit back and enjoy it without feeling guilty, even if they find themselves alone through partners dying or, in my case, buggering off with younger models."

"Such a large percentage of the maturing population is alone these days."

"Both men and women," Jo and Hattie agreed.

"Most people don't want to be alone," Hattie said, "look at all the people we know who are single at our age."

"Everyone wants to have company, to be needed."

"Exactly! I'm going home to nothing. No one needs me, you have new things to consider but my life will stay the same."

A germ of an idea had come into Jo's head.

It sat like a seed, freshly planted in warm soil and as it nestled into place, tiny shoots began to sprout and she felt a tingle in her veins.

"I've had an idea!" Jo announced. She turned and faced Hattie and reached for her hands.

"Oh Lord... you're not going on tour with Long Tom?"

Jo ignored Hattie's comment.

"I think it could it work," Jo looked excited as the idea took root and began to grow.

"What could work? What are you banging on about?"

"Boomerville!"

"Boomerville?"

"Yes!" Jo leapt to her feet and dragged Hattie up too. "Kirkton House is perfect for it."

"Perfect for what?"

"It will become a residence for independent boomers who need company, friendship and respect."

"Just like us..." Hattie whispered. She was beginning to see the light.

"We could turn the hotel into rooms more suitable for long-term guests. Boomers could stay for a week, a month - maybe they have a reason to stay longer."

"Or want to stay for a season or a lifetime."

"You've got it!"

"You could open the restaurant up again."

"The outbuildings could become studios and workshops for both residents and their guests, we could open to the public - areas where people can come together and learn or do something meaningful."

"There could be cookery classes."

"You could run classes on how to style your hair in corn rows..."

"Now you're being bloody silly," Hattie laughed but she held onto Jo's hands and began to jump up and down.

"We don't have to face the boomer woman years on our own, I could come back to work, I'd have a purpose," Hattie said.

"So would I, but it would be different. With more permanent residents we'd have to choose carefully."

"Oh, think of the fun, we'd accommodate boomer men too!"

"It would breathe new life in the old place."

"It would breathe new life in both of us."

The two women turned and looked at each other.

"Boomerville!" they both cried.

"We could have Boomers in Barbados for folks wanting a bit of a sunshine frolic," Hattie was on a roll. "Your Jimmy's beach house is far too big for him to roam around in on his own, he could find a nice apartment and with a bit of a conversion..."

"The possibilities are endless," Jo laughed.

"This calls for a celebration, where's Malibu? I need one of his finest pina colada's," Hattie tucked her arm into Jo's and led her along the beach. She was bursting with ideas and couldn't stop talking.

Rain fell lightly, caressing Jo's skin and as Hattie ran ahead to shelter in the bar, Jo turned and looked out at the sea. Pink lightning flashed across thunder filled clouds and the horizon turned dark, the elements all powerful as an angry storm gathered.

For that moment, far from their sun-drenched bay, Jo felt a different world emerging and knew that her time on the island was, for now, at its rightful end.

She didn't need to leave Westmarland to do something new. She'd found a purpose and would bring Kirkton House back to life, but in a different manner and in so doing, with luck, help others who were also in danger of losing their way.

Jo smiled as she watched the distant storm. The Caribbean had healed her, Barbados had wrapped her in its magical charm but now it was time to go home.

She had much to do.

26

Long Tom turned his phone off and placed it on a side table in the drawing room of his London town house. He wandered over to the doors that led out to a wrought iron balcony and undid the latch. As he stepped out, he looked at the steady hum of traffic that circled the communal garden below.

Hilary was in Ireland.

She'd extended her stay because work was well underway on the renovation of an ornamental lake and, as she'd explained in their short conversation, she wanted to be on hand to ensure that her instructions were carried out to the letter.

Long Tom was annoyed. He'd purposefully flown back to London to spend some time with her before he began work to finish his album. Was it too much to expect his wife to be waiting for him?

He leaned on the railings and as he watched a couple walk hand-in-hand through the garden, he thought of Hilary's renovations to the lake and hoped that she didn't disturb the peacocks that lived there. They'd been his salvation in the years following his rehabilitation, companions that sensed his moods and made no demands other than to follow him as he paced, day after day, around the grounds of the crumbling Flatterly Manor.

Hilary had been a saviour too.

She'd come into his life as he emerged from his self-imposed exile and his attraction to her had rid him of the demons that had impaired his ability to perform sexually - a problem following years of drink and drugs. But Long Tom wanted more from their short marriage and he'd imagined Hilary at his side, not emerged in the Irish countryside, where she seemed able to run her business as well as being completely obsessed in rebuilding his former home.

He looked up at the grey skies of the city and remembered the glorious sunsets on the east coast of Barbados, as he'd sat on Eddie's verandah with Jo. He wondered what she was up to and knew that she'd left the island and would now be back in Westmarland.

Jo had told him a lot about her life. He was aware that she'd been blissfully married but the shock of her husband's sudden death had sent her into a vortex of change.

Long Tom sighed as he thought of their days together at Eddie's lovely plantation. It had been as happier a time as Long Tom could remember, to enjoy an uncomplicated woman who made no demands on him. Hilary, although wealthy in her own right, was spending money as fast as he earned it and Long Tom wondered to what end. A home meant nothing without love, and these days she seemed totally absorbed in making Flatterly Manor one of the finest properties in southern Ireland, with little time to spend on what really mattered to Long Tom - a relationship with her husband.

Long Tom shut the doors and sat down at his piano, letting his fingers skim over the smooth surface of his beloved Steinway. A sense of well-being flooded over him as he began to play, he thanked god for his music and recovery! He knew in his bones that things would work out and had faced the worst that life that thrown at him. Going forward, he would handle whatever challenges arose.

Calypso notes tinkled from the keys and as he remembered his days in the Caribbean with Jo, he began to sing,

THE SUN IS GOING down on this great unknown
    I'm out of sight and all alone
    Don't forget me!
    Don't forget me...

∽

ZACH STOOD in the kitchen and waited for the kettle to boil. He looked out at the little garden on the balcony and was pleased to see that the herbs he'd planted had taken to the sunny corner and established themselves well. Pots of mint stood amongst basil, chives and coriander and a woody bunch of thyme had spread over an old stone trough. Even a frail bunch of parsley had revived and Zach remembered the old wife's tale about parsley thriving in a household where the woman wears the trousers.

He smiled and reached for the coffee.

Pouring milk into two mugs, Zach added hot water and stirred.

Poppy appeared from the bedroom. She wore an old chambray shirt that belonged to Zach and as she walked across the lounge, she rolled the sleeves.

"Nice," Zach said as he gazed at her long slim legs, "office wear?"

"No stranger than Lottie's creations," Poppy replied. "She wore a potato sack last week, belted at the waist and tried to convince Bob it was straight off the cat-walk."

"Bob..." Zach muttered and as he handed Poppy a mug he was thoughtful. "We may have a problem."

In recent days Zach and Poppy had become inseparable.

On the night of Heidi's birthday, Poppy had thrown caution to the wind and instead of piling into a late-night club with the others, she'd asked the taxi driver to take her to Zach's flat. Zach, who'd been chatting to his brother on the phone, had been astonished when he saw Poppy standing nervously at the door.

They'd fallen into each other's arms and in no time, Zach's bed, where they made up for all the lost time that they'd been apart.

The following day, Poppy dutifully went off to work and despite being exhausted, managed to get through Britain's Best Baking Show and ensured that the agency's clients were well represented. But Zach had insisted she forget work for a few days and they invented a food poisoning bug and when Poppy called in sick, a concerned Lottie said that she hoped Poppy would soon be feeling better. Zach told Bob he was hard at work with research for the book and having created precious time together, the pair had hardly come up for air in the days that followed.

Zach had been able to explain to Poppy why he'd had to end things so suddenly and now, knowing the risk to Poppy's job, they decided to keep their relationship secret. Poppy didn't want to jeopardise her career and she certainly didn't want to lose Zach.

For the moment, no one need know.

"What's cooking today, Chef?" Poppy asked, wrapping herself round Zach who'd spread out on the sofa.

"Today, we experiment with desserts," Zach said as he wound a lock of Poppy's thick hair round his finger. "I'll tempt you with elderflower ice-cream and wild berry tart."

"Sweet and delicious, like you," Poppy kissed his fingers.

"And in that little pot in the kitchen is a handful of guarana which I'll add to the icing on my beetroot muffins, it's an aphrodisiac and known for its stimulating action."

"You'd better not eat any," Poppy giggled as Zach's hands roamed under her shirt.

"I don't need any," Zach said and grabbing Poppy's wriggling body lifted her with ease and headed towards the bedroom.

The doorbell rang and Zach stopped abruptly. He put Poppy down and held a finger to his lips as they waited for the caller to go away.

But a key turned in the lock and the door began to open.

Zach and Poppy froze.

"Only me!" Heidi called out. "Thought I'd look in and see how the book is coming along," she stopped in her tracks and stared at Zach. Poppy was hiding behind him.

"Shit…" Zach whispered, "I'd forgotten Heidi had a key."

"I thought you'd be hard at it... Oh bloody hell," Heidi said as she took in the scenario. "You obviously are. Bob's going to throw a wobbler!"

"Bob doesn't need to know," Zach grabbed Poppy's hand.

Heidi sighed and walked over to the kitchen where she reached for the kettle. "I need a strong coffee," she said and flicked a switch as she pulled out a stool. "Is something burning?"

"Oh bugger!" Zach remembered his muffins and raced across the room to rescue them.

The trio sat in the kitchen and sipped their drinks. Zach sliced the muffins and pushed a mound towards the girls.

"Bloody lovely," Heidi said and licking her finger, traced the crumbs on her plate. But she looked at Zach and frowned. "I'm in a very difficult position," she said.

"You don't have to say anything to Bob, surely?" Zach asked. "Only while we decide what we are going to do?"

Heidi shook her head. "Well you're obviously joined at the hip, but Bob will let Poppy go as soon as he knows about this, is that what you want?"

"No, of course not," Poppy said, "I love my job."

"For now, could we keep it to ourselves?" Zach pleaded.

Heidi was sympathetic. It was a ridiculous rule. What difference would it make to the agency? But she knew that Bob and Hilary thought a single young chef had more appeal to the masses and Zach's contract forbade him to have a relationship with agency staff.

"Well, I won't say anything but you must never implicate me." Heidi hopped off her stool, "And I suggest that Poppy gets back to work, there's only so long that Bob will run with food poisoning."

Heidi wandered into the lounge and asked how Zach was getting on with the book. She was pleased when he took her over to his office area, where a pile of recipes sat beside Zach's laptop. The recipes were all tried, tested and ready to be typed up.

"Good to see you making progress," Heidi said looking at Zach. "Let me know if you need anything." She glanced over to Poppy, "both of you." She leaned forward and gave Zach a peck on the cheek, "I must get back to work."

"Thanks for everything!" Zach and Poppy called out as Heidi disappeared out of the apartment.

"It's going to get hot in the kitchen," Poppy cast a worried look towards Zach.

"I work best under pressure," Zach replied and wrapping Poppy in his arms, kissed her forehead. "It will all work out," he said, "you'll see."

27

Pete walked into the arrivals hall at terminal two and checked his watch. The information board showed that Jo and Hattie's flight was on time and he decided that he would grab a cup of coffee and perhaps glance at a newspaper while he waited.

The coffee was smooth and strong and hit the spot. Pete scanned the headlines without registering the day's news and tried not to think about Jo.

Rob had been full of himself in the pub the previous evening, as he celebrated the sale of Kirkton House and Pete had felt like throttling him. He knew that Rob was pushing to get the paperwork finalized. There was a large commission coming his way and he was keen to have Jo sign on the dotted line and complete matters.

Pete sighed as he pushed the paper to one side.

It was time to face the music.

He strolled over to the arrivals area, where a stream of weary travellers made their way towards waiting family and friends. The golden glow of faces recently exposed to a tropical sun and lightweight clothes of warmer climes, suggested that they'd come off the Barbados flight.

"Taxi for Contaldo and Edmonds!"

A voice boomed out of the throng and the crowd parted as Hattie appeared and shoving her trolley to one side, made her entrance.

"This way, Jo!" she yelled and threw her arms around Pete like a long lost lover.

Pete was engulfed in layers of swirling kaftan and mounds of Hattie's deeply tanned flesh. Her hair was plaited and as she whipped her head round to search for Jo, a burst of tiny beads flicked across his face.

He closed his eyes and waited for the tornado to subside and when he looked up again, Jo standing in front of him.

Pete stifled a gasp. His heart began to pound and as he peeled Hattie away, he resisted the urge to scoop Jo into his arms and spin her round.

She looked stunning.

The sun had added golden highlights to her hair and the copper tresses cascaded over her brown shoulders. Her green eyes sparkled and as she stepped forward to kiss Pete softly on the cheek, an aroma of coconut and the Caribbean sent his pulse soaring.

"Never mind all that nonsense," Hattie said petulantly. She gave Pete a nudge. "Get your hands round this lot." An overflowing trolley was shoved in his direction. "At least you haven't brought the daft mongrel to the airport."

"How is Meg?" Jo asked.

"Oh, aye, she's alright," Pete replied. He was struggling to contain a swell of emotion he'd determined not to display. "She's packed her bags and is sitting patiently in her box by my kitchen stove," he sighed. "We'll pick her up on the way back."

"Now don't go looking so smack-arsed," Hattie grinned as she swept ahead. "Madam here has got some news that will put a smile back on your face."

"Come on," Jo said, "our news can wait, let's get this lot in the car."

Pete steered the trolley through the terminal and as they waited for the lift to ascend to their floor, he wondered what the news could be. Jo was busy telling him all about Jimmy's bar and how much they'd enjoyed the island, when Hattie, who was watching Pete carefully, interrupted.

"For heaven's sake, put him out of his misery," she said. The lift had stopped and they stepped into the car park.

"I've decided not to sell Kirkton House," Jo announced.

Pete stopped dead.

"I need to let Rob know as soon as possible," she went on, "I expect I'll have to compensate him for his time, he's worked hard to get the sale."

Pete listened to Jo as she mumbled on. He was finding it hard to believe that she was casually talking about her future as if life-changing decisions were made every day. He stood by his car and opened the boot.

"So, what's brought this on?" Pete asked as he began to load the cases.

"I think Kirkton House could have another use."

"Happiness Hotel!" Hattie yelled and squeezed herself into the passenger seat. "Boomerville!" she added.

Pete ensured that his passengers were comfortably seated then closed the car doors. He walked around the vehicle to the driver's side and glanced heavenward. Thank you! He whispered and punched the air as his face cracked into a broad smile.

They left the airport and began the journey north. The motorway was busy but Pete was oblivious to the heavy traffic as he listened to Jo's plans.

"So, what do you think?" Hattie poked Pete on the arm and indicated that he should pass the tube of mints that lay on his side of the dashboard.

"It's different," Pete replied. He didn't really care if Jo opened a circus. The fact was, she was staying put and he was absolutely delighted.

Hattie filled Pete in with details of their holiday. She regaled the finer points of the places they'd visited and spoke excitedly about the glorious beaches and wonderful weather. She was careful to edit any details about the more personal exploits they'd both experienced but realised that Pete wasn't really participating in the conversation; he was distracted and kept glancing in the rear view mirror at Jo.

"You're like the cat that's got the cream," Hattie hissed to Pete as they pulled into his drive. "Don't bugger it up - I've worked hard on this, for both our sakes," she climbed out of the car.

Barking could be heard from inside the house and Jo ran towards the kitchen. Pete reached for the key then threw open the door and a furry mass hurtled towards Jo, knocking her to the floor.

"Steady on lass," Pete said and reached for Meg's collar, but the dog was not to be stopped and had pinned Jo in a position where every bit of available skin could be licked.

Her mistress was back!

Jo swung onto her knees and cuddled Meg's head. Oh, how good it was to be reunited with her adorable dog!

Hattie and Pete stood side by side and watched the performance.

"Right, that's enough of that," Hattie said, "I'm collapsing with jet leg, time to go home." She turned and walked out of the kitchen.

"Or even jet lag," Pete said and smiled.

He helped Jo to her feet and they collected Meg's things then piled into the car. The old dog was glued to Jo's side and as Pete put the car into gear and accelerated onto the road, Meg lay her head on Jo's lap and nudged her hand into a constant stroking motion.

Hattie was the first to be dropped off. She unlocked the door of her house and glanced around then flung her cases into the hall and disappeared up the stairs, claiming she was exhausted and in need of immediate rest.

Pete placed a box of food on the kitchen table.

"This should keep her going for a day or so," he said, then raised the blind over the kitchen window to let light into the room. Jo adjusted the thermostat on the boiler and when they were sure that the house was cosy for Hattie to wake up to, they let themselves out.

As Pete drove to Kirkton House they chatted comfortably and Jo caught up on local gossip and was pleased when he told her that the garage sale was about to complete.

"You'll be a man of leisure," Jo said as she looked out at a maze of dry-stoned walls across the fells, marking patchy fields as far as the eye could see.

"And you'll be as busy as ever."

"I need to be busy and I'm not ready to settle for a quiet life." Jo was thoughtful as she continued. "I hope I can do something to help the community."

"Well providing all those jobs will be a good start, will Zach be back to head up the kitchen?"

Jo spun round and looked anxiously at Pete.

"We saw that he'd hit the headlines," Pete said softly.

"His life is in London, I can't control what he does."

"Nor should you, it looks like he's having a good time."

Pete had turned off for the village of Kirkton Sowerby and slowed down as they approached Jo's home.

Meg, who sat upright on the back seat, began to bark.

"Everywhere is still in one piece," Pete said as he unloaded Jo's bags and followed her across the drive to the side door of her house.

Jo began to open curtains and windows as Pete placed Meg's box in the hollow under the stairs. "It's like you've never been gone," he looked around. "Do you want me to walk through the hotel with you?"

"No thanks, I think I'll have a lie down then unpack and wander round later, I may have jet leg too," Jo smiled as she turned to Pete. "Thanks for everything, I do appreciate it."

"Aye, I know lass and I'm very happy that you're staying put." He reached out and gave Jo a hug.

Steady on... Pete told himself, plenty of time now!

Jo stood at the window and watched Pete drive away. Meg placed her paws on the sill and looked out too as Jo gently stroked the dog's head.

Another chapter in her life was about to begin, who would have thought it at her age? But first she needed to catch up on some much needed sleep and with Meg racing ahead, Jo wearily headed up the stairs to her bedroom.

28

Bob had a nagging inkling that all was not what it seemed in his working environment. Poppy, who was back at work after her food poisoning bout, had set to her duties in an exemplary manner, often working late to make sure everything was done perfectly and arriving at events earlier than required.

Bob smelt mischief.

He decided to turn up unexpectedly at the company's in-house studio, where Poppy was assisting Prunella Gray. The food writer was working on a new book about how to look good in your fifties and Poppy was a runner for the two-day photo shoot.

Prunella had come up with a collection of recipes that promised eternal life and her image would soon be seen on billboards around the country, extolling the virtues of her secret formulas and encouraging the middle-aged to try her elixirs. As Bob watched Prunella pose and pout in front of the camera, he had to admit that she looked amazing for a woman who swore to fifty-something but would never see sixty-five again.

He had high hopes for her new book. Secretly, he knew that she used the same cosmetic surgeon in Harley Street as her lover, Nancy

Nevis. Both had the same rigid foreheads, slightly startled smile, puffed up cheekbones and baby-jane pouts.

Poppy had been surprised to see him.

She was mid-text, huddled in a corner with a grin plastered across her face, when Bob rounded on her. Shoving her phone into her bag, Poppy coloured deeper than Prunella's lipstick and grabbing her notebook, threw herself back into the shoot.

Something was certainly afoot.

Bob decided to pay a surprise visit to see Zach and to the young chef's credit, found him up to his neck in a forest of strange ingredients, creating the savoury chapters for his book. Bob sniffed and pulled a face and wondered if the weed-like offerings could really be used in a serious recipe but with Zach's two Michelin stars safely under his taught designer belt, Bob decided that chef knew best.

"Do these have a hallucinogenic effect?" Bob asked and picked an odd shaped mushroom from a bowl on the kitchen counter.

"Try one, they're delicious raw," Zach replied and focused on a sauce reduction, keeping the liquid at exactly the required temperature with a thermometer, whilst making notes on a lined pad.

Bob popped a mushroom in his mouth and wandered around the living room. He remembered eating mushrooms many years ago in the mountains of Nepal, happy times, most of which were a complete blur.

A T-shirt lay on the arm of the sofa and Bob studied it with interest. He glanced at Zach, but the chef was engrossed in his sauce. Bob reached for the garment and shook it out. It was tiny with capped sleeves and would probably fit Lottie. Certainly not a garment from Zach's wardrobe.

He looked up.

Zach was staring at him.

"Very fetching, dear boy," Bob said. "But possibly a tad tight?"

"There was a girl in the pub..." Zach mumbled and looked sheepish.

"A man has needs," Bob replied and admired the way his client's eyes sparkled, despite his embarrassment.

"Come and try this sauce," Zach deflected.

Bob returned the T-shirt to the sofa but not before inhaling its soft perfume.

Poppy wore the same.

Heady and spicy, the perfume was unusual and distinct and Bob, who had a remarkable nose and considered smell his best sense, couldn't recall it worn on anyone else that he knew.

Now he had a dilemma.

Love was clearly not affecting the work of the young lovers. In fact they seemed more productive than ever. But how long would their secrecy last? Bob had no desire to spoil their fun but they were clearly flouting contractual rules and ridiculing the company they had pledged loyalty to.

Hilary would go bonkers.

Bob scooped the sauce onto a plate and let it join a slither of sautéed venison, then popped it into his mouth. The flavour combination was as stimulating as sex and Bob knew that he would sell his soul to the devil for a plateful of this amazing dish, to hell with stupid contracts and forbidden love!

"Good eh?" Zach asked.

Bob opened his eyes, and despite the exquisiteness of the dish, came back to earth and reality. He made a mental note of the T-shirt and decided that it would have to be dealt with, but all in good time. At the rate Zach was working, the book would be in the bag long before Nancy's tight deadline and nothing must upset Zach's delivery.

"Very good," Bob replied, "but I think the venison could be a little rarer." He didn't want Zach getting above his station and Bob, after all, was boss. "Keep up the good work, dear boy, and I'll be in touch."

Bob gave a little wave and smiled at his protégé and with a last glance at the heavenly offerings oozing over every surface in the kitchen, turned and left the apartment.

FAR AWAY IN SOUTHERN IRELAND, Hilary relaxed on a lounger and read a book. A jug of iced gin sat on a table beside her and periodically, she topped up her glass with the cool restorative nectar. A little dish held fresh limes, cut into neat slices and Hilary popped one into her drink.

Long Tom's wretched peacocks squawked from the other side of the garden, they loathed their new home in a field beyond the ornamental lake. But Hilary could no longer bear the continual need to clear the droppings that soiled her carefully manicured lawns.

It was too humble a task for Seamus, her new head gardener.

Hilary put her book to one side and stretched luxuriously, the sun was warm for the time of year and she closed her eyes. The gentle rays caressed skin unused to ultra violet and felt pleasant.

She let her thoughts drift to Long Tom, back in London.

His Caribbean stint had been a success and proved a nice little earner, taking away any guilt she may have felt about the extortionate amount of money she was spending. The ornamental lake, which had been completely redesigned and was now twice its original size, had massive stones imported from a quarry in Germany, lining one side of the water and formed the start of an exotic garden. Seamus and his team were working tirelessly to follow Hilary's precise instructions on the layout and planting of many valuable, and carefully selected, rare species of plants.

She'd spoken to Long Tom on his return and he'd told her that he was would stay in London to work on his new album. Hilary argued that he could work on it in Ireland but knew that realistically, he needed to be in a London studio with his band. It didn't really matter to her and she promised to catch up with her husband soon. At least she could run her business remotely and Ireland seemed the perfect place. Hilary had never had a retreat away from the city and for the first time in her life was enjoying the countryside. Flatterly Manor was shaping up and with her concentrated efforts and a top London designer, would be one of the finest houses in an area stuffed with tax-dodging exiles, actors and pop stars.

She thought about the agency's latest client, Zach Docherty.

Bob was handling the young chef well and it was only a matter of time before money would start to flow in serious amounts. The media loved a naughty boy and Zach ticked all the boxes. Combined with his roguish good looks and incredible skill, Hilary envisaged constant TV work, best-selling books and wall-to-wall sponsors. If they could get him lined up with a supermarket endorsement, they would be home and dry.

She reached for her drink and sighed happily.

Seamus was heading towards her. Sweaty and hot from his exertions in the garden, his shirt clung to a taut six-pack, muscles in his forearms rippled. He held out a purple fountain grass and his body seemed to sway sensuously with the gentle waving motion of the fronds.

Decisions were needed on planting. Hilary swung her legs over the side of the lounger and eased herself upright.

What a perfectly pleasant way to spend an afternoon!

HATTIE SAT IN HER LOUNGE, snuggled into a fluffy onesie, and wriggled into a comfortable position on the La-Z-Boy. The onesie was a Christmas gift from a daughter-in-law and designed to resemble a sheep, with soft cream fleece and a hood that sprouted ears.

Hattie was absolutely drained and wondered if the long flight was catching up. She'd slept the clock round, only surfacing to re-fuel and was grateful to Pete for leaving much needed supplies to keep her going.

She fiddled with a remote control and the television sprang to life.

Hattie flicked through the channels until she came across a house-swop, in the Caribbean of all places! She dunked a biscuit in a mug of milky coffee and settled down. Hattie couldn't imagine how the neat and comely, semi-detached family from Wimbledon would adjust to a ramshackle split-level, high in the hills of Jamaica and what would the gentle Rastafarian family make of suburbia? But as the camera panned around rolling hillsides, where palm trees swayed lazily under a tropical sun, Hattie began to lose interest.

Her thoughts wandered back to Barbados and she realised that she missed Mattie terribly.

Hattie placed her mug on the floor.

She closed her eyes and imagined Mattie's handsome smiling face. His ease of patter, spiked with a sharp intelligence that often surprised Hattie, seemed to wash over her as if his spirit was in the room. Thank goodness she hadn't any wacky-backy to hand, or she would be soaring on a spiritual cloud and visualizing herself back in his comforting arms. As he crooned lilting lyrics about his faddah and his muddah and how happy he cuddah make her...

Hattie sighed and sat up. This wouldn't do.

She flicked to another channel then in frustration, turned the TV off.

Hattie had called her sons the previous evening and all seemed well in their lives. She planned to visit them soon but they'd not suggested any dates and Hattie hadn't pushed. Jo was banging on about a trip to London to see Zach, before she took any further action on her new plans for Kirkton House and would be away for several days.

Hattie felt redundant.

She stood up and stretched. The room felt cold after the scorching temperature in the Caribbean and zipping her onesie tightly, she pulled the hood over her head and contemplated running a bath to warm up. Perhaps she'd wash her hair. But she reasoned that it would take ages to remove the beads from her hair and get the tangle back into some sort of order, suitable for a supermarket trip in Marland.

It was too much of an effort.

Perhaps she'd go shopping and treat herself to some warmer clothes? It seemed a shame to waste this fabulous tan but it was far too cold to nip out to the chippy in a kaftan.

She grabbed another biscuit.

It was time that Jo got moving with the new plans for Kirkton House. Hattie couldn't wait for Boomerville to open, but in the meantime, it was just another day in dreary old Marland. She searched for her coffee to dunk the biscuit and accidentally knocked the mug over with her foot.

"Bugger!" Hattie swore and crouched down to dab at the stain on the carpet with her sleeve.

A commotion at the window startled Hattie and she spun round to see Reg, the window-cleaner, who had placed his ladder against the wall and was now leering through the glass. He was puffing furiously on a roll-up and the grubby chamois in his hand was perilously close to his crotch.

"Sending me smoke signals?" Hattie yelled. She was mortified that Reg had caught her on all fours, dressed as a sheep. His eyes gleamed beneath thick bushy eyebrows and Hattie sighed as she grabbed the La-Z-Boy and pulled herself upright, well aware that she had just fulfilled one of Reg's ultimate fantasies.

She walked over to the window and grabbed the curtains.

"Baaaa!" Hattie yelled, "I'll leave tha' money in the usual place!" And with force, she closed the curtains.

As she turned back to the living room she wondered if Jo would be running any boomer courses on sexual fantasies and giggled as she caught her reflection in the mirror. There would be no shortage of takers round here.

29

P   ete stood at his kitchen door and looked out over the fells. A
       dawn mist hung in the valleys as sunlight hovered beyond
       the rolling peaks. Birds soared overhead and in the distance
Hardwick sheep grazed contentedly on rich pasture, stretching for
miles. It was a picture postcard moment and he sighed with pleasure.

He missed Meg and it surprised him.

The old dog had been a true companion in the last few weeks and
it seemed odd not to have her nudging against leg, begging for a
biscuit or edging Pete out for a walk. In fact, walks were lonely
without her. He thought about Jo and was pleased that she'd asked
him to have Meg again, while she went to visit Zach in London. Meg
could easily stay home for a few days with Hattie and the gardener
popping in to take care of her, but Jo obviously felt that the dog was
better off with Pete.

Round one accomplished.

Now if he could only move on to round two.

He was taking Jo to the station shortly, she'd insisted on a taxi but
as he was collecting Meg then going on to the garage, it wasn't out of
his way and she'd agreed. He'd only spoken to her on the phone since
her return and he longed to see her. Naturally, he'd have all the time

in the world now that she wasn't moving away but at their age, time was a privilege and Pete didn't want to waste a moment.

Jo had never referred to his drunken telephone call and for that, Pete was grateful. But it meant that she was aware of his feelings and had shown no reaction, which clearly was a worry. He wondered what had happened in Barbados? Both women had looked wonderfully refreshed on their return. The holiday had clearly been a tonic, but Pete was curious to know exactly what had put such a glow on Hattie's cheeks and enabled such a transformation in Jo.

The grieving widow was long gone.

Pete turned from the view and searched for his car keys and briefcase. The garage sale completed in a week and he had a lot of paperwork to go through, including a meeting with his solicitor. It would be strange not driving over to Marland each day, stranger too with no work to focus on. Still, he was sure he would adapt and the spare hours would allow him more time to tinker on his tractors.

And more time to pursue Jo.

Pete glanced at the clock. He should be on his way. Jo's train left at seven and she would be waiting. He paused to run his fingers through his hair and to check his reflection in a mirror.

There's life in the old dog!

Pete smiled and with a wink to himself strode purposefully out to his car.

Jo jumped on the train at Marland and found her seat in the busy compartment then settled in for the long journey south. She'd chosen to travel first class and wondered if it was a luxury she would soon have to think twice about.

Kirkton House was going to cost a bomb to convert.

She picked up a complimentary newspaper and glanced at the headlines. Jo felt as though she'd been out of the loop for a long time and was only now stepping back into the real world.

She was so looking forward to seeing Zach!

Her youngest son had been ecstatic when she announced that she'd like to visit and he'd assured her that he would be waiting at the station. Jo was anxious to catch up with Zach's life and ached to hear about everything that had happened since he'd left Westmarland.

An attendant poured coffee and Jo pushed her paper to one side and sat back. The drink was refreshing and as she watched the Westmarland countryside hurtle by, she thought about Pete. He had kindly taken her to the station and to her relief, would be keeping Meg for the few days that Jo was away.

The old dog had howled when she saw the weekend case and guilt swept over Jo.

Pete still made no reference to his declaration of love but Jo could see in his eyes that he yearned for her to address the issue, to talk to him and let him know if he was in with a chance.

Jo knew that she should make a decision. Pete would be a catch for many women. Handsome and healthy with plenty of money and a fine property, Jo was amazed he hadn't been snapped up.

But his heart seemed set on Jo.

She wondered why she was dithering. There may not be too many chances ahead and they had been friends for so many years, surely that counted for something? But as Jo watched the countryside slip by her thoughts drifted to sunnier climes and she remembered her days with Long Tom.

It had been a precious moment in time.

Somehow, he'd brought her back to life, reminding her that she had feelings and that it was good to love again. She felt no guilt in regard to John and knew that he would want her to be happy, Long Tom had been a breath of fresh air and she was grateful for the interlude. It had woken her up and enabled her to see the future with clarity and now, she knew that her plans for Kirkton House were right and she had a fresh purpose. As soon as her visit to Zach was over she would return home and crack on.

Rob had been pacified with a very generous payment for his inconvenience and Julian Struthers seemed to think Jo's reluctance to sell was par for the course for a dithering middle-aged widow and within a year, she would be begging him to take it off her hands at a much reduced price. Jo was pleased that she'd never met Julian and believed Pete's comments that the man was an arrogant prat.

She pulled out a notepad and reached for her pen. Jo had nearly five hours to kill and would use the time to start making plans for Kirkton House. There was a great deal to be done. Folk in the village had already heard the news and rumours were rife. Jo hoped that past employees would come forward and take up new roles, for they'd been like one big family in the past.

She thought about Hattie too and hoped that her friend was happy.

Hattie had so enjoyed Barbados and coming back to Marland was like ricocheting to earth from a different planet, a hard reality check for her friend. But Jo knew Hattie couldn't wait to be involved going forward and this would give her a new lease of life. Hattie was a perfect hostess and with her no nonsense attitude and streak of naughtiness and fun, guests loved her and Jo was confident that Hattie would soon be welcoming new faces to Kirkton House and leading them to levels of comfort and delight way beyond their expectations.

Jo smiled. There was so much to look forward to!

Breakfast appeared and as Jo tucked in, she thought about the day ahead. She was pleased that she'd made an effort with her outfit, as Zach had told her that he was taking her to lunch. It was ages since she'd been to London and she had no doubt that he would choose somewhere special, perhaps a restaurant that he was familiar with, somewhere discreet where they could catch up and share each other's news.

How good it was to be busy again!

ZACH STOOD on the crowded Tube and braced himself as the train raced along the northern line towards Euston station.

He hoped that his mother's train was on time.

Zach had booked a table at Ranchers Restaurant, confident that Jo would like the buzz of the popular eatery. He knew that Bob was wining and dining with Prunella Gray and Nancy Nevis today, to celebrate the successful launch of Prunella's new book and Zach hoped that Bob would find time to pop over and meet Jo.

The Tube slowed and as Zach prepared to jump off, he noticed two girls nudge each other. They were nodding in his direction.

Was it his imagination? Everywhere he went he seemed to create attention, surely his one TV appearance and various media articles couldn't have stirred up this much interest? He wondered what was going to happen when his television series came out and as he ran towards an escalator he also wondered about Poppy and how on earth they could keep a lid on their relationship. He couldn't bear it much longer and yearned to take her out and be seen publically, to eat in a restaurant, walk in the park and maybe ask her to move in to his apartment.

Zach reached the station concourse and looked up at the arrivals board and decided that he would tell Jo all about Poppy and the stupid agency rules.

She would know what to do.

JO GRABBED her suitcase from the luggage rack and stepped down onto the platform. She'd worked hard on the train and now had a clear idea of the rebirth of her business. Kirkton House would be open to people of a certain age, 'boomers,' as Hattie liked to call them. It wasn't a rest home for the elderly. Kirkton House would be a temporary retreat for those in mid-life. People on their own, capable and able, but in need of company and stimulation, a place to spend quality time, before returning relaxed and refreshed, to their day-to-day lives.

"You'll have a marriage bureau on your hands!" Hattie had said. "Distinguished dating, well-heeled introductions, back-to-back-bonking... It will go mad!"

Jo smiled as she hurried along, remembering Hattie's premonitions.

As soon as she got home she would get in touch with the planning department and confirm that she could open and trade at Kirkton House again. There was little to do structurally, as the current rooms lent themselves to her ideas. The restaurant would remain, as would the conservatory, bar and reception rooms. They were all lovely communal areas for everyone to enjoy and Jo hoped that non-residents would dine in the restaurant, alongside hotel guests and enjoy the many workshops she planned to open to the public. They would offer terms from weekly to monthly or longer and clearly specify in the marketing material their mission and aim - to help mid-life boomers evaluate and stimulate their lives as they entered their later years.

Dear Lord, I hope I've got it right! Jo thought as she joined the masses heading towards a flight of steps that led out to the station. But all thoughts of Kirkton House were soon abandoned as she caught sight of Zach, twenty feet ahead.

"MUM!" he yelled and raced forward to scoop her into his arms.

Jo dropped her suitcase and hugged her son. They rocked from side-to-side and laughed as he welcomed her to London.

"Oh, it seems an age since I saw you," Jo said. "Your hair has grown long."

"So much has happened," Zach grinned.

"You look so grown up and handsome."

"But you look stunning…" Zach twirled Jo round and admired her suntan and pretty lace dress. He grabbed her case and taking her by the arm, hurried her down a flight of steps to the taxi rank. "Lunch is on me, I hope you like it," he said as they settled into the back of a black cab.

"I'd be happy with a chip buttie," Jo grinned as she stared wide-eyed at the traffic and hordes of people hurrying by.

"You sound like Aunty Hattie."

"She sends her love and hopes you are getting up to plenty of mischief."

"Well, she taught me plenty," Zach laughed. "I can't wait to hear all about your holiday, we've so much to catch up."

The taxi pulled up in Covent Garden alongside a discreet doorway, where a simple plaque announced the entrance of the legendary Ranchers Restaurant. A commissionaire held the door ajar and Zach led Jo down the dimly lit stairway to the restaurant's reception desk, where he deposited her case. The maître d' greeted Zach and led them past packed tables and through the New York-style interior to a raised centre booth that overlooked the room.

Jo wriggled onto the curved banquette and stared at the exposed brick walls and dark wood, plastered with show posters and photographs.

"It's lovely," she whispered.

"It's OK, Mum, no one can hear you," Zach grinned. "I think we'll start with some bubbles."

"This is a very nice table," Jo said as she looked around the room.

A man nearby gave a little wave as two women, dining with him, looked on.

"That's my agent, Bob Puddicombe," Zach said as he watched a waiter pour their drinks. "He'd said he'd stop by a little later."

"Oh how lovely, I can't wait to meet him." Jo picked up her champagne. "Here's to you, my lovely son and to your precious brother."

"Here's to all of us," Zach raised his glass, "and your new venture!"

They studied the menu and after placing their order, Jo sat back. "You can see everyone from here," she said as she recognised faces from the world of theatre and television.

"This is Hilary's table; Bob wanted us to have it today as it is such a special occasion. Hilary is his business partner."

Jo froze.

Mention of Hilary's name sent her spiralling back to Barbados and nights of passion with Long Tom.

"Hilary lives most of the time in Ireland now, she's married to a rock singer, you may have heard of him - Long Tom Hendry?"

Jo downed her drink and held out her glass for a refill.

"She's taken quite an interest in my career. In fact it was

Hilary who insisted that Bob 'discover' me." Zach went on, oblivious to his mother's paling complexion and trembling hand.

"Yoo hoo!" A voice rang out and made Jo jump.

"Only me," Bob said and edged onto the banquette beside Jo. "I am so thrilled to meet Zach's mummy and can see where he gets his delicious looks from." He held out his hand and leaned in to peck Jo on each cheek. "I'm not stopping; I don't want to disturb your family time."

"Have some champagne, please," Zach indicated to the waiter. "Mum has been longing to meet you."

"Well just one glass," Bob said. "I mustn't leave the dragons for too long, you never know what they'll get up to without me." He grinned and nodded towards Prunella and Nancy who raised their glasses in acknowledgment.

"Whatever Happened To Baby Jane?" Jo muttered and smiled at the two women.

"They are alive and well, my dear - both of them!" Bob whispered back. "I hope you like Hilary's table," he continued. "You can't imagine the grief the Janes have given me."

Jo thanked Bob and said he really didn't need to give up the table for her. His guests, who were clearly not suited with a lesser banquette, would be very welcome to join them.

"Does your mum enjoy eating razor blades?" Bob asked Zach. He turned to Jo. "You enjoy your precious time with our protégé, I'm sure you have masses of gossip to catch up." He finished his drink, "Oh my, look who's just walked in."

The trio turned simultaneously.

A tall figure, wearing a black leather jacket and Stetson, had made an entrance and diners nodded and whispered as he walked through the crowded room.

Jo gasped.

An invisible punch to her chest rendered her speechless. Long Tom, accompanied by Boss and two suited males, was heading in their direction.

Jo's winded heart thudded and threatened to bounce out along the banquette. She suddenly had the urge to hide under the table.

"Didn't know you were in town," Long Tom said. He stopped and stared at Jo as he shook Bob's hand.

"Do you two know each other?" Bob asked.

"No," said Jo and lowered her head.

"Yes," replied Long Tom.

"How interesting," Bob raised his eyebrows and introduced Zach.

"Er, I can't remember where…" Jo stammered and looked gratefully at Boss who had discreetly kept walking and now sat with his companions at the far side of the room.

"How's Hilary?" Bob asked.

"You tell me," Long Tom smiled lazily. He nodded at Zach, "Nice to make your acquaintance," he said and turned back to Jo. "Good to see you again," he whispered softly and lifting her hand, kissed it.

Long Tom grinned, winked and suddenly was gone.

"I'll tootle off then," Bob said, making a mental note of the exchange. "Wonderful to meet you," and with a little wave, he slid off the banquette and returned to his guests.

"Mum, you've gone very pale."

"Should we have another bottle of champagne?" Jo took a deep breath and trying hard to regain her composure, looked anxiously at Zach, "I think we've both got rather a lot to talk about."

30

Jimmy sat on the flat-topped rock by the beach near his house and watched a Boeing 747 make a gradual descent along the south coast. It was a Virgin flight and as familiar with flight times as his Aunty Hattie, he knew that at this time of day, it was the red-eye flight coming in from Manchester.

The gentle giant soared across the brilliant blue sky and Jimmy thought about the passengers on board. Many would be taking their first glimpses of this 'Treasure Island' and there would be great excitement as they looked down on the soft white beaches and turquoise waters rolling to shore.

Jimmy resisted the urge to wave.

His heart was heavy today and he missed his family. England seemed light years away and he yearned for his home. It had been wonderful having Jo and Hattie around, family meant so much, and he'd loved being with them and sharing precious moments. At times, even though everyone thought he was living the dream in this tropical paradise, he'd welcome the colder wet days of Westmarland, tucked up in a pub by a roaring log fire, with a glass of real ale and a hearty meal.

Jimmy thought about Jo and her brief relationship with Long

Tom. He hoped it had been good for her. Leaving the island, she'd seemed happy and refreshed and ready for new challenges. A far cry from the sad, thin, pale person who'd arrived several weeks earlier. Perhaps she would find someone suitable in Marland? Long Tom would be embarking on a European tour soon and the two were unlikely to cross paths again. It had been so good to have his mum on the island and Hattie, who embraced life and whatever came her way, had kept him smiling. Jimmy stared out at the sea and thought about Zach and all that was happening to him too, he missed his brother and longed to catch up.

The tall handsome fellow, with waist-length dreadlocks who lived further down the beach, approached and grinned, "Yo, man!" he called out.

"Yo, Rasta," Jimmy replied.

"Homesick?" the man asked and looked up at the plane.

"A little," Jimmy marvelled at the man's intuition and smiled.

"My belly button buried in Barbados," the man said. "Yours too, yu' see..."

Jimmy remembered the old custom that Bajans, on the birth of a new child, buried the umbilical cord in their back garden to ensure that the child would always return.

"Go see yu' folks, but yu' sho' be back."

The man reached out his hand and they touched knuckles.

"Bless," they both said and Jimmy watched the man stroll away.

There was something unique about the islanders and something special about Barbados and Jimmy knew that he was lucky to be living there. With a lighter heart and a spring in his step, Jimmy turned and went back to his house.

HATTIE SAT on the desk in Pete's office and stared at her phone. She frowned as she fiddled with the screen and in frustration, threw the phone to one side.

"I can't work these phone emails out, why can't she write me a note?" Hattie said crossly as Pete approached with Meg following close behind.

Hattie had stopped by the garage for elevenses and watched Pete as he carefully placed two mugs of coffee on mats, before making himself comfortable in his office chair.

"We'll use my computer and I'll print it off," Pete said. He watched Hattie move a pile of paperwork to one side and spread her ample behind across his work space. She reached for a drink and began to sip.

"No biscuits to dunk?" Hattie asked.

"Bottom drawer."

Hattie leaned over and shoving Meg's inquisitive head out of the way, reached for a packet of bourbon creams. She took one then placed the packet on her lap and dipped the biscuit in her coffee.

"What's your email address?" Pete asked as he reached over and pulled a laptop towards him. He knew that Hattie and the internet didn't blend well and as the email she was trying to read had come from Jo, he was keen to assist.

"Hotlipshattie at Hotmail," Hattie mumbled and she licked wet crumbs from her lips.

"Password?"

"Pickpick."

"What?"

"Just type, it's all lower case."

Hattie's email account sprang to life on the screen and Pete scrolled past several messages from Mattie-the-dred-lover-man, to find the mail from Jo. He pressed print and handed the page to Hattie before logging out of the screen.

"Blimey," Hattie said. "She's been busy. I've got a great long list of things to do." She reached for another biscuit and Meg nuzzled her knees. "I've got to start sourcing people to run courses."

"What sort of courses?" Pete asked as he made himself comfortable. Anything related to stability at Kirkton House was music to his ears.

"Yoga, meditation, art, creative writing, drama, health & lifestyle, cookery... It goes on and on," Hattie pulled a face. "She wants to turn the meadow into a sanctuary for those searching for their souls in the solitude, then there's another list of titles and I'm to find stuff in the local area."

"And what's she got on that one?" Pete closed his eyes and thought about the many fascinating historical buildings close by and endless hikes in the wonderful countryside.

"Great Gardens of the North, Hiking in the Fells, Victorian Marland, Wine Tasting in the Lakes - there's loads and she wants me to add my own ideas to the list."

"No doubt you have plenty," Pete reached out and took a biscuit. He broke a piece off and held it out for Meg.

"Dating for Deadbeats, springs to mind," Hattie rummaged around at the bottom of the packet and retrieved the last biscuit. "I don't think Jo understands that her retreat for middle-agers could easily become a retreat for those looking for a bit of nookie with some cultural classes thrown in."

"I'm sure she's thought of that," Pete said but he could see that Hattie had a point. "There are lots of folks our age glad of a change of scene, a bit of company and learning something new to take back into their own lives and enrich themselves with the experience."

He quoted Jo.

"Well, whatever it is, I'm up for it and can't wait," Hattie said and leapt off the desk. Meg careered to one side. "She's absolutely right that folk at our age need to keep active and involved, it would be so easy to sit back, thinking you're all washed up." Hattie drained her coffee. "I mean, look at you - working days nearly over, money in the pot and what are you going to do with it?" She looked at Pete. "You'll spend every day in your shed talking to tractors and nights in the Red Lion with Moaning Marlene leering over you. Is that how you want to finish up?"

"Aye, all right," Pete replied. "I know what you are saying and it's not for want of trying but Jo avoids any situation that involves talk of us and I've already made a fool of myself by telling her how I feel."

"God loves the man who tries."

"Aye, I'll try a bit harder."

"Get yourself on the creative writing course and write to her."

"Very bloody funny," Pete pushed his laptop to one side and reached for the bundle of papers that Hattie had strewn across the desk. "Haven't you got work to do?" he said. "I've a business that closes in a few days and I need to get on."

Meg placed her head on Pete's knee, her eyes fixed on the remaining piece of biscuit in his hand. Absentmindedly, he held the biscuit out and she wolfed it down.

"Well that will take you all of ten minutes," Hattie looked around at the empty office and deserted forecourt. "Then you'll be off on a tractor with that daft object riding pillion."

"Each to their own," Pete smiled but knew that Hattie was probably right.

"Well, she'll be back from London in a day or two and from what I've heard, you need to keep your wits about you, you're not the only one on a mission." Hattie drained her coffee and placed the mug on the desk then folded the email in two and tucked it in her bag. "Be seeing you!" she called out and strode out of the office.

"Aye, no doubt you will," Pete said softly as he watched her go.

Meg was licking his hand and he stroked her head. Hattie's words had jolted him and he wondered what was behind them. Had Jo got another admirer? Had something happened in the Caribbean? He sighed and looked at the dog. "I think we need to step things up a notch, Meg," he said.

Meg yawned and seeing that the biscuit drawer was staying firmly closed, retreated to her blanket in the corner of the office and slumped down.

In moments, she was snoring.

"It's a dog's life," Pete thought as he picked up a pen and reached for his paperwork. He looked across at the sleeping animal, "But we've work to do, old lass!"

∾

Jo SLIPPED into her dressing gown and tied it at the waist. She glanced in the mirror in Zach's bedroom and stared at her reflection as she ran her fingers through her tousled hair. The face that looked back had puffy eyes and a tired expression.

It had been a heavy night.

She wandered into the living room and tiptoed past the sleeping forms huddled under a duvet on the sofa, their bodies entwined as one. Zach and Poppy had insisted that Jo have the double bed and despite her protestations, were unanimous that she made herself comfortable in Zach's room.

Jo yawned as she made a cup of coffee then sat on a stool in the kitchen and thought back to the previous day. She had no idea what time they'd left Ranchers Restaurant, people kept stopping by their table to chat and drink and after the shock of seeing Long Tom, Jo had been happy to avoid Zach's questions and divert the conversation to the frivolous banter that followed. But they'd continued their evening at an underground cocktail bar, in the seclusion of a cellar booth. The barman performed theatrically and produced a series of unusual and mind-numbing drinks which weakened mother and son. Both admitted to their exploits and soon knew that the situation was tricky.

"Why did you sign the contract?" Jo asked.

"I never thought I'd meet Poppy," Zach replied.

They'd pondered long and hard as they watched a smoking vessel arrive then sipped warm tobacco flavoured liquid, through two straws.

"Why did you sleep with Long Tom?"

"I didn't know he was married to Hilary."

"We're buggered!" they both said and laughed as they fell back on the soft leather seating that circled the booth.

But in the cold light of day, Jo wondered what they needed to do to remedy the situation. She glanced over at Zach and Poppy and watched their angelic expressions as they slept.

These two must have a chance!

Jo remembered the long chat they'd all had, late in the night.

Poppy was a lovely girl and clearly mad about Zach. Jo thought it nonsense for them to live in the shadows and had decided that she would arrange to meet with Bob and sound him out. Surely the contract could be adjusted? No one, especially Hilary, need know about her time with Long Tom and as Jo would soon be heading back to Westmarland, there wasn't a chance that she'd meet with him again.

She made up her mind to give Bob a ring today and see if she might call by the office. She was here for a couple of days and he'd seemed like a very amicable man.

Jo felt sure that he'd help.

Feeling more positive, she decided to make a full English breakfast to mop up her hangover. She'd take breakfast in bed to the young lovers then let them get on with their day.

Finding everything she needed in a fridge bulging with unusual vegetables and spices, Jo began to cook. It reminded her of cooking for her family when all her men were at home and she smiled as the bacon sizzled and sausages browned. Family was everything to her and the memories reinforced Jo's mission to protect her sons and do something to help those, at her age, who needed new company and direction in their lives.

And that would include Hattie.

How she would enjoy this breakfast, Jo thought fondly as she dished up. Her friend would be salivating as she tucked in, finding as much pleasure in good food, as she did in life. Kirkton House was going to be a fresh start for them both and Jo couldn't wait.

A sausage slipped off Jo's fork and rolled to the floor. She glanced around for Meg then shook her head as she remembered that Meg was far away, keeping Pete company. She missed the old dog terribly and couldn't wait to get out on the fells again with her faithful hound by her side.

"Something smells good!" Zach called out and Poppy popped her head out from under the duvet.

"Oh, you're awake, come and join me," Jo said and dished up.

Plans for the day were made as they ate. Jo was going to an exhibition that she wanted to see, followed by a couple of galleries and shopping in Knightsbridge. Zach and Poppy would join her for lunch in Harrods and Jo would buy Hattie some biscuits in the food hall. Pete would probably enjoy a bottle of red wine and no doubt there was something for Meg in the pet department.

Zach suggested an evening bar meal at the pub.

"Let me have the chat with Bob before you go out together in a public place," Jo said, hesitant for the young lovers to be seen in the local pub, "I'm sure he'll agree to amending the contract, after all you can't live all your days like this."

"If he sacks me, I'll just have to find another job," Poppy said.

"Let's worry about that when we have to," Jo replied and smiled at the couple, who were staring lovingly at each other as they ate.

"It's a shame Aunty Hattie isn't here," Zach said. "She'd love London."

Jo imagined Hattie in London.

You could take the girl out of Westmarland but would never take Westmarland out of the girl. She smiled as she envisaged the mayhem Hattie would create.

"Ten minutes to get ready?" Zach looked at Poppy and Jo. "I'm first in the bathroom." He slid off the stool and disappeared.

Jo looked at Poppy and laughed, together, they collected the dishes and cleared the table.

It will all work out! Jo told herself and prepared for her day.

31

"Well, how did you do that?" Hattie asked a puzzled potter as he stood by a wheel, both hands covered in fresh, wet clay with a perfectly formed vase on a table beside him.

The potter looked bemused.

Hattie had decided to throw one or two ideas of her own into the mix on Jo's list of courses. She had arrived in the studio of a local business that specialized in running pottery classes for beginners and those wanting to learn more intricate techniques, and now sat astride the wheel. Hattie had followed the potter's instructions to the letter, but the phallus-like object rotating in her hands looked nothing like his vase and the potter looked nervous as he leaned over to help.

"You need to make a hole in the top," he said and plunged a finger in.

Soft gooey clay shot over the apron that strained across Hattie's chest and splattered onto her face and hair.

"Blimey," Hattie said as her phallus erupted, "I think this course is a winner."

She tidied herself up and agreed that she'd be back to collect her masterpiece when it had been fired in the potter's kiln then, adding a tick to her list, jumped into her car and sped away.

Never mind creative writing and arty farty classes! Hattie was confident that Jo's new clientele would benefit from wandering off the cultural improvement path and she was enjoying doing some research of her own.

Her next meeting was with a Shaman, who held mind-altering classes in a teepee on top of a Westmarland mountain and promised to communicate with the spiritual world.

Hattie couldn't wait.

She wished that Mattie was with her, the class was sure to offer some mind-altering substances that would be new to Mattie and fun to try. No wonder the course cost so much! Still, Jo's lot wouldn't be short of a bob or two and whilst they were dancing in a tent with their dead granny, Hattie would be making sure that their direct debits swelled the coffers in Kirkton House's bank.

She thought of Mattie as she drove and wondered what he was up to. New holiday makers, brave enough to experience his island tour, would be full of memories far removed from the traditional beach holiday. Word spread and it was no wonder that he was much in demand.

Hattie missed him.

Mattie made her feel alive and adventurous and there wasn't a man in Marland who could match up. She sighed and knew that he would be in the arms of another by now and in no time at all, would rotate his romances as new arrivals stepped tentatively in his direction.

You've got to make the most of whatever comes your way! Hattie told herself as she followed a hand-painted sign of a teepee and began her ascent up the mountain.

She'd spoken to Jo earlier and hadn't been in the least bit surprised to hear that Long Tom was in town. There was a space that needed watching! Jo would have her work cut out to keep that one at bay and Hattie wondered if she'd been right to let it slip to Pete that he needed to sharpen his arrow. Cupid would never wing Pete's way if he didn't get in on the action. It was no good dallying around where Jo was concerned. She never knew what she wanted till it stood in front of her. Take Long Tom for example. He was a man on a mission who hadn't taken no for an answer. And look how she'd buggered around over John! It had taken a snowy, star-lit night, a diamond ring and a head-over-heels gypsy to make her mind up. Hattie smiled as she remembered John and Jo's sudden engagement one New Year's Eve. Pete needed to set something up that would give him an opportunity to make a deeper impression on Jo. Hattie wracked her brains for a solution.

But first she had a teepee to find.

Hattie's car groaned as it tackled the almost vertical summit, scattering a bag of sweets on her lap. Just as she feared the vehicle would flip over backwards, the road levelled off and the teepee came in sight at the far end of deserted field. An Indian-looking man wearing a long dark coat, stood beside a tall wooden pole covered in feathers and pieces of bone. He beckoned to Hattie and indicated that she should park.

"Crikey!" Hattie said out loud and took a nervous gulp as she stepped onto the damp wet grass.

"Namaste," the man said as he placed the palms of his hands before his heart and bowed his head. "The god in me greets the god in you."

"Charmed, I'm sure," Hattie replied and returned the greeting.

Jo's going to love all this spiritual clap-trap! Hattie thought happily and headed towards the tent.

LONG TOM SAT at his Steinway in the music room at his London town house and thought about Jo. He couldn't get her out of his mind.

His fingers brushed the smooth cool keys and he began to play.

The sun is going down on this great unknown
I'm out of sight and all alone

Don't forget me!
Don't forget me...

He repeated the chorus of his new song and wondered what she was doing. It had been quite a shock to see her in Ranchers Restaurant when he'd automatically turned to Hilary's table and with surprise, recognised Jo immediately.

She had shone in the dimly-lit room.

As he'd approached, he watched her smile and laugh with son, her hair catching the light as she turned, illuminating her lovely face and Long Tom had longed to pull up a seat and join in.

He wondered how long she was in London. He wanted to meet up and had already decided to give Jimmy a call to get Jo's mobile. Perhaps she'd have dinner with him?

Long Tom's PR people had arranged a trip back to Barbados. They'd lined up a busy publicity schedule to promote the new album, including a photoshoot at Eddie's plantation, a series of interviews for leading publications and filming for Long Tom's channel on YouTube. He'd be flying back there soon.

He wondered if Jo might go with him.

He knew that he was playing with fire and if Hilary found out it would be the kiss of death to his marriage. But where was Hilary? Her business and husband were in London, yet she insisted on staying put in Ireland. God knows what kept her there. At the moment, absence wasn't making his heart grow fonder and his annoyance grew each day.

Long Tom played on.

He was confident that the new album was going to do well and was looking forward to a European tour, his recording company already talking about America the following year to celebrate his rebirth. Long Tom's career had come back to life at a time when he thought it was all over and he gave thanks each day.

If only his home life could be as successful.

Long Tom stopped playing and picked up his phone then pressed Jimmy's number. His life had been in the lap of the gods when he was stoned and drunk and he took whatever came his way. But after rehab he'd learnt to take control and now it was time to step up again.

The phone rang and he waited for Jimmy to pick up.

"Hey man, just an old reggae rocker calling, I need your help."

Long Tom smiled as he wrote Jo's number down.

Jo's heart was heavy as she hugged Zach and Poppy. A taxi was waiting to take her into Soho to meet with Bob and then she would head to the station and catch her train back to Westmarland.

They'd had a wonderful time the previous day on Jo's whirlwind tour of London and she'd managed to see and do all of the things she'd planned. The exhibition at the Victoria and Albert Museum had been fascinating and the galleries fun. In Harrods, Jo had shopped till she dropped and tried not to think about what she had spent before joining Zach and Poppy for lunch.

The young couple assured Jo that they would visit Westmarland very soon and Zach promised that he would oversee the menus and opening of the kitchen when Kirkton House re-opened. Jo told them that she was sure Bob would go along with her suggestions to ease the clause in the contract and would let them know as soon as she left his office.

"Let love win out!" Zach called as Jo climbed in the taxi.

"Get back to work on your book, I've taken more than enough of your time." She blew them both a kiss, "See you soon!"

The journey to Wardour Street was slow and traffic dense and Jo was thoughtful as she watched the sights of London slowly pass by. It was a heavenly day and tourists thronged the streets taking in the rich history of the city. Jo contemplated her meeting and felt confident that all would be well. Instinct told her that Bob was a decent sort and would see things her way.

Her phone rang and Jo reached into her bag to retrieve it.

"It's thirty four degrees in Barbados."

An icy shiver ran down Jo's spine and she closed her eyes. Long

Tom's voice was rich and sensual and as he spoke she found herself melting into the seat.

"Can you come out to play?" he asked.

"I'm heading home," Jo replied.

"That was a short trip."

"I've got a lot to do, like making a new life. How did you get my number?"

Long Tom paused. He didn't want her to hang up.

"I've got to go back to Barbados, come with me," he said.

"Are you crazy? I've only just come back."

"Just crazy for you babe."

"I can't talk now," Jo's emotions catapulted around the taxi and she opened her eyes. She must stay strong! "I have to go," she said.

"I'll call you back, think about Barbados, please?"

Jo ended the call and took deep breaths to try and stem her racing heart. Why did he do this? They'd agreed to end their relationship in Barbados and now he wanted to start things up again, just as she was on her way to his wife's offices!

The phone rang again and Jo answered quickly.

"Yes?" she barked.

"Hello, lass," Pete said, "I was going to suggest you don't eat too much today and I take you out for dinner when I pick you up later. Are you OK?" he was perturbed by Jo's tone.

"Oh, sorry Pete, I thought you were someone else," Jo replied.

"Alright, no bother, but what do you think?"

"About what?"

"Dinner later."

"Oh, I can't think about that, I've got stuff to do and I'll be tired when I get home." Jo cut him off, "Is Meg OK?"

"Aye, Meg is fine," Pete replied. Unlike me! He felt peeved. He was no more than a damn dog-sitter and it was wearing very thin. "I'll see you at the station, text me your train time." He hung up.

Jo stared at the phone.

Had the last two conversations really happened? Long Tom said he was crazy about her and Pete had put the phone down. Oh heck, she thought as the taxi pulled into Wardour Street, and now I've got Bob to face!

Jo paid the driver and stood on the street looking up at the offices of Hargreaves & Puddicombe Promotions. The gold-embossed sign was intimidating but Jo told herself that this would all be over in an hour or so and then she could head home and sort out the mess she'd made with Long Tom and Pete.

Let love win out! She remembered Zach's words and braced herself, then took a deep breath and pressed the bell.

32

Bob cradled his prayer beads in both hands and let the smooth stones drop comfortingly from one palm to the other as he thought about a call he'd had with Hilary the previous evening. Hilary was across the water in Ireland, in the garden at Flatterly Manor and Bob chatted to the butler while he waited for someone to find her. He'd met the butler, a very decent chap, the previous year when visiting a food festival with Hilary. A short time before Hilary married Long Tom.

"I see Long Tom is back in town," Bob said when Hilary finally came to the phone.

"He's making a new album," Hilary replied. She seemed distracted.

"He certainly wasn't making music when he sauntered into Ranchers."

"A man has to eat."

"Shouldn't you be by your husband's side?" Bob hesitated and wondered if he'd overstepped the mark.

"Well he won't come to Ireland till the album is finished and I'm too busy on the garden," Hilary snapped. "How are things with Zach

Docherty, have you got a supermarket interested yet?" she diverted the conversation.

"All in good time, dear."

"He starts filming soon and when that hits the screens with his book on the shelves, it will be like printing money so make sure a supermarket is lined up for a hefty endorsement!" Hilary was in a foul mood and Bob counted his prayer beads and breathed slowly as she barked out orders.

"Get your finger out now and you'll have your pension pot sorted by the end of the year." Hilary said and hung up.

Bob closed his eyes and whispered a soothing mantra. He refused to let Hilary upset him and hoped that she'd stay put in Ireland. Hargreaves & Puddicome Promotions was running perfectly well without her.

"Wake up! Your eleven o'clock is here," Lottie stuck her head round the door and grinned. She wore a headband covered in dazzling star shapes that sparkled as she moved.

"Be a poppet and organise some coffee," Bob said and placed his beads in a velvet bag, pushing them to one side.

He was looking forward to seeing Zach's mother again and straightening his shirt cuffs, he sucked in his stomach and stood. "Show her in," he called out.

Jo stepped into Bob's office. She'd left her case and coat in reception and moved her bag to her arm as she reached out to shake Bob's hand.

"Oh, let's not be formal," Bob laughed and grabbing Jo's shoulders kissed each cheek. "My, how your son takes after you - such looks!" He settled Jo into a chair and took his place on the other side of his desk. "And here's our lovely Lottie with some coffee."

Lottie carried a tray, laid out with smart white china and a pot of freshly brewed coffee. The cups wobbled as she walked.

"Marvellous outfit," Bob smiled and studied Lottie's long dark dress and flashing headband. "You look like a constellation."

Jo was amused as she watched their exchange.

Bob poured the coffee and handed a cup to Jo. He asked Lottie to close the door on her way out but Lottie had picked the empty tray up and with both hands full, left the door slightly ajar. Unperturbed, Bob turned his attention to Jo.

"Have you enjoyed your time in London?" he asked.

"Yes thanks, it's been great." Jo chatted about the previous day and said she'd enjoyed lunch in Harrods with Zach, omitting to mention that Poppy had been with them. Bob asked about her holiday in Barbados and how she'd liked the island. For the next fifteen minutes they made small talk.

"Now my dear, you wanted to speak to me," Bob announced and turning his chair to face Jo, looked straight into her eyes.

"It's about Zach."

"Go on."

"He seems to have a silly clause in his contract."

"I think I'm familiar with the clause you're referring to."

"Can we take it out?"

"Is there a reason to?" Bob raised his eyebrows.

"I think we both know there is," Jo came clean.

Bob folded his fingers into a pyramid across his chest and looked thoughtful. "It's tricky," he said. "My partner, Hilary, believes that a client of Zach's age has far more commercial appeal if he is single, which we could of course overcome, but..." Bob paused, "As a company, we have a strict rule that staff and clients do not fraternise. It's a contractual agreement for both and should either break that rule it is considered to be gross misconduct."

"Have you ever been in love?" Jo spoke softly. She wanted to appeal to Bob's softer side.

"Unconditionally and I married my partner," Bob replied. He returned Jo's gaze and wondered how far he should go. "My business partner married recently too."

Jo stiffened at the mention of Hilary and Bob caught the movement. He'd hit the nail on the head!

"Her husband was in Barbados recently and I could see from your reconciliation at Ranchers that you know Long Tom quite well." Bob was wading into water and was unsure of the depth.

Jo knew the game was up. Whatever she did now was damage limitation and she had to put Zach first.

"I didn't know Hilary was Zach's boss," Jo said.

"Really?"

"Of course, it would never have happened had I known."

"And what did happen?"

"We had an affair, a few brief days. He was lonely, I was numb. He helped me come alive again."

"I see..."

Both Bob and Jo were deep in thought, neither saw the door move and gasped when it slammed back against the wall, almost shattering the glass panel.

Hilary entered the room.

"Jesus!" Bob said.

"Oh hell..." Jo winced.

"No, it's me." Hilary stormed into the office. "What have I told you about open doors, Bob?" She walked over to the window and opened it slightly, then reached into her bag for a menthol cigarette and placing it in a holder, dragged deeply as she lit it. "I thought I'd pay you a visit after our telephone conversation last night."

"You've started smoking again!" Bob was aghast.

"You've stopped obeying company rules!" Hilary flung back. The room was silent as she stared out of the window and blew smoke above the traffic in the road below.

"I think I should go," Jo said.

"I think you should." Hilary turned and glared.

"Not until we've sorted this out." Bob stood and tried to pacify the two women.

"Get that woman out of here!" Hilary hissed.

Jo leapt to her feet and grabbed her bag. "I'm sorry..." she mumbled and knowing that she was about to burst into tears, fled from the office and slammed the door.

"Bitch!" Hilary flicked the butt of her cigarette out of the window and faced Bob.

"I think you should take a seat, dear."

"Not until I've called Poppy and sacked her."

"That won't be necessary," Bob took Hilary by the arm and placed her in the chair that Jo had occupied.

"I need to call my lawyer and start divorce proceedings."

"Oh really?" Bob returned to his seat and made himself comfortable. "The media will love that, imagine the headlines: 'Rocker's Recipe For Love!' with a celebrity chef, his mum and agent boiled together in the mix..." He looked out of the window where a plane could be seen in the sky overhead, heading to Heathrow. Bob stared at the gliding giant as it made it's descent over the city.

"A little bird told me that you're enjoying more than the fresh Irish air at Flatterly Manor," Bob said quietly. He thought about his conversation with the butler and waited.

His words hung menacingly in the tense atmosphere.

Hilary whipped her head around. Bob could almost hear the bones in her neck as they cracked.

"What do you mean?" she asked.

"I think you know what I mean," Bob replied. "You've employed a gardener by the name of Seamus? I hear he's laying more than turf by the ornamental lake."

"I don't know what you are talking about," Hilary stammered.

Bob spun round to face her.

"Don't balls this up!" he was angry. "Zach Docherty is a decent man and will be the making of this agency for years to come. So he's fallen in love, so what? Poppy is a darling and works hard for us. Rules can be changed. You've screwed your marriage up, can you blame your old man if he looks for pastures new? You're never anywhere near him! He's an ex-addict. He's always going to be addicted to something, perhaps this time it's love? He'd be a fool to ignore Jo, she's stunning and a beautiful person, don't blame her because you're crap at relationships!" Bob sat down. "He's a rock star for god's sake - what did you expect?"

Hilary was silent.

Bob had taken the wind out of her sails and after the shock of overhearing a conversation that had staggered her, she suddenly felt exhausted.

"Coffee anyone?" Lottie lit up the doorway.

"SHUT THE DOOR!" Bob and Hilary both shouted and Lottie, staggering under the verbal avalanche, backed away.

33

"Just like old times!" Hattie announced as she made her way through the office door at Kirkton House and grinned happily. "I never thought we'd be sitting here again." She held a tumbler in each hand and placed one on the desk beside Jo. "That kitchen needs a good sort out." She nodded backwards as the door closed. "It's time to get your Zach out of London for a couple of weeks."

Jo looked up. Hattie had pushed a glass of vile looking liquid across the desk.

"Sup up," Hattie said and took a slurp of her drink. "Delicious!" she announced as a dark purple foam clung to her top lip. "Buggers your lippie up though." Shiny red gloss mixed with the foam and Hattie wiped it away with the back of her hand, smearing it across her face.

"You look like a road accident," Jo said. "What on earth is in this?" She held the glass up and studied the muddy contents.

"The secret of eternal life," Hattie replied and tipped her drink to down the remains. "I read about it in the paper, that posh food writer, Prunella something-or-other, reckons it will take years off. I might buy her book."

"You've obviously never seen her," Jo muttered and pushed the glass away.

"By heck, it feels good to be back here." Hattie looked around the office then leaned over the desk that partitioned the office from the reception area and looked out. "It's a bit spooky though." She glanced towards the cocktail bar where dust sheets covered mounds of furniture and bar fittings. "You need to open the shutters and jazz things up."

Jo looked up from her paperwork.

Hattie was right. There was a great deal to be done. She'd had a meeting with the planning officer that morning and he'd accepted that there was no reason why Kirkton House shouldn't open as soon as possible, no structural work was required and as it would be offering accommodation and meals again, no change of use either. The outbuildings were in good order and would only require a coat or two of paint and some decoration to enable Jo to run classes. Overall, he'd thought it a splendid idea to re-open. Kirkton House was an asset to the area and he hoped that Jo would be successful.

It was time to bring the place back to life.

"Not drinking that?" Hattie asked and picked up Jo's glass.

"All yours," Jo shook her head. "Enjoy it, any more and you'll be sucking a dummy."

Hattie drank the energising drink slowly, savouring each mouthful as it slid comfortably into her stomach. It would take several of these to bring her back to life that morning. She'd spent an interesting few hours in the teepee with the Shaman, an experience she might edit when updating Jo on her progress with courses. Jo would have a heart attack if her guests signed up to that particular experience and she'd need to double the public liability insurance.

"Is that a tattoo on your chest?" Jo raised her eyebrows and frowned as she reached out and pushed Hattie's blouse to one side. A strange swirling line danced over the contours of Hattie's bosom before disappearing into her cleavage.

"Just been mucking about with an eyebrow pencil," Hattie fumbled with her buttons, securing the blouse firmly under her neck.

She silently cursed the Shaman and his henna wand, grateful that Jo couldn't see the rest of her body, and prayed it would wash off.

"So, Pete closes his doors today," Hattie quickly changed the subject. She pulled out a chair and placed her feet on the desk. "End of an era," she sighed and thought longingly of the gallons of free petrol she'd had over the years.

"I don't think he's speaking to me."

"Who could blame him?" Hattie flicked a compact and began to apply lipstick. "He's probably hearing the beat of Long Tom's bass guitar pounding out a new love song about love and lust under a Caribbean sun."

"I don't think he has a clue about Long Tom," Jo reached for Hattie's lipstick and applied a coat to her own lips. "This has got foam on!" She winced and wiped it away with a tissue.

"Like hell," Hattie closed her compact and stared at Jo. "The poor sod knows he's got competition, but as yet, he doesn't know who."

"Oh, why does it have to be so complicated?" Jo stood up. "I'm going for a walk and when I come back can we please get stuck in? I'm planning on opening this place as soon as possible and there's a ton of work to be done."

She pushed Hattie's legs to one side and walked into the hallway. A dust sheet moved in the bar and Meg, who was asleep on a sofa, appeared and wagged her tail. Jo reached down and stroked the dog's head.

"Come on sweetheart, let's get some fresh air."

Hattie waved goodbye as the pair disappeared through the conservatory and out into the garden. It was so good to be back at Kirkton House! She loosened her blouse and headed for the kitchen. Hattie was feeling peckish and it must be way past lunchtime.

JO CLIMBED OVER THE WALL, beyond the meadow and strode out across the fields. Meg bounded along with her nose to the ground, in pursuit of the dozens of rabbits who watched tauntingly from the hedgerows, safe in the knowledge that the old dog's hunting days were well and truly behind her.

It was an overcast, grey sort of day and Jo looked down as she plunged her hands in her pockets and walked briskly, trying not to let her spirits match the mood of the weather.

She felt bad about Pete and knew she'd upset him. He'd hardly spoken to her when he met her at the station, merely asking politely if she'd enjoyed London and what news she had of Zach. Jo wanted to tell Pete all about Zach and Poppy and how happy they were and the good news she'd received on her way home, that Bob wasn't sacking Poppy. But she knew it would lead to complications, there would be a lot of explaining to do and the whole story might come out. Jo had no idea whether Hilary had confronted Long Tom and was fearful of being named should their marriage flounder and the news hit the press.

Long Tom had phoned several times and Jo had ignored the incessant ringing, turning her phone to silent, for she still didn't trust herself to speak to him and subconsciously worried that she'd let her heart rule her head and would jump at the chance to join Long Tom in Barbados and hang the consequences.

Meg ambled ahead and Jo looked up from her thoughts as the dog threw herself to the ground and began to roll in a crusting cow pat, her rickety legs waving in the air as she embraced her favourite pastime.

"Oh, bloody hell," Jo said crossly and went to scold her pet but the look of bliss on Meg's face made Jo stop in her tracks. She shook her head and sighed.

There are some things you can't change, she thought and smiled. How she adored her old dog! Meg's unconditional love was a constant and with a flood of emotion, Jo watched the animal roll over, stand and career towards her, tail wagging with happiness as she accompanied her mistress over their favourite fields and fells.

Together they turned and began to walk back to Kirkton House.

The old house appeared from a mist that clung to the pale pink stones. It looked ghostly in the ether and seemed to beckon Jo home.

As she wandered through the wrought iron gates, across the meadow and along a path that divided two acres of freshly cut lawns, Jo felt happy. Her home was coming back to life and would soon be filled with people.

John would be proud of her.

Hattie stood at the door of the conservatory and waved when she saw Jo. "Let's saddle up and go and wish Pete all the best," she called out. "I've made a cake!"

Jo hurried down the steps and ran across the croquet lawn to see what Hattie held in her outstretched hands. A chocolate cake, with a very sunken middle and finger marks on the butter cream, sat on a large round tray.

"How kind," Jo said and beamed. She tried not to think of the state of the kitchen. "Let's surprise him!" She called out to Meg and in moments the trio had locked the house and climbed into Jo's car.

"The way to a man's heart is through his stomach," Hattie said as the cake bounced in her lap. "This will knock him sideways, he'll be eating out of your hand again in no time."

Jo glanced at her friend.

Hattie's face was covered in icing sugar and there was chocolate all over her blouse. It was kind of Hattie to make a cake and Jo hoped that they'd be in time to catch Pete. Perhaps he would soften and they could be friends again? After all, he didn't know about Long Tom and, with luck, never would. She pressed down on the accelerator and the car thrust forward.

The sooner they got there the better.

HILARY STARED out of the tiny window and watched the plane's propeller spring into life. She sat back as the aircraft taxied down the wet runway, then felt it gather speed and become airborne, lurching into the low-lying cloud above.

She'd spent the night in London with Long Tom and it had been a difficult few hours.

Long Tom was surprised to see her when she appeared in the music room. He looked up and smiled but continued to play a tune she wasn't familiar with, the notes sweet under his fingers as they moved gently over the keys.

Eventually he'd stopped and closed the lid on the Steinway.

"Didn't know you were back," he said, making no move to stand or touch her.

"I've been to the office," she replied. "I had something to sort out."

"All well with the new chef?"

"He's fine."

Hilary longed to light a cigarette. Until this morning, she hadn't smoked for over a year and her craving was intense, the nicotine demon demanding attention.

"You look tense," Long Tom said.

"Just tired, I've not been sleeping."

"Peacocks keeping you awake?"

"No, not at all," Hilary snapped. She daren't say a word against Long Tom's beloved peacocks even though she'd love to wring their necks. She thought about Seamus and turned away as a flush burnt into her skin, she'd hardly had a wink of sleep in weeks.

They'd dined in the kitchen where Long Tom made a salad with tomatoes and leaves from the garden, then added cooked chicken breasts. Hilary poured herself a glass of wine as she watched him cut a chunk from a wedge of creamy brie and warm it gently before spreading over the chicken, finishing the dish with a drizzle of sesame oil.

The wine tasted good and she poured another.

"Not hungry?" Long Tom asked as he sipped water and watched Hilary push her food around the plate.

"It's delicious," she replied. "But I must be coming down with something, I've no appetite."

Long Tom looked up, "For food or for me?"

Hilary dismissed his question and began to tell him about Flatterly Manor and how grand it all was. The house had been redecorated, the garden looked glorious and the ornamental pool was nearly finished. He'd soon be able to stock it with fish.

"I have to go back to Barbados." Long Tom topped up her glass, picked up their plates and carried them to the sink, where he stacked them for the housekeeper. "Then I've a tour to Europe, I'll be away for two or three months."

"I'll join you in Europe," Hilary took an interest. "A couple of nights in Paris would be lovely." She cringed as she heard herself speak, this was no basis for a marriage.

And later that night, as they made love, Hilary knew that her marriage was on life-support. Long Tom went through the motions but the physical act was over in moments, the passion gone for both of them. Hilary fought hard not to think about Seamus and his young, athletic body that took her to heights of ecstasy she'd never experienced before.

Long Tom wasn't the only one with an addiction.

Her marriage, which had been joyous and fun, was in grave danger. She knew about Jo and didn't doubt that Long Tom knew about Seamus - unions that were probably meaningless, for Hilary at least.

Perhaps she should have stayed on to try and talk to her husband?

The plane banked and Hilary was jolted from her thoughts. As the rugged coast of southern Ireland came into view, Hilary looked down and caught sight of a twinkling estuary that led to the little town of Kindale, where Flatterly Manor lay in a valley beyond the small port, amongst lush green fields and deserted country roads.

Hilary smiled.

Twelve months ago she never thought she'd leave the cut and thrust of the city but now she found herself yearning for the comfort blanket of their Irish home and couldn't wait to get back, after assuring Long Tom that she'd go through his tour schedule and be with him very soon.

She sighed and remembered the way Long Tom had stared at her wine the previous evening and even though she was sure he'd never indulge again, she'd had a nagging doubt.

As the plane came to a stop and people scrambled for their belongings, Hilary shivered. For the first time in her life, she wasn't at all sure how things were going to work out and the feeling made her cold and uncomfortable. She braced herself and hurried to the luggage carousel.

At least business was booming with Bob at the helm.

She found her bag and walked through the arrivals hall and out into bright sunshine. A new Range Rover was parked in the pick-up area. A door held open. And as the sunshine warmed her bones, Hilary's body began to relax.

Ireland was weaving its magic and Hilary was still under its spell.

∿

ZACH AND POPPY sat at the busy bar and tucked into a huge bowl of chili. A grain of rice clung to Poppy's top lip and Zach leaned in to kiss it away.

"Seconds?" Poppy asked. Their body language was clear to everyone in the packed pub, the couple were besotted with each other.

"Only if you're on the menu," Zach replied and tearing a piece of garlic bread, dipped it in the rich dark sauce and held it out for Poppy.

"Your mum worked wonders with Bob to re-write the contract," Poppy said, taking a bite.

"Seems to have done," Zach replied. "You've kept your job and our relationship is public. Bob has even agreed that we can work together on some projects."

"She's amazing."

"Yes, Mum weaved her magic."

Zach thought about Jo and wondered exactly what had happened in Bob's office when Jo went to see him.

Bob had called Zach and said it had been lovely to have a little chat with his mother and that he'd spoken to Hilary who was so happy that their new chef was in love, she'd agreed to overlook their strict agency rule.

Zach had been puzzled, he hadn't expected Hilary to change her mind and had been sure that Poppy would lose her job, but the news was excellent. It was fantastic to show Poppy off and he'd asked her to move in. Zach felt delirious with joy that they were together and knew that his work would flow now and he'd be well ahead of Nancy's strict deadline.

Poppy was helping with the book and as she understood his job, they were going to make a cracking team.

He was due on location in a few days to start filming the TV series and couldn't wait to begin. The six-part programme would be shot over the next few weeks and the producer wanted one episode to be filmed on Zach's home turf in Westmarland. There was no gossip in the office that Hilary's marriage was in trouble and Zach suspected that Jo had managed to keep her relationship with Long Tom under wraps.

All was well.

"How's your brother?" Poppy asked.

"Working hard, probably playing harder," Zach replied. "I really miss him, I wish he'd come home for a visit, I'd love you to meet him." Zach made a mental note to call Jimmy and tell him about Poppy. He knew his big brother would be pleased.

"So your mum is opening the doors of Kirkton House again?" Poppy pushed their plates to one side. "Will you be helping?"

"Yes, I've said I'll sort the menus out and make sure the kitchen team knows what they're doing. If I fit it in on days off, it will work out OK, and I might even be able to do it when we're filming there. I want you to come with me."

Zach was looking forward to going home and knew that Poppy would love Kirkton House. Jo had told him that their old cook, Sandra, had already agreed to come back, on the understanding that she had younger chefs to work with.

"Your dad would be pleased," Poppy said softly.

Zach thought about his father and had no doubt at all that John would be happy that the old place was coming back to life. The restless gypsy had settled at Kirkton House and found new roots when he fell in love with Jo. He'd loved the very bones of the building and Zach knew that John would be watching from above and smiling down on them all.

But Zach couldn't help wonder what his father would have made of Long Tom.

"I'm sure Dad's happy," Zach nodded. "Should we have another bottle?" He held up his empty glass.

"That would be lovely," Poppy smiled and kissed Zach gently on the lips.

34

Pete was thoughtful as he drove along the motorway, it had been an odd sort of a day and he would be grateful to get home, kick off his shoes and settle down with a glass of wine to think it all over.

His business had gone. Over three decades of trading had ended in the office of Mann & Co, in Carlisle, where Pete had just handed over the keys.

"You'll be a man of leisure now," Rob said as he shook Pete's hand and wished him good luck. "No doubt you've plenty planned to fill your days."

The truth of the matter was that Pete had bugger all to fill his days. In fact nothing in the pipeline, having hoped to be spending much of his newly created free time with Jo. But his plans were now in doubt as he felt sure that Jo had found another, even though he had no idea who it was.

He was angry with her for not giving him a chance.

She had been all over the place emotionally when he'd met her at the station and Pete wondered what had happened in London. Jo was in no mood for talking and he'd been in no mood to ask. They'd hardly spoken on the journey home and he hadn't seen her since.

Pete sighed with frustration, he should be happy, the sale had gone smoothly and he was now a free man. He'd passed the morning packing the last of the boxes of paperwork from his office and saying goodbye to his staff and many of his clients, who had stopped by to wish him well. There was a sombre atmosphere in the garage, for everyone knew that the building would have bulldozers moving in soon. The very fabric of a life they'd all enjoyed for so many years was making way for progress and the site would be unrecognisable in the weeks to come.

Pete had been subdued as he stood quietly and thanked the people that he'd come to know so well.

He would miss them.

Suddenly, out of nowhere, a car had sped across the forecourt, tooting its horn and to Pete's joy he saw Jo and Hattie waving as they skidded to a halt, catapulting Meg from the back seat onto Hattie's lap.

"Get that smelly thing off me!" Hattie yelled as she threw the door open and fell out of the car. She gripped a sticky looking object and jabbed frantically at Meg, who had pinned Hattie to the ground. Jo hurried to the rescue and pulled Hattie to her feet.

"Thought we'd come and wish you good luck," Jo said as they rushed in. She held a fancy carrier bag and Hattie gripped a tray.

As angry as he was with Jo, Pete couldn't help but smile. Her hair was tussled and her cheeks flushed. She wore an old hiking jacket and jeans and rubbed her hand fondly along Meg's head as she greeted everyone in the showroom.

"Sorry about the smell," Jo apologized, "Meg and I have been for a walk."

A muddy-looking substance was caked along the fur on the dog's back. Several people clasped their hands to their nose as Meg sat happily, thumping her tail on the polished floor. Pellets of hardened cowpat and soil scattered across the tiles. She wore a pink leather collar, which looked new to Pete, despite the mud-encrusted diamante studding. He wondered if Jo had been spending. Jo thrust out a bag to Pete and as he dismantled the package, a bottle of vintage wine appeared. It was neatly stored on a bed of straw, in a posh wooden box, engraved in gold lettering from Harrods.

"I thought you could toast your new life," Jo said.

"That's grand," Pete replied, "thanks very much."

"Better than my blasted biscuits," Hattie said, "not worth a dunk, they didn't last five minutes, even if they were from that snobby food hall." She held out her cake to Pete, "Get your laughing gear round this little lot, now this is something to sweeten your day."

Pete looked at Hattie's offering and contemplated handing it straight to Meg, but Hattie's expression was serious and she had a look of concern.

He reached out and took the cake then leaned in and brushing a layer of icing sugar away, kissed Hattie on her cheek.

"Thank you, Hattie, that's a very kind thing to do," Pete said softly then turned to Jo, "I appreciate the wine too."

More people had arrived and wanted to talk to Pete and he didn't notice when Jo and Hattie slipped away.

As Pete drove home, he wished that he'd had a chance to talk to Jo. He needed to clear the air and he also needed to know if she had found someone else. There was no point in him holding a torch if her heart lay elsewhere.

Pete decided that he'd take the turning to Kirkton Sowerby. It wasn't the day to be talking to Jo, but he'd go past the old house anyway. After all, from today, with his business gone, he'd have no real reason to be driving by.

With a heavy heart, Pete pulled off the motorway and made his way to the village.

~

"WELL I'M sure he appreciated our visit," Hattie said as she stood with Jo on the drive outside Kirkton House and stared up at a large sign that hung on a wrought iron frame.

"I've no doubt he did," Jo replied, "but I've no time to think of

Pete, we need to get to work." She paced up and down, contemplating the sign.

On the drive home from Pete's garage, Jo had determined to get moving, it was time to throw off the dust covers at Kirkton House and bring the place back to life. She'd decided that they could be open within weeks if she ran a tight schedule, possibly a month. Work would absorb and divert her from matters of the heart, and Pete and Long Tom could go on a back burner.

Jo had much to do.

"The sign needs re-painting," Jo said and made a note on her pad. She paced over the gravel with Meg at her heels and studied the herbaceous borders that lined the driveway. The gardens had been maintained since Jo closed the property but not to hotel standard and Jo looked at the about with fresh, critical eyes.

"I'm good at weeding," Hattie chirped up. She pulled at a plant and looked thoughtful.

"The only weed you're familiar with is in one of Mattie's roll-ups," Jo said and brushed Hattie's hand away from the lush Lady's Mantle.

"Ah, happy days..." Hattie sighed.

"Do you miss him?" Jo stopped and looked at her friend.

"Like plants need rain. I was as smitten as a kitten." Hattie's eyes were misty, "Mattie was my man."

Jo was moved. She walked over to Hattie and placed her arm around her shoulder. She'd been so wrapped up in herself lately, she hadn't stopped to consider that the Caribbean had left its mark on Hattie and her heart was clearly still bouncing along its shores.

"But, he'll be off with a new plane load of tourists, charming his way around the island." Hattie looked up at the sky where a plane flew high overhead. "I can't mope around."

"You can mope as much as you like," Jo said and distracted by the plane, stood alongside and remembered Hattie's antics with Mattie during their holiday.

The two women were lost in thought and hadn't noticed that Meg had wandered away. She stopped by the edge of the driveway and twitched her nose.

Meg smelt rabbit.

On the other side of the road, a bunny had hopped into the long grass leading to the village green, its soft fluffy tail glinting in the sunshine. In moments, the old dog was reliving her youth and with a puppy-like pounce, she shot out of the gates and hurtled across the road.

A white van came around the corner.

The driver had his eyes on the road but when a large black shape leapt across his vision, there was nothing he could do. He threw himself on the brakes and was torn with fear and horror as the shape hit the bonnet of his van with a heavy thud, then spun into the air.

Jo heard the squeal of brakes and shot round. As she looked anxiously for Meg she heard Hattie swear.

"Oh, Christ... NO!" Hattie's voice seemed to come from the distance and man was running towards them.

"Don't look love!" he shouted and held out his arms to try and grab Jo as she moved forward in a trance-like state. "I didn't stand a chance, it leapt out," the man said.

Jo pushed him to one side and ran to the kerb.

The white van stood at an angle with the driver's door flung wide. Meg had been tossed to the side of the road and lay on long grass on the other side. Her prostrate body was still but her paws twitched.

Jo's head spun and her heart pounded so hard that she thought she would fall and fighting the dizziness that engulfed her, threw herself beside her pet then gently placed her head on the silky body.

Hattie raced over the road and knelt beside her.

"Get the vet," Jo whispered.

Meg's eyes were open and her breath came in slow pants and Jo stoked very gently, terrified of hurting the dog further. "It's alright my old beauty," Jo whispered as her lungs filled and sobs threatened to rack her body, "I'm here, I'm here..." Salty tears cascaded onto the motionless fur. A wound on the side of Meg's body seeped over Jo's legs.

Hattie stood back.

Thank god she had her mobile in her pocket. She'd phoned the vet and prayed that he would jump in a jumbo and arrive at any minute. Half the village had arrived and keeping their distance, looked anxiously on as Jo lay alongside her dying dog. The van driver was shaking and muttering that there was nothing he could do and someone held out a mug of sweet tea, encouraging him to take a sip.

The minutes seemed like hours to the assembled crowd.

PETE ROUNDED the bend and was surprised to see a commotion in front of the hotel.

There must have been an accident.

A van was skewiff across the road, its door flung open and a crowd had gathered to one side. He slowed down and unable to get near the hotel, parked in the pub car park and ran towards the scene.

Hattie hurried towards him.

"Oh, thank god you're here!" she cried.

"What's to do?" Pete looked anxiously at the crowd.

"It's Jo, well Meg..."

Pete needed no further words and pushed his way through the throng as people stood back to let him through.

His heart collapsed when he saw Jo and Meg.

Jo lay prostrate on the grass, covered in blood and was soothing the injured dog. Pete moved swiftly to her side and knelt down.

"It's alright, lass," Pete said softly, "I'm here now." He felt for a pulse on Meg's neck. It was faint but there was no doubt in his mind that the animal only had moments. He heard a car pull up and a voice called out.

"Here's the vet!"

Pete put his arm around Jo and together their fingers entwined as they gently stroked the cooling body.

"Let me through!" The vet could be heard and Pete was aware of the man kneeling alongside.

But Jo was not to be moved and Pete indicated that the man should hold back. Meg's breathing had slowed and her eyes closed.

"She's gone," Pete whispered and held Jo tighter. "It's all over, lass, she's gone."

35

In the days and weeks that followed Meg's death Jo threw herself into her work. She was courteous and polite with the reappointed staff and civil to the painters and decorators as they worked their way through the refurbishment schedule. Blinds, flooring and furniture were ordered for the outbuildings, which now housed six good sized workshops and Sandra had returned to the kitchen to take charge of recruiting a new team.

Everything was going to plan and with a new website up and running, enquiries began to pour in.

On a mid-week morning, Hattie had been dispatched to Butterly to pick up new lamps for the workshops and as she lumbered under the weight of her packages, she bumped into Pete wandering down the high street.

"Bleedin' hell, Pete Parks," Hattie exclaimed when she saw him, "you look like a lost dog wandering about."

"Poor choice of words," Pete replied as he reached out to help with the packages.

"Shite, I'm sorry," Hattie shook her head. "Fancy a coffee?"

They made themselves comfortable in the Lemon Drop Cafe, where Hattie ordered a mountain of toasted teacakes. It was a damp and miserable day and she attempted to lighten the mood.

"Started dating yet?" Hattie asked.

"No," Pete replied as Marlene approached with their coffee.

"You want to get yerself on t'internet. Hattie took the steaming mug from Marlene and reached for the sugar, "Wall-to-wall crumpet online, all gagging for a man, eh Marlene?" Hattie looked up. "How's your Jack's prostate?" Marlene glared at Hattie and flounced off.

"I'm not dating anyone," Pete said firmly.

"Well, maybe get yourself on some of the courses Jo's got set up, bound to be a surplus of singles, middle-aged, well-heeled, up for a bit..." Hattie trailed off and bit into a teacake.

Pete shook his head. It wasn't worth getting into a conversation on the subject of dating. He'd never date again, unless it was Jo.

"How's is she?" Pete asked, hardly able to say Jo's name.

"Like a steel door," Hattie replied. "I've never seen her like this before, the shutters are down and she's not coming out."

Hattie took a sip of her drink and thought about her friend. Jo was going through the motions with work but seemed to be in emotional shutdown since Meg had died. "Perhaps it's brought back John's death too and she's mourning all over again."

"Aye, more than likely," Pete agreed. "It can do that to you."

He'd hardly seen Jo since the accident. When he called at the hotel, she'd little time for him and was always busy, refusing any invitations to go out, claiming that she had much to do and deadlines to meet.

"It'll pass," Hattie said doubtfully. "Not eating that?" she stared at the teacake beside Pete's coffee.

"Help yourself." Pete pushed the plate across the table. Crumbs flew as Hattie tucked in.

Marlene sidled over and flicked at the table with a cloth. She leaned in and began to pick at Pete's lapel where a crumb had landed. Her cleavage lay inches from his face.

"You need a housekeeper," Marlene whispered, "don't be letting yourself go."

"I can manage," Pete moved back.

"I can spare a few hours a week," Marlene winked. "If you know what I mean..."

"I've told your Jack he can get some Viagra from the doctor," Hattie said, "with his condition being so bad." She pushed her empty plate towards Marlene. "You need some new buttons on that blouse."

Hattie stood up and Marlene, glaring at her old enemy, curled her rouged lip in a snarl.

"Thought about trying t'internet yerself?" Marlene snapped. "Try deserted-and-desperate-dot-com."

"Nowt desperate about me," Hattie grinned. "I've still got the old magic, eh Pete?" She rummaged around for her packages and with Pete's help made her way out of the cafe.

"Silly cow," Hattie said as they stepped out onto the street. "Look, it's brightening up a bit."

They crossed the road and strolled over a bridge where the river Bevan meandered below.

"You'll be coming to the grand opening?" Hattie's car was parked at an angle, on double yellow lines. She turned to study Pete.

"Am I invited?"

"Well, I'm inviting you even if she doesn't get her finger out and ask those that matter."

"Then I'll be there."

"Good, it's only two weeks away and god knows how we'll manage it, but she wants to preview the place to the locals and the press before we officially open the doors."

"Sounds grand."

"It'll probably be mayhem but nowt we can't cope with," Hattie said as she watched Pete bend to stack the packages neatly on the back seat. As he closed the door and turned to her, Hattie reached out and touched his arm. "Don't give up, she needs both of us," she said earnestly.

"She makes it damn hard," Pete replied.

"I'm sure you'll think of something to bring her back to life."

"Aye, lass, you're right, I shouldn't be moping about, there's plenty to be getting on with." Pete thought about the farm sale at Marland the following morning, there were a couple of old tractors that he'd got his eye on.

"Well, keep well away from that one!" Hattie nodded towards the cafe and grinned as Pete burst out laughing. "You'll have more than crumbs on your lapel if you get lost down that wrinkled old cleavage." Hattie turned and opened the driver's door. "Now bugger off and find something worthwhile to do!"

She slipped behind the wheel and started the engine and as it roared into life, Pete leapt back on the pavement and watched Hattie take flight across a line of oncoming cars.

"I'll see thee!" She waved through an open window.

"Aye, lass," Pete said and raised his hand. "I'll see thee, too."

~

LONG TOM WAS IN TURMOIL. For the first time in years, he wanted a drink. He stood on the patio of his west coast hotel and looked out at the sparkling sea beyond.

The last time he'd stepped on the silky soft beach, Jo had been with him.

He thought about their picnic on the boat and blissful days at Eddie's plantation and as he remembered, his heart was heavy and he knew that the only thing that would make him feel better lay waiting, like the devil, in the bar next door.

In recent days, he'd completed his media sessions. Photography to promote the new album had been done and his PR team was delighted. Interviews would appear in relevant journals and newspapers throughout Europe to promote his forthcoming tour. There had even been time for a video to accompany his new song. Filmed at Eddie's plantation, it was short and simple, with a melancholy Long Tom playing the grand piano in the guest suite. As he sang, linen drapes billowed, while his words drifted across the shaded room, out through the open doors and over the magnificent views of the east coast below.

Don't forget me... Don't forget me....

It was a moving and poignant few minutes of film and Long Tom's record label were confident that they had a massive hit.

Eddie had left that morning to spend time with his family at their London home and now there was only one interview remaining. It was with an American journalist and scheduled for that afternoon.

Long Tom turned from the beach and stepped into the apartment. It was his usual suite and very familiar, but everywhere he looked, he could see Jo.

The concierge, having been unable to locate Jo after she left, had kept her red dress and delivered it on Long Tom's return. It hung on a hanger in his bedroom and despite having been cleaned, still smelt of her perfume every time he buried his head in the silky folds. He remembered her soft, yielding flesh and ached with a hunger he'd never known. It was all-encompassing and corrosive and Long Tom felt emotionally ripped apart by his obsession, fearing that the only thing that would soothe his demons was just a phone call away.

How easy it would be to order a bottle of Jack Daniels and give in!

Jo hadn't spoken to him since he'd seen her in London. His calls rang out and despite leaving messages she never got back to him. He couldn't recall ever feeling this way before, even when he met Hilary.

Hilary.

He could hardly bear to be with her.

What a dismal experience it had been in London. She was obsessed with the property in Ireland and Long Tom was happy to let her get on with it. Boss had told him to keep an eye on the gardener over there, but Long Tom barely took interest. As long as his peacocks were OK, she could do what she wanted. The marriage that he'd longed for, to help him through his later years, was failing and he couldn't summon up the energy to try and save it.

Just a sad old man... Long Tom thought as he waited for the American to arrive.

He'd spent the previous day with Eddie and the kids and even the gentle calm and faith of his Caribbean family hadn't improved his mood.

They'd travelled in trucks to Bath, a resort on the east coast. Setting out and driving through the lovely countryside until they found the perfect picnic spot alongside a party of cheerful Bajans, also on an excursion. Women of all sizes, dressed in bright clothes and children with pretty beads in their hair, held coolers and baskets, while men carried their drinks of choice to blankets and fold-up chairs, laid out by the sea. The breeze was balmy and the sun hot as the adults sat and limed in the shade, the children played happily in the shallows of the sea.

It should have been perfect but Long Tom had been restless and spent most of the afternoon pacing the beach. Eddie, sensing his friend's anxiety, tried hard to talk, but Long Tom had diverted the questions and refused to be embroiled.

A knock sounded on the door of the suite.

Long Tom sighed.

He'd showered and changed and made an effort but the last thing he wanted to do was sit and talk about his life. He opened the door and stood back.

A tall blonde stepped forward, "Long Tom Hendry," she said, "pleased to meet you." She smiled as she walked past.

Long Tom thought he might explode and had to get out of the suite. It was beyond him to be interviewed in a room where memories of Jo hung like the dress in the closet.

"Don't sit down," he said. "We can do the interview on the move, I feel like company." He picked up his Stetson, closed the door to the suite and walked purposefully ahead, with the blonde struggling to keep up.

At the concierge desk, he asked for a car.

"Yes sir, Mr Hendry, where are you going to?"

"The Lime Inn," Long Tom said and reaching for his Stetson, placed it on his head then moved quickly out of the foyer.

"This is a first!" the blonde exclaimed as she ran to keep up.

"And probably a last," Long Tom whispered as he climbed into the waiting car.

~

EXCITED to be getting out of London and heading north, Zach and Poppy held hands as Zach drove steadily through the heavy streams of traffic. Their destination was Westmarland and they planned to arrive by early evening at Kirkton House.

Zach had been filming over the last few weeks and his series would soon be complete with an episode to be filmed in the north, where Zach would trace his roots and forage on his home turf, perhaps even cook in the kitchen of the house that had led him to restaurant fame and earned him his Michelin stars.

He couldn't wait to get home.

The trip coincided perfectly with his mother's plans for the grand opening and he would have time to discuss menus with Sandra and work with her new staff.

"You'll love Kirkton House," Zach told Poppy.

They'd stopped at a Starbucks on the motorway and sat in a window booth sipping frothy cappuccinos. The film crew would be staying in the pub over the road and Zach anticipated the excitement in the village as word spread of the prodigal's return.

"Mum doesn't sound herself though," Zach said. He thought about recent calls home and how flat Jo had seemed. Meg's death had hit her hard and Zach hoped that it hadn't stirred up too many painful memories.

"She'll be happy to see you, it will cheer her up," Poppy said as she licked chocolatey froth off her lip.

She reached for her tote bag and brought out a folder. It contained proofs for Zach's book and together they poured over the pages, hardly believing that the stunning artwork compiled in the draft of, Foraging with Friends by the Gypsy Chef, was attributed to Zach's recipes and written text. Nancy had certainly pulled out all the stops with her team and the book would be ready for publication to coincide with transmission of the television series.

"Better get going," Zach said and helped Poppy to pack the book back into her bag.

As they linked arms and wandered out to the car, Zach's phone rang and he dug deep in his pocket to retrieve it.

"Hi Zach, Heidi here, I've got some interviews lined up for you while you're in the north."

"I'll put Poppy on, she can take details."

"Don't worry, I can email stuff over. You're going to be busy, local-boy-makes-good and all that sort of stuff, the northern press can't wait!"

"That's great, is Bob happy with everything?"

"Ecstatic. He keeps talking about his pension pot, I think you're about to hit the big time."

"What about Hilary?" Zach thought of the other partner in the business who, having been hell-bent on signing Zach never seemed to take much interest.

"She seems to be on some sort of sabbatical," Heidi's voice softened. "I've heard a rumour that her marriage is in trouble."

"What sort of trouble?" Zach tensed.

"I don't know, but she is married to a rock star, anything could happen."

Heidi wished them both a safe journey and ended the call.

Zach jumped into the car and started the engine.

"Is everything OK?" Poppy asked.

"Yes, fine," he replied as he reversed out of the parking space, but he made a mental note to speak to his mother. Had she really ended her relationship with Long Tom? If not, there would be fireworks if Hilary ever found out.

Perhaps there was more to Jo's doldrums than met the eye. Zach hoped that she wasn't about to be named in a media divorce case, the press would love it: Celebrity Chef's Mother in Affair with Chef's Boss!

Zach decided to phone Jimmy later. His brother would know

what the buzz was and if he didn't he'd have good advice on how to deal with it.

Determined to stay light-hearted, Zach winked at Poppy and pressing his foot down, accelerated onto the motorway and continued their journey.

36

Jo was on a mission. Her determination to re-open the hotel and keep to a tight schedule, strengthened as the days went by. Surprisingly, it hadn't been as difficult as she had first thought.

The old place was still in good order and despite having been closed up for over a year, with the cleaning team reinstated, they'd soon given everywhere a complete overhaul and in no time the rooms and hallways had come back to life, which is more than could be said for Jo.

Meg's death had been devastating.

Jo kept telling herself that it was only an animal. A family pet, neither human nor related and she couldn't understand her feelings of complete and utter anguish and despair. Determined to keep her feelings private, Jo carried on with her daily duties and smiled and chatted with the staff, as deliveries came in and plans began to fall into shape. But at night, she couldn't stop crying and her pillow was wet as her troubled mind finally fell into a deep and unsettled sleep. Hattie tried endlessly to help and encouraged Jo to talk, but that seemed impossible and Jo knew that Hattie felt helpless that she couldn't help her friend.

It will pass... Hattie had told Jo. Be patient.

Pete buried Meg in the garden.

In the meadow beyond the wrought iron gates, a mere pounce away from the stile that led to the fields and fells, where Jo and Meg had spent so many happy times, enjoying their daily walks.

Jo wandered down there each day at dusk and stood beside the mound of dark earth that now had a shadow of new growth. She'd scattered wild flower seeds and soon all traces of her pet would be buried beneath a carpet of colour, blending in with the surrounding wildness.

John's ashes were scattered in this meadow too and as the sun set, Jo spoke to him and asked him to help her find her way. She knew that what she was feeling was grief. A deep pain, soothed and subdued by the Caribbean holiday, had returned and memories of those she'd lost, including her parents, haunted Jo.

Meg's shocking death had been a catalyst, a jolt.

A reminder of loves she'd never know again, both parental and personal, for Jo was sure that she'd never love anyone as she'd loved John.

An old gypsy caravan stood in the corner of the meadow. Our vardo, John had called it, using the gypsy term for the pretty, horse-drawn painted home on huge wooden wheels. The caravan was derelict now, the wood rotting and iron frame rusting as it stood unprotected from the elements. Jo remembered how they used to escape from the hotel, running hand-in-hand to the meadow to hide from the world. Giggling as they locked the door and made love in the afternoon with children, family, business, cares and worries all put to one side for a few stolen moments that had kept their marriage alive. In recent years, Meg had always bounded alongside and howled when they closed the caravan door, lying at the base of the steps then leaping with joy when they reappeared and made a great fuss of their faithful animal.

Now, Jo couldn't bear to go near the vardo and it sat as a ghostly reminder of times she'd lost. She knew she should have it restored. Guests would love it, it could be a real novelty item, but she hadn't the heart and kept her distance.

Jo couldn't think of Pete or Long Tom.

She knew that she should but her emotions were numb and her heart in no place to make amends. Pete, who had been so kind and gentle with Jo when Meg died, looked forlorn whenever he called round. He subtly made suggestions that maybe she'd like a change, perhaps a meal out. But Jo turned him down each time and in doing so, felt worse and the guilt doubled. Long Tom had left so many messages, Jo had lost count and hadn't returned any of his calls, the feeling of reproach heightened her anxiety but she didn't know how to deal with it and in so doing, did nothing.

The only thing that kept her going was work.

Soon, Kirkton House would be back in business and Jo couldn't wait. Work had always been her salvation and her therapy and no doubt would be again.

The grand opening was around the corner.

Already they had enquires for rooms and the first few bookings were trickling in. Hattie, to Jo's amazement, had taken herself off on a course and was now computer literate. When the new booking system arrived, Hattie had taken charge and with the help of two new recruits in reception, was fully conversant in marketing and promotions and had set up a data base from the old hotel guest ledger. Newsletters had been sent out, detailing prices and courses and Kirkton House even had a Facebook page and Twitter account.

Zach would be back and although Jo knew Sandra had a team that could easily manage the kitchen, he would wave his magic and soon the kitchen would be filled with amazing smells and creations that would be the talking point for miles around. Sandra was far too long in years to work full-time but she was thrilled to be part of the business and her new recruits seemed eager to learn, especially as they knew that a chef with two Michelin stars was coming home to head-up the new menus and train them all. And he would make regular visits in times to come. Sandra couldn't wait for her favourite young man to come back and Jo knew that the faithful cook was counting off the days.

There was much excitement in the village too.

Word of the film crew's imminent arrival had become more than a rumour. The landlord of the pub had broken the news that the production company had confirmed that they would be taking all his rooms for several days. The first episode of, Foraging with Friends by the Gypsy Chef, was to be based in Kirkton Sowerby and as most of the villagers knew Zach, they were brushing up on their knowledge of wild herbs and plants and hoping to be in on the action. Jobs were available at the hotel and many of those who'd worked there before soon found themselves reinstated. New positions would become available too, when the workshops opened and courses were running. The village had come alive again!

Now Jo needed to come alive again too.

But as she went about her daily chores, the sadness seemed to deepen and Jo wondered how on earth she was going to shake herself out of it.

She tried to remember Hattie's words.

It will pass...

She repeated them like a mantra, and hoped and prayed that it would.

37

J immy was enjoying an evening out. The rum shops on the east coast road lay ahead like magnets and together with a group of friends, he planned to sample them all.

He turned off the main road and headed to Consett's Bay. The truck was full and the boys on the flat-bed had already opened a case of beer as they prepared for their sunset rum shop hop, while Mattie sat in the passenger seat and stared out at the road that tumbled towards the coast. Jimmy had agreed that Mattie would take over the driving, it was good for Jimmy to have a night off to relax, the club was busy and there had been too few nights out of late.

Mattie was quiet as he stared out at the rugged cliffs surrounding the bay. The sea was at low tide and he remembered walking along the beach with Hattie, pointing out shells, unusual shaped drift wood and pretty coral. Hattie had been in awe of the tranquil environment, with only the sound of trees, waves and the occasional boat. Mattie visualized her excited face glowing with childlike joy as they'd wandered hand-in-hand and watched shoals of flying fish leap out of the water.

He missed his English rose.

Hattie was different to the rest. Tourists came and went, on the island for a couple of weeks, searching for pleasure and fun, regardless of the cost, both financial and emotional. Women spent their money and Mattie pandered to their emotions, ensuring that their memories of Barbados left them with warm happy thoughts for the dark winter days at home. But this time the emotion had left Hattie's footprint on his heart and for the first time that he could ever remember, it hurt.

"You're very quiet, man," Jimmy said. He leaned one arm out of the window as he maneuvered the truck down the steep winding track. Whoops and shouts could be heard from the flat-bed as the boys braced themselves and held onto their beer.

"Fuh' real," Mattie replied.

"What's on your mind?"

Mattie refused to be drawn and pointed to a bar, tucked away behind a building that was used as a fishery for boats unloading the day's catch. "Go-across," he said and sat forward to checkout the gaggle of men gathered round an upturned box, placed on a stool. They slapped domino counters down and gesticulated in between sips of beer and rum.

"Want to talk about it?" Jimmy asked as he parked up.

"Man, yu hurtin' up my head," Mattie snapped and leapt out, "get me a Ju-C." His phone rang and he wandered away to find a quiet spot.

Jimmy left Mattie to his call and went over to his friends at the bar. Flasks of dark rum had appeared with bottles of water and ginger ale, alongside an old plastic box filled with ice and, once drinks were poured, the group toasted each other and began to tell jokes.

Jimmy looked up.

Mattie was hurrying towards him and as he moved, he held up his hand and indicated that Jimmy join him.

Jimmy picked up his drink and walked out.

"Yes man, what's going on?" Jimmy said.

"Everythin' cool but tha's a rock singer in the bar."

"Long Tom?"

Alarm bells rang.

"Fuh' real," Mattie replied.

"How long has he been there?"

" 'Bout a quarter of a bottle of JD."

"Jesus!" Jimmy threw his drink to the ground and reached in a pocket for his keys. "Can you sort the boys out?"

"Sho' t'ing," Mattie replied and reached for his phone. As Jimmy explained that he had a problem at his bar, Mattie arranged alternative transport for the party and in moments the pair had leapt back in the truck and thundered up the road.

"I can't believe he's fallen off the wagon," Jimmy said as the countryside flew by. Local Bajans taking their evening stroll, jumped back as dust billowed up from the fast-moving vehicle. "I think we might be too late to help him."

"Fuh' real," Mattie whispered. Fuh' real...

JIMMY SWORE at the traffic as he flew along the highway. Half of the population of Barbados seemed hell-bent on taking to the roads for a night out and amongst the stream of cars that moved slowly ahead, an old bus had collided with a bollard at a junction, spilling several rows of church-going passengers off their bench seats.

Old ladies, in their finest, bearing bonnets, bags and brollies descended on the driver and began to curse. Their freshly starched dresses and tan-coloured stockings a stark contrast to the hot dark tarmac on the road.

"This is mayhem," Jimmy said as he weaved carefully through the throng. "We'll never get there."

"Take a chill pill," Mattie muttered and pointed to a gap in the traffic.

Jimmy mounted the kerb and with Mattie clinging to the dashboard, hit a hard left. The tyres on the truck screeched as they sped along a narrow alleyway that opened to a series of steep and winding roads, before finally linking up with the south coast road.

They were moments from the club.

"Who the hell served him?" Jimmy yelled into his phone. The call was on loud speaker and Mattie shook his head as he listened to the conversation between Jimmy and a manager.

"He brought a bottle in with him," the distraught manager replied. "An American girl got it next door, you know we'd never go against your orders and serve him alcohol."

"Cheese on bread..." Mattie muttered and sucked on his teeth.

"He's making one hell of a scene out here on the deck," the manager said anxiously.

"I'm on it." Jimmy floored the gas pedal.

His heart was pounding and he felt desperate to help Long Tom, the man was a friend and if he'd fallen off the wagon, something big had happened to cause it. Jimmy thought about Jo but refused to linger on Long Tom's relationship with his mother.

Right now, he had to get to his club!

The Gap was backed up with traffic and the sidewalk spilled a mass of people, dressed in their finery as they slowly promenaded in a busy procession, heading for popular bars and night clubs. Jimmy cursed and threw his hands in the air in frustration, as the vehicles ahead came to a standstill in the hot and humid road.

For once, Mattie ignored the profusion of beautiful women sashaying before him. He grabbed the steering wheel and shouted, "Yu go!" then pushed Jimmy to one side and leapt into the driver's seat.

"Drive around the back!" Jimmy yelled and began to run in a snake-like path to get to his club.

In moments, he'd arrived.

The hostesses either side of the entrance stairway, looked nervous and stood back as Jimmy took the steps two at a time. He stopped on the outside deck and looked above the swaying mass of people, who were being entertained by a six-piece jazz band, playing on a raised platform in the corner.

In the centre of the band stood Long Tom, his eyes closed as he threw back his head and sang.

The crowd went wild.

Despite Long Tom's garbled verse and staggered motions, they were exulted and surprised to have free entertainment from such a famous artiste. They cheered and clapped and begged for more.

Long Tom held a glass in one hand and the rich amber contents spilled onto the floor as he staggered around the stage, slurring his words. He paused and downed the remains of his drink, then held out the glass for a refill and a tall blonde sprang forward to top up the glass with the final drops from a bottle of Jack Daniels.

Jimmy made eye contact with the club's plain-clothes security guards, who wore discreet microphones to communicate between themselves and the club's management team. The band had begun an intro for another song and the lead saxophonist jumped on a table to belt out the familiar opening bars. With the crowd momentarily diverted from Long Tom, Jimmy gave a signal and as the rest of the band hit the high notes and the music became deafening, the guards moved in.

Within seconds, Long Tom had disappeared and the American found herself out on the street.

Jimmy made his way to the back of the club, greeting familiar faces as though nothing was wrong. He high-fived his way past the packed dancefloor and through the crowded bar and when he reached the kitchen, shook the hand of his head of security who stood like a mountain, guarding the door.

"He's not so good, boss," the man said and indicated to the rear of the kitchen.

In a corner, Long Tom was hunched over a deep sink.

Mistress Nysha, the head cook in the kitchen, held onto his shoulders and rubbed hard on his back.

"Lawd help muh," she said. "Daddy, yu sho got it bad."

When she was sure that there wasn't an ounce left in Long Tom's stomach to be projected into her pot sink, she nodded to the two security men either side, then very carefully, they lowered the crumpled figure onto a chair and supported his lifeless body. Long Tom's head hung limply to one side and tears poured down his cheeks. His face was ashen.

Jimmy leaned down and reached for the rock singer's hand, "You OK, buddy?" Jimmy asked and searched the traumatized face for a sign of recognition. He knew that this sudden bout of drinking could be fatal if it continued.

Long Tom's eyes were closed and his breathing shallow but Jimmy felt a tightening of fingers around his hand.

"I want to be sober..." Long Tom whispered and opened his eyes. The haunted look of pain that implored for help, sent shivers down Jimmy's spine and his heart gave a desperate lurch as Long Tom held on.

"It's done, it's all OK, buddy, I've gottcha..." Jimmy whispered and with the greatest care, as if handling a new born, pushed his arm under Long Tom's shoulder and eased him to his feet. Strong hands and muscled torsos reached in and helped and within moments Long Tom was carried discreetly through the dark corridors of the arena and out to Mattie's waiting vehicle.

"Cheese on bread," Mattie said as Long Tom was laid on the back seat. Mattie shrugged off his jacket and folded it into a pillow, which he placed under the comatose singer's head. Mistress Nysha had found a blanket and tucked it gently around the sleeping body.

"Yu' look after dat boy, he sure is ill." She looked sad as she shook her head and made a little sign of the cross across the front of her starched white jacket, "My good Lord, help him."

Jimmy turned to thank his team.

He hugged Mistress Nysha and embraced the security staff, then touched knuckles with his manager. They all nodded solemnly and stood respectfully back as Mattie fired the engine. Jimmy knew that the night's events would never be gossiped, his staff were as loyal as Mistress Nysha's Lord.

He leapt into the passenger seat and Mattie slowly inched the truck forward. Large doors were opened and the vehicle passed through.

"Where to, man?" Mattie asked.

"Eddie's plantation," Jimmy replied, "but we have to make a stop on the way."

"Sho' t'ing," Mattie said and paying careful attention not to jolt or disturb his sleeping cargo drove swiftly into the night.

Under the protection of Jimmy and Mattie, Long Tom was whisked across the island to Eddie's plantation and met by the house-keeper, who had been alerted and hurriedly unlocked the deserted house. She stood discreetly to one side as they carried Long Tom to the guest room, where they'd laid him carefully on the bed.

"I should send for a doctor," Jimmy whispered as he went around the room, opening shutters to let the cool night breeze waft over Long Tom.

Mattie stared at the inert figure and shook his head.

Long Tom was sweating profusely and tossing around, he groaned as if in agony, while his limbs twitched and hands shook.

"Yu' need to get him to drink," Mattie said.

They stared at a bottle that Jimmy had placed on the bedside cabinet.

Beyond the glass, in an old-fashioned receptacle, a dark brown brew, with a layer of muddy-looking froth, lay menacingly.

"I don't want to kill him," Jimmy replied.

"Have faith, man."

THEY'D MADE a stop on their way to Eddie's plantation and Jimmy had leapt out of the truck. A little chattel house stood alone in the moonlight, with thick vegetation spilling out from lop-sided bricks that supported the rickety structure. Jimmy heard a dog howl and shivered as he looked around at his surroundings.

The humid night air was cloying and sinister.

A noise from the porch made him turn and as he approached the steps to the house, he heard the sound of a rocker, creaking slowly in the night.

"Wha' de white boy dun now?"

A voice cried out and startled Jimmy.

The old woman began to cackle as she swayed gently from her position on the porch, "He sho' is stupid," she said.

Jimmy moved forward and searched in the darkness until the bulky shape became clearer, "We need your help."

"Sho' t'ing yu' do," she replied. "He need fix-up good dis time."

"Alcohol," Jimmy stated, knowing that whatever psychic powers the old woman possessed, they were already one step ahead of him.

"Yu' find help in de kitchen."

She continued to sway, her hands knotted over the folds of a stained cotton dress that covered her ample frame.

Jimmy hesitated as he stepped into the one-roomed shack, then remembering his cargo in the car, moved quickly and began to search. He didn't need to look far. Beside a dusty cupboard, on a cracked work surface, covered with bits of twig and leaves, a little bottle stood. A silver beam peeped out from behind a dark cloud and illuminated the glass in the moonlight and Jimmy was certain that the bottle gave off an iridescent glow.

As if in a trance, he was drawn towards it and reached out.

The bottle felt warm and his fingers tingled as he gripped tightly. Shaking, he turned and fled the room but pulled up abruptly by the old woman.

"How much?" Jimmy asked.

The sum she requested made him gasp, but he counted out the notes and tucked them into the claws of her leather-like hand.

"Make sho' he drink it all," she warned and resumed her rocking.

Jimmy thanked the old woman and fled to the truck. Within seconds Mattie had started the engine and they pulled away.

Now the two men stared at the bottle. It seemed to shimmer in the dimly lit room.

"Wake him up," Jimmy said.

They moved forward and reached out. Mattie shook Long Tom's shoulders as Jimmy picked up the bottle and removed the cap. Long Tom groaned and shook, his body was on fire and perspiration oozed from every pore. His skin had a deathly tinge and for a moment Jimmy wondered if he should have hospitalised the singer but, urged on by Mattie, Jimmy reached for Long Tom's head and put the bottle to his lips.

"Come on buddy, take a drink..."

Long Tom thrashed and kicked and it was all that they could do to steady the man and hold his head in a vice-like grip.

"Drink man, drink!" Mattie cried as Jimmy began to pour.

Long Tom spluttered and swore and the acid-like liquid splashed on the pillows.

"Christ, we'll kill him!" Jimmy watched the dark stains eating into the fabric.

"Keep pouring!" Mattie shouted and with strength neither knew they possessed, they gripped Long Tom and tilted his head, thrusting the bottle into his mouth.

The liquid slowly disappeared.

Long Tom stopped thrashing. His limbs became still and his head rolled to one side. They gently lowered him back on the bed and Jimmy reached for a sheet. He placed it around Long Tom and together with Mattie, moved back to study the motionless form.

Long Tom had stopped breathing.

"He dead," Mattie announced.

"Oh Christ..." Jimmy felt the room sway before him.

"Man, we killed him!"

"Oh Jesus..."

"Dem gods don't help yu' now," Mattie eyes were wide and he stared with horror at Long Tom.

Jimmy began to walk backwards. He wanted to look away but was transfixed by the lifeless body.

Mattie grabbed hold of his arm and hissed, "What de hell we gonna do?"

They stumbled to the open doors and pushed the muslin drapes to one side. The east coast lay ahead, under the cover of night, and as Jimmy heard waves crashing on the distant rocks, he contemplated throwing himself off the balcony.

"Where's my Stetson?" A voice called out and Mattie fell to his knees, garbling every prayer he could think of to all his Rasta gods who'd sent the ghost of Long Tom to haunt him.

Jimmy spun around.

His jaw fell as he looked on the smiling face of Long Tom, who'd moved himself into an upright position.

"You're alive!"

"Could murder a fruit punch," Long Tom said and closed his eyes.

Mattie heard the word murder and groaned, then collapsed onto the polished floorboards. Jimmy stepped over the wailing Rasta and reached out for Long Tom's hand. The skin was warm and fingers strong.

"Thank god," Jimmy whispered.

"I'm kinda tired," Long Tom mumbled.

"You rest buddy, I'll make the punch." Jimmy tucked the sheet carefully then stepped away from the sleeping figure.

He leaned in to turn off the lamp by the bed and glanced at the old woman's bottle, now discarded and strewn to one side. The glass was dull and cracked, with dirt caked around the neck. As Jimmy picked it up, the bottle felt cold and appeared aged, the edges around the neck rough and sediment lay in the bottom.

He shook his head in wonder.

Only in Barbados... Jimmy muttered for the umpteenth time in his life and with a glance towards Mattie, closed his eyes and thanked whatever spirits had aided them that night.

38

T he garden at Flatterly Manor was show-stopping, especially late evening and had she been a more social person, Hilary would have opened the grounds to the public, to share her new-found joy with the countryside.

Until recently, Hilary had shown no more interest in flowers than the cost of the florist delivery from her local Knightsbridge shop, but now, she was entranced by the marvels of nature and what could be achieved.

But as the sun finally set and Hilary walked over the manicured lawn to the ornamental pool, she felt anxious. She hadn't heard from Long Tom in days and even when they hadn't been getting along, they had communicated in a fashion, if not by phone, by email or text.

She knew he was still in Barbados.

He was due back any time and Hilary wanted to talk to him. She needed to find out where he was going to be, so she could join him. But the last thing she wanted was a long flight to the Caribbean and hoped that he'd be back in London soon.

Hilary had been giving her marriage a great deal of thought.

The relationship with Seamus seemed pointless. He'd fascinated her with his gardening knowledge and achieved a great deal in a short space of time, no doubt due to the ridiculous amount of money she was paying him. But she'd been impressed with his green fingers that had wandered over more than the beds and borders at Flatterly Manor.

Already, she regretted their brief affair.

Sex with Seamus was like riding a rocket to the moon, a drug of frightening necessity in the short time she'd experienced it. It was illicit, brutal and completely without depth and had given Hilary an experience like no other. Now, as the novelty wore off, she thought of Long Tom and remembered his soft tender manner.

Love-making that went far beyond a quick shag behind the hollyhocks.

In their early days, Long Tom had been unable to perform. A symptom from his drug and alcohol addiction, but they'd soon overcome that and although he would never make love like a twenty-year-old again, there was something far more appealing and romantic in the ways of the Long Tom she'd known.

What a bloody fool she was! She wanted to have her cake and eat it and in so doing, had fallen in love with Ireland and out of love with her man.

Bob's conversation with Jo had deeply shocked Hilary. She'd tried hard not to break down when she stormed into Bob's office, but her heart had done somersaults as she glared at the beautiful woman who'd found a place in Long Tom's heart. Only now did Hilary understand what she stood to lose, how she'd taken her husband for granted and she realised that she desperately wanted him back.

Despite everything, she knew that she still loved him with every bone in her body.

Hilary paced the lawn furiously and when Seamus appeared through the darkness on his sit-on mower, bare-chested and beckoning her over, it was all Hilary could do not to raise her middle finger and yell at him.

It was time to talk to Bob.

He would know what to do. She would call him tomorrow and

with his cool karma-like attitude and wise words of wisdom, Hilary knew that he would find a solution.

As Hilary hurried back to the house, she hoped that she hadn't left it too late.

~

ZACH'S HOMECOMING was a quiet affair. He'd arrived with Poppy late evening, after a torturous journey north. The motorways had been congested with hold-ups, road-works and accidents, slowing the traffic to minimum speeds for most of the way and although the young couple felt tired, they soon picked up when they arrived safely at Kirkton House. After being welcomed by Jo and settled into Zach's old room, they'd quickly showered and changed, then joined Hattie in the bar for a drink before supper.

"Mum seems very subdued," Zach said as he watched Hattie expertly pour a pint of draft beer.

He sat on a tall stool alongside Poppy and nibbled from a bowl of nuts.

"Still mourning that daft mongrel," Hattie replied. "It seems to have set her off again."

Hattie didn't want Zach to know how worried she was about Jo. Over the last few weeks she had watched the plans to bring Kirkton House back to life being run with regimental-like precision, with Jo as the sergeant major. But it had been done without any feeling or passion, as though Jo was on a soulless military-style mission to get the job done.

Hattie pushed the pint across the bar towards Zach then poured similar for herself. She mixed a gin and tonic for Poppy.

"Cheers!" Hattie held up her glass, "bloody marvellous to have you home."

Zach toasted Hattie and Poppy and as he studied his surroundings, a glow warmed his soul.

The old place looked magnificent.

The ghost-like feel that had pervaded throughout in the days and months following his father's death, had gone.

The dust sheets were well and truly off.

Kirkton House felt alive and vibrant again and would soon be filled with people, enjoying the warm and welcoming atmosphere that so many had thrived on in the past. Zach thought that the new-look business was a great idea and was proud of his mother for finding a purpose that she believed in. The workshops would benefit not only residents, but locals and visitors alike and anyone fortunate to stay at the hotel would be pampered and cosseted, just like the old days when Kirkton House was a popular and much sought-after venue.

Zach couldn't wait to see Sandra in the morning and spend time with his mentor, he'd come up with some cracking ideas for the restaurant menu and hoped that she'd approve. Bob had told him that the production company wanted to film the reopening and use excerpts in the first episode of, Foraging with Friends by the Gypsy Chef. It would lend substance to the series and be a great promotion for the hotel too.

"Where is Mum?" Zach asked and reached for the nuts, "I'm starving."

"She's coming in from the garden now," Hattie said, nodding towards the conservatory where Jo could be seen, beyond the open doors, as she wandered along the path from the meadow. Her hands were tucked into her jacket pockets and her head held down. She looked a sad figure as the evening sun cast long shadows across the lawn.

How Hattie wished that the sun would rise and shine again for Jo.

"Have I kept you?" Jo asked as she stepped into the bar.

"Yes," Hattie said bluntly. "Now get yer gob round this and give us a smile." She handed Jo a large glass of Cointreau, a drink that had been Jo's life-blood in days gone by.

"To happy days!" Zach said as they all clinked glasses.

"I'll second that," Hattie replied and downed her pint.

They dined by candlelight in the panelled dining room. A light supper prepared earlier and left on a low heat in the Aga oven in Jo's kitchen. Sandra had made Zach's favourite comfort food, knowing that he would be tired after his long journey.

Hattie tucked in to the velvety smooth topping on the deep cottage pie and piled her plate high with baby carrots and tiny peas, harvested from Sandra's own garden. Pudding was a lemon meringue pie with a tangy filling and crisp sweet pastry.

Jo ate sparingly, pushing her food to one side.

"Absolutely delicious," Zach sighed happily and sat back. "Sandra hasn't lost her touch."

"The restaurant is already filling with bookings for the first couple of weeks and over half the bedrooms are taken," Hattie said, looking smug. Her new found computer literacy was working wonders in reception. Gone were the days of double-bookings and cock-ups with seating plans, Hattie had never really mastered the old-fashioned charts in years gone by and more latterly, left the computer technology to younger staff, but this time round she was taking control and was hugely satisfied with her work to date.

"How are the courses being received?" Zach asked.

"Back-to-back bookings," Hattie poured herself a glass of wine. "Pottery has sold out!"

She thought about her own creations that sat on windowsills either side of the workshop door. The masterpieces would entice the punters on other courses and they'd soon be queuing for a place with the potter.

"I didn't think the Shaman course would work," Jo said absent-mindedly, "but lots of places seem to have been taken."

Hattie coughed and began to clear the table. Word had got round about Hattie's experience in the tent and she hadn't mentioned to Jo that the course wasn't exactly as detailed in the prospectus. She also knew that a teepee on the croquet lawn was probably going to take a bit of persuasion, but Hattie decided that she would cross that bridge when they got to it.

"Would anyone like coffee?" Hattie asked.

"No," Zach said, "I think I'll be heading off to bed, we've got a very busy day tomorrow."

"Me too," Jo said. "The Cointreau has made me tired, leave the dishes, I'll sort them out in the morning." She pushed back her chair and with a half-hearted wave, disappeared through the door to her house.

Zach and Poppy kissed Hattie goodnight and followed.

Hattie picked at the crumbs on her plate and eyed the last portion of pie as she heard Jo heading up the stairs to bed.

"Oh, if only we could hear the patter of paws behind her," Hattie whispered out loud and sighed. She reached for the pie and began to eat.

"Woof, woof! Meg, can you hear me?" Hattie looked towards the ceiling, "I never thought I'd be pleased to see that mongrel but what I would give for her now."

PETE SAT by the fire in the Red Lion and stared into the flames. He too wished that he could look down and see old Meg lying by the hearth, thumping her tail in her sleep as she dreamt of chasing rabbits.

But her last rabbit had been a chase too far.

Pete remembered that horrible afternoon. Jo had been inconsolable and when her tears eventually dried up and Hattie managed to persuade her to change out of her blood-soaked jeans, she'd huddled into a dressing gown and sat motionless by the fire, not saying a word. Pete sat beside Jo and handed her a brandy as he quietly explained that Meg was safe and comfortable in the meadow, where he'd buried her. But Jo hardly seemed to hear his words.

And it seems that she'd been much that way ever since.

He'd received a hand-written note thanking him for his kindness, as had the driver of the van. Hattie told Pete that the poor man had appeared the next day with a bouquet of flowers, still clearly upset from the accident but Jo had calmly told him that it wasn't his fault and there was nothing anyone could do, he mustn't blame himself. It was her own fault for not having Meg on a lead.

Pete had called in several times since, on the off-chance of catching Jo alone, but she'd been busy with all the preparations for the opening and barely stood still. There'd been no opportunity to talk.

"Fancy another?" Rob appeared and sat down beside Pete.

"Aye, don't mind if I do."

Marlene, who had been hovering, flew with whippet-like motions across the bar to pour their drinks.

"You look like you've lost a tenner and picked up a pound," Rob said.

"If only it was that simple."

"I heard about the dog, bad business," Rob shook his head, "no doubt she's distraught?" Rob thought of Jo with concern. He'd been disappointed that he'd not achieved a sale but he'd been generously compensated for his time and in truth, was delighted that Jo was staying in the village as his family had always enjoyed events at Kirkton House.

"Tight as a clam, nothing gets through."

"Not been out on any fancy pub dinners then?"

"Only in my dreams," Pete didn't bother to deny his feelings, his friends were very well aware that retirement wasn't all Pete had hoped it would be.

Marlene appeared and placed two frothy pints on the table.

"I'm finishing early tonight," she whispered to Pete.

"Aye, that'll be nice for your Jack," Pete said. "He'll get to see a bit of you." He glanced at the low-cut neckline thrust out before him, "Not that there's much left to see."

"You don't know what you're missing, Pete Parks!" Marlene said angrily, tired of the tactics she'd painstakingly employed in the past. "Simpering over that skinny bit with the fancy hotel, hardly got you anywhere has it?" Her face had become puce and she glared at Pete before turning on her heel to storm off.

"Ouch!" Rob said and picked up his glass. "Cheers!"

"Not much to cheer about," Pete said.

"Not like you to give up."

"I can't see much point in pursuing it."

Pete stared into his pint and wondered if Jo was mourning for more than the dog. He'd many unanswered questions spinning around in his head. Had she set her heart on another? Pete was sure something had happened in Barbados and she'd behaved very strangely when she came back from London. Perhaps whoever it was had knocked her back and this, combined with Meg's death, had caused her to spiral, trapped in a place of emotional despair, resurrecting a thousand memories of John's pain and sudden demise.

"Death does funny things, probably brought some grim stuff back for her," Rob said, mirroring Pete's thoughts.

"I'm no psychiatrist, I give up."

The two men stared into the flames and nursed their drinks.

"I've had a thought!" Rob suddenly announced.

Startled, Pete looked up, "Well don't keep it to yourself."

"I think I know a way that might jolt her out of her darkness and put you in a very handsome light." Rob finished his drink.

Pete was puzzled and looked curiously at Rob's empty glass.

"I think it might work," Rob smiled.

"Marlene!" Pete called out when he'd heard Rob's solution. "Two pints of whatever he's drinking," he pointed to Rob's glass. "And take one for yourself." With a smile Pete settled down to discuss the finer detail of Rob's newly hatched plan.

Operation Parks was soon to be deployed.

ob fidgeted from side to side on his old office chair and
studied the rail timetables on his laptop. If he left on an
early morning train, he could be in Marland shortly after
lunch. He flipped open his leather-bound note book and began to
make a list. He'd need country wear for the north and must
remember to pack a few vests and perhaps some thermal long-johns.
It was no doubt chilly in the evenings at Kirkton House.

Bob felt happy as he scribbled away. Things were going swim-
mingly and he was looking forward to his trip. It was kind of Zach to
invite him to the reopening of Kirkton House.

Jo seemed an entrepreneurial sort of woman and Bob was
intrigued with her plans for a hotel that catered to those in their
middle years, who wanted to improve their mind and body and make
new friends. It sounded a perfect venue for Bob and his partner to
spend some time in the future and Bob wondered if there were
courses on meditation, perhaps he could get Anthony to finally
indulge? Bob had studied the course prospectus and amongst the
many interesting things to study, Sharing with the Shaman, had
jumped right out.

He couldn't wait to make a booking.

Lottie knocked on the door and popped her head into Bob's office. Her newly-dyed pink hair was fluffed out like candy floss and Bob gazed in wonder at the apparition.

"Would you like a chicken panini?" Lottie asked.

"Lovely darling, get me a cappuccino too."

They were both working late, the office had been busy for weeks and Bob had a mountain of paper work to catch up on. He turned to his inbox and set about answering a long list of emails. Business was booming and Bob was over the moon, Hargreaves & Puddicombe Promotions was running perfectly under his direction.

A chime sounded and Bob reached for his mobile, the dong-like sound soothed and he took a calming breath before answering the call.

"I need to talk to you!" Hilary yelled down the phone.

Bob winced and held the phone away. He reached into a drawer for his prayer beads and with them safely nestling in the palm of one hand, turned his attention to his business partner.

"Calm down, sweetie," Bob said. "Let's start at the beginning."

For the next twenty minutes, Bob listened carefully. He made soothing noises where appropriate until Hilary's tale finally came to an exhausted end.

"Quite a pickle, dear heart," Bob said as Lottie wobbled in with Bob's food. A fur boob-tube covered a long pink taffeta tutu and on her feet, Lottie wore matching fur boots.

"It's a disaster," Bob announced.

"Oh, thanks!" Hilary cried. "That's really helpful," she said bitterly.

"Not you darling, your receptionist."

Lottie's tutu wobbled as she approached and with faltering fingers, set the lunch out. The cappuccino spilled onto the desk.

"Tissues!" Bob cried, "Quickly!"

"Is she crying?" Hilary whispered.

"No, the silly mare has spilt my drink, now where were we?" He waved Lottie away and dabbed at the soggy stain on his blotter.

They spent the next half hour analysing Hilary's situation and Bob was relishing the task. It was like the old days, when their scheming and plotting had won many a client over.

"I think I've solved your problem," Bob said suddenly. A golden light seemed to fill his office and as he fondled the soft smooth stones in his hand, he let his intuition flow.

Hilary listened intently to Bob's plan. She had several arguments to fault it but in the end, agreed that it was worth a shot.

It was probably her only shot.

And with luck, Bob thought as he ended the call, she might fire a bullseye.

Operation Hilary was underway!

~

HATTIE WAS UP EARLY. She'd stayed over at the hotel and following Jo's long held rule that staff should always know the workings of every bedroom, had enjoyed a comfortable night in a four-poster bed.

Lucky sods! Hattie mumbled to herself as she unlocked the back door of the hotel and set about the short walk to the paper shop. They'll certainly get their money's worth.

She thought about the guests who would arrive in the coming weeks and settle into their luxurious surroundings. From Jacuzzi baths to finest Egyptian cotton linens and comfortable antique furniture, they'd be wined and dined in style in the newly-opened restaurant and entertained with a variety of life-enhancing courses to dabble in whenever a whim took their fancy.

"Morning all," Hattie said as a bell rang above the paper shop door and she stepped into the little emporium. Faded postcards were stacked in a wonky wire frame and jaded looking vegetables lay in wooden crates at a far corner of the room. An assortment of odds and sods were displayed on shelves, with the more intimate items in a glass fronted cabinet behind the counter.

As Hattie stood in line and waited patiently for a group of gossiping women to disperse, she glanced at the cabinet and wondered how much demand there was in the village for The Ultimate Pleasure Pack, a large packet of condoms, both flavoured and ribbed.

"I see you're checking the new products," the shop owner nodded and gave Hattie a wink. "We're getting ready for the hotel to open up again. The ladies here were just talking about it." Several heads turned toward Hattie.

"Aye, it's going to be a very inspiring venue," Hattie said. "I trust you ladies are all signed up for pottery and art?" She looked around at the enthusiastic faces and nodding heads. "Oh, and don't forget to try something very different," the gaggle leaned in, "Sharing with the Shaman, is going to be a best-selling course, so make sure you book your places soon."

Tight perms and grey heads nodded and a lady wearing a purple bandana whipped out her diary and made a note. Hattie thought of the Shaman and wondered if she should warn him to stock up on henna, this lot would be queuing down the road once word of his wandering wand got out.

She moved to the counter where the newspapers were laid out and idly scanned the headlines. Photos of several anorexic film stars at a movie premiere sat alongside government warnings that obesity was crippling the health service. Hattie yawned and was about to move to the magazine rack when a headline screamed out:

Reformed Rock Star Rebels!

The article, written by an American journalist, detailed Long Tom's massive fall from grace on a night out in the Caribbean. The ageing rock star who, after a spell in rehab and a long period of sobriety, was seen consuming large quantities of alcohol in a bar and was as drunk as a skunk and revelling in it. He'd attempted to perform with a jazz band before a group of party goers at a popular island resort.

A slightly out of focus photo showed Long Tom. He appeared to be falling over a saxophonist. The journalist went on to explain how her camera had mysteriously disappeared on the night in question and the photo had been taken by a tourist.

Hattie stared wide-eyed at the report.

Shite! She whispered to herself and slapping some money down on the counter, picked up the paper and hurried out of the shop.

Hattie ran all the way back to the hotel and threw herself into the kitchen where Zach and Poppy stood in their dressing gowns, making coffee and toast.

"Where's your mam?" Hattie asked.

"She's getting dressed," Zach said as he buttered a thick slice of Sandra's granary bread.

Hattie ran through the bar and restaurant and flung the door to Jo's house open. She half expected Meg to peep out from her box and cursed as she flung herself on the stairs.

Jo sat at her dressing table. She wore a short tunic dress and held a brush in one hand and looked up when Hattie fell into the room.

"Whatever's the matter?" Jo asked.

Hattie sat down on the bed and caught her breath. She reached into her bag for the paper and handed it to Jo. "You'd better read this," she said.

Jo took the paper and laid it on her knees. As she scanned the headline, her jaw fell open and she gasped, "Oh my god..."

Hattie sat quietly and let Jo digest the information contained in the article. She watched the colour drain from her friend's face as the words sank in.

"Why?" Jo said.

Hattie stood and walked over to the window. She looked out to the garden where the gardener was trimming the edges of the croquet lawn, in final preparation for the party that would be held in a few days' time. She drummed her fingertips on the sill and thought carefully about what she was about to say.

"But why would he do it, Hattie?" Jo repeated, tears running down her cheeks.

"WHY?" Hattie cried, unable to contain her emotion any longer.

"Why? That's a very good question." She stomped across the room to stand in front of Jo and took a deep breath as she began.

"Has it ever occurred to you that you might be the reason why the poor bugger is drowning his sorrows?" Hattie yelled. "You hole up with him and have the best sex you've had in yonks, no doubt for him too, and openly admit that the affair has buried a million demons and couldn't have come at a better time, then when he phones, you won't pick up and talk to him and never return a single call - can you imagine what that does to a man with an addiction?" Hattie snatched the paper from Jo's knees and shook it. "God knows what journey he's got to face to get better, assuming that's what he wants, and we can confidently say that his marriage is up shit creek without a paddle, Hilary will never put up with that sort of public humiliation. I hope your Zach's contract is water-tight, I can't imagine what Hilary will do if she gets wind that you're behind this."

Jo bit into her lip and gripped the hairbrush as she listened to Hattie.

"And while I'm giving you a telling-off," Hattie went on, "we might as well get it all out in the open."

She turned away from Jo and tucking her hands in her pockets, crossed her fingers before carrying on.

"What are you going to do about Pete?" Hattie asked. "The poor bugger is besotted and you barely throw him a crumb from your table, heaven knows why he keeps simpering back, I'd have kicked you into touch a long time ago." She tightened her fingers and wondered if she was going too far, but now she'd begun, she couldn't stop. "Alright, we all know John died, it was terrible and a tragic loss, but stuff happens and people survive and get on with their lives. The daft mongrel has gone too and as much as I know that you loved it like a child, you have to move on, Jo."

Hattie turned to face Jo. She was surprised to see that Jo was sitting up and looking directly at her.

"After all," Hattie softened her voice and sank down on the bed. "Look at everything you have got - this place is fantastic, it's got your name all over it and is set to succeed but it will never be a success unless you get some passion back and stop feeling sorry for yourself."

The words were out and Hattie closed her eyes as she finished her statement. She counted to ten, half expecting Jo to have stomped off in a rage.

"What would I do without you?" Jo whispered as she stared at Hattie's flushed face.

Hattie half-opened one eye and looked up.

"Blimey," Hattie said and uncrossed her fingers, "I thought I was going to get a swipe round the ear with that hairbrush."

"You probably deserve it, but not from me." Jo moved over and sat beside her friend. "Have I really been that bad?"

"Worse, I've been creeping round on egg shells and you know my size nines were never meant to do that."

"I'm so sorry." Jo put her arm round Hattie and hugged her. "Meg's accident seemed to send me all over the place but you're absolutely right, I've got to stop feeling sorry for myself."

Hattie returned the hug, then turned and faced Jo.

"I don't know how you are going to sort things out, both with Long Tom and Pete, but I suggest you make a start by putting your lippie on and sticking a smile on your face. We've got people arriving for the party soon and this place needs to be at its best."

"You're absolutely right," Jo replied.

"Well I'm starving, all that emotion has drained me."

Hattie retrieved the newspaper and folded it carefully. She placed it on the dressing table then made for the door. "Fancy a fry-up?"

"Too right I do," Jo replied. "Give me a couple of minutes and I'll be straight down."

The door closed behind Hattie.

Jo stared at the headline again and thought about Long Tom and prayed that he was in safe hands. She glanced over to a photograph of Meg and thought about Pete. He'd been so kind and taken care of everything when Meg died, thoughtfully burying her in the meadow by the caravan, where he knew Jo would spend many quiet moments in the times to come.

As she looked out of the window, past the garden walls and out to the fells beyond, Jo told herself that it really was OK, the time to be happy was definitely now. She didn't have to feel guilty or sad, and when she didn't know what to do, she must remember John's words and let the universe sort things out.

Jo stared at her reflection in the dressing table mirror. A weight had been lifted and she had Hattie to thank for it.

God bless her friend...

Remembering Hattie's words, Jo reached for a lipstick and smoothed the pretty pink wax over her mouth. With colour restored to her face, she brushed her hair and smoothed out her dress as she stood.

Jo took a deep breath and smiled.

"Here's to the rest of my life," she said and with a new spring in her step hurried to join her loved ones.

40

Zach stood beside a gnarled birch tree in the Westmarland forest and smiled at the camera.

"And, action!" The director called as everyone stood quiet and still to watch the gypsy chef.

"So when you drill into the tree and insert a tube, don't forget to have a vessel handy for the other end of the tube to catch the sap as it drains."

Zach pointed to a plastic bottle taped to the tree.

"Would this work better if he took his shirt off?" the director whispered, conscious that the predominantly female audience might like a six-pack to go with their birch sap brandy in months to come.

"Probably help the ratings," Bob mused as he watched Zach skilfully hammer a cork bung into the tree.

"Don't forget to plug up the hole to prevent infection," Zach continued. "We don't want unwelcome fungal spores gathering and ants will amass around any exposed sap."

"God forbid!" Bob squirmed and scratched at his skin.

They'd spent a busy couple of days filming in the countryside around Kirkton House and Zach had explored many different habitats and foraged in woodland, fields, fells and river banks. The footage made a wonderful start to the series. Foraging with Friends by the Gypsy Chef, and provided an introduction to Zach's home environment, showing the habitats and haunts he'd discovered with his father and brother, where he learnt about wild plants and how to harvest them.

"He's incredibly knowledgeable for one so young," the director commented as they waited for Zach to remove his shirt and the home economist handed Poppy a bottle of olive oil to rub across Zach's chest.

"Oh Lord, dear heart," Bob said as the scene was shot again. "Pulses will be pounding over the pans and throbbing through the Home Counties when this gets aired."

Zach paced across the forest floor and explained that many toxic plants could be rendered edible but it was essential that you knew what you were looking for. The camera panned around, then zoomed in as Zach picked a succulent looking mushroom and licked the cap, before popping the whole thing in his mouth, grinning wickedly and flicking back his lush dark locks as he turned to search for another.

"Too sexual?" the director asked.

"Absolutely perfect," Bob purred and hoped that they'd move to the river bank, where Zach might be persuaded to skinny dip.

Bob reached for a handkerchief and wiped his brow, he wished he hadn't worn his long-johns. The Westmarland forest suddenly felt like an Amazonian jungle.

"Plants give life and nourish the body and have also been used to flame the passions, express love and ignite latent desire," Zach spoke as he foraged in the forest.

"Be still my beating heart..." Bob whispered as he watched the young chef swoop on plants Bob would normally have trodden on. Zach's muscles rippled and glistened under the camera lights.

Zach was on a roll as he held up a variety of misshapen leaves and strange looking roots, "But they can also act as potent weapons in the fight against many common ailments."

"Totally unscripted, I love it," Bob clasped his hands together. "The countryside will be free of weeds in weeks, with women foraging the world over when this goes global." He thought about the abundance of endorsements for Zach and media opportunities that sat on his desk.

The filming wrapped up for the day and as the crew made their way back to the pub, Zach, Bob and Poppy headed for Kirkton House.

"Come on in and get warm," Jo greeted them with mugs of mulled cider. "You must be freezing after standing around in the damp old forest all day."

There was a roaring log fire in the Red Room and they piled in and made themselves comfortable on soft leather chesterfields, either side of the hearth.

Bob sank into the padded sofa and sighed with pleasure as he sipped his drink. He was enjoying his sortie from the office, London felt light years away. He wondered what Hilary was up to and if she'd given their plan further consideration. News of Long Tom's shocking slip back into old habits must have upset her, but she'd told him that Long Tom was in safe hands and expected back soon. Bob wondered what had caused the alcoholic to return to his old ways and had a feeling that the affair with Jo, and Hilary's stand-offish attitude was no doubt behind it.

Bob watched Jo as she moved about the room, cosseting her guests and making sure that they had all that they needed before she disappeared to check on dinner. She was a beautiful woman and he could easily understand why men fell for her.

Bob stared into the fire and smiled. He was looking forward to the party in a few days and would use the time before then to do some walking in the Westmarland hills. It would help his karma and clear his mind. In the meantime he was enjoying the hotel facilities and making the most of having the run of the place, Kirkton House was a wonderful building and Jo had done a magnificent job of restoring the property. Bob adored the Georgian rooms with their bold colours and lovely antiques. The front of the property was a later addition and, as he'd discovered, the building had a wealth of history having begun life in the 17th century. It was great fun to wander through the periods, appreciating Jo's attention to detail, including the addition of state of the art bathrooms and flat-screened TVs discreetly positioned in the bedrooms, to bang up to date computer facilities and all those wonderful classes and courses to dally with. He idly wondered if he could run the business from his suite for a few weeks.

"Dinner will be ready in an hour," Jo announced.

"Perfect, my dear," Bob said, "I have time to shower." He stood and picked up his drink and gave a little wave to the love-birds on the sofa.

Life is sweet... Bob muttered and headed up the stairs.

PETE WALKED along the long sandy beach in the bay of Abersoch, on the Llyn Peninsular, and breathed in the tangy salt air. Wales was pretty at this time of year and he gazed with interest at the chalets that stood on the edge of the dunes dipping down to the bay. Pots and troughs on sea-facing patios spilled tumbling geraniums and flowering fuchsias, an abundance of colour against the wind-swept scenery. He wondered what Jo would make of this area, which was a popular place for a weekend break, with the warm gulfstream running into sheltered waters. It was perfect for water sport and sailing enthusiasts.

Pete watched an old tractor head out along the beach. It towed a speedboat down to the water's edge then turned and reversed the vessel safely into the sea. Billowing black smoke, the tractor chugged back up the beach, lurching and coughing out fumes.

Needs a bit of TLC! Pete thought as he heard the owner cursing.

He watched as the man dismounted and kicked at a tyre in frustration. The vehicle was an old John Deere and Pete shook his head, the tractor would be worth a fortune if looked after properly and restored with care. Still, it wasn't his problem and he had more pressing things to consider.

He'd spent a number of evenings with Rob, poring over the internet and making a few calls and now found himself in Wales, hoping to conclude his mission. He wondered how things were with

Jo and if she was any brighter, he also wondered if her heart was still fluttering in another's direction or if events that had seemed to weigh her down, were ongoing.

Pete sighed.

There wasn't a lot he could do at this distance, but he hoped that when he got back she'd feel more like seeing him and with luck he might eventually find a way to her heart. The party at Kirkton House was coming up and he was looking forward to the event.

Pete gathered his jacket around him and stepped up his pace. He'd a meeting in an hour and wanted to be ready, he'd a little bit of shopping to do too. As he passed the disgruntled tractor owner, who had the bonnet up on the hood and swore loudly at the engine, Pete was tempted to help, but he'd waited too long for an opportunity to win Jo over and nothing was going to stop him today.

He'd finish his walk and be on his way.

41

Jo held a clipboard tightly and slipped out of the side door of her house. She stepped across the drive until she reached the front of the hotel then, standing with her back to the road, stared at the building and ran a critical eye over the smallest detail. With only a day to go, she wanted to be sure that everything was perfect for the opening party.

Windows gleamed and paintwork shone.

The brass fittings on the front door dazzled in the sunshine, alongside two tall urns of flowering lavender, a heady scent to welcome guests as they arrived at the hotel. The borders surrounding the car park were neat with recently pruned plants and climbers trailed over honey-coloured walls. A freshly painted sign swung under the old oak tree and would soon announce that Kirkton House was open.

Jo made a serious of ticks on the notes attached to her clipboard.

A car screeched to halt on the road then accelerated onto the drive, spraying gravel in Jo's direction and she jumped back, cursing as deep indentations appeared in the freshly raked surface.

"You look like Simple Simon standing there!" Hattie yelled as she climbed out of her car. Several sweet wrappers fell to the ground and Jo walked over to pick them up. "Met any pie men lately?" Hattie grinned, "or been to any fairs?"

"It's hopeless trying to keep the place tidy with you chomping your way through a tin of toffees every time you set foot out of Marland," Jo bent down and began a collection.

"Oh, it's good to have you back to your old self," Hattie replied. "What are you doing prancing around out here? There's heap to do." She reached into the back of the car and gathered a box. "Got the new brochures from the printers, they've come out great."

"I'm having a final check through. I want to make sure everything is perfect for tomorrow." Jo looked curiously at the box, "Let's have a look then."

Hattie swerved away.

"Not till I've had me elevenses, is your Zach in the kitchen?"

"Up to his eyes with Sandra and team, they're putting the final touches to tomorrow's buffet."

"Grand, I'll get the coffee on." Hattie headed for the front door and placing her bottom on the handle, made a wriggling motion until the door flew open. "Don't mess about out here," she shouted, "come and have some cake!"

"I'll catch up with you in a bit."

Hattie disappeared and Jo stepped into the hallway to continue her perusal, determined that every detail should be checked and double-checked.

An arrangement of oriental lilies stood on a mahogany console table, beside a gilt-framed mirror, and Jo stopped to breathe in the heady aroma and caught sight of her reflection in the mirror. She certainly looked better than she had a few days ago, the tiredness and stress seemed to have lifted and her face looked less anxious. She put her clipboard on the table and ran her fingers through the chestnut curls that tumbled onto her shoulders.

She thought about Long Tom and how he'd loved to stroke her hair when they were together in Barbados, she could almost feel his touch. Jo had been shocked to hear of his downfall and was wracked with worry for his health and state of mind. She'd tried to contact him and had tracked Boss down in London. He told her that Long Tom was in seclusion, not to be disturbed, and when she'd spoken to Jimmy he gave the same answer. There was nothing she could do but hope and pray that Long Tom was alright and would find the strength to overcome his demons. Her heart ached as she imagined his pain and anguish; this was a time when he needed to be reassured that everything would come good, with loving arms waiting for his return. Jo wondered how Hilary was reacting to the news but decided not to dwell in that direction.

She also wondered where Pete was.

Hattie said that Pete had gone away for a few days. He hadn't said where and Jo thought that Pete too might need some seclusion to gather his thoughts, as he headed into a different phase of his life.

She missed him and was used to having him call in and check on her. Jo feared that she had abused his friendship in the last few months and never given him a chance. Long Tom had been passion and fireworks, and Pete a security blanket, like a comforting hug. She sighed and turned from the mirror, she hadn't time to dwell on the dismal failings of her love-life, there was still a great deal to do. Dignitaries and guests from all over the county would be arriving tomorrow, alongside local press and Jo expected most of the village to turn out too. Hattie had arranged for the course tutors to be in situ in their workshops, to chat to guests and demonstrate examples of their work during the event, which would begin early in the afternoon and no doubt carry on into the evening.

The front door suddenly flew open and a gust of wind whooshed past Jo. Warm fur seemed to caress her leg and startled, Jo looked down.

Was Meg sitting beside her?

Jo's heart lurched and she reached out. But her hand felt nothing; there was neither a soft warm head, nor thumping tail, and Jo squeezed her eyes tightly to try and stop the tears. Would she ever stop missing her dog?

Hattie's head appeared around the door in reception and she called out, "Coffee's ready!" she said, "and there's cake!"

Jo picked up her clipboard.

Enough! She told herself and put thoughts of men and dogs to one side. She hadn't made much progress with her checks, but there was time to have a quick break. "On my way," she replied and closed the front door.

She found a hub of activity in the kitchen.

Sandra stood by the stove and poked a wooden spoon into a pot, then blew on the sticky orange mass that clung to the spoon. Zach stood by and looked at her with expectation.

"Good?" Zach asked as he watched Sandra taste his lavender marmalade.

"The best one yet," Sandra smiled and patted Zach's arm. She was in heaven. Kirkton House was about to reopen and her boy was home and standing right beside her. All Sandra's motherly instincts kicked in when Zach was around, after all, she'd watched him grow up and trained him at her table. His talent knew no bounds in her eyes and she was as proud as punch that she'd been instrumental in inspiring him. The elderly cook had a new lease of life and even though her work would be on a part-time basis, she couldn't wait for the kitchen to swing back into action and residents to arrive.

But first they had a buffet to prepare.

Guests who were coming to the party would enjoy mini bites of many of the dishes from Zach's menus. Working alongside Zach, Sandra and her team had been busy testing and tasting and were confident that the recipes, now in a neat file in Hattie's new computer system, all worked perfectly.

"Slap one of those over here," Hattie whispered to one of the chefs who stood beside Zach. The smartly attired young man, in a crisp white jacket with the hotel logo embroidered on the pocket, slid a goat's cheese crostini, wrapped in Westmarland ham, onto a palette knife and handed it to Hattie.

The offering disappeared in one bite.

Hattie moved around the stainless steel table and noting that all eyes were on the stove, leaned over and took a generous slice of smoked trout roulade. Mascarpone oozed from the corners of her mouth and she sighed with pleasure. She spotted a tray of Butterfly Bangers and drooled as she noted that the sausages were roasted to perfection - all ready for a marmalade accompaniment.

Hattie grabbed the fattest on the tray and popped it into her mouth.

Sandra, who'd seen Hattie out of the corner of her eye, spun round and took a wide swipe with her spoon. Chunks of marmalade flew and landed in Hattie's hair.

"Bleedin' hell!" Hattie's sausage went flying. "It's boiling!" she yelled as the sticky mass clung to her ginger locks.

Jo turned and watched Hattie run to the back door to shake her head furiously over the cobbles.

"New hair gel?" Jo asked and smiled as Hattie gesticulated with two fingers and swore under her breath. Jo turned to the chefs and looked around for her coffee. "Is this one for me?" she asked and pointed to a steaming mug.

"Try a slice of this, Mum," Zach pushed a plate forward and Jo picked up a slice of dark, fruity cake. She closed her eyes as the rich coconut flavour exploded in her mouth.

"It's our Kirkton Caribbean Cake , in honour of Jimmy, to make sure that he's always in our hearts even though he's thousands of miles away."

Sandra and the chefs stood silently beside Zach and looked at Jo with expectation. It had taken days to get the recipe right and they all held their breath.

Jo wanted to cry. The cake was the nicest thing she'd ever eaten and Zach's sentiments and kindness towards his brother touched her heart.

"It's absolutely sensational," Jo said. "We must send some out to Jimmy as soon as possible."

"Not until I've had a slice!" Hattie came into the kitchen and snatched a piece of the cake. Her hair was glued together and stood at right-angles to her head. She glared angrily at Sandra, "I need a shampoo and set now," Hattie moaned and stomped out of the kitchen.

"Tha' needs to get tha' mouth wired," Sandra replied and turned back to the stove.

Jo winked at Zach, who was chuckling as he lined up jars on the stove, to warm for the marmalade. She picked up her coffee and resisting another slice of cake, smiled at the chefs then walked out of the kitchen to carry on with her day.

LONG TOM LAY on an old wooden chair on the verandah at Eddie's plantation and looked out at the view. It was a scene he would never tire of.

A green monkey sat in a nearby tree. The little creature eyeballed Long Tom with interest as it fidgeted amongst the branches.

The garden was a perfect habitat for the monkey.

It was a delicious palette of fruit and flowers, lizards and insects, all easily to hand to be plucked and stolen. Long Tom remembered Eddie telling him that in a parish on the coast, monkey was a delicacy, cooked and served as a stew by locals in a particular rum shop. The illicit fare was on the menu by invitation only.

He wondered what it tasted like.

As if reading Long Tom's thoughts, the monkey screeched then leapt out of the tree to land on the grass and scamper away.

Long Tom smiled and shook his head. Don't worry little fella, you're safe with me.

It was only a few days since Long Tom's relapse and he knew that he was lucky to be alive. In rehab they'd told him that further drinking would undoubtedly kill him, the shock too much for his damaged body to bear. Long Tom couldn't recall much of the night when his demons had overcome him and hadn't a clue how Jimmy and Mattie had brought him back from the brink of death.

For he knew that, at one point, he'd passed over.

But a miracle had happened and just as his light seemed to be fading and transcending into another dimension, strong arms had reached out and embraced him.

It wasn't his time.

Now he was back, on a mortal coil that felt good. He was tired but energised and it didn't make sense. The only thing that made sense was gratitude and relief and Long Tom knew that he was a fortunate man.

He gazed at the east coast below and wondered at the stark contrast to the Caribbean calm of the west. Long Tom watched the Atlantic as it crashed onto volcanic rocks, the bottle-green breakers pluming clouds of spray and he sensed the movement and heard the sound as the power and beauty combined.

Thank god he was alive.

His conscience told him to call Hilary. They'd spoken briefly since the incident and he'd assured her that he was alright, but his marriage was far from his mind as he lay looking out to sea.

A truck was winding its way up the steep, hilly road, and Long Tom followed the trail of dust as it got closer. Jimmy leaned out of the driver's window and waved as the truck came to a halt beneath the verandah, then leapt out and raced up the stairs.

"You're looking good, man!" Jimmy grinned and leaned down to hug Long Tom.

"And you look like my saviour," Long Tom sat forward and smiled.

Jimmy placed a large bag of mangoes, coconuts and breadfruit on the deck then produced a neatly wrapped package from a cool box.

"Fish fuh days!" Jimmy laughed, "To quote Mistress Nysha, she sent it for you and says it will make you strong." He peeled the wrapping off the parcel and the men gazed at a fat mutton snapper. The fish glistened like the sea that had raised it, the belly meaty with a healthy red tinge.

"Looks good," Long Tom nodded.

"Are you hungry?"

"Sure am, will you join me?"

"I'll get cooking," Jimmy grinned. He picked up his packages and disappeared to the kitchen.

Long Tom watched Jimmy move away. The young man had so many mannerisms that reminded him of Jo. His eyes danced when he spoke and his mouth smiled in a certain way.

The fruit don't fall far from the tree...

Long Tom's heart was heavy.

He thought of Jo with an aching affection and wondered how her new plans were working out. He wished that she'd walk across the deck towards him, arms held out to embrace, body welcoming in his hour of need.

For Long Tom knew that Jo was the reason for his downfall and he was ashamed for blaming her.

Jimmy had told him that she'd phoned several times and Long Tom was pleased that she cared. But he couldn't blame her for his relapse. He was responsible for his own actions and he remembered the twelve steps that he'd learnt in rehab. Certainly, a greater power had restored his sanity but Long Tom wondered what the hell Jimmy had given him that night? Whatever was in the concoction had cleansed his body in record time and left him in a calm and healing frame of mind. It had made him determined that it would never happen again. Jimmy had tried to talk to Long Tom, to figure out why he'd fallen off the wagon that night, but Long Tom refused to discuss the matter, he couldn't land his failings on Jo and her family.

"Try some of this cake," Jimmy said as he carried a plate across the verandah and placed it beside Long Tom, "Mistress Nysha says it's full of goodness and glory."

Long Tom bit into the thick sponge. A shred of coconut clung to his mouth and he licked it away, "Glory be!" he said, "tell Mistress Nysha that it sure is good."

"Caribbean cake, made with love," Jimmy smiled, "great eh? Lunch won't be long." He reached for the empty plate and returned to the kitchen.

Long Tom closed his eyes and the balmy scented air lulled him into a doze. When he woke, he saw Jimmy beckoning to a corner table.

"Grub's up," Jimmy said and placed a serving dish on a raffia mat.

Long Tom swung his legs over the side of the chair and grabbed the decking rail. A gardener, trimming the lawn below, looked up and waved, delighted to see that the house guest was up and about.

"So what's the plan?" Jimmy asked as he served up snapper ceviche.

"I need to go home."

"Home to Ireland?"

"Yes, in time, but there's something I need to do first."

Jimmy looked wistful as he thought about his own home. It seemed a very long way away and he wondered how Jo and Zach were getting on with their preparations. There was a party coming up and Jimmy tried to visualise the old house as it came back to life. The bonds of familiarity tugged hard, he'd grown up at Kirkton House, it had been his boyhood home and the rock that Jo had built to nurture and protect her family.

"Sure going to miss this place, though," Long Tom tucked into the food. "It's been kind of Eddie to let me use it."

"You'll be back," Jimmy said. "Your bellybutton's buried in Barbados."

Long Tom looked up. He raised his eyebrows and considered Jimmy's words. "That line would make a good song," he tapped a beat on the table with his fingers.

"It's got reggae-hit all over it."

The two men looked at each and simultaneously burst out laughing.

"Yes, it has," Long Tom said and looked around. "You're right and there's one thing I am quite sure of, his eyes gazed out at the view, "I don't know where my bellybutton is buried, but I do know, Barbados - I'll be back."

42

P ete stared at the mess in his kitchen. It looked as though a tornado had struck. The rugs were rucked up and items scattered all around and he sighed as he bent to straighten things, a task he'd been repeating over the last couple of days.

Rob had called round earlier and Pete had offered him a beer. They'd sat in the yard and supped the refreshing ale then made small talk about Jo's hotel and Rob gave an update. He knew most of the staff that had returned to their old jobs and everyone was talking about the party.

"That's a fine piece of metal you've got there," Rob said idly as he cast his eyes over the old Massey Ferguson that stood in one corner. The fresh red paintwork gleamed in the sunshine.

"Aye, she's worth a few bob now," Pete nodded his head in agreement and thought about the hours he'd spent in his workshop, restoring the vintage tractor to former glory.

"You'll be having a spin out no doubt?"

"She's filled up and ready to roll," Pete said as he twiddled the engine keys in his jacket pocket.

"An impressive beast," Rob said.

"That's me!" Pete grinned and turned to Rob. "Another?" he nodded towards Rob's empty glass.

Rob followed Pete into the kitchen, stepping carefully over the debris. He shook his head as he noted a book face down, the pages torn and scattered all over the floor.

"Bit of work to do here," Rob commented.

"True," Pete replied as he poured a can of beer, "not for much longer though."

"Don't be too sure."

"To the new Kirkton House!" the friends said in unison and raised their glasses.

"May she rise again," Pete added with a smile as he downed his pint. "Let Operation Parks begin!"

HATTIE HURRIED up the path to her house and placing her packages by the front door, searched in her pockets for the key. She thrust the door open and fell into the hall then unloaded her hoard in the lounge and hurried into the kitchen to make a reviving drink.

Shopping was hard work.

Hattie flicked the kettle on and searched for coffee and milk then reached for a mug.

Suddenly, she had a feeling of déjà vu.

Was it only a few short months ago that she'd crashed a mug into the sink? The mug that she'd broken had reminded her of Maurice. So much seemed to have happened since then! Hattie recalled the feelings of loneliness and boredom she felt, which had now been replaced with excitement and wonder. Were there enough hours in the day?

Thank goodness Jo was reopening the hotel.

Hattie couldn't wait. She'd enjoyed a wonderful holiday in Barbados and now had a job to look forward to. It was just like the old days.

She stared at the mug in her hand and remembered the words

embossed on the side - Maurice's Mug. Hattie stared harder and the letters seemed to swirl, jumbling of their own accord. Suddenly the words, Mattie's Mug, appeared and her heart gave a lurch.

Hattie jumped back and dropped the mug in the sink.

"Bugger..." Hattie swore as another mug smashed. "Sod the coffee!" She reached for a glass and poured a shot of rum. The rich amber liquid was soothing and a comforting glow warmed her throat and calmed her pounding heart.

Hattie closed her eyes and thought of Mattie. "Here's to you, lovely man," she whispered and raised her glass. Mattie's handsome face seemed to be smiling and she let her imagination run free as she remembered their happy days together.

A hand rattled against the window and startled Hattie.

She jumped back from the sink and glared out as a scruffy chamois moved slowly across the pane.

"Bleedin' hell, Reg!" Hattie shouted, "not you again! Can't you knock or something?"

"Just did," the window cleaner grinned, a roll-up wedged between a gap in his teeth, "day-time drinking and dreaming of a lover?"

"Mind yer own business," Hattie snapped and felt her face flushing.

"I do extras..." Reg gave Hattie a knowing wink. "Tha's gone puce just thinking on it," he leered hopefully.

"I must have the cleanest windows in Marland, now pack up and piss off!" Hattie yelled and in one swift movement reached for the roller blind and let it thunder to the sill.

"Only a matter of time..." Hattie heard Reg faintly mumble as he continued to daub the windows.

She flew into the living room and closed all the curtains.

Reg had the biggest gob on the estate and she didn't want him to see all the packages that were strewn around the room. As she gathered them together, she began to feel calmer. Her shopping trip had been fruitful and she could hardly wait for the party the next day.

Hattie smiled as she thought of her new outfit.

Classy and well cut, it was just the job to impress Jo's prospective punters and get everyone into the spirit of the party. Hattie was confident that she'd cut quite a dash and shine in her resurrected role as manager of Kirkton House. She grabbed her purchases and headed up the stairs. A long lazy bath lay ahead, with plenty of pampering too.

Operation Hattie was in progress!

Hilary sat in the music room at Long Tom's London town house and stared out of the French windows to the garden below. This place had never felt like home. She wondered if she should have taken more interest, instead of dallying off to Ireland to spend all her time at Flatterley Manor.

The town house décor looked tired but Long Tom seemed to like it that way, just as he'd liked Flatterly Manor in a dilapidated state. Hilary stared at the worn fabrics and jumble of rock memorabilia spilling over mismatched furniture. Everything cried out to be homed in a more fitting tribute to a life-long career in the industry.

Hilary thought of her luxurious apartment in London.

It had been rented out when she married Long Tom and brought in a substantial amount of income each month. Furnished with lovely antiques and a state of the art kitchen, the letting company had placed the apartment on the market and within hours, a foreign diplomat had snatched the opportunity to live in such a prestigious part of the city. But now, Hilary wondered if she would need to reclaim her former home.

She sighed and stood, then crossed the room and paused by the grand piano as her fingers strayed over the keys and struck the notes of a childhood song. How she wished she'd kept up with piano lessons! There were so many things that she was beginning to wish she had done and Hilary was unsettled by the way her life was unfolding.

Even the business was successful without her.

Bob had triumphed at the helm of Hargreaves & Puddicombe

Productions. It was thriving and she was somewhat redundant. Zach Docherty was heading for success and would in time, be their number one client as Bob had handled the young chef's career quite brilliantly.

But wasn't that what she'd wanted?

She'd set things up so that she could have a life with Long Tom, but she'd let it slip away. And now, he'd fallen off the wagon in a spectacular manner and she hadn't been there to pick up the pieces. She'd been too immersed in a stupid affair in Ireland and hadn't seen what she'd lost. Hilary was certain that Zach's mother was the cause of Long Tom's drinking bout. She'd found a place in her husband's needy heart that his wife should have occupied and worked at maintaining.

Hilary could hardly bear to say the woman's name.

When she saw Jo in Bob's office and overheard their conversation, she'd known that all was about to be lost. Long Tom was closing down and Hilary was powerless to stop him.

She yearned for a cigarette and her fingers fumbled hopefully in her pocket. But the pocket was empty as Hilary had known it would be. All smoking paraphernalia had been thrown in the trash. If Long Tom was conquering his demons again, she would too. It was a tightrope that seemed set to threaten the rest of their lives, never knowing if one slip would cause an irreversible fall.

A clock chimed the hour and startled her. She needed to get on! She closed the lid of the piano and moved swiftly to lock the French doors.

Hilary glanced around the room and imagined it with a refurb. She would hire an interior designer and bring the house back to life. But could she do the same for her marriage?

She caught sight of her reflection in a dusty old mirror.

The face that stared back looked worried and strained and remembering her conversation with Bob, Hilary grabbed her coat and bag then flew down the stairs to step out into the square to summon a taxi.

Hilary had too much to lose and she wasn't prepared to go down without a fight. She'd taken her man for granted and now she wanted him back.

Bob's Operation Hilary, needed to work and she would do everything in her power to ensure that it did!

BOB SAT on a comfortable Queen Anne chair in the bay of the Green Room at Kirkton House and stared out of the curved windows to the driveway and village beyond.

There was a great deal of activity.

Deliveries were coming and going via the kitchen entrance and staff buzzed to and fro. A gardener watered baskets and tubs that brightened the hotel brickwork with a mass of flowering plants and an old charabanc, covered in hand-painted murals, rattled to a halt on the gravel. The driver, a native Indian-looking fellow, asked directions and was guided to the rear of the hotel.

Bob was intrigued.

He sipped his Earl Grey tea and felt a flutter of excitement as he nibbled on a scone. Jo's opening party was finally here and by the look of things, was causing much excitement.

The film crew had wrapped up that morning, after shooting the opening for the episode of Foraging with Friends by the Gypsy Chef. They would be back the following day to film Zach at the party.

Bob was glad that he was staying on to celebrate the event. He thought about his call with Hilary earlier and was pleased to note that she sounded as though she had a new spring in her step. Bob hoped that at last, she was seeing sense.

Tyres crunched and Bob leaned forward to look out. A taxi had glided to a halt by the front door and the occupants spilled onto the drive.

"Oh my goodness!" Bob exclaimed as he saw Lottie lean across the back seat. Her bottom protruded as the driver held the door, his eyes averted from the mass of frills on Lottie's knickers. She wriggled out backwards and finding her feet, turned to face the hotel.

Lottie wore a flimsy T-shirt over a short red dress and Bob winced as he read the words emblazoned across her chest, I love Tipsy Gypsies! A red heart improvised the word love and Bob wondered where on earth Lottie had found it.

"Heaven help us..." Bob mumbled and shook his head. Had it been a mistake for Zach to invite office staff to the party?

Bob finished his tea and wished that it was something stronger. He hurried to the front door.

To his relief, Heidi appeared. She'd paid the driver and having organised their luggage, moved smartly across the threshold. Immaculate as ever in a smart Barbour jacket, silk scarf and tailored Capri pants, Heidi beamed when she saw Bob.

"Darling heart!" Bob squealed and pulled Heidi into a warm embrace. "You've arrived and I'm so pleased to see you." He examined her head to toe and smiled approvingly. Turning to Lottie, Bob raised his eyes and clucked his teeth. "Oh well, we could pass you off as the cabaret," he sighed, "come here." He pecked Lottie on each cheek. "We need to lose the T-shirt though."

"I've got one for everybody!" Lottie trilled and jumped up and down.

"Over my dead body..." Bob imagined the photos in the local press covering the event. "Now you must tell me about your journey and I want the office gossip," he reached for a suitcase, "but first let's get you both settled."

They trooped into the hotel and Bob indicated that the girls follow him up the stairs.

"Jo has asked me to show you to your rooms," he said. "Everyone is busy with preparations but we're all meeting up in the pub later."

"Oh wow," Lottie exclaimed as Bob led them round the curve of the stairs to a wide gallery, then threw open the door to a twin-bedded room. She jumped on the bed in the far corner and began to bounce up and down.

"It's lovely," Heidi said as she looked at the richly polished mahogany bedroom suite, "and so huge!" She walked over to the sash windows and reached out to stroke the thick chintz curtaining.

"Well, make yourselves at home, shout if you need anything," Bob gave a little wave then gently closed the door.

There was one scone left on his tea tray and with luck, he could squeeze another cup of Earl Grey to go with it.

With a contented smile, Bob hurried down the stairs.

Jo stood in the dining room and made a final tick on the notes on her clipboard. At last, everything was ready and she knew that all her efforts had paid off.

Kirkton House looked splendid.

Guests would be welcomed tomorrow in the reception rooms then taken on a tour of the property, which would end with drinks and food in the cocktail bar and Rose Room restaurant, no doubt spilling out into the conservatory and gardens if the weather stayed fine. The preparations were completed and with only the kitchen to kick in on the day, Jo was confident that all of her carefully laid plans would fall into shape. The staff had been briefed and everyone seemed as excited as Jo.

She stepped through the French windows that led to the patio overlooking the croquet lawn and stared at a teepee that occupied a large section of lawn. It had been erected that afternoon by an interesting looking gentleman, who suddenly appeared from the folds of the tent.

This was Hattie's Shaman.

"Namaste," the man bowed slightly and Jo returned his greeting, mirroring his actions by placing the palms of her hands over her heart. She introduced herself and told the man that she was looking forward to his courses; there was a lot of interest and Hattie, having experienced his work, had high praise - it was kind of him to bring a teepee to the party.

Jo thanked the man and made a mental note to ensure that the teepee was erected further down the garden when the courses commenced, as there wasn't a prayer that anyone would negotiate a croquet ball around the huge structure.

She walked briskly down the garden and as she inspected the manicured lawns and neatly trimmed hedges, she thought about Meg. How the old dog would have relished all this activity on her patch!

In the meadow, the vardo had been freshly painted and restored. The brightly coloured caravan looked delightful against banks of wild flowers and Jo smiled as she got closer, knowing that John would have loved this scene too.

She sat on the wooden steps of the vardo and looked around.

Kirkton House stood proud and tall, the evening sunshine glistening like a halo over the rooftops and chimneys as birds circled overhead.

Jo smiled as she stared at her business and family home and knew that she had done the right thing. She was merely a custodian of the old manor, there to preserve the central hub of the village which gave employment to so many and provided shelter, food and warmth for those who passed through its doors. Soon it would provide education too and Jo intended to use much of her profits to help those in need in the county.

Jo thought about Pete, she hadn't heard a word from him even though Hattie had told her that he was back from his break.

She hoped that he would come to the party.

There was no word from Long Tom either and Jo had a heavy heart as she thought of the anguish that he was going through.

However did she end up falling for two men? It seemed only moments since she'd stepped out on holiday with Hattie, scared for her future as middle-age nudged on, a grieving widow who never imagined that romance would come knocking on her door.

Whatever would she do without Hattie? None of this would have been possible, they'd come through so much together over the years and Jo thought fondly of her friend, whose loyalty never wavered, no matter how tough things got.

Jo stroked the gleaming paintwork on the vardo and remembered so many happy times in this garden with John, watching the boys over the years, grow into the fine young men that they both were today.

The time to be happy is now...

John's words whispered and Jo looked up.

Let the universe take care of the how...

The words seemed to float across the meadow and touching her fingers to her lips, Jo blew a gentle kiss to the heavens.

It was time to make her family and guests happy and on this occasion, she would take over from the universe and personally take care of the how.

43

Hattie sat in reception and fiddled about with the computer. She checked the guest list for the umpteenth time, noting that all the invitees had accepted their invitation and many had begged for more tickets.

They were going to have a very busy afternoon.

A delicious smell drifted in from the kitchen and Hattie could hear the chefs as they called to one another and made final preparations for the scrumptious buffet that would be served later that day. She leaned over the desk, until she had a clear view of the cocktail bar, and saw that staff had set up trays of glasses for champagne cocktails to be served when the guests arrived and the bar was fully stocked. The florist had put final touches to lavish arrangements throughout the reception rooms and the housekeeper, smart in a new uniform, busied about with a duster, ensuring that everything glistened and gleamed.

So far, all was going to plan.

Jo was taking a bath and had left Hattie in charge and as Hattie glanced at her watch, she noted that she had a bit of time to spare before she needed to get ready.

She sat back and yawned.

Her tummy rumbled and she contemplated slipping next door to make a sandwich, or see what she could nick from the buffet, anything to mop up the alcohol swirling about in her stomach. She was beginning to regret the amount she'd drunk the night before.

Mind, it had been one hell of a get-together!

Hattie closed her eyes and remembered the previous evening. Those film people certainly knew how to party and many of the locals in the pub had never seen anything quite like it before. Hattie thought fondly of the little lass from London, who'd so kindly bought T-shirts for everyone, not that Hattie had expected old Bob to wear one when he was dancing on the bar.

What a sport he'd turned out to be! Buying drinks for everyone and picking up the tab for their meals.

That Poppy was a poppet too, no wonder Boy Wonder was stuck to her like glue. They made an adorable couple. They'd announced their engagement in the pub and Jo, who was so overcome for her youngest and his lovely fiancée, burst into tears and bought champagne for everyone.

The front door bell rang. It startled Hattie from her daydream and she reluctantly dragged herself to her feet. A delivery van was parked outside and the driver stood in the porch holding a huge arrangement of flowers.

"Delivery for Ms's Docherty and Contaldo," he said, peering round the vast pile.

"Blimey," Hattie gasped, "it's a long time since anyone sent me flowers." She stood back and asked the driver to place the delivery on the console table.

"Have a nice party," he said and closed the door.

Hattie picked the arrangement up and staggered down the hall. She fumbled her way through the bar and restaurant and opened the door to Jo's house.

"Get your arse down here quickly!" Hattie yelled up the stairs. "This arrangement is setting me allergies off."

Jo appeared at the top of the stairs. She was wrapped in a towel and looked puzzled as a forest of flowers moved slowly across her lounge.

She grabbed the banister and ran down to assist.

"Gosh, who on earth has sent these?" Jo asked. She guided a staggering Hattie to the table and together, they gently placed the floral display down.

"There's a card," Hattie sneezed and reached to retrieve a little envelope.

"Oh my, you'll never guess..." Jo's eyes were welling as she read the note.

"Not unless I've got a crystal ball up me jumper." Hattie snatched at the card and quickly scanned the words.

With our love to you both on this special day
Wishing we were with you but sending some Caribbean sunshine to
celebrate the re-opening of Kirkton House.
Jimmy & Mattie xx

"Well I never," Hattie whispered, her eyes filling too.

"How kind," Jo mumbled.

They both stared at the flowers, letting the heady scent take them back to their island holiday. Jo reached out and put her arm around Hattie's shoulders as Hattie looked up and reached for Jo's hand.

"Not tempted to jump on a plane?" Jo asked. "I'm sure he'd be waiting for you."

Hattie shook her head and sighed, Mattie clearly on her mind. "He'll be shacked up with a whole cast of new holidaymakers now," she sighed, "but I can't deny that I miss him, I wish he was here."

"He'd certainly liven Marland up," Jo grinned.

"Oh, my god, could you imagine?" Hattie smiled too. "The weed wagon in Westmarland!"

"They'd be queuing to get in his taxi, he could go global!"

"Reggae Reggae Rides on Mr Lover Lover's Lakeland Tours..."

The pair shook with laughter.

"Never mind me and men," Hattie said, "what are you going to do about Pete and Long Tom?"

"Perhaps you could whip that crystal ball out of your jumper and guide me?"

"You're blind when it comes to love. The only thing that can guide you is a dog," Hattie shook her head. "Now what about a quick livener as we put our party dresses on, my throat thinks my gob's been glued up."

"Champagne it is!" Jo disappeared to her kitchen and returned with a bottle and two glasses, "Let's get glamorous!"

THE PARTY WAS in full swing. Guests had arrived promptly on the dot of two and a crowd formed on the driveway, waiting patiently to move forward when the doors opened.

Jo and Hattie stood either side and welcomed everyone as they were ushered into the reception rooms for champagne and canapés.

"Darling! You look absolutely ravishing," Bob cried and air-kissed Jo on both cheeks. He took care not to mark her makeup, nor smudge his own discreet layer of tinted moisturiser, then stood back and admired Jo's outfit. She wore a calf-length cocktail dress in a shimmering red silk. The dress skimmed her curves and accentuated the chestnut highlights in her hair.

"And Hattie, dear, you look..." Bob was lost for words as he studied Hattie's unusual outfit, "Interesting and lovely too." He raised an eyebrow and studied Hattie's cotton blouse, cut dangerously low and tied at the waist, above a tiered ruffled skirt that was edged with fine lace.

"I think you look smashing," Jo said encouragingly.

"This is afternoon wear, for a posh party," Hattie said, "nothing too flamboyant, something that I can adapt." She smiled mysteriously and moved forward to greet more guests.

"Yoo hoo!" A voice called out above the crowd and Jo and Bob turned to see Lottie sliding down the banisters. She still wore her T-shirt from the night before and as she landed in a pile at the bottom of the stairs, a local journalist, who represented a county glossy, whipped out a camera and asked her to stick out her chest and smile.

"I think we can safely say that as far as the press is concerned, we're fucked!" Bob grinned and Jo burst out laughing.

"Who's fucked?" Zach appeared and put his arms around Jo and Bob's shoulders.

"No one you'd know, dear boy," Bob replied and touched Zach's arm fondly. "Congratulations again on your engagement, Poppy is a darling girl."

"Cracking night at the pub," Zach said as he watched the guests still piling in. "I hope the crew caught your bar-top pole dance on film." He winked at Bob.

"I didn't know there was a pole on the bar in the pub?" Jo looked puzzled.

"There isn't," Zach and Bob said in unison and Bob held his hands to his brow, "I need a drink," he mumbled and catching the eye of a passing waiter, reached out for a glass of champagne. "Cheers, darlings, to you both!"

THE AFTERNOON PROGRESSED and Jo and Hattie took groups of guests on a tour of the hotel and the new facilities. Many of the ladies from the local WI were fascinated with the Shaman and several in Hattie's group disappeared into the teepee.

"There's smoke coming out of the tent!" Jo whispered to Hattie as they passed in conga-like fashion on the lawn. Jo pulled a face as she inhaled a whiff of something herby.

"Probably just a few josh sticks," Hattie mumbled and hurried by with the remains of her group.

Jo paced confidently through the new studios and introduced the tutors, who patiently explained their course content to her group.

At the door of the pottery class, Jo stopped. Was she imagining things or were there really two penis-shaped vases on the window sills, either side of the door?

"Pottery is sold out!" Hattie whispered as their groups crossed over again. She nodded at the clay phalluses and grinned.

Jo swiftly moved on and eventually came to the meadow, where she opened the wrought iron gate and stepped aside. As her guests meandered around, enjoying the tranquil setting, Jo spotted a man staggering down the steps of the vardo. His face was white and he seemed to be in a hurry to get away from the caravan.

Jo looked up.

Hattie stood at the door. She wore large hoops in her ears and a headscarf over her head and gathered her ruffled skirt in one hand, whilst fondling a crystal ball in the other. She beckoned one of the eager guests forward.

"What's going on?" Jo hissed as a woman mounted the steps and disappeared behind a red velvet curtain.

"Don't shoot the messenger!" Hattie hissed back, "It's a new course, fortune telling for the over forties, booked up for weeks!"

Jo looked on in disbelief as Hattie winked, then gathered her scarf tightly around her shoulders and followed the woman into the vardo.

As THE DAY progressed and having completed all the tours, Jo and Hattie found themselves in the dining room thanking all the guests for attending, as the local press lined Zach up for a photo next to the Mayor of Marland and several other dignitaries. The atmosphere was buzzing and as staff served the buffet, Jo grabbed a glass of champagne and wandered out to the patio.

"I thought Pete might have turned up," she said sadly. Hattie stood alongside. She held a plate piled high and began to tuck in.

"Aye, nowt so queer as folk, have some of this." Her mouth was full and she held the plate out.

Jo reached out to take a canapé but the loud hum of an engine made her suddenly turn. A tractor was chugging along the cobbles in the courtyard and approached the gates to the patio.

Several guests stepped outside to see what all the noise was about and saw the magnificent machine gleaming in the early evening sunshine, as smoke puffed from the funnel.

Jo held her hand to her eyes to shield the sun and as she tried to make out who was making such an entrance, the tractor moved forward and Jo realised that Pete was at the wheel. Standing behind him on the running board, stood Rob, holding a tartan covered bundle in his arms.

Pete cut the engine and stepped down. He looked dapper in a smart suit and polished shoes and grinned as he walked smartly towards Jo. Rob leapt off the running board and Pete turned to take the bundle Rob held out.

"Blimey, would you credit it..."

Jo heard Hattie mutter but her eyes were fixed on the bundle.

It seemed to be moving.

"Hello, Love," Pete said. "You look gorgeous."

Jo's heart missed a beat. Pete looked incredibly handsome and as he stood before her, his blue eyes sparkled.

"I've brought you a present." He lifted the edge of the tartan rug and a little brown head peeped out.

Pete stepped forward and placed a wriggling puppy into Jo's arms. The puppy was anxious and whimpered plaintively as she left the security of hands that had safely held her for days.

Jo's heart was melting and threatened to pool all over the puppy. She lifted the soft little body to her face and kissed the top of her warm head.

"She's a chocolate brown Labrador, eight weeks old and came from a breeder in Wales." Pete said. "She's got a fine pedigree." But Jo hardly heard his words as she murmured soothing coos to calm the trembling body.

"She's adorable," Jo finally spoke. The puppy was licking Jo's hand and seemed to have settled comfortably into the crook of her arm. "I don't know how to thank you..." She stared at Pete and a rush of love ripped through the core of her body. Startled by the sudden emotion, Jo moved forward to embrace him.

"MUM!" A voice shattered the calm in the garden and Zach ran out. "MUM!" Zach yelled again as he rushed to Jo's side. "You'll never guess who's here!"

Jo turned and looked over Zach's shoulder.

She thought that her heart would explode and the air around suddenly seemed to mist as she fought hard to focus on the figure in the door of the conservatory.

Long Tom stepped out onto the patio.

Jo looked at the tall, tanned figure, clad in a leather jacket, faded jeans and his trademark Stetson and as her knees buckled, she thought that she was going to faint.

"He's flown over on a private jet to Carlisle!" Zach said excitedly, but Jo could hardly take in his words as she gripped the puppy and stared at Long Tom.

Pete stood back.

He looked at Long Tom and then at Jo and comprehension flooded over him. "I'll catch you another time," Pete said quietly and turned away.

"Don't go," Jo heard herself say but the tractor had fired up and Long Tom had reached her side.

"Nice dog." Long Tom smiled. He stared at Jo then looked over at Pete, but Pete had already reversed and was making his way out of the courtyard.

Jo had no time to reply when a scream rang out. It reverberated around the walled garden and made several people gasp. Jo spun round to see Hattie, her eyes wide in shock as she held a hand to her mouth.

"OH, MY GOOD GOD!" Hattie screamed again, her plate of food flying over the lawn.

Lazily strolling through the door and meandering towards Hattie, came Mattie. He held his strong arms wide in greeting and beamed. The smile was like a beacon and lit up his magnificent face. In a flash, Hattie threw herself in the air and leapt into Mattie's embrace, her legs circling his waist.

"Got me a jump-up on a jet," Mattie said as he swirled Hattie round. "De Barbados flight has landed!"

"Fuh' real!" Hattie cried and covered his face with kisses.

"GOT ANY CARIBBEAN CAKE LEFT?" Another voice cried out from the direction of the Rose Room and Jo turned in astonishment.

Jimmy stood by the French windows.

He held a glass of champagne and grinning wickedly at his mother, raised it. "Congratulations, Mum," he said, "our home looks magnificent."

Zach had propelled Jo forward and she fell into Jimmy's arms. Tears coursed down her cheeks as she welcomed her eldest son home and listened with incredulity as he told her that Long Tom had chartered a plane to bring their loved ones over for the celebration.

Laughing with joy and wiping her eyes, Jo disentangled herself from Jimmy's embrace and asked Zach to hold onto the puppy for a moment.

She looked around to find Long Tom.

He stood on the lawn, admiring the garden as Hattie and Mattie disappeared into the teepee and a stream of newly tattooed ladies ran out and began to dance around the croquet lawn.

"Nice place," Long Tom said and smiled at Jo.

"I can't believe that you're here."

"Wanted to get the boys home for the celebrations, I owe them my life."

"That was an incredibly kind thing to do."

Long Tom shook his head. "It was nothing. I wanted to see you, Jo."

They stared at each other and Jo longed to wrap her arms around the man who stood humbly before her. She could feel the chemistry that they'd experienced in the Caribbean and it tore at her heart.

Jo knew that Long Tom felt it too.

"Yoo hoo!"

Bob called out to them and Jo heard his crisp footsteps on the patio. Reluctantly she turned.

Hilary stood beside Bob.

Jo gasped as Hilary stared. Her look was icy and Jo reeled from the venomous look that coiled across the lawn and ripped into her soul.

Hilary had been watching Jo's exchange with Long Tom.

"Look who's here!" Bob exclaimed and shoved Hilary forward.

Jo quickly gathered herself and remembering her manners, greeted her new guest. "I'm so pleased to see you," she said and prayed that Hilary wouldn't cause a scene to replicate their last meeting.

"I wanted to congratulate your clever son." Hilary had composed herself and smiled sweetly as she leaned in to air-kiss Jo on each cheek, "I can see where he gets his talent from. You have a wonderful place here." She made a sweeping movement with her arm. "But the real reason for my journey is to see my husband." Hilary moved over to Long Tom and took his arm, "We've been apart for too long and I want to get him home, where I can look after him." She looked lovingly at Long Tom then turned and glared at Jo, laying down a challenge.

"Come on, darling, I have a car waiting," Hilary said and with a smug little smile, led Long Tom away.

Bob watched from a distance.

Back of the net! He whispered, telepathically congratulating Hilary as she gripped Long Tom's arm and guided him out of the garden. Bob reached for his prayer beads and fondling them gently, began to say a chant of thanks. His plan had been for Hilary to chase Long Tom down and show him that she loved him and just as she was about to board a flight for Barbados, Boss told her that Long Tom was heading to Carlisle on a jet. She'd soon changed her plans and a chauffeur-driven car had whisked her speedily up the motorway and delivered her to the hotel in the nick of time.

Bob sighed happily and as the dancing ladies whirled past, he reached out and placed his hands on a pair of plump hips and with a whoop and a wiggle, joined in.

Long Tom allowed himself be led away. But as he stepped into the conservatory, he turned back to look at Jo.

She stood alone on the lawn and stared at Long Tom. The sun

caught her hair and her lovely body cast a shadow almost to his feet. He reached out with his fingers to trace the shape of her silhouetted curves, then looked up and saw the pain in her eyes.

Goodbye... Jo whispered.

Long Tom looked long and hard, embedding her image forever.

Don't forget me, he whispered back. Don't forget me...

But in truth, Long Tom knew that Jo probably would forget him, for he'd seen the way she'd looked at the man on the tractor and the old rocker knew when he was beaten. A touch on his arm told him that Hilary was still beside him and with one last look at Jo, Long Tom reluctantly turned and walked away.

A few weeks later...

Jo stood at the kitchen door and looked out at the fells beyond. In the distance, a tractor chugged through a field, while birds hovered overhead and a dog ran in circles, chasing their shadows. The last few months had been tumultuous and Jo wondered how she'd got through. She'd fought to keep her sanity and diminishing family close but miracles happened and time and friendships had been kind. She waved to Pete as he got closer and called out that dinner was on the table. She smiled as he leapt off the tractor and scooped the puppy into his arms.

"Coming sweetheart," Pete waved in reply. "We'll be home in mo..."

ALSO BY CAROLINE JAMES:

If you enjoyed this book, you may also enjoy reading more from Caroline James

Coffee Tea the Gypsy & Me

So, You Think You're A Celebrity... Chef?

Jungle Rock

The Best Boomerville Hotel - coming soon!

Join the shenanigans at Boomerville, a retreat for discerning clients of a certain age. Find out if it is fun to be over fifty, single and serious about making the most of the rest of your life...

"Britain's answer to The Best Exotic Marigold Hotel!"

FREE BOOK

Enjoy a FREE Kindle Copy of JUNGLE ROCK

"A FUNNY & FABULOUS FEEL-GOOD READ"
By Caroline James

Join Caroline's Newsletter here to receive
your free copy to download:

www.carolinejamesauthor.co.uk

THANK YOU

If you enjoyed this book Caroline would be
hugely grateful if you would share your thoughts with other readers
by leaving a review on Amazon or Goodreads.

CAROLINE JAMES

Caroline James

Caroline James was born in Cheshire and wanted to be a writer from an early age. She trained, however, in the catering trade and worked and travelled both at home and abroad. Caroline has owned and run many related businesses and cookery is a passion alongside her writing, combining the two with her love of the hospitality industry and romantic fiction. She writes fun, romantic fiction and is a member of the Romantic Novelist's Association and as Feature Editor, writes a regular column for a lifestyle magazine. Caroline can generally be found with her nose in a book and her hand in a box of chocolates and when not doing either, she likes to write, climb mountains and contemplate life.

CONTACT

Twitter: @CarolineJames12
Facebook: Caroline James Author
www.carolinejamesauthor.co.uk

Caroline James Author - Amazon

Printed in Great Britain
by Amazon

27156842R00202